EVERYONE

I Kissed

~~~~~~~~~~~~~~~~~~~~

SINCE YOU GOT

Famous

EVERYONE
I Kissed

SINCE YOU GOT
Famous

A NOVEL

MAE MARVEL

ST. MARTIN'S
GRIFFIN
NEW YORK

First published in the United States by St. Martin's Griffin, an imprint of St. Martin's Publishing Group

EVERYONE I KISSED SINCE YOU GOT FAMOUS. Copyright © 2024 by Mae Marvel. All rights reserved. Printed in the United States of America. For information, address St. Martin's Publishing Group, 120 Broadway, New York, NY 10271.

www.stmartins.com

Designed by Omar Chapa

The Library of Congress Cataloging-in-Publication Data is available upon request.

ISBN 978-1-250-89468-7 (trade paperback)
ISBN 978-1-250-89469-4 (ebook)

Our books may be purchased in bulk for promotional, educational, or business use. Please contact your local bookseller or the Macmillan Corporate and Premium Sales Department at 1-800-221-7945, extension 5442, or by email at MacmillanSpecialMarkets@macmillan.com.

First Edition: 2024

10 9 8 7 6 5 4 3 2 1

To everyone who almost kissed their best friend and then finally, finally did. Or they kissed you. For everyone who thought about it during late-night talks and driving around with no destination. For our yearning imaginations and vulnerable hearts.

EVERYONE

I Kissed

~~~~~~~~~~~~~~~~~~~~~~~~~~~~~~~

SINCE YOU GOT

Famous

Chapter One

"Wil, either take off your sunglasses or stop fidgeting."

Wil Greene slid her sunglasses down her nose, squinting over six rows of people who were talking and laughing so loudly, she couldn't hear herself think. Hundreds of lights hung from crisscrossing catwalks overhead, illuminating the cavernous space. She turned to her mother, Beanie. "Explain."

"The squirming is ruining your cool." Beanie pointed up and down at Wil in her good jeans and leather jacket. "If that's what you're going for."

"Naturally, that's what I'm going for. Did you see my new boots?" Wil stuck out her feet, making Beanie roll her eyes. "It's just that it's so incredibly bright in here," Wil explained. "There must be three hundred lights."

The stage their chairs faced was painted severe black and backdropped by a truly massive screen, bigger even than those in a movie theater. Just in front of it were two mid-century-style chairs that looked quietly expensive. Dozens of cameras and mics ringed the stage, with bored-looking press standing around tapping on tablets and phones. Wil didn't watch TV news, but she recognized several faces, including a morning show anchor who turned out to be surprisingly tiny in person, balanced on sky-high nude heels with bright red soles.

It was surreal. Even though Wil had never been on a sound-stage in her life, and even though the lights were so much brighter than any she'd seen before and the crowd was bigger than she'd known to expect, waiting for Katie Price to walk onto a stage still felt completely familiar to Wil's body.

As though no time had passed at all. When actually it had been at least, what? A dozen years. A little longer. Thirteen.

Wil hadn't actually laid eyes on Katie in thirteen years.

God.

She stashed her sunglasses into her bag and bussed her mom's cheek. "I guess I'll go look at the set."

Beanie gave her a quick cheek kiss back. "Good. Ask questions. All these film students are very eager. They feel bad if you don't talk to them and act impressed. Do your best to make up for the massive student loan debt they're facing after graduation."

"Got it. You want me to scare them with an object lesson in what happens to a person when they don't follow their dreams." Wil stood, one hip cocked to make it obvious that she was talking about herself, and Beanie smacked her thigh with her program.

"If you want to talk about that, let's talk about it. I saw a diner down the street. I'll buy the coffee and pie. Jokes like that aren't as cute as you'd like them to be, Wilifred Darcy Greene."

"Obviously, I know better." Wil kept any comedy out of her voice and conceded the point to Beanie, who was looking at her with a lot of knowing.

"You do," Beanie said. "Because I'm amazing, which can only mean you're amazing, too."

Wil reached down to squeeze her mom's hand, then minced along the aisle, passing Beanie's best friend, Diana, who Wil had known her entire life, and who was pretending that she hadn't heard Wil's conversation with her mom. She made her way past the long row of folding chairs that had been set up on the concrete floor of a giant soundstage in Chicago's Studio City.

Having navigated her way free of people's knees and bags, she flashed the lanyard Diana had given her at a security guard, who permitted her into a roped-off area, giving Wil access to the set, a retro 1970s family home where they filmed the hour-long weekly drama *Mary Wants It*.

Wil pointedly did *not* look past the brightly lit set to the moving shadows of people behind the stage and screen.

She wouldn't be able to tell, anyway, if one of those dark silhouettes, out of reach of the studio lights, was Katie.

The interior of the set's living room area was remarkably like a real living room, except without a ceiling or fourth wall. As soon as Wil crossed the threshold, a staffer made enthusiastic eye contact. "Do you have any questions?" The student's smile was embroidered by several glinting piercings against a goth-white complexion and framed by a genuine *sheet* of glossy black hair.

Mindful of Beanie's encouragement, Wil put her hand on a coatrack hung with a collection of vintage coats and tried to think of a good question.

"What do you do for the show, and how important are you?" she asked. "But be gentle with me when you explain it. I only recently figured out that there weren't tiny people living inside my television, letting me take a peek into their lives for my entertainment."

The student laughed. "Oh, wow, no. I don't work for the show. My roommate's girlfriend is a PA for it, but she mostly just works from home on compliance—you know, keeping track that everyone on set has worked the right number of hours and has the right credits and all of their paperwork. I'm a very unimportant screenwriting student at the University of Chicago. I have an internship here."

"At Studio City? That seems like kind of a big deal."

Wil had been amazed when they arrived and Beanie parked in a huge lot. A golf cart picked up Wil, Beanie, and Diana to take them to the VIP entrance for this afternoon's event. She'd also been amazed by how enormous the Chicago-based film studio lot was and how many famous shows and films were made here, including *Mary Wants It*. Wil hadn't thought of Chicago in the same breath as LA or New York, but something was obviously holding its own here.

Her observation earned Wil a bigger smile from the student. "I beat out two hundred other people just as awesome as me, honestly. Although, who knows why I got the internship? I think they put our apps in a random-number generator."

"Well, congratulations." Wil straightened up from where she'd been leaning close so she could hear the student, who was short. Then she felt fingertips touch her wrist.

"I'm Sasha." The student held up her lanyard with her name and pronouns and a bright red bar featuring the word INTERN. She gave Wil another smile, a flush of pink racing up from the collar of her white button-down to her cheeks. "I'm not usually so cringe, I guess, but are you doing something after this?"

Oh. Wil cleared her throat and glanced involuntarily toward the back of the stage again.

This had backfired. When Beanie and Diana asked questions of twentysomething film students, it did not come across the same way, apparently, as when Wil did it in her leather jacket and new boots, leaning in close and smiling.

Sometimes she didn't realize she'd activated her flirt mode until things had gotten to wrist touching. Her moves had become habitual.

"I'm so completely flattered. I'm—"

"Don't even. You don't have to." Sasha's voice *was* very brave now, her eyes big and serious. She moved her hand away from Wil's wrist. "It's just, I was thinking, you probably have some really great party to go to after this." Sasha pointed at Wil's VIP lanyard. "I know there's that meet and greet with Katie Price, or you have something, I mean, *somewhere* booked in the city." Sasha nudged Wil's shin with her knee. "And unless you also have a *someone*, I'm a really good date at fancy parties."

Wil had to laugh. Sasha had some moves as well. "I have no doubt. Actually—"

Sasha waved her hand in front of her face, grinning. "Listen to me, oh my God. But I had to shoot my shot, right? Or I'd regret it forever. Also, you need a better camera person, because *fuck me*, you are hot. I knew you were hot, but TikTok is not doing this justice." Her hands flapped at Wil's body, her neck bright red now, while Wil slowly caught on to what was happening, which was not, in fact, a direct consequence of her game.

She'd been *recognized*.

Despite having well over a million followers on her channel, Wil-You-Or-Won't-You, it didn't happen often. Maybe because she rarely left Green Bay, Wisconsin, where she'd lived most of her life. It wasn't unusual for Wil to be recognized in Green Bay, of course. She got recognized for all kinds of things. The scandalous cheer routine she'd choreographed in high school to Ke$ha's "Take It Off" that nearly cost her her spot as valedictorian, for example.

Sometimes, driving her Bronco around town, she'd get a familiar wave from someone she didn't recognize and then wonder if the wave was actually for her dad, who'd driven the Bronco before her, or if the person waving was someone she'd met through work and forgotten. Wil had taken a lot of reports of trees falling through the roofs of garages in her job as an insurance adjuster.

But also, Wil suspected that even when she *did* get recognized in Green Bay for her TikTok, most everybody in her hometown was too Midwest polite to mention where they knew her from. Not least of all because it would mean they'd have to admit they followed her channel.

Green Bay was really Catholic.

She turned her attention back to Sasha, taking a breath so she could be completely present in the moment. The huge studio and the lights, the slight fug left over from the three-hour car ride from Green Bay, and her jumble of unlabeled feelings about being here at all had shattered Wil's usual focus on one thing at a time.

She looked—really looked—at Sasha, who was definitely a little bit nervous after hitting on Wil, but still meeting her gaze. She noticed the way Sasha's eyes watched her face for changes in expression, which told Wil that Sasha wasn't shy, but she wasn't indiscriminately extroverted, either. Wil realized Sasha was most likely being humble. There would be good reasons why she had this coveted internship, and also why she'd recognized Wil right away in a sea of strangers, placed her, and felt confident enough to approach her.

Sasha was smart. Really smart. And she took in details, and she knew she was *good*.

In any other circumstances, Wil would have absolutely asked Sasha to kiss her.

"Honestly, it's not that I wouldn't seriously consider the offer if I were able to." Wil kept her voice matter-of-fact, because no one really liked being treated gently or condescended to. "And it's not because I have any kind of glamorous commitment after this. It's just that my ride here was my mom and her best friend, so this is strictly a family outing today. To see Katie."

Just in time, Wil stopped herself from looking toward the back of the stage again.

She hadn't expected to feel such a pull.

"You're big Katie Price fans?" Sasha asked. "What am I saying? Of course you are. You're humans in the twenty-first century. Well, I can tell you that she only got here thirty minutes ago, but I caught a glimpse of her going into what we set up as the green-room, and she looks like she's had twelve hours of sleep and has strolled off the runway for Ralph Lauren's fall sportswear collection. No kidding, it's unreal. Stars are *not* like us."

"Yeah."

Her answer didn't even make sense, but when Wil tried to think of something else to say, she couldn't.

What *was* Katie like now? That was the question Wil kept circling back to in the car on the way here, tuning out Beanie and Diana's chatter to look out the window at the farm fields rushing by I-43 and wonder if becoming a star had transformed Katie Price into someone completely unfamiliar, or if she would still *feel* like Katie.

Like the Katie who Wil had once known better than anyone.

A bar of lights hanging from the three-story ceiling flashed twice.

"Five minutes," Sasha said. "You should go back to your seat. Hey, could I get a selfie?"

"Yeah," Wil said again. She took Sasha's phone, since she was so much taller, and pressed her cheek to Sasha's while firing off a bunch of pictures. Sasha gave her a hug. Then Wil was weaving around bodies to go back to her seat. She made it just as the lights over the audience lowered.

Wil glanced behind her at the endless rows of filled chairs that went all the way to a huge garage-style door in the side of the soundstage. There had to be at least five hundred people here. For Katie. At an event so elite, it wasn't even public. Today's viewing and the interview to follow were restricted to invited film students, industry professionals, media, and people like Wil who'd been put on a list by Katie or Katie's inner circle.

In this case, by Katie's mom, Diana, who'd been Beanie's best friend since kindergarten.

Diana leaned forward, her ash-blond hair slipping over the shoulder of her sweater set. Diana's skin, direct from her Norwegian ancestors, was struggling under the intense lights. Even the tip of her nose had turned a startling red. "Katie just texted me to make sure we'd been well taken care of. She said to tell you hi."

Katie said to tell you hi.

Katie said to tell you she wished she could've made it.

Katie said to tell you she wished she could've seen you, but she had to get back to Los Angeles.

Katie said to tell you she's so, so sorry about your dad, and she wanted to make sure you got her card and flowers.

Diana had been telling Wil what Katie said for fully thirteen years. Or, even more often, Beanie told Wil what Diana had told her Katie said.

"Tell her I said to break a leg." Wil smiled.

Diana started typing, and Beanie patted Wil's knee, which meant that she'd responded correctly. Versus, say, blurting out, *Tell Katie she could give me her number.*

Beanie leaned closer. "After this is over, Diana's going to fly back with Katie to LA for a couple of days. So get ready for a nice long talk on our drive back to Green Bay." Beanie smiled at Wil with an eyebrow raised.

"I love that for us. Do you want to hash out a rough agenda or stick with the classics?"

Beanie laughed. "I do like the classics, but maybe we could mix it up a bit. After the part where I gently ask you what you're going to do with the rest of your life, and I remind you that I'm tired of hearing about your TikTok at my workplace from people I try to avoid talking to, then we could try out—and I'm just workshopping this, so do feel free to offer feedback—I don't know, processing some of our feelings about losing your dad and the love of my life?"

"Oh, wow. Okay." Wil nodded, staring at the still-darkened stage. "Or, option B, we could talk about Katie's thing. Our observations and deeper contemplations about what we're about to witness." Wil gestured toward the stage. "Enlighten ourselves with the arts."

"Sure, sure. Except, this is you and me, right?" Beanie leaned back and smiled. "We might as well get a sack of burgers at a drive-through and turn the stereo up super loud."

"That," Wil said. "Let's do that. It's been working for years. Why mess with our amiable and pleasant mother-daughter bond?"

Beanie pursed her lips. "Your deflection is noted for the record."

A beam from a hidden projector lit up the screen, and a lush sound system filled the cavernous concrete-walled studio with the opening theme of *Mary Wants It*.

Wil had seen this episode.

She didn't follow the show, but she'd watched the two episodes Katie guest directed. The first one was part of last season, and Katie later won an Emmy for it. Wil had watched the Emmys, too, because she made sure to watch all the awards shows where Katie had been nominated. Usually she curled up next to her mom on Beanie's sofa, a bowl of cheese popcorn between them, reminiscing about when Katie had first seen the Oscars when she was eight. She'd made Diana buy her a trophy from Green Bay Awards and Trophies so that she could practice holding it while giving invented acceptance speeches.

This episode of *Mary Wants It*, Katie's second as guest director, had broadcast a couple of weeks ago. It was notable for having aired live, in a continuous take, with no commercials except for a ten-minute intermission. No doubt the producers thought of it as a bit of a stunt, but in the dark of Wil's bedroom, streaming the show on her laptop, she'd cried.

It wasn't something Wil was accustomed to doing. Crying at shows or music or movies. It felt weird. And amazing.

Very familiar feelings in the category of Katie Price, Wil remembered. Katie was, and had always been, a weird and amazing person.

The episode was even more overwhelming on the huge screen, which exaggerated the high-definition, hyperreal way Katie had filmed it. The actors seemed to throw off visible energy that wasn't fully controlled. It felt almost like they would inevitably have to mess up or break, but the longer they didn't, the more Wil's throat got tight. It was relentless, and beautiful, and probably would put Katie's trophy-holding skills to good use this year.

The episode ended. Beanie sniffed and wiped at her cheeks. The lights over the audience stayed low, but the screen light gave way to stage light that was somehow the same color as fall sunlight. The shift brought the press corps to attention, buzzing around their equipment as the audience applauded.

Before Wil could even get ready to anticipate it, Katie stepped onto the stage, tall, as tall as Wil in a pair of stacked heels and an outfit Katharine Hepburn probably had had three of, with high-belted drapey trousers and an understated ivory silk button-down unbuttoned past her sternum. Casual ropes of pearls and soft gold chains layered against her peachy skin. Her dark blond hair—longer than her mother's and somehow always a little warmer, a little wilder—was caught in a casually disintegrating braid over her shoulder that looked like it had been styled by angels while she was sleeping.

It had been so long since Wil had seen Katie in person that she saw this Katie—waving at the roaring crowd in the artificial autumnal sunshine, her smile glowing—and Wil's brain supplied a memory, as clear as if it were happening now, of Katie in the *real* fall sunshine of their senior year of high school, folding up her long legs on the bleachers set up by the football field, a script on her thigh, her hair in a messy braid over her shoulder, watching Wil's cheerleading practice while she memorized her lines for the school musical.

Then Wil's throat felt tight again, and she made herself look away for a minute so she could take a deep breath to slow down her racing heart.

It had been a long time since she'd taken those kinds of memories out and thought about them.

The audience clapped and whistled and shouted until Honor Howell stepped onto the stage. Wil looked at Honor with interest, dazzled in spite of herself at this glimpse of Hollywood royalty. The Howells were mentioned in the same breath as the Barrymores, Coppolas, Warners, and Disneys. Members of the Howell family had been breaking the race barrier in Hollywood for a century. Honor herself was the daughter of Gordon Howell, the most famous director in Hollywood for all of Wil's life, at least, and the first Black man to direct a film with a budget in the $300-million range.

Honor Howell, Diana had explained on the drive south from Green Bay, had made her mark in Hollywood as a "dreammaker." She'd funded and invested in some of the most well-respected production studios in the world, and her own media corporation, Cineline Carnegie Howell, had recently edged out the Murdochs' empire, pulling ahead in stock value due in large part to Honor Howell's impeccable savvy.

Honor's signature inky bob gleamed under the lights as she waved at the audience with a pair of tortoise-framed glasses in her hand. Her warm, deep brown skin, snatched jawline, and broad cheekbones would mean she remained effortlessly gorgeous for decades. She slid the glasses on as she sat down in one of the chairs.

Paired with the glasses, her perfect red sweater and trim dress pants gave her a look that Wil associated with the hardest professor on your college schedule—the one who ended up being a favorite despite handing out Cs like they were gifts.

Katie settled back in her own chair with a command of the space that meant the audience started quieting without being asked. "Everyone!" Katie said at the precise moment the crowd was perfectly calm. "So many everyones are here!"

Boom mics moved like birds over Katie's and Honor's heads, but the women didn't give them even a glance. "You're very popular," Honor said, smoothing her hands over her lap. "Aren't we on your home turf, nearly? You're a Midwestern girl, if I remember correctly."

"Born and bred in Wisconsin," Katie agreed. "They say everyone in Hollywood is really from the Midwest."

Katie came home a few times a year on an unpredictable schedule. Wil almost never knew she'd been in town until afterward, so fiercely did Diana guard her daughter's privacy.

It had always made Wil a little, just a *little* bit, irritated that even though she had been to so many of Katie's children's theater performances, had shared an orbit with her growing up because their moms were best friends, and the two of them had spent almost every minute of their senior year together, Diana never invited Wil over.

As if Wil would disturb Katie's privacy.

Maybe Katie wanted it that way. Her life had changed unfathomably, completely, almost the minute she left home the summer after high school. Wil had sometimes thought to ask Beanie about it, but Beanie protected Diana, and Diana protected Katie, and that was the way things were supposed to be.

It didn't surprise Wil—not at all, not in any way—that Katie Price was one of the most famous women in the world. Wil had grown up believing that Katie's success was a foregone conclusion. Katie would be a star. She would move to Hollywood. Wil would see her in the movies.

All those predictions had come true.

She slid off her leather jacket, the giant room warming up with the big audience and stage lights. Katie and Honor were obviously wrapping up their preliminary banter. Honor crossed her legs and leaned forward just as Katie smiled at her, and it must have been a signal, because Honor smiled back and asked her first real question.

"A lot of people considered the initial episode you directed of *Mary Wants It* to be publicity for the show. But I would point out that no one wins an Emmy for publicity, and I was there. I visited the set to check you out. I've known a lot of actors who believe they're directors, you see. I was pleasantly surprised to find you *directing*, in every sense of the word. You were behind the camera, you blocked every scene, you ran the crew. You were more than comfortable with the tech and the practicals. The shoot for that show was tight and, in many ways, groundbreaking. Where did you learn to do that?"

Katie nodded once. "You mean, because I hadn't done it before."

"Of course. Though I doubt that's true. Perhaps because you hadn't done it when someone else was paying for it and everyone would see the result."

"And I'm not a product of a place like this—" Katie swept her hand in a circle to indicate the vastness of the studio. "Of the University of Chicago or UCLA or anything like that."

"No. You are not."

"And there isn't any *possible* way that I would notice, take in, or observe how the tools and skills work and come together, as someone who was acting in front of a camera?"

Katie smiled at Honor, who smiled back. They were conspiratorial and very vicious smiles. A soft wave of mostly feminine laughter behind Wil told her others in the audience had noticed, too.

"No, of course you wouldn't," Honor agreed. "The lights are too bright, your makeup is too pretty, and your costars are too handsome."

Everyone laughed.

Katie let it die down, making a knowing expression at the audience. "To be clear, your question is one reserved for a woman. A Black actor. A Latine actress. Maybe for someone very young. 'What gave you the authority to decide to do this? Also, what's his name?'"

Honor nodded, beaming at Katie as though she were Honor's favorite protégé, and Wil leaned back in her chair, glad she had come. She liked this Katie—the Katie who spent the next hour talking about how to translate the technical into what the audience felt. The one who confessed she'd thought she would be terrified to direct a live episode but found that the pressure quieted her brain and made her vision easier to access.

Katie was getting an A from the hardest professor.

In all the hours Wil had spent watching Katie be interviewed, looking at clips on Beanie's phone of the latest talk show appearance, or flipping through a story in the copy of *People* she'd picked up while she waited to check out her groceries at Woodman's, she'd never heard Katie talk about acting and directing like this.

The audience was riveted. And, Wil distinctly sensed, astonished. Because even though Katie didn't say anything particularly outrageous—even though every word out of her perfect signature-pink lips could have been a six o'clock news sound bite—no one in the room except Wil, Beanie, and Diana had ever heard Katie Price take herself, and her work, so seriously.

"So what's next?" Honor crossed her arms. "What is Katie Price's next project? Acting or directing?"

There was a look Wil couldn't interpret on Katie's face, and Wil felt, rather than saw, the press lean in closer and focus their cameras for a tight view of her dark blue eyes fanned with impossible lashes and winged with sharp black eyeliner, looking for a flaw that Wil couldn't imagine they'd find.

Wil glanced over at Diana, who had gone completely still in a way that was as noticeable as if she'd started dancing. She had hinted, in the car, that "dreammaker" Honor Howell might be considering making a dream come true for Katie, but Diana wouldn't say much more than that.

"Something scary," Katie said. "That's all I can tell you right now."

Honor raised her eyebrows and looked at the press, sending them into a sudden, buzzing frenzy that Katie silenced by nodding at the morning anchor Wil had recognized earlier, inviting her to ask the first question.

"Thank you, Katie," the anchor said. "I have to say, the scariest thing I can think of for Katie Price is if you've finally considered the role of someone special's girlfriend! We have to know, are you seeing someone?"

The smile that Katie plastered on her face in response to the anchor's question made Wil's neck tense. *This* was one of the reasons why Wil watched Katie's movies but only looked at clips of her interviews.

"May I have another question?" Katie's voice remained scrupulously smooth and polite, as though she were asking a dinner companion to pass her the salt.

There was a nervous titter from the audience and the press.

Honor Howell recrossed her legs.

"Katie!" A man raised up his finger. "Thank you. Ben Adelsward recently mentioned to *Variety* that you were starting a production company. I can only imagine he has the inside scoop for a good reason. Have the two of you set the past aside to work together again?"

Diana softly gasped. Beanie slid her hand over top of Wil's, which was when Wil noticed she was gripping her own knee, her knuckles bloodless. Diana started tapping rapidly at the screen of her phone.

"No." Katie delivered this single syllable with absolute finality. "Linda?" She looked at an older woman at the edge of the press pool.

"Hi, Katie. Honestly, I have the same question. Ben seemed to know a lot about what you were up to."

"Asked and answered." Katie smiled, her shoulders fascinatingly relaxed, her expression satisfyingly bored. But Honor Howell had turned to stone across from her.

These were two very powerful women transmitting—or, in Katie's case, *concealing*—a lot of intense emotion. Wil didn't know what the whole story was, but the stakes of whatever was going on between Katie and Honor were palpable.

Also, Diana was completely freaking out.

"Zara! How nice to see you." Katie nodded at Zara Hurst, a former actress who Wil had grown up watching in dark indie teen movies. Zara now had a wildly famous podcast where she interviewed celebrities about their secret special interests.

"Hey! So, I think I speak for everyone when I tell you that we *have* to know if your beautiful cat children, Phil, Trois, and Sue, are as welcome on set when you're directing as they've been when you're in front of the camera. Do they have their own trailer? Do they get brand-new producer credits?"

This reference to Katie's cats, who were internet famous, and whom Katie talked about in all her interviews, made Katie laugh. The audience followed suit, approving the question with their own delighted laughter, and Beanie's hand let go of Wil's knee. Finally,

Honor Howell's posture relaxed, and Diana made a noise somewhere between a laugh and a sigh.

It was strange, Wil thought, how obvious it was that no one in this enormous room, Honor Howell included, seemed to want Katie to be forced to talk about Ben Adelsward.

And yet the questions never stopped coming, even all these years later.

"Only Phil gets producer credits," Katie said. "After his profile in *Vogue* last year, he signed with my agency, so *he* has a contract."

The cat question, and Katie's response, signaled the tone and permissible subject matter of the rest of the press questions, which didn't last long before Honor stood abruptly, indicating that the interview was complete. The lights came up to half intensity over the audience. Wil watched as Sasha and the other interns set up microphones in the aisles for students to line up behind.

Katie looked into the audience, waving a bit, and Wil watched as she clocked her mom, beamed, and gave her a tiny finger wave. Then her gaze swept to Beanie and—as Wil's breath caught—to her.

Katie didn't hold her gaze, or wave, or make any expression beyond pleasant interest in the crowd. But then she looked completely away and smiled in a way she hadn't smiled yet.

Wil bit the inside of her cheek to school her expression as she felt Beanie's attention hone in on her. She didn't really want her mother's insights and observations right now. She wanted to take that smile of Katie's and think about it all by herself. As many times as possible.

Something new to go with the old memories.

Later, after they skipped the meet and greet because Diana said it would distract Katie to have "people from home" there, and after Beanie dropped Wil off at her house—their conversation from Chicago to Green Bay having remained as safely in its lane as Beanie's Prius—Wil didn't let herself think about Katie.

She didn't think about Katie the whole time she pulled out two chairs in front of the white bedsheet she used as a backdrop, or turned on the secondhand photographer's lights she'd picked up at an estate sale, or clamped her phone in its tripod, getting ready to film for her TikTok channel.

She didn't think about Katie when the doorbell rang, or when she let in the pretty woman with big brown eyes who she'd met in a parking garage next to the library a few days ago, giving her directions to the YWCA and then, on an impulse, inviting her over tonight.

She especially didn't think of Katie Price after she pressed the phone's red record button and kissed this woman, softly, and then much more seriously and deeply.

But she wanted to.

Chapter Two

"Good morning, tiny babies!" Katie Price clapped her hands together and surveyed her three cats. Cat breakfast was one of her favorite times of day.

"I think for this morning," Katie said, opening the cat cabinet, "we'll go with the mousse puree texture, in deference to Sue's adventure at the dentist. She seemed to struggle a bit with the shreds yesterday. What do the three of you think?"

Sue had her sleek brown-and-black back to Katie, which, fair. She had gone in for a tooth cleaning earlier in the week, and she hadn't looked Katie in the face since. She was enraged at the little shaved-off area around her leg from the IV, so Katie was giving her space for now.

Katie definitely understood how it felt to be betrayed.

Since none of the cats voiced an objection to puree, Katie rubbed their heads—asking Sue politely for permission first—lined up their bowls, and gave them their breakfast. She took a minute to listen to their wet eating purrs before she broached the subject she needed to talk with them about.

"So, my darling peanuts, while you eat, I have to tell you something." Katie walked over to the large array of buttons she had set up on a credenza outside the kitchen's cased opening. The credenza faced the wall of glass that looked out on the pool and the bird feeders she had installed to provide her indoor cats with enrichment.

The buttons were mounted to interlocking foam mats of the type preschoolers sat on for circle time. Each button was a plastic circle, about three inches across, that played back a brief recording when depressed.

Almost two years ago now, Katie had begun with one button—a recording of her own voice saying the word *treat*—and she had patiently and painstakingly trained the cats to associate the word with the action of getting a treat.

Then they'd learned to push the button themselves when they wanted a treat, which was, conveniently, always.

After that, it was easy. One by one, Katie had added more buttons to the array, known among speech therapists as an Augmentative and Alternative Communication board, until she had more than fifty concept-words that she could use to communicate with her cats.

And which her cats could—and did—use to communicate with her.

Katie pushed the large buttons while she said the words out loud. "Cats," she said as she pushed the *Cats* button. "Mama. News."

The cats looked back at her. Trois, a three-legged calico who was the most active and adventurous of Katie's cats, swished her tail in anticipation. Phil finished eating, stretched, and let out a long, multipitch report on his feelings.

Sue jumped down from the counter and leapt onto the credenza. She was often the spokescat for the rest of them. She was the chattiest on the AAC, and Phil complained the most.

"Mama. Trip. Cats. Trip." Katie pushed the three buttons, then surveyed the cats for reactions. Trois, naturally, looked excited. Phil dropped back into his loaf.

Sue approached the buttons. "No. Kennel. No."

Sure. They had been here before. Katie's work as an actress meant that she'd taken her cats on a lot of airplanes to a lot of different destinations—enough that they understood the significance of her announcement. Sue was not a big fan of having to spend time in her kennel, whether in a car, on the airplane, or visiting the vet.

"Yes," Katie said, pushing the button. "Cats. Kennel. Airplane." She rubbed Sue's head to soften the blow.

Sue pushed the buttons again. "Sue. Mad. Mad."

"I know you don't love the smaller airplane kennel, Sue. But it *is* a direct flight, on a chartered plane, so you'll be with me the whole time." Katie pushed the buttons. "Mama. Cats. Together. Plane. Your reward is that, just like I told you, none of you had to say good-bye to Nana Diana for long." She pushed the button for *Nana Diana*. "Because that is where we are going. You like it there, even at Christmastime when it's cold. You will be spoiled, and I will be with you the whole time! No meetings. No visitors you don't know. Just me and you. Because, as you are aware, I am supposed to be writing, and if I have to barricade myself in Green Bay with my mom's cooking to pull it off, I will."

Katie pressed her hand against her belly to head off the buzzy, cold shiver of nerves that hunted her whenever she thought about writing. Really doing the thing. The secret thing that she'd told five hundred super-smart film students was scary, that every one of them would give a vital organ to get to do, and so she better do it well, right?

Because the very last words that Honor Howell said to her, before she got inside a sleek navy car, were, *We'll soon see if your script is better than the* unpleasantness *we suffered on that stage, Katelyn. I do wonder how ready you are for work out of the spotlight.*

Sue gave a short, huffy meow and jumped down from the credenza.

"I love you, Sue," Katie said.

She cleaned up the cats' dishes and then got out the truly massive breakfast burrito she'd ordered on Uber Eats the night before to have now, slathered with warmed-up white queso and covered with an avocado from her tree in the conservatory. It didn't matter that Katie had lived in Los Angeles for almost thirteen years, her Wisconsin soul would never, ever get over that she could grow her own avocados in her sunroom—in December!—and how good the breakfast burritos were here. Ever.

Katie loved breakfast burritos. There had been no such thing growing up in Green Bay unless you counted the ones at McDonald's, which were emergency breakfast burritos only.

She'd fixed her burrito and pulled out her phone, wiggling in her dining room chair with delight at her chance to have burrito-and-phone time, when a FaceTime request came through from Madelynn, her primary publicist.

Katie gave a very, very tiny sigh. Madelynn was tremendously talented, but publicists were such that even if you got the best ones, if you had any scruples at all, you'd end up running through them. Madelynn was Katie's fifth publicist.

She was Katie's publicist forever, her *last* publicist, because she listened when Katie told her that she didn't want anyone manufacturing anything that wasn't true, and she wanted 99 percent of the publicity focused on her projects.

Also, Madelynn would never make Katie talk about Ben. In fact, Madelynn had quietly released a few dozen photos of Katie in Chicago in her serious director outfit, some of them with smart pull quotes that Katie almost couldn't believe she'd said. There was a fat series of shots of Katie posing with or talking to film students with bright, interested faces, and even some of Honor Howell looking at Katie with interest and a smile.

But if Madelynn was calling her early on a Saturday morning, this was a call about something Katie didn't want to talk about.

"Hi, Madelynn!" Katie said. Then she put a very big bite of burrito in her mouth. Pointedly.

"Katie, good morning." Madelynn Soh was forty, with one of those pixie cuts that made everyone ask their stylist for a pixie cut. She had a whole wardrobe of glasses. Today, they were orange frames with little fried eggs where the jewels would go. "I'm calling about your secret project. Specifically, I am calling about the fact that the existence of your secret project leaked to Ben Adelsward, thereby fucking up your appearance in Chicago."

Madelynn never beat around the bush, which Katie appreciated.

"It's perplexing, for sure." Katie dabbed her mouth with her napkin. "Have you googled 'secret'?"

"I have. A *secret* is information no one else but your publicist knows. That's from *Merriam-Webster's*." Madelynn raised one of her eyebrows, so sharp they could noiselessly bifurcate a tabloid rumor with the slightest contact.

"So obviously there *are* no secrets"—Katie made an expansive gesture with her hand—"because it turns out everyone knows about my project, *somehow*." Katie sighed over the tight pinch in her stomach. "What did my mother bribe you with to keep you off my back for a week?"

"She sent me a basket of peanut butter meltaways from Seroogy's."

"Damn. That is a good bribe." Seroogy's was a candy store, local to the Green Bay area, particularly well-loved for their meltaways. Katie took another huge bite of burrito. Sue jumped up onto the table and inserted herself in the frame.

"Katie."

"Mm-hmm." Katie chewed. She offered Sue an opportunity to investigate the burrito, but Sue was more interested in the queso, which she licked delicately from the edge of Katie's plate. Madelynn shuddered at Sue's proximity to Katie's burrito.

Madelynn did not feel the same way about cats that Katie did. It was hard to find a Madelynn who also loved cats.

It was hard to find a Madelynn, period.

Katie put another bite of burrito in her mouth, because she knew there was no way to have this conversation with Madelynn without talking about Ben Adelsward, and she was not interested in doing that. It had been enough for her, more than enough, to spend three years dating the twelve-years-older, tall, dark, and handsome leading man who'd swept her up and moved her to Hollywood and "given" her a career.

He had also given her an STI, a broken heart, and a lot of trauma that she'd been diligently working on with her therapist every Tuesday for almost a decade.

Katie hadn't dated anyone since Ben, seen anyone, fallen in love with anyone, fucked anyone. It felt right to her to take this time, and lately she and her therapist had been talking through some super-interesting ideas about gender and sexuality that were helping Katie get a bead on why that was.

But *Entertainment Weekly* was not a fan. The entire Hollywood gossip complex had spent Katie's ten years on break from romance flipping back and forth between "Katie's still in love with Ben!!!!" and "Katie's a freak and the reason Ben has been dating eighteen-year-olds ever since!!!!"

Meanwhile, no matter how often she changed her number, the cockhead kept texting her. He did it every time Katie was nominated for or won an award or got a project with a salary north of $15 million.

Hey, Katie.

She was always tempted to text him back something cutting, but she did not do that. She blocked and walked.

Yet even when Katie did everything she was supposed to do to take care of herself, Ben Adelsward inserted himself into her story. He'd told the press she was starting a production company—information that Katie and her agent, April Feinstein, had controlled as tightly as they could—and his decision to do so had derailed Katie's event in Chicago.

Leaks were inevitable, no matter how trustworthy her inner circle was. But the fact that Ben had managed to get his hands on this particular news and release it at a moment that Katie had expected to be *hers* left her feeling deflated, unimportant, and trapped.

That was his goal.

Ben had brought her all the way to Hollywood and put her in front of everything she had planned on earning for herself, and then when she did get those things, *earning* them despite him, despite all of it, he wouldn't stop reminding her that it was really because of him. Even now, a decade later, he wanted her to feel like she could never get away from him. He wanted her to feel like everything she had, she had because he'd given it to her.

That was Ben's thing. It was what made *him* feel like a Hollywood god.

The worst part was that he'd caught her up in this bullshit when she was eighteen and barely knew who she was. When all of her experiences, despite being a *legal adult* (Ben's point), were those of a child. Katie had managed to win herself a spot in an elite summer stock program outside of Chicago before she was supposed to go to the University of North Carolina's School of the Arts in Winston-Salem. All of it was already a big deal for someone who'd never even left the band of states around the Great Lakes, and then there was Ben, so yes. She'd fallen for him, their acting teacher. She'd fallen for what he said about how mature she was, with all the authority of a thirty-year-old A-list actor who "still did independent projects."

His self-effacing humor. His charming patter, as though he were always sitting with one ankle crossed over his knee, a mug of coffee in his hand, exchanging quips with a talk-show host in a careless display of male whiteness. His broody dark eyes, his three-days-of-stubble beard, his pouty mouth and full head of dark hair that looked like he'd just raked his fingers through it.

To Katie, Ben Adelsward had seemed like someone who knew everything she was so desperate to learn, and at first, what she'd fallen for was what he told her about herself.

She hadn't known the difference between his grooming and her own awareness that she had something special. Ben singling her out for attention, praise, had felt, at first, like confirmation. Katie *had* it. Ben said so.

But then, gradually, there had been a shift in what Ben told her about herself. He'd started to say she would be such a beauty *one day,* that she had the *ungerminated seeds of potential talent,* if only she would learn how to use it. She did so many things wrong. But lucky for Katie, Ben was generous and brave enough to tell her the bald truth that no one else would say.

Lucky, lucky Katie Price.

She didn't judge the girl she'd been with Ben. Not anymore. There had been some difficult years of panic attacks and waves of shaky shame when Katie couldn't convince herself, some days, that she was truly *real.* When she felt like a body moving through space, a character to be dressed and pushed out under the footlights.

The work had saved her. She kept making movies, kept reaching inside herself to find a way to feel and think and talk like another woman, and doing that reminded her of what it meant to be human.

She never judged the characters she played. She couldn't judge herself.

But Ben Adelsward simply wouldn't go away.

Also, she'd once accidentally left something very sentimental to her by a soap dish in his apartment in New York when she was washing her hands, and he'd never returned it.

Katie sighed. As much as she wanted to, she couldn't avoid this conversation with Madelynn. Business was business. "How bad is it?"

"I'm a publicist. Nothing is bad, everything is simply a pivot." Madelynn smiled. "Our plan was a good one. Get you behind the camera? Check. You helped make that even better by winning that Emmy. Then option one of the best-selling novels in America for you to adapt? Check, check. Get you in front of the camera again, this time with the fire of a live audience licking at your heels, and oh! my! Is that *Honor Howell* who happens to be on set, watching the birth of the best auteur of your generation? Yes. Yes it is. What a wonderful coincidence!"

Katie laughed. Madelynn enjoyed putting on the occasional show. "I'm with you."

"Enter Marisol Gonzales," Madelynn said. "She's an auteur in her own right, and she has a script everyone wants. But Marisol has something no one else in this town has, which are values. So she's shopping. Marisol talks to Honor. Honor mentions you. The word is put out by a discreet and extremely fancy source—courtesy of me—that you and your longtime agent, April Feinstein, are starting a production company. You're shaking off the scales of the dinosaurs of Hollywood for something real, inclusive, hot. It's going to be amazing."

"It is," Katie agreed.

"Of course it is. So Marisol talks to you. Oh! *Interesting.* She suggests the world might need to start to learn a little about your vision. Calls are made. Chicago is booked. It's just a small appearance, but it conveys a serious, important message. Honor Howell interviewing. There are pearls and eyeglasses and trousers. An elite but fun-funky collection of press are on hand. It's all ripe for a small but intriguing mention at the best places. Did you hear Marisol Gonzales is working with Katie Price's new production company? No! But *oh, yes*. Honor and Katie? Hmm . . . hmm! All of it setting the stage, after Honor reads your script and loves it, for a big fat check signed by Ms. Hollywood herself, and an announcement in the form of a long-form profile in *Hollywood Reporter* accompanied by another pearls-and-trousers glamor shot of you in a director's chair." Madelynn sighed. "It was such a lovely, lovely dream."

Katie put her fork down. "But now, pivot."

"Indeed," Madelynn snarled. "I wonder who booked him that sham of an interview in *Variety*? It was *Variety online*, mind you, so it must have been some hasty work. All so Ben could run with the leak of your project." Madelynn brightened and smiled. "Doesn't matter. Pivot."

Katie nodded and started cutting her burrito into bite-sized pieces. Her eyes were burning a little bit, because it felt as though Madelynn had just delivered the funeral requiem for Katie's dream. Or, at least, the version of Katie's dream that Ben Adelsward had no part in.

But they could pivot. They had to, because Katie wanted this. She wanted it all the way down. She wanted to write the script and direct it. She wanted Honor Howell to back her production company. She wanted Marisol Gonzales to knock on her door. She wanted the *Hollywood Reporter* profile and the pearls.

What Katie really wanted, most of all, was to make something that was hers. That was *her*. She wanted something she wasn't even sure she could do. "What's your new plan?"

"You won't like it, but the only way out is through."

"No." Katie knew what was coming. She and Madelynn had been here before.

Madelynn rubbed her eyes under her glasses. "The fuck of it is, Katie, I like you, and I don't like anyone I work with. I'm a sanitation worker. I pick up the garbage. But you don't make me do that. You either don't produce garbage or you're composting everything, I don't even know, but you're a pleasure to work for, mainly because work is all you do. But my liking you so much means that it is especially egregious to have to deal with the same fucking story over and over again forever, especially when that story is, at this point, an impediment to you getting what you want. I have a dartboard with Ben's face on it. I actually throw darts at it."

Katie looked down at her breakfast. She reminded herself to keep her shoulders loose, her jaw relaxed. She pressed her feet into the rough wool of the rug under her dining room table.

Madelynn leaned back. "Listen. I want this not to be a thing. I want you to let me salt it out of your fields forever so you can do some coy project when you're fifty and look like a goddamned icon while also subtweeting him so hard, and then everyone notices his neck has fallen so far that you can't see his bow tie anymore."

"Wow," Katie said. "Don't hold back."

Her sarcasm fell flat. Probably because of the cold fear rising up her spine.

"Greta Gerwig thinks you're a burgeoning directing genius."

"Did Greta say that? Tell me word for word."

"She said, 'Katie Price was born to see the world from behind the camera, even though there's a good reason the world loves her in front of it.'" Madelynn had a convenient eidetic memory, both a bad thing and a good thing in a publicist.

Smiling, Katie put her head down on the table next to her burrito. "Can you text that to me?"

"No. I won't. I won't because no matter what Greta Gerwig says, it won't mean what you need it to mean until no one fucking cares what Ben Adelsward says."

"Madelynn."

"Listen to me. I have never seen the kind of organic buzz like you got after that live episode aired. Never. My people's people were Korean immigrants with big ideas. They ended up in Hollywood so they could collaborate on the first movies alongside Jewish optometrists from Manhattan who were running cameras they'd bought on payments from the lens equipment man. Which is just to say, I have been in this business my whole life, so I know. *You* made that buzz, and you're going to have to build a new shelf to hold all of the awards your live episode is going to generate. It was the work of a moment to get that Chicago Studio City gig for you so that you could talk about what you did and what it meant to you and what the world should prepare for, *from your perspective*. Everyone wanted to hear what you wanted to say."

Katie swallowed over the burn in her throat. It took all of her training to hold onto the tears caused by her heart swelling big and tight in her chest.

The smallest, smallest hint of feeling what it might be to get what she wanted.

"Three out of four people in this town are fucked up, but mostly in a delightful way," Madelynn said. "Ben is the other kind of fucked up, the kind who weaponizes absolutely everything he does so that he stays at the top by virtue of the bodies under his feet. I told you again and again that it's my job to remove any impediment to you getting what you want, and I am telling you that ignoring Ben, holding our breath until his next move, exhausting yourself with this ridiculous business of creating a pristine image, is *not sustainable*. Also, it's not how you can possibly build a production company, make a mark as an auteur, or meet any of the goals that it's my job to help you accomplish. Big goals require big risks. You have to give yourself some fucking margin for mistakes. Right now, the only room you are giving yourself is for silent perfection, and honestly, if that's all you're ever going to do, you don't need me."

Startled, Katie met Madelynn's eyes, and Madelynn smiled.

"Please. Going after what you want will feel a whole fuck of a lot safer if you will let me obliterate Ben Adelsward like a bad ghost floating through a cloud of sage."

Katie laughed, an involuntary sound that came from her heart, where Madelynn's vision of what Katie could have had released a surge of warm, bright hope.

But Katie had to press her palms flat against the surface of the table to keep them from shaking.

Every day this week, she'd sat at this table with her laptop open in front of her while her assistants and staff operated in hush mode, keeping their footsteps soft and their interruptions to a minimum. She'd downloaded a program that blocked the internet and filled the whole screen with a Zen-like blank field while playing soothing music.

Katie didn't have a single word saved. She'd written a hundred different versions of the opening scene—the stage direction, the establishing shot, the first lines of dialogue—and then highlighted them and pressed delete.

It wasn't just Ben. Her secret project was also scary because she didn't know if she could pull it off.

I do wonder how ready you are for work out of the spotlight.

"I love your passion," she told Madelynn. "But you and I both know that the last time Honor Howell agreed to back an actor's production company, it collapsed in a MeToo-fueled meltdown over the actor's bad behavior. Honor wants the people she works with to center the work and keep their personal lives utterly out of the public eye. The only reason she's interested in working with me is that I talk about my cats and my work and literally nothing else."

Madelynn pursed her lips. "Honor Howell knows you have a life. She isn't asking you not to, but she does need to know if your life belongs to you. She needs to know if, behind the scenes, maybe *you're* the one who's manufacturing leaks, amplifying the story of your connection to Ben Adelsward every chance you get, even as you pretend to be over him."

Katie clenched her hands and then released them, her heart racing.

Madelynn must have seen something in Katie's face, because she sighed and said, "I can handle Honor Howell."

"I haven't asked you to," Katie said much more tartly than she felt. "So here is what *I've* got, as far as the pivot. The inside scoop, Madelynn. Next steps. What I'm doing. What you're doing. Are you ready?"

"So ready."

"In a few hours, I'm flying to Green Bay with my three cats to stay at my parents' house and write an Oscar-winning script when the last thing I wrote was a paper in high school about the pros and cons of solar panels. I'll probably eat a lot of bratwurst. We will open presents on Christmas Day, not Christmas Eve—that is for monsters. I've purchased a number of beautiful things for my babies, but I'm still on the lookout for something extra special for Trois, here. I will bring the AAC board so my children and I can keep working on expanding the horizons of human-animal communication."

And maybe I'll see Wil, Katie thought.

She'd never run into Wil on any of her earlier trips home. There were the years with Ben, when Katie didn't go home because Ben didn't want her to, and she didn't want to do anything Ben didn't want. Then, the years after that, when Katie had needed her parents to be simply, completely hers. She'd needed to go home and be fed, be talked to and fussed over by people who knew her and loved her *only* as Katie, their daughter.

But recently, Wil's TikTok, which she published under the handle Wil-You-Or-Won't-You, had done something to Katie's memories about her last year living in Green Bay. Namely, reminded Katie that the year she was eighteen hadn't been *all* about Ben.

Then, in Chicago, looking for her mom and Beanie in the VIP rows, she'd seen Wil. Her impossible white-blond hair gleaming in the light, curling against her neck. A flash of black leather. Her smooth skin, on first glance just as white-girl ordinary as Katie's, but with a secret golden undertone that could ripen to a tan that looked perfect against tank tops and in a cheerleader's uniform. Her serious, plugged-in expression, which Katie had spent months of their senior year of high school actively soliciting by talking to Wil about absolutely everything she could think of, because the experience of Wil listening to her thoughts, considering her ideas, taking her seriously, had felt so good as to be addictive.

To realize that it was all coming at her again, in that moment on the stage in Chicago, being *Katie*—well. She'd been seriously disappointed not to see Wil at the meet and greet after the event.

Madelynn narrowed her eyes. "I can't make a story out of any of that. Maybe 'Christmas with the Prices,' and I could send a photographer to take a picture of all of you, sans cats, in front of the tree with a few pull quotes about Midwest Christmas comfort foods, but I'd leave out 'bratwurst.'" Before Katie could laugh, Madelynn narrowed her eyes more. "But there's something else. About going home. Just now, I saw it. Something you're not telling me."

Katie schooled her features. "Is this what you wanted to do when you were little, Madelynn? Contemplate how 'bratwurst' plays in the media?"

"You're hiding it from me even as you speak." Madelynn sighed. "But to answer your diverting question with the same utter honesty I would like to receive from you, what I wanted when I was little was to be a spy." Madelynn said this with the smallest hint of a dimple that told Katie she had decided to let Katie off the hook. For now.

"Really?" Katie looked at Madelynn carefully. "*Are* you a spy?" she whispered.

"Torture me with one more cat headline, and maybe I'll give myself up."

Katie laughed, Madelynn signed off, and Katie looked out through the French doors toward her pool. Her house was quieter than usual, her staff already gone for the holidays in anticipation of Katie's flight later today. It was nice to have the place completely to herself. It gave Katie the space to find her breath, center herself after the phone call with Madelynn, and let her mind drift.

All three of the cats had settled into favorite spots, Trois and Phil cuddled together in a bed that caught a beam of early morning sunlight and Sue deep inside the wool pod at the very top of the cat tree in the corner, where no one could get at her unawares, but she could see everything.

Katie had often thought how pleasant it would be to have a cat tower of her own, with a wool pod to hide inside.

She finished her burrito, stacking avocado on top of every bite, savoring the taste, which she'd miss in Wisconsin. When she'd pushed her plate aside, she picked up her phone and swiped through her social media—not her real-name accounts, but the accounts she'd created for her own private enjoyment, where she could leave a "like" on an ad for a cat toy or a post by the person who'd inspired her to set up AAC buttons for Sue, Trois, and Phil without setting off a maelstrom of weird effects.

She saved TikTok for last.

There was only one account she followed on TikTok. It posted Wednesdays and Saturdays. No fixed time.

Wil's TikTok.

She let herself wonder, just a little, like she did every time she opened the app to Wil's channel, if Wil wondered if Katie watched her videos.

Because, *because,* what a completely ambrosial thought. Wil, posting, watching hearts come in, wondering if one of them was hers.

Katie knew, of course, that Wil had seen her movies. Everyone saw her movies. Diana liked to tell her what people said, and a few times she'd mentioned Beanie and Wil in the same breath in the context of what they thought of one of Katie's movies, and Katie had imagined asking her mother a million breathless questions about exactly, *exactly* what Wil had said, but she never did.

It was more fun to imagine Wil watching. So many times, in so many audiences, Wil had been there, watching Katie.

Then, in Chicago, Wil was right there, and Katie had basked in the familiar feeling—right up until she got the first question about Ben. Then, Katie hated that Wil was there. Wil did not belong in a world that Ben had corrupted.

Wil belonged in her own sparkly world.

But this past year, for the first time, Wil had been sharing a part of her world with everyone else, which meant that Katie got to be a part of *her* audience.

Twice a week, Wil kissed someone. Never the same person twice. The camerawork, from a directorial perspective, left something to be desired. It would be close up and never pull back, or it would be six feet away and never zoom in. Katie assumed there was no one operating the camera, just a cell phone on a tripod, probably, set up wherever Wil and the person she was kissing today decided they wanted to put it.

There were no captions but *Wil + blank,* with the other person's name in the blank, followed by the person's pronouns. There was no music.

There was sound, though.

The videos were edited into four fifteen-second segments that told the story of the kiss, beginning, always, with the *before.*

Lingering in the moment where Wil and the person she would be kissing had to confront what was happening.

Today it was *Danya, she/her.* Danya was small, a white woman with short frizzy dark hair and big dark eyes.

The people Wil kissed were not introduced. They just appeared, sitting across from Wil on one of two wooden stools or standing facing her, always in front of the same wrinkled white studio backdrop.

They looked at Wil, or they didn't look at Wil, or they tried to figure out whether to look at Wil or not. Sometimes they held hands. Some of them talked.

I'm so nervous, do we just do this? How do we do this?

You tell me. Tell me what to do.

Are you filming?

Is this happening?

Today, Danya didn't say anything. She put her hand at Wil's waist, splaying her fingers over the soft blue of Wil's T-shirt, and stepped close enough that Wil had to bend down. Wil was tall, at least a foot taller than this woman, whose face she cupped in her hand.

Then it just started. Their mouths met. Katie watched Wil's fingers flex against Danya's face—an involuntary reaction, surprise, or pleasure—and the intensity of the kiss shifted.

Katie felt heat race up her chest and neck.

The film cut. Now Wil's fingers were in Danya's hair, spread out over her nape, and Danya's arms had come up to wrap around Wil. Wil's blond hair had fallen down over her eyes. Her body curved around Danya's, one knee bent, and Katie couldn't figure out what to look at, it was all so good. Wil's hair and jeans and motorcycle boots, Danya's short skirt rucked up a little bit, her top coming away at the waistband, her hands roaming like she couldn't figure out what to do with them, what she wanted, what was next.

Another fifteen seconds, the same. The tension made Katie's heart race. She'd never been able to watch porn, there was too much choreography and something she couldn't put her finger on that felt like violence, but she'd had to make a rule for herself that she could only watch these videos one time, or else watching these videos would be the only thing she ever, ever did.

So she tried to memorize them. How Danya went up on her tiptoes and gripped the fabric of Wil's T-shirt across her shoulder blades, pulling her closer. How Wil adjusted the angle of the kiss, took it deeper, until Danya made a muffled noise, and then the energy shifted again.

Katie was pretty sure Wil had a timer in her head that told her how long sixty seconds were. Because there was always this part—this part where she stroked her hand down the person's head, or eased her hips back, or pulled away to smile, her nose against the person's nose, her forehead on theirs, and maybe laugh.

There was always the last fifteen seconds, when they figured out how to pull away. How to go back to who they'd been before they started kissing someone they'd never kissed before, someone they didn't know, or barely knew, or had never known like this.

It was the part Katie liked best of all. Watching two people figure out what they needed in the moment. Watching Wil tuck someone's hair behind their ear, or run her hand over their shoulder, letting them know that everything would be okay.

They stepped apart.

Katie let out a breath.

The video faded to black.

Chapter Three

Wil piled her plate with German potato salad, some kind of sausage that was in an electric skillet on the buffet table with a lot of apples, those sliced cucumbers in the white dill dressing stuff, and three of Diana Price's giant soft rolls, which she dragged across a plate that held three sticks of room-temp butter rather than bothering to cut off a portion with the butter knife.

She was going to find a good spot and smash this food so hard.

Wil surveyed the Prices' truly ginormous living room. Katie had purchased this place for them several years ago in a tony new development on the east side of Green Bay. Wil worked for the agency that insured the Prices, so she had a good idea of what she was looking at. She'd actually recently come out here in her role as an adjuster to document where a tree branch had taken out a corner of their new LeafGuard gutters on the four-car garage.

There was a trio of forest-green oversized chairs by the front windows, and Wil went to claim one near her mother, snagging an overstuffed pillow to put on her thighs, drape her napkin over, and make a tray for her food so it would be closer to her mouth. She speared a piece of sausage, kabob'd it with a chunk of potato salad, and stuffed the whole thing in, closing her eyes. "Fuck, that is so good."

"Wil, Jesus Pete!" Beanie poked her hard in the shoulder. She was smaller and scrappier than Wil, but otherwise they were a mother-daughter copy-paste. "Try something other than pure Neanderthal. I'm not even asking for manners at this point, just basic human behavior." Beanie knifed and forked her own piece of sausage and took a bite. "Fuck. That *is* so good. What the hell does Diana put in this?"

"Even if you knew," Wil said, "you couldn't replicate it."

Beanie pointed her fork at Wil. "Don't I know it. And yet you grew to adulthood."

"God bless Marie Callender," Wil and her mother said in unison.

Wil surveyed the room. She knew a lot of the people, most of them old friends or work colleagues of the Prices. She'd been to a version of this event a lot of times as a kid. "So I've been meaning to ask you, what made Diana decide to get back in the holiday party game? With Katie visiting, I thought the policy was strictly no guests when Katie's home, forever and ever, amen."

"Mmm." Beanie finished chewing. "Katie's idea, apparently. She's hoping to be home for almost a month instead of a short visit. Diana didn't want so many people here, but I got the sense Katie gave her a guest list and insisted." Beanie looked at Wil significantly.

Wil applied herself to her plate, skipping her mom's scrutiny. If Beanie was implying that Katie had wanted Wil here, and wanted her here for some reason Wil had access to, in the hope that Wil would tell Beanie what that reason was, Wil could not help her mother.

Of course, if what Beanie wanted was for Wil to confess that she was glad she'd made Katie's guest list, and that she'd given herself goose bumps wondering if this meant she and Katie would talk to each other or somehow *connect*, Beanie would have to live without that satisfaction. Wil would never confess such a thing to Beanie, which Beanie must know, since she had known Wil from literal birth.

Wil looked around the room, considering each of the guests again from the angle of knowing Katie had requested their attendance. There was no one else even close to Wil's age. This was a room full of Diana and Craig Price's oldest friends and—judging by all the blond in the room—most trusted relatives. No one else Wil and Katie had known in high school. Just Wil.

She had been thinking about Katie noticing her at the Chicago event for days. Now she was finding out Katie had especially invited her tonight.

"You're thinking." Beanie softly kicked her. "You're making thinking face."

Thinking face was what Beanie had called it when Wil's dad dropped into the depths of his own head, sometimes for long minutes at a time. The memory made Wil's throat catch, so she focused her attention on her dinner roll, refusing to blink until the threat of having feelings in front of her mom had subsided. "I'm eating and not talking. It doesn't mean I'm thinking."

Beanie laughed. "It's hilarious that you're still trying to dodge me like this, like I have just fallen off the turnip truck."

"I thought that saying involved a potato truck."

Beanie furrowed her brows like she was trying to remember, then kicked Wil again. "Don't distract me. Tell me what you're thinking about."

"Where's Katie?"

It was a question Wil had asked a million times when she was with Beanie, and Beanie was with Diana, and Wil—dying of boredom—was trying to figure out if she could play with Katie as a survival strategy.

Not that there was anything wrong with playing with Katie, it was more that Katie was always off doing her own thing. Reading a book in her room. At a voice lesson. Practicing piano.

Wil had played softball or volleyball or had cheer camp in the summer. She relentlessly pursued straight As and otherwise favored sedentary pursuits. Streaming shows, video games, computers, food, music.

They hadn't been, in any way, the same type of kid, which was why Beanie and Diana had given up matchmaking their friendship before they hit middle school.

"She's here somewhere," Beanie said. "She got in Saturday night. She had to get her cats settled into the suite downstairs."

"*There's* a reason to have a shitload of money. I could take Almond Butter anywhere." Wil's cat was sixteen and the primary recipient of Wil's expendable income in the form of consistent, high-quality geriatric vet care.

"You have plenty of money," Beanie said. "Enough that you could buy yourself a place like a grown-up. Hell, you could buy the place you live in now and keep the housemates. Or get a new car. Your dad would roll over in his grave if he knew you were still driving that Bronco."

Wil's Bronco was the secondary recipient of her expendable income. Her dad had willed it to her, mostly as a joke. He'd died when Wil was in college after battling Huntington's his whole adult life. They had been very close, and Wil had learned how to drive on the Bronco shortly after her first lesson, when she dropped its transmission.

She loved that truck.

"I love you, Mom," Wil said, and leaned over and kissed her mother's cheek.

"I do know that. I just feel it's my duty to occasionally say important mom things like 'Don't drive a 1984 Bronco' or 'Maybe stop kissing people on the internet.'" Beanie grinned at her. It was a smile that said, *I know you're thinking about your dad. I would so much like to hear what you're thinking. And feeling. Tell me about your heart, Wil, I'm your only mother.*

"I take it all under advisement." Wil had to wrinkle her nose, just a little bit, to keep the sting from traveling to her eyes. "I am well advised."

Now that the parenting part of her evening out with Beanie was over, Wil ate her delicious food and wondered if she'd only see Katie from afar or if she'd actually have a chance to talk to her.

She'd just let her third roll dissolve in her mouth, swiping her finger through a pool of melted butter and dill dressing, when there was excitement by the huge granite breakfast bar that poked into the living room. The excitement was Katie, in black leggings and a black T-shirt with no bra, and a lot of cat hair, visible even from across the room. She was talking and smiling with a woman Diana was introducing her to.

Katie looked good. Wil was grateful for her outfit, actually. Her outfit helped. If Katie had come into the room as Hollywood Katie, Wil wasn't sure she'd have been able to talk to her. Katie in interviews and talk shows was a creature so lovely, she was hard to understand as human. Her long limbs, awkward and too much in high school, turned out to be made to occupy drapes of precious fabric in impossible configurations under bright lights. The angles and planes of Katie's facial structure—Upper Midwest by way of Norwegian immigrants—had always seemed, in person, back then, a little strange, but the camera caressed Katie's face like it had been looking for those cheekbones and shadows its whole life.

But here, in the living room, with more than a dozen years between then and now, Wil could see that Katie's body was seriously hot, and Katie had learned how to use it so that it looked like something gleaming and soft, *and* she knew how to wear leggings—even covered in cat hair—like they were a gift of joy from the baby Jesus.

She had the same layered, shaggy, casually expensive blond-brown hair as in her photographs, but without styling, the track lights caught the halo of shorter, unruly hairs frizzed through it, and without makeup, Katie's face was a fascinating kaleidoscope of Katie then and Katie now, shifting as she laughed and talked.

Wil couldn't stop looking at her.

"Go say hi," Beanie said. "Everyone else here is old. And get me a piece of the coconut cake."

"Okey-doke." Wil stood, determinedly not fixing her hair or otherwise preening such that Beanie would know exactly what she'd been thinking. "I assume you also want 'just a teeny slice' of the chess pie."

"The teeniest. But not too teeny."

"Got it. A regular slice of chess pie."

Beanie winked at her.

Wil started across the huge room, arrowing toward Katie, who'd begun slowly making her way to the buffet. She was curious to find out where this would lead. Curious to notice just *how* curious she felt, considering the circumstances.

She wasn't someone who had a problem approaching people. It was her ease with new people, combined with her lack of long-term romantic prospects, that had made one of her housemates say that Wil would never be able to really *be* with a person, even if she made out with a hundred people.

That had gotten Wil's attention.

Probably someone else would have followed up on that observation in a different way, like reading self-help or scheduling counseling, for example, but Wil felt that her housemate had set out a very clear proposal for how to look at this issue, and the proposal intrigued her. She'd actually always loved kissing.

So she'd started the kissing TikToks as kind of a lark. A year into it, however, Wil was starting to understand that the project was *doing* something to her. Probably the kissing TikToks were why she'd said yes when Beanie invited her to Chicago to watch Katie.

All of which meant that as Wil made her way to the buffet, she felt like something new was happening, something important, but she wasn't afraid. Not exactly. She was searching for how to let Katie know that she'd been thinking about her for a long time— more very recently—without suggesting that Katie should have been doing the same.

But also, Wil *had* seen Katie's smile after she spotted Wil in Chicago, so she couldn't believe this would go entirely unfavorably.

Katie had arrived at the buffet now. She had a platter in her hand, not a plate—like the kind of platter you put on your wedding registry to put a whole turkey on—which made a surprised smile break across Wil's face, because what kind of courage did that take? For Katie Price, Hollywood movie star, to tell Diana after all these years to throw one of her old-school holiday parties, then to show up in casual clothes, no makeup, and pile up a whole platter full of food. It was such a move.

It said, *Look at me. I'm still me.*

It said, *Don't treat me any differently than you used to. Don't sell me out.*

Plus, Katie Price with a big platter of food was delightfully familiar. Diana was probably the best cook Wil had ever met, and she never cooked on a small scale. All the Prices could eat. Their buffets were the only buffets Wil had ever been to that *had* platters.

Just as Wil was close enough to Katie that she couldn't plausibly pretend she'd only been approaching the buffet to get dessert, Katie looked up and saw her.

This time, Katie's gaze didn't move away.

They made eye contact. In a single heartbeat, Wil knew that she hadn't been invited to this party as an afterthought. It was no coincidence she was the only person here who was Katie's age. She was the only person at this party *for Katie*. Everyone else on the guest list was for Craig and Diana.

Then, like thirteen years had never happened, neither one of them could stop smiling.

"Guess what?" Wil stepped into the spot next to Katie at the buffet and picked up two dessert plates, conscious of the fact that standing next to Katie Price at her parents' holiday party and pretending like thirteen years had never happened was the best feeling she'd had inside her body in a really long time.

Katie put down the serving spoon in the big tureen that held German potato salad and turned to face Wil. They were nearly the same height.

She was right there, and Wil was right here.

Wil watched as Katie looked her up and down. It was a surprise. The look was not guarded, it was appraising, and slow enough that Wil had to remind herself to hold still and take it. God knew that plenty of people looked at Katie.

Katie set her platter down. "What?" she asked. "Tell me."

Well, that was hot. Wil looked more closely at Katie. She was so interesting to look at with her wide-spaced eyes and her full mouth. She was breathing a little fast, her lips slightly parted. Wil couldn't remember what she'd thought she was going to say before, because she couldn't think past this moment, right now, standing with Katie, conscious all at once of how much she'd fucking *missed* her.

But she had to say something, so she said the first thing she thought of when she thought of senior year Wil-and-Katie, what they'd talked about obsessively, cracking each other up in the front seat of the Bronco until Wil's cheeks were bright red and Katie had to wrap both arms around her stomach against the ache of it.

"I saw Andrew Cook at Java! Java! with Brunette on Monday. Before you think I've been stalking him since we were in high school, let me say this is the *first* time I've seen him since then. He was whispering in Brunette's ear."

"You're serious."

"As an AP exam."

First semester of their senior year, Wil and Katie had both found themselves in Mr. Andrew Cook's U.S. Government class. Mr. Cook was young and relatively new to teaching, but he already had a reputation around East High as a teacher who sliced students down with negging, passive-aggressive bullshit, and unfair grading.

Katie had been a bit scared, because she needed the A to get some part of her scholarship package approved for her school in North Carolina.

Wil had been pissed because she just hated bullies like Mr. Cook.

Katie lifted an eyebrow and gave Wil a look that was wide-eyed and almost incorruptible, except that the arching eyebrow made it a little dirty. "Did his mouth touch her ear when he whispered, or was it polite, we're-in-a-theater whispering to anyone?"

The low and conspiratorial way Katie spoke made Wil's middle finally relax, her chest and neck go warm, and her personal space disappear. Like it always had. "Lips to lobe, Katie. And she turned and smiled at him after."

Katie wrinkled her nose. No one had liked Mr. Cook, but Katie least of all. "Okay. Go on."

It only took the first day of class to establish that Mr. Cook was a bully. He'd pretended not to know about accommodations for Jen Diver's IEP when everyone in senior year knew exactly what Jen needed in class and also loved Jen. Mr. Cook actually sent her out of the classroom instead of teaching her.

That had led to Wil calling him out for ADA violations and Mr. Cook implying that Wil didn't have brains because tits and blond hair leached them from the cranial region of a woman's body. He hadn't said the last part, but he'd said something similar enough that the class had started to make noise, and Wil was ready to shit-kick her 4.0 to the curb.

That's when Katie had stepped in, affecting a persona that Wil could only describe as "oldest girl in the one-room Wisconsin prairie schoolhouse attempts to affiance the country teacher." To everyone's shock, it worked. Katie's bottomless, generous, approving attention mellowed Mr. Cook right out. From then on, in that class, he did whatever Katie implied would make her happy. Or make her willing to be his bride? It was a bit confusing. But Katie had saved that class for everyone. It was one of her best roles, really, and only fifteen people ever saw the performance.

Outside of Mr. Cook's class, Katie, that last semester of their senior year, had her first light schedule since she started tap in the first grade, so they'd partnered on a project.

They hadn't been able to see it through to the end, though.

Wil had almost forgotten all about it until she saw Mr. Cook canoodling with Brunette at the coffee shop, and it brought the memories of their senior-year deep dive into Mr. Cook's personal life back in vivid detail.

"So I took in the vibe," Wil said. "This was not a platonic vibe."

Katie nodded. "You must have googled, right?"

"Absolutely I did. He's still in the school directory, but they shut down the details now. You can't see anything but a name and what subject he teaches. If you want to send an email, they won't even give you the address. You have to fill out a form. So, naturally, I dug around, and I found a Facebook for his wife."

"When you say you found his wife's Facebook, you mean Official Wife?" Katie hadn't taken her eyes off Wil. It was starting to make Wil's heart race in a way that was pleasantly familiar, but also confusing, because what was this? Flirting?

Were they flirting right now?

Wil wasn't used to being confused by flirting. For the past year, she'd talked two strangers a week into kissing her on camera. Flirting was pretty familiar ground.

Katie was pretty familiar ground, too, but Wil hadn't really thought about the way she used to talk to Katie about Mr. Cook as *flirting*.

She decided to throw caution to the wind. Worst-case scenario, she wouldn't get invited to next year's holiday party. Best-case, she got to see what happened if she brought her fullest, most charismatic game to the project of flirting with one of the hottest people in America.

"Yes, Official Wife, and on her Facebook, she's got recent pictures with him. Still blond. Same woman. Their kids are thirteen years older. No Brunette in sight."

Katie looked up at the ceiling. She was thinking. Her leggings had a hole in them by the hipbone. Wil thought it was probably from a cat claw. Up close, she looked a little tired, but her skin was like a fucking Rembrandt. Spilling light.

At some point, someone had fixed the tiny chip in the corner of her front tooth, which was too bad.

Then Katie put the rest of the potato salad on her platter, and sausage, and took the three rolls that Wil handed her, and wrinkled her nose at the cucumbers. "What's your plan?"

"Don't have one." Wil smiled. "We agreed not to investigate on our own. That's where we left it back then. That's where it stands today."

"Make a plan," Katie said. "I'm here for a month. Though, you know"—Katie stepped into Wil's undefended personal space—"I was never actually sure if our investigation of Mr. Cook was an investigation so much as it was a way to spice up hanging out in your Bronco."

Wil grinned, almost laughed. "Did hanging out in my Bronco need to be spicier?"

Katie didn't answer that question, but she did give Wil a smile not unlike the one Wil had seen on the stage in Chicago. "My original objection still stands."

"Your original objection being there's no evidence this is a second family. It could be an affair. Now well into its second decade without being discovered by Official Wife."

"That's my position. Although I suppose they could be polyamorous." Katie put a slice of coconut cake next to the potato salad. Her platter was going to start groaning. "A little unconventional for Green Bay, but we've seen more of the world, haven't we, Wil? So we can come at this from a new angle and apply the benefit of our extensive experience."

The look she gave Wil very unexpectedly made Wil go hot all over.

But Wil recovered, because she was *Wil Greene*. "I still have the Bronco."

Katie's eyes widened in genuine surprise, forgetting she was cage-match-flirting with Wil. "Like, it runs?"

"Smooth as an old lawnmower, Katie."

Katie grabbed a fork and looked at the ceiling again, grinning, just like she used to when Wil said something that enormously pleased her and she had to take a moment to feel her big feeling inside herself. "Pick me up where the driveway goes around to the back at eleven. Bring supplies."

"Tonight?" But Wil wasn't seriously incredulous. She was getting what she wanted, what she'd figured out she *could* want when she made eye contact with Katie at the buffet and they both broke out in smiles.

Katie was home for a month, and Wil was going to make the most of it.

"Time's a-wasting," Katie said. "What? We're going to let this affair go on for another thirteen years without interference or violating an entire family's privacy?"

"What you mean is, we're going to find out once and for all that Mr. Cook has two families. Right here in Green Bay. And not in the sister wives way, but in the traveling salesman or sailor way."

Because this had been the debate. They agreed 100 percent that Mr. Cook was the absolute worst kind of human. Where they differed was on the question of whether they'd inadvertently discovered he was committing straightforward adultery—Katie's position—or whether he was actually a bigamist.

There had been a fantasy, shared between them, of figuring out the truth so they could tell both women and free them from their disastrous attachment to the terrible human they mutually seemed to love.

"I never bought the two families thing. Still don't." Katie took a big bite of potatoes. "Oh my fucking God. No one cooks like my mom."

"No one does. I would take a bath in the potato salad."

"Would you?" Katie stabbed a sausage. "Would you actually? Would you fill even an average-sized bathtub up with my mother's German potato salad and then take off all of your clothes and, like"—Katie mimed, *incredibly* well, squishing into a bathtub full of wet potatoes—"into the potato salad?"

"You've only made it more attractive." Wil said this with her best smile, the one she'd been accused of deploying for nefarious purposes, and then watched Katie's eyes widen a fraction. "Now I'm not going to be able to stop thinking about it. I knew a woman once who'd filled a tub with Doritos. It was a whole thing for her. I can't say that it sounded bad."

"German potato salad tub *is* weirdly hot, now that I really commit," Katie said. "Like Roman hedonism meets capitalist excess. Midwest German–style."

Wil gave herself a minute to thoroughly stare at Katie Price.

Katie stared right back at her, spearing her fork into a bite of potato salad and eating it without taking her eyes off Wil.

There was an element here that Wil didn't understand. An under-the-surface thing coming from Katie, not from her. Wil wasn't much of an under-the-surface person.

Whatever it was, it felt good. She liked it.

"So now that we do have more experience, as you say, maybe we raise the stakes of this investigation." Wil started filling the dessert plates.

"You mean a bet." Katie raised an eyebrow. "To pile on the spicy."

Wil laughed. "Right. I mean, it has to be interesting."

"Well, to be *interesting,* we both have to get vulnerable." Katie put half a roll in her mouth. "This is what I've learned from acting. Only human vulnerability is interesting and creates stakes. Everything else is dull."

Wil had a million TikTok followers who agreed with Katie 100 percent. But probably Katie didn't know about her TikTok.

This didn't seem like the moment to mention it.

"Where do you want to hash this out?" Wil asked.

"Come sit with me on the sofa with the mallards on it. It's really fucking comfortable."

Wil gave Beanie her desserts and accepted her compliments for entertaining Katie, and then she took her own giant piece of pie and peanut butter cookie and sat beside Katie on the mallard sofa.

Wil remembered this sofa from the Prices' old house. They'd moved it to the new house, probably because it was the best sofa Wil had ever sat on. It made her want to slide underneath it and write her name on some part of the framing so that, when the Prices wore it out and carried it to the curb to donate, they'd see Wil's dibs and give her a call to pick it up.

Katie pulled her legs up into crisscross applesauce and turned completely sideways to face Wil. "I have a confession."

"Good. What could it be, famous actress Katie Price who I haven't seen in thirteen years, that you have to confess to me?"

Wil's wry tone made Katie look up from her plate, her mouth almost smiling in a way that put Wil on alert. "I've seen your Tik-Tok."

Wil closed her eyes. Yeah. Yeah, that was a good confession. She liked that. "When you say you've seen it . . ."

"I mean I look at it twice a week. Every time you post."

Good *goddamn*. "That makes it so easy for me to know what I want to bet."

Katie was looking right at Wil, making perfect eye contact, her cheeks almost red and her eyes incredibly soft. "I'm willing to put that on the line."

Wil did not, for one moment, believe that Katie meant what she was saying. But it didn't matter. This, like their plan to ride around in the Bronco later, was all for fun. Part of what made it fun was knowing there weren't any *real* stakes.

Wil told herself.

And tried to believe.

"You would come on my TikTok and be my Wednesday. Or Saturday." Wil could not let herself think too hard about this proposition right now, on the mallard sofa, in the middle of Diana and Craig Price's holiday party. She was going to have to save it for when she was alone in her bedroom.

The thing that Katie probably didn't understand—or maybe she did, but Wil *really* did, in every part of her body—was how long a minute lasted when you were kissing someone for the first time.

"I would if I lost," Katie clarified. "If I'm wrong about Mr. Cook, and he's not just having an affair, because he has a whole second family." Katie's voice was a little rough. She hadn't stopped looking at Wil. "But you know this would explode your entire life."

"Maybe my life needs exploding." Wil meant for this to be a line—the kind of thing she might say to catch someone's attention—but it didn't sound like that, and she was tuned in enough to Katie's changes of expression to watch Katie's gaze sharpen as the words landed.

Maybe my life needs exploding.

Of course her life needed exploding. Wil wasn't even meant to be here.

Katie had left for Chicago, bound from there to Asheville to Los Angeles with a possible stop-off in New York City, and Wil had gone to Michigan. She was supposed to have gone to law school after that. She was supposed to have clerked for the Supreme Court.

She was supposed to be somewhere else, doing something else. Something big.

But her dad had died, just like they'd always known he would, and Wil had stayed in Green Bay, even though that was never the plan.

It was just what had happened to her, somehow, in the years since Katie got famous.

Katie leaned forward. "I have to tell you something else." Her voice was low. Soft. "I didn't mean to not see you after your dad died. I thought I would. There was a reason I didn't make it back for the funeral, a reason I didn't have control over, but I've regretted it. I regret that I didn't make it." She blinked. Her eyes were shiny. "I really liked your dad. He was the only grown-up who would ever do karaoke with me. He had such a beautiful natural tenor."

Wil nodded. She couldn't think what to say. She looked down at Katie's plate and noticed the hole by her hipbone was all stretched out. She could see a teal elastic from what had to be very small underwear.

She cleared her throat. "I didn't hold it against you."

Katie nodded. She reached out one finger and tapped it against Wil's knee, and that tap echoed through Wil like Katie was knocking on a door, asking Wil to let her in. "Tell me more, then. Tell me why your life needs exploding."

Well, that was easy. Wil conjured up her mother's list. "I rent. I still live with housemates. I still drive the Bronco, like, as my full-time ride. But not because of money. I could afford better."

"What do you do for work?"

"I'm an insurance adjuster. I came up for a promotion two years ago that would put me in charge of all the adjusters for my company in the Fox Valley, but I'd have to change to another office, so I haven't taken it. They ask me every eight weeks like clockwork. I don't know." Wil shook her head. "There's probably something with Almond Butter, too."

"You still have Almond Butter?! Oh my God! I love Almond Butter! Do you have a picture? Gimme." Katie held out her hand, so Wil fished her phone out of her pocket, unlocked it, found a picture of Almond Butter, and handed it over.

"Oh, she looks so good! I can't believe how good she looks! What would she be, sixteen? Seventeen? I forget her birthday." Katie was swiping through Wil's photos, one after the next, and it was true most of them *were* pictures of Almond Butter, but it wasn't a photo set. It was Wil's whole camera roll. There was other stuff. Random shots of things like receipts or her health insurance card she'd had to upload for a medical appointment.

Also, pictures from kissing sessions. Some stuff that had happened *after* kissing sessions a few times.

Katie swiped, and one of those pictures filled the screen of Wil's phone as though Wil had conjured it with her thoughts. Katie's perfect eyebrows shot up. "God." She looked at Wil. "I remember him."

"Them."

Katie nodded. "Sure. I remember them. That was a good one. Holy shit."

Her finger hovered over the screen of Wil's phone as though she wanted to keep swiping, to flip through a slideshow of what had happened between Wil and Emory after they finished filming the TikTok.

"That's the only picture." Wil took a bite of peanut butter cookie, because she couldn't think past the heat in her cheeks and between her legs.

Katie put the phone to sleep and handed it back to Wil. "Okay. So, I am very sorry for invading your privacy. I get excited about cats, but that is not an excuse, just an explanation."

"No worries."

"All right." She did an exaggerated nod, her whole torso bouncing up and down with her head. There was no food left on her platter. Wil wasn't sure where she'd put it. Or when. "Hammering this out, then. If I win, you do adulting things. Fix your renting and housemate situation, buy a real car, take the promotion, maybe make an end-of-life plan for Almond Butter?" She looked at Wil with a question in her eyes.

"Yeah. The vet suggested this might be a good idea."

"And if I lose, which I won't, because there's no way a teacher at East High has carried on a double life in a town of a hundred thousand souls for a dozenish years, I will go on your TikTok. I should warn you that if that happens, it's not going to be a small event in your life. It will be everything that happened before you kissed Katie Price on TikTok"—she gestured to the left of her body—"and the aftermath"—she gestured to the right.

Then Katie went still, frowned, and blew out a long breath that let Wil see the tiredness around her eyes again. "Actually, even if you don't kiss me on TikTok," she said. "Even if someone takes our picture when we're out in public together. It could be a lot of things, and they'd all mean exposure, the kind of exposure that's not in your control."

The kind of exposure, Wil assumed, that would throw her name into the morass of speculation around Katie's love life and her breakup with Ben Adelsward.

Because Katie's press, when it wasn't about her current project or her cats, was always about Ben. Wil had never, on any level, understood the appeal, but she'd figured at the time he swooped Katie away to LA that if Ben Adelsward made Katie happy, that was good.

It had been intimated over the years between Diana and Beanie, however, that this was not the case.

"Maybe we should walk this back," Katie said. "It's fun for me to see you, but I don't want to get carried away and cause problems for you."

Wil looked across the room. Beanie was still by the front window, talking to Diana and a man with a mustache. There was Christmas music playing quietly in the background.

Katie was the one who lived in Los Angeles, but Wil couldn't help thinking *she* was the one who wasn't supposed to be here. At Diana's for a holiday party with Katie Price. In Green Bay.

Healthy and whole, with her whole life in front of her.

"I don't want to minimize," Wil said. "I know that it's not anything in my experience to have literally everyone on the globe not only watching you but also talking about you, having their lives changed by your work, thinking about what you made them feel. But I will say that there are ways my own life didn't even start until recently. I don't know what to do with it yet, but what I *have* done, so far, is let a lot of people look at me. And I don't mind telling you that I haven't stopped letting them, and it's not because of the passive creator income stream from TikTok. Also—"

She stopped herself. Wil had already said more than she would have ever guessed, and she still wasn't sure what everything she said was headed toward. Going this deep wasn't normally how she talked to people.

It was how she'd talked to Katie. Ever since the day at the beginning of senior year when she'd pulled up alongside Katie in the Bronco. Katie was walking away from the high school, in the opposite direction of anywhere Wil had been able to think she'd want to go, and when Wil slowed down to get her attention, she'd seen Katie wiping at her eyes.

So she pulled over, leaned across the seat to open the passenger door, and asked, *You want to get in?*

It was the beginning of what they'd had together that year.

"Also, what?" Katie sounded a little dreamy. She hadn't taken her eyes off Wil the whole time Wil was silent, thinking.

"I've missed you." Wil put her palms on her thighs. Breathed in, breathed out. "But I don't want to make you feel any kind of way about that. It's not to make you feel guilty. It's just something I'm figuring out right now."

Katie covered Wil's hand with her own, just for a moment, and the contact pushed a shockwave of heat through the middle of Wil's chest. "I was waiting in my publicist's office flipping through *People,* and there was one of those splash pages with a roundup of social media accounts to follow. Nothing I would ever typically stop on, but I recognized you in a grainy two-by-two-inch screenshot photo from one of your videos, Wil. And I stopped on the page, and I read the two hundred words *People* magazine had written about your account over and over until I just tore away the part of the page with you on it." Katie leaned into the back cushion of the sofa and smiled at Wil. "I missed you, too."

Hearing that was a big enough gift, it gave Wil the push she needed to ask her next question.

"Are you into girls?" Wil had no idea. Katie hadn't dated in high school, and Katie also hadn't dated since Ben Adelsward—or if she had, the press didn't know, and Diana wasn't talking about it. "To be clear, I'll kiss you either way. But I'm curious."

"I don't know how to answer that. Are you?" Katie was leaning her side against the back of the sofa, and now she bent her long legs up, stretching her leggings tight over her knees. She hadn't looked away from Wil even once.

"I haven't met a gender I'm *not* attracted to yet," Wil confessed. "It used to be that I had to get to know someone, but the kissing thing has rearranged my brain on that. I think I could have a relationship or a fling or anything with almost anybody. There don't seem to be any barriers there. The only barrier I've got—and I've challenged it with some very wonderful people a few times—is monogamy. I'm a pair-bonder. I blame my dad for that."

Wil could feel the back of her neck get hot in a way that was a precursor to blushing, which surprised her. She'd talked about this kind of thing a lot, with a lot of different people, but there was something about the way Katie was looking at her face.

Katie nodded. "I don't know. I've only come with one partner, and I think even that was more about me than him. There hasn't been a single one of your videos that hasn't turned me on, but I haven't looked at why. There's something in me I don't get yet, but to be honest, I'm not worried about it."

God, Wil thought. *God.* This—what Katie was calling vulnerability, getting vulnerable—was, in fact, Wil's kryptonite milkshake.

Katie looked like she knew it, too, or at least as though she was thoroughly pleased with Wil's reaction. Wil resettled herself on the mallard sofa, looking wildly around the room to make sure none of the guests were paying attention to the unfolding drama between her and Katie.

They were not. This was a crowd of people who'd spent a lot of time ignoring Wil Greene and Katie Price and their various shenanigans.

"What do you . . . when you . . . ?" Wil cleared her throat and wondered how she could possibly walk this back.

Or walk it forward much more quickly.

"When I masturbate?"

Wil needed to lie down. Maybe if she lay down on top of Katie, every part of herself matching up to every part of Katie, right on the mallard couch, it would resolve the problem she was having.

It would create some new problems, though, given the number of people present.

Katie had stopped looking at her and was nibbling on one fingernail. She pulled her hand away from her mouth and stared at her manicure, then caught Wil's eyes again and suddenly— surprisingly—laughed. "That is not an interview question, Wil Greene. I was *not prepared*." She fanned at her cheeks, but she was smiling. "Sometimes I turn on music I love, really loud. Then it's just all sensation. Sometimes I loop on a moment in a book or a movie or a play or something I see in public, not a sexy thing necessarily, it can be an awkward thing or a tender thing. Like a look. Like—"

"The first fifteen seconds of my videos," Wil suggested.

That earned Wil another overwhelmed-Katie-ceiling-smile. "*Yes.*" She looked back at Wil. "Like that. Maybe more the last three seconds *before* the next fifteen seconds."

Oh.

The buildup.

The just-before.

The maybe-this-won't-happen moment.

It was Wil's favorite three seconds, too.

"What are your pronouns?" Wil felt like she was barely keeping up with this conversation and all of the urgent things she needed to know. It was not what she'd expected.

It was what she should have expected. Wil had forgotten what it was like to have Katie Price's full attention.

Now she remembered.

She remembered, too, what a revelation it had been in high school when she'd picked Katie up in the Bronco and driven her around, and they'd talked more that first night than they'd talked to each other in all the seventeen years before.

"Professionally, right now, my pronouns are she and her," Katie said. "For just myself, privately, I'm not sure. I don't think I care. I don't mean that in a flippant way, or a way that would ever dismiss or stand in for something that others have fought hard for. I mean, I guess, that when I reach into that, it's sunbeams. Oxygen." Katie made a series of gestures that looked like dancing, watching Wil until Wil laughed, but also completely understood what she was trying to say. "What are yours?"

"She and her."

"Why? I'm sorry if that's rude." Katie waved her hands in front of her face like she was trying to stop herself or slow herself down, but her voice was too delighted-sounding to make her attempt serious.

Wil shook her head, smiling. "We're in it now, Katie. No apologies. I guess it's because *she* and *her* make sense to how I feel about sex with myself and with other people. For me, even though it's not necessarily true for others, my gender and how I feel about sex are twisted together."

Every time Wil said the word *sex* out loud to Katie Price on the mallard sofa, in the middle of a room full of people, she felt a fraction more reckless, as though at any moment she might grab Katie by the hand and pull her out of here into the nearest dark room with a door that locked.

Katie drew a small circle over Wil's denim-covered knee. Wil felt that fingertip in every cell of her body until she ached everywhere. "To get back to this bet we are pretending is serious, and its spoils, I think it's all a pretext for Bronco time."

"Right." She looked at Katie, considering. She should put down this bet right now, because Katie was right. They *were* playing a game.

Except she'd never played at anything with Katie.

And she didn't want to put this bet down.

Katie's warnings were an attempt to make it clear that her celebrity made regular things, even fun things like a bet, kind of impossible. A gamble. Loss. Temporary. A little unreal.

Still. Wil wanted the chance to kiss Katie the way Katie had been watching her kiss other people. *And* she wanted the chance to see what would happen between them if the bet stayed in place—if they couldn't, or wouldn't, kiss until Katie lost. After all, Wil's TikTok was for *first* kisses.

It was also for *onetime* kisses with near-strangers.

Katie wasn't a stranger. If Wil kissed her, it would be because she wanted to kiss her more than once. Also, Wil had already made it clear to Katie that she was monogamous.

What that meant was that if Wil somehow, in the next month that Katie was in town, got all the way to kissing her, she wouldn't be making TikToks anymore.

She would be exploding her life just as she was seeing what the pieces of it actually were.

"Oh, no," Katie said, her expression caught somewhere between excitement and fondness. "I just watched you think through something with your whole brain. You made the face. Whenever you did that in high school, what happened after was always so, so good. We are getting somewhere here."

"I'm not sure where."

"I'm not sure either, but"—Katie stood up, her eyes bright and daring—"definitely, *definitely* pick me up at eleven."

Wil blew out a breath.

When this inevitably fell apart and Katie went home to Los Angeles, Wil hoped she would have some good memories to tide her over through the next thirteen years.

She should probably be much, much more worried than she could make herself be.

Chapter Four

"I'm loving the comedy for you, and Kennenbear is hot, hot, hot. He has three upcoming joints." April, her agent, flipped through a script. Katie could see her Persian cat behind her, sitting on a cat tower, and another tail just off-screen.

"Are we saying that, for real? 'Joints'? It's so dudeish, it makes my back teeth ache."

"Why your back teeth?" April leaned so close to the camera that Katie could make out the dusting of freckles across her milk-pale skin. April had her bright-red, super-coily hair piled up on her head, and she wore a bear onesie over her plus-size, six-foot-tall, screamingly hot body.

Sometimes it was hard to believe that everyone in Hollywood listened to April Feinstein, but they did. Katie knew for a fact that April scared people, though her reputation was that she was funny, warm, and scrupulously kind. Equitable. But no one fucked with her.

April was the agent Katie had found after she left Ben and had to fire the agent she shared with him. April had been such a boon, too, directing Katie to projects that had gotten her awards, challenged her, kept her out of harm's way, and made money.

"Like, because you grind your back teeth in response to dude things. Maybe." Katie was sitting on the floor of the suite her parents had built into the walkout basement of their house. She'd set her laptop up on the little coffee table in front of the squishy love seat. After her mom's party, she'd come back down here to its pink and gray and white womb-like squishiness to cuddle her cats, talk to April, and—

There had been the thing she'd done before she cuddled her cats. In the small suite's tiny, blissfully blackout-shaded bedroom with its gray gingham wallpaper and crispy white duvet, with the door closed and locked, and a pillow she'd ritualistically folded in half and straddled, her hand under her shirt, thinking about the white-blond baby hairs along Wil's hairline that she'd noticed when Wil had run her fingers through the hair at her nape, a little nervous in response to Katie's questions, and the way her breath had been soft against Katie's cheek when they'd quickly hugged good-bye at the end of the party.

Katie still felt warm from how hard she'd made herself come.

Before Wil left, Beanie had taken a picture of them together with her phone, and Diana had clearly tried to stop herself from reminding Beanie not to show anyone the picture she had just taken, and then failed, making Beanie visibly embarrassed she had taken the picture at all.

The exchange had made Katie's stomach cramp into a sharp ball. The old guilt at what she'd put her mother through ten years ago, as fresh as ever.

Sometimes Katie still had dreams where she woke herself up crying for her mom to come and help her, the phantom feeling of tears slick against the glass screen of the phone taking ages to fade.

When she came back to herself, April was studying her closely. "And Kennenbear makes your teeth ache in this manner?"

Katie smiled, but she could see herself in the little thumbnail screen, and her smile wasn't convincing. "It's mostly the term *joint*, but yeah, maybe also Kennenbear. I'm a little iffy on the whole 'written and directed by a man' situation at this point."

"Like you are literally referring to a joint." April smiled.

"I know. Because words like *auteur* and *film* aren't good enough anymore? Or cool enough? I forget the difference."

"Fuck him. Fuck Kennenbear." April said this decisively. "Besides, the man is a multimillionaire, get a fucking pedicure. Those Jamaica pictures still haunt me."

"I'm intrigued by the Latener project." Katie sifted her hair away from her ear and shoulder, her mood lifting with her thoughts about the beautiful script she'd read on the plane on the way to Green Bay. "I love Gloria Latener, and I love the script."

"But?"

"Hmm. There's no buts, actually. It's something that would be a top-of-the-pile, one-hundred-percent yes at literally any other moment."

"But we want more." April smiled again.

"We do."

Katie looked away from April and ran her hands over Phil's body, stopping at his tail base to give him the scritches he asked for at the end of each pet that turned his purr motor on high. Her conversation with Madelynn had raked up a lot of feelings. A lot of knee-jerk risk aversion that had led to her calling this meeting with April to consider roles in the first place.

A fallback.

For when she fell.

But she hadn't told April that. If she did, April would want to brainstorm it, workshop it, challenge it, call someone in. But Katie didn't want that.

She'd always loved reading scripts. She loved how it felt in her brain to make them live in her head, loved making the characters and rewinding and rereading and lingering over little moments, writing down snippets from them to say out loud to herself and think about.

She loved memorizing them and letting the words saturate her body before she ever began working on the character, even, just sitting with the words, and she loved when the character started talking just to her, then inside of her, and how the world around her began populating with the story and engaging with the character in her body.

Since she was a little girl, she'd had these feelings and sensations reading books, sometimes listening to other people tell a story, watching people, reading scripts and play texts and song lyrics. The stories worked inside of her like a mill, pulling feelings and ideas out of the depth of herself and letting her look at them.

Every single moment of guest directing *Mary Wants It* was one that Katie had relived and relived, her brain humming with pleasure. She'd loved the tools, the camera, she'd loved taking the script to the set, to the table read, she'd loved building the vision for the episode in layers and layers in her mind's eye. Working with the actors from behind the camera made her feel hot and giddy every day she was on set.

After her first guest direction stint earned her an Emmy, it had been an open secret that Katie wanted a feature film project. But she was still considered too young, too big a commodity by most studios as a leading lady box office draw. She felt the responsibility of that, the jobs her craft made for so many, including her team.

But making a whole entire film would *also* make jobs and opportunities for others, giving Katie the chance to break open what was a very conservative and backward town and guide other creatives over the rubble to make something even bigger than a film.

She could do that, just as long as she kept Honor happy, wrote an amazing script, and perfectly played her most important role ever as the woman in Madelynn's imagination—the one sitting in a director's chair, vetted, funded, *trustworthy*.

April was watching her again. Katie had been silent for too long.

She sat back and gave her agent a smile that looked weary, even in the tiny square floating above April's head. "Don't worry about me. I've got this."

"Hmm." April reached up and pulled the pencil out of her curls, gathered her hair up again, and stuck the pencil through it. Her thinking move. Very dangerous. "You talked to Madelynn."

Katie narrowed her eyes. "You already know that. All of you"—Katie made a wild, circling gesture with her hand—"talk to each other, about each other, *at* each other."

"Yes. But Madelynn *talked* to you."

"April."

"Katie." April raised her eyebrow. "I want to get this thing out of first gear. To be clear, by 'this thing,' you know that I mean our company, your projects, your script. I want to get to the part where we're not spending our own money. I want to take the meeting with Marisol Gonzales that she requested after Ben's horrible *Variety* piece, because on the phone, she definitely implied that her Emma Tenayuca biopic that Universal, New Line, and Columbia are fighting over would be a better fit for whatever we're doing, and she wants to know how we could make that happen."

Katie felt a hot flip of pleasure in her chest, followed immediately by sick self-doubt. "It's much too soon. We need to have Honor completely on board first. Without Honor, there's no way we could fund a period epic like that, with hundreds of cast, and get it right, really right, get it as good as what Marisol does. She's seventy. She doesn't suffer fools."

"You need to think more about what it would feel like to walk into that meeting and less about what we would tell her. Marisol directed her last Oscar-winner with a one-point-five-million budget at a closed hotel in Guatemala. She's interested in our vision, not if we have the latest in camera drones and post-production compositing. This is what we *want*. Right? This is what we've always talked about. Don't shut us down before we get to one meeting. And I know I've said this before, but I really think if you let Madelynn do her job and skewer that hangdog-eyed starlet stalker Adelsward, you'd find that the world is a lot bigger and brighter than you—"

"April." Katie shook her head, interrupting April before she could say more. Before she tried to encourage her to step through a door that opened into a freefall.

"Just let us keep talking, okay?" April said.

What she meant was, *I understand that I just scared you, and I am backing down. I also understand you're hiding right now, and you know I'm worried about that, but as long as you keep talking to me, I won't push it.*

"But I'll talk to Latener, too," April said.

Katie let out a long breath and tuned her body in to the feeling of Phil's heavy weight on her lap. She felt guilty for putting her team in a place where they had so many concerns, and she felt even worse that she couldn't make an immediate and clearer plan for what they wanted, but she couldn't. She'd gotten this far considering every angle of every move. "Yes, that's good. Talk to Gloria. See what it would look like to fit the project in."

"Are you writing?"

"I am. Ish. I am writing in the sense that people on the internet, in their writing memes, say is writing. Meaning I am deleting. And making myself snacks. And reading other people's writing and feeling bad."

April laughed. "This part, I'm not worried about at all. You are the reigning queen of finding a way. Remember when Dick Mayhew stopped taking my calls because he said he wanted a lead who could pull off eighteenth-century Dutch? And he didn't think that could possibly be you? And so then you followed him into that patisserie looking like a Vermeer with honest-to-fuck panniers under your skirt and ordered in a perfectly accented noblewoman's Dutch? Surely writing is easier than that."

"Wellicht," Katie said, the Dutch for *perhaps* coming smoothly to her as soon as she thought of the character she'd played in that film, which had earned her a second nomination from the Academy.

April laughed again, and Katie had to admit she did feel a little better. "So what's next this evening?" April asked. "Writing? Slipping into a food coma? Your mom sent me a box of cookies that I've proposed to."

"I'm going out with an old friend." Katie smiled.

April raised her eyebrows and did jazz hands. "Do you have a hometown fuckbuddy, Katelyn Rose Ellis Price?"

I wish, some version of herself, deep in her chest, whispered.

Except, first of all, she didn't want a *fuckbuddy,* never had, and, second, the idea of Wil Greene occupying a role so trivial wasn't something that would ever feel true or possible. Even if it had been thirteen years.

Katie didn't hide her smile, but she kept it cool. "She's the daughter of my mom's oldest friend. We went to high school together. We're going to ride around in her truck and soak in nostalgia."

"You didn't answer my question. You used heteronormative assumptions to dodge my question, in fact." April grinned, leaning back in her bright pink gaming chair, pleased with herself.

Katie looked away, but only to better sift through a few memories so she could tell something to April that was true, even if it wasn't everything.

A tumble of emotion-tight images gathered somewhere in her chest. The way Wil would break out into laughter at the end of every cheer at games, jogging back to the sidelines with her poms at her hips, her high ponytail bouncing, and pull a motorcycle jacket over her uniform to stay warm, which was impossibly cool, and how Katie would feel the phone in her hands vibrate because Wil had sent a text, making Katie nearly explode with the delicious knowledge that the first text the head cheerleader sent from the sidelines after halftime was to *her,* Katie Price, when Wil was literally sitting right next to the most popular and interesting girls at school.

Wil Greene could drive a stick shift. Wil Greene wore a two-piece dress to homecoming that showed her belly button. Wil Greene got straight As in her AP classes but wasn't stuck up.

That Wil Greene had belonged to Katie Price. For a little while.

This Wil Greene wasn't hers, not anymore, but Katie couldn't imagine her as anyone's anything on the side. She was too big, too charismatic, too engaged when she listened, too . . . Wil Greene.

Katie decided to go with the scaffolding of the truth. "Wil and I hung out in a pretty intense way my senior year. Nothing happened. I've started thinking about her again lately because of something she's involved with. When I saw her tonight, I wanted to see her again."

April leaned forward. "This would be Wil-You-or-Won't-You?"

Katie's heart stopped, then started back up with a slow, blood-draining thud. She put her hand over her mouth. She probably shouldn't have been surprised that April had guessed, or known, but years of guarding everything, *everything,* meant she was rarely caught off guard and hated it when she was.

And until April guessed, Katie hadn't talked to anyone, at all, anywhere, about Wil or about Wil's TikTok. Both had been just for her.

"How?" The word came out a bit of a croak. "How did you guess that?"

"You said 'Wil,' you're in Green Bay, my niece and I trade Tik-Toks all fucking day long. That shit is hot. Is she repped?"

"You"—Katie pointed at her—"are both mercenary and also *a lot* for me at this moment."

"I bet. A lot of reality coming at you if *Wil's* your plan, tonight, in the dark, driving around Green Bay, Wisconsin, the air cold, the cab of the truck warm, the radio softly playing."

"Write your own script, April." Katie pointed at her again.

"I am." April's grin was fully salacious. "I'm writing it, and I'm feeling it inside of my body, and I like it, Katie. I like this script. Also, give me the heads-up if you're going to make out on her channel, and I'll be the one to tell Madelynn. I feel like I'm a bit of a Madelynn whisperer, honestly. I can give her stuff like this and make it feel like a career opportunity. For her. That's why she likes me."

"Are you finished?" Katie tried for imperious, but it just came out resigned. April sounded and looked supremely pleased with herself, and of course she should be, given the enormity of what she'd just pried out of Katie.

"Not really. Also, you've noticed Wil is incredibly beautiful, right? Like, in the cartoons, where the tongue rolls out and the eyeballs pop and the horn goes *wah-wah-wah-wuh*. Her handle is hilarious to me, 'Wil-You-or-Won't-You'—of course I fucking will. There must be a line to her front door that backs up into Ohio." April sighed. "Now I'm done."

Unbidden, the picture Katie shouldn't have looked at on Wil's phone swirled into focus like ink dropped into water. Wil with both her hands on Emory's nape, her tongue just past her teeth, Emory's hand either pushing down into the front of Wil's pants or dragging back out, their fingers pressed into the skin of her belly.

Fuck.

Incredibly beautiful didn't completely cover it.

"Say hello to Meryl and Viola for me," Katie said, referring to April's cats. "Tell them that Sue, Trois, and Phil say hi from Green

Bay." She flashed the tiny, prim smile that meant she'd finished, and the conversation was complete.

April broke out into a grin. She was the one who'd taught Katie how to do that. Years ago, when Katie was reeling in the months after leaving Ben, she'd complained to April at one point that every interaction, every interview, seemed to end with someone getting more from her than she wanted to give them.

Stop fucking talking, April had said. *You're an actress. Act like it's over.* Then she'd made Katie show her what that looked like, trying on one expression after another until they settled on this one.

Katie's victory smile, April called it.

"I love you, honey. Be careful," April said, waving.

Katie stood up and stretched, then attended to her cats' bedtime needs. Phil and Sue had medicine, Trois had eye drops, and their litters needed to be scooped. Katie talked to them with and without the buttons, watching them to make sure they were well settled in. They had stayed in the suite before and seemed unbothered. Katie made sure that she turned on all three heated cat beds on low so they would have a warm place to sleep. It was no small thing to acclimate to Green Bay's winter.

Then Katie brushed her teeth and her hair, pulled on a sweatshirt because she hated coats and always had and it was only thirty-eight degrees—though that was balmy for a Midwest winter—and put Uggs on her bare feet. She turned out the lights and waited for Wil's truck, watching out the back slider, her skin buzzing.

It was a familiar feeling, waiting by a door for the lights of Wil's Bronco to sweep through the window.

By her senior year, Katie had maxed out the regional and local acting workshops. She'd learned everything she could from the instructors who would work with kids. She'd earned a lead in every local theater, which was as many leads as she was going to get, because no company in the Midwest was going to give the same child *two* leading roles. Katie remained committed to doing the work for her dance and music teachers, but when she got accepted to summer stock in Chicago for the summer after senior year, she realized she wanted to do high school. She hadn't even tried out for the East High School plays or the musical.

Diana was surprised, but thrilled, and tried and failed not to give Katie too much social advice as though she needed it, which she did, and in the end, the only advice Katie took on from her mother was to stick close to Wil Greene.

She's very involved at East and could help you figure out what extracurriculars you might like.

The subtext was that Wil could also introduce Katie to the people Katie had only observed from a distance since kindergarten but had rarely talked to because Diana drove her to Milwaukee and Madison and even Chicago multiple times a week for acting obligations, and probably those kids thought Katie was horribly stuck up.

They did think that, it turned out. They told her as much in the hallway outside the theater the afternoon of the first rehearsal for *Seussical the Musical,* in which Katie had been given the role of the Cat in the Hat. Katie had tried to casually strike up a conversation with a few of the theater girls right after the rehearsal, and they told her she'd stolen the part from one of the girls' boyfriends, who actually deserved it, and thereby ruined the musical, and probably Katie had only been given the part because Diana had agreed to make costumes.

Katie was snot-crying and walking on a cold September evening after this unfortunate event when Wil picked her up. After that, Katie didn't really see the need to stick close to anyone else. Wil was everything she needed and a lot of things she didn't realize she'd missed out on. Plus, Diana was right, as always, because everything got a lot easier after Katie and Wil were friends.

Nothing, nothing, had been that easy since.

The headlights on the Bronco lit up the backyard before Katie saw the truck pull in. Its orange and brown and yellow paint job filled her with so many feelings, she thought she was going to black out. She ran out to meet it after setting the alarm on the slider behind her.

Wil leaned over in the cab, and the door opened from the inside.

"Hi!" Katie climbed in. The woven fabric bench seat felt exactly the same. It smelled, like always, like wintergreen Altoids and the Aveda rosemary shampoo Wil used. Katie grabbed the seat belt and buckled herself in.

"Hi, yourself." As Wil put the Bronco into gear, Katie looked at her manicure. Wil wore her nails short, in pretty ovals. Her ring finger was maroon with a perfect white circle, and the rest of her nails were buff clear, with perfect maroon circles. The TikTok people loved to talk about Wil's nails. Katie was certain Wil had influenced all kinds of trends and fads.

Wil wore jeans that fit her exactly right, and her black motorcycle boots, and an unbuttoned gray waffle Henley, different from the tee she'd had on earlier, cleavage pushed up just so. Her soft, pale blond hair was styled in an artful, femmey mullet that drew Katie's eyes to her perfect mouth, which literally everyone on the internet was talking about, the bottom lip so full, it creased in the middle.

"You must have so many offers," Katie said. Because she knew the business. She saw what April saw. Everybody had seen it in high school.

Cool, beautiful, smart Wil.

"To ride in the Bronco? Less than I would expect, but I'm biased."

Katie laughed. "No. Entertainment offers. Offers from people who want to gift wrap what you've got going on and act like they invented you."

Wil wrinkled her nose. "A few."

"Not good?"

"I mean, it's interesting trying to figure out the what and the why of the offers." Wil took a detour in Katie's parents' neighborhood to avoid getting to the main road via a steep hill that was always covered in ice this time of year. Katie's dad took the same detour. "Some are obvious. The porny stuff, for example, sure, inevitable. Those are easy to pass on. But there's stuff from cosmetics people, streaming people, completely random ad people. What do they want? What do they think I can give them? How far will they go to try to exploit me?"

Wil tapped the steering wheel. Her smile was small, private. Katie felt like she'd been invited inside Wil's mind, which was a delightful feeling.

"I ended up reaching out to some other creators on the platform," Wil said. "That led me to a pretty intense deep dive into all the ways the people making the content are getting screwed over. I actually spent most of a four-day weekend off work one time just reading the terms of service from beginning to end, marking them up, making sure I completely understood everything. Now every time they update, I'm on it, checking it against my notes. I'm all up in the forums, leaving comments for other content creators, helping them sort through their problems or understand their situation better. It's the same thing I do at work all week. Cut through red tape. Simplify complex situations for other people."

Wil glanced at Katie and smiled right at her. "I like fighting for other people, figuring out how things work and looking for ways they could work better," she said. "But as far as making decisions about anything beyond just basic ad packages on my channel, I don't have a decision tree for any of that stuff."

"Do you want one?" As soon as she asked this, Katie realized she wasn't sure she wanted to give Wil a decision tree for media offers. One of the things she liked best about Wil's channel was that everything about it had been decided by Wil. It was hers. She'd made it, in the most absolute and basic way that Katie never got to make anything.

"I need a decision tree for my entire life." Wil laughed. "I'm not irresponsible or impulsive or anything, truly. I have a tendency to stick? I guess."

"Like in a rut."

"Like in what's comfortable, mostly because I really enjoy everything. I genuinely like my job, for example."

"As an insurance adjuster?" They had picked right back up the conversation they'd started earlier. It was as if everything they said to each other was part of one long, continuous talk that never ended.

"I love being an insurance adjuster. I love knowing all of this ridiculous, industry-specific language and going out to places and taking my pictures, writing the report. Fixing something simple with money. I also love that no one cares, at least in my company, what I'm like, or how I dress or spend my time."

Katie listened, watching Wil drive.

Once, all those years ago, Wil had taken her hand off the gearshift and put her arm along the back of the bench seat. Then, when it was time for her to shift again, just as she was taking her arm away, she'd softly pulled Katie's hair and slid her fingertips down Katie's arm.

It had been the first time Katie had ever spontaneously felt herself get wet. She hadn't felt strange about it. Being with Wil had been incredibly fun, easy. Getting turned on like that before she even knew what she wanted from, well, anyone had only been interesting. They were leaving for college soon. Everything was golden hour.

Looking at Wil now, in the dark, Katie wondered, though,

about all that intensity then. Why she remembered everything about the cab of this truck down into the deep sense memory parts of her brain.

"Every day is different," Wil said, still answering Katie's question. "I don't even mind that the clients calling in are often upset, or angry, or both. It feels like what I can do is useful. Document. Listen. Look. I don't make the money decisions, not really, or the policy ones, but I can advise clients."

"I can see that. But you're doing this creative project, so I wonder if something's not all the way stuck down."

"Maybe. Or a lot of little things aren't? Living in the same place, which, again, I like. I like how the space feels, and my landlord, who I've known for a long time, and I've been interested in my different housemates, and some of them have become friends. But."

"But." Katie smiled.

Wil rolled her shoulders and grinned at Katie. "Something isn't fitting right. Even the TikTok, I can feel there's a way that it wants to be something else, and it's happened faster than anything else in my life, that shift."

Katie liked looking at Wil this way, in the Bronco, with the only light coming from the street. Even more, she liked looking at her live and in person instead of on the tiny screen on her phone. It seemed inconceivable that she hadn't spent any time or talked to this woman in thirteen years.

It felt like something else Ben had taken away, something Katie hadn't even realized Ben had taken away.

But also, once things had settled—once there was an April, once her mom wasn't flying out to LA at least once a month to stay and help Katie get on her feet again—there hadn't been anyone who'd thought to tell her that if she wanted to be comfortable in this new normal, to stick with Wil Greene.

Wil was gone by then, of course. In college. Three years and thousands of miles away from the Wil who Katie had known, somewhere in the middle of her junior year, living a college life Katie had only seen—and wasn't that ironic, wasn't that funny?—in the movies.

Wil had pulled up to the intersection that fed into the loop in front of their old high school and waited for the light to change. She pulled into the loop, followed it, and then parked in a spot where they were facing the front of the building. Wil unbuckled her seat belt and turned to face Katie. There were lights all around the school filtering into the cab. "Did you get my care package?"

Oh.

Katie had to draw on her training to school her expression when what she wanted to do was close her eyes. Lean her forehead against the cold passenger window.

That care package was the last thing she'd had of Wil before she didn't have her anymore.

It arrived in Chicago a few weeks after Katie did, the smallest Priority Mail box you could get from the post office, with Katie's name and address printed in Wil's handwriting. There was a staff member for the summer stock program who passed out the mail, who handed Katie the package when there was a whole group of other actors standing together, joking, laughing, and of course they asked her who it was from, wanting to know if she had a person back home, but their teasing had an edge to it.

The package came the morning after Katie had said yes to Ben. As much *yes* as an eighteen-year-old girl could give a thirty-year-old acclaimed actor who had just been named *People*'s Sexiest Man Alive. Already, her peers that summer had stepped away from her at the same rate Ben stepped to her. She didn't have anyone to tell what had happened. She could hardly admit it to herself.

Inside the box, there was a wide, intricate green-and-pink

friendship bracelet knotted with the words KATIE KAT. It had a button clasp with a bead shaped like a cat's head, and there was a scribbled note from Wil on a piece of misprinted law office stationery that Beanie kept in a box in the kitchen for scratch paper.

Katie didn't remember what the note had said. She remembered the paper. She remembered Wil's handwriting. She remembered the catch in her throat and the feeling that she was lost, and it wasn't just that she'd graduated and left home, it was more.

She was *lost*.

She'd put the bracelet on in the middle of the room where all of them were waiting for Ben, her throat thick and her eyes burning, and she'd wanted more than anything to be on one of her late-night drives with Wil, pretending to investigate Mr. Cook, but really talking, just like they were now.

Katie hadn't thanked Wil for the package. She hadn't even texted her that whole summer. She'd wanted to, but Ben was so preoccupying. Everything was so, so much. And when she thought about texting or calling Wil, she felt like she wasn't even the Katie who Wil knew.

Or that Wil wouldn't understand.

Now, Katie smiled. "Yes. I did. I wore the bracelet every single day until I left it at Ben's accidentally, and he claimed to have never seen it when I asked for it back. Maybe he didn't, but he knew how I felt about that bracelet, and no cleaner would throw something so obviously personal away."

Katie touched her left wrist compulsively.

She'd even called Ben's brother, a man who had always been kind to her, to ask Ben for it back, more than once. But it was gone.

Or it would be a prize if she'd get back together with Ben.

"Was it . . . Are you okay?" Wil pushed up the sleeves of her Henley and turned down the blasting heater.

She was so pretty, so Wil. Gorgeous and blond wrapped up in

boots and waffle weave, minty and self-assured and thinky, wanting to know. Always wanting to know.

"It was the worst, and I'm okay," Katie said. Then she changed the subject. "And you went to the University of Michigan like you planned."

Wil nodded. "I did."

"What did you major in?"

"Pre-law."

Katie leaned forward and smiled, giving Wil her full *tell me everything* treatment. It made Wil roll her eyes and squirm in a way that shot Katie through with tingles.

Wil was the same in this way, too. Forthcoming until you hit on something. Until Wil didn't know the *answer* to something. Katie had spent so much of her time trying to stump Wil like this, just so they could go deeper.

"I got into Michigan Law," Wil said. She obviously couldn't hold Katie's gaze, so she looked out the windshield at the high school. "I got the adjuster job the summer before. They had a temp program that was a decent bit of cash, and I thought it would be good starter money. I moved into the place I live now. It *was* good money. The job had so many of the types of people and fixing problems and tiny details that attracted me to law, and maybe . . . It was hard. I felt like Beanie couldn't be alone. I was tired, I think. Because, you know, I had lost my dad at the end of college, when I was away. So I deferred for a year. Then I couldn't defer again. If I reapplied, I'd have first consideration, but I haven't."

Katie had been in Paris when Jasper Greene died. The apartment they were shooting in was one that had been owned by a minor aristocratic family until they fled the German occupation and never returned. It became the lavish set of the intimate marital drama that was the first big project April found for Katie, within the year after she left Ben, and Katie's costar—an intense, serious

method actor who never broke character—would not have toler-
ated Katie's leaving the set to attend a funeral in Wisconsin.

Diana had called her the day after and described everything in
detail, because Katie had wanted to feel as though she'd been there.
But she hadn't been there.

"Do you want to reapply?"

Wil looked back at Katie. The blue of her eyes was always
so interesting with her pale brows and lashes. Under her left
eye, Wil had a new patch of freckles—evidence, along with the
sharper bones of her face and the lushness of her body, that she
was older.

And evidence that there wasn't anywhere on her face that
wasn't good to look at.

"Sometimes I do. More and more sometimes. But it doesn't feel
possible anymore. Just a scattered, diffuse, regretful feeling." Wil
said this while rubbing her hand over her throat.

"Is that where you feel it?" Katie reached over and touched
Wil's hand.

Wil smiled. "Maybe."

"Something I've learned to do is think about where I feel
something in my body. It's so you can take care of that part of your
body, regulate it, and maybe be able to safely address the feelings."

Katie thought about Wil's Altoids habit. Her kissing. Always
having someone around to talk to. Her mouth. Her throat. Places
Wil was trying to take care of in the absence of not giving them
what they needed.

A voice.

This time, she reached out and touched Wil's throat directly
with the tips of her fingers. It made Wil laugh, just a small laugh,
and look away again, thinking.

That was okay.

Katie adjusted herself in the seat to have a better view of the school. She'd never been back after graduation. East High was a massive early-twentieth-century brick fortress with honest-to-God statues on the rooftop. Looking at it made Katie wonder why she'd had to let go of everything, absolutely every part of her life, when she left Ben.

Hadn't there been a way to keep more than just her parents and her career?

They were quiet until Wil's phone made a series of chimes, and she pulled it out of the back pocket of her jeans.

"What is it?" Katie asked after Wil had been tapping and swiping for more than a few moments.

"I'm sorry. It's just that the video I shot this morning posted, and there's always a bit I have to do when it goes up."

It was Wednesday. Traveling had made Katie's schedule feel slippery.

God.

There was something completely unanticipated happening to her, knowing there was one of Wil's videos up while she was sitting next to Wil. Talking to her. Looking at her. Thinking about her.

She must have gone silent for too long, because Wil finished and then looked at her—looked at her in a way that Katie could *feel,* even though she was trying to keep her gaze trained on the school building.

"Hey, Katie?" Wil asked.

"Yeah." She said the word the way she felt it, wrapped up in nostalgia, longing to get back what she'd lost.

"Do you want to watch it with me?"

Chapter Five

Wil put her arm along the back of the Bronco's bench seat and scooted closer to Katie, who smelled like Diana Price's house, some kind of holiday potpourri that had baked into Katie's sweatshirt and was releasing now in the blast of the Bronco's overenthusiastic heater.

Cinnamon and nutmeg and oranges.

Wil had known this outing would be a trip down memory lane, but she had failed to understand what a trip down memory lane would feel like, which was like her throat had shrunk to half its size, and her middle wouldn't stop flipping like the times on a train station arrivals and departures board.

Time kept crumpling and buckling in a way that was fucking her up.

Katie had pressed her shoulder against Wil's chest, the side of her head so close that Wil could smell Katie's skin instead of Christmas potpourri. Soapy and herbal and warm. She was moving restlessly, and if Wil's body hadn't perfectly recalled the sensation of Katie constantly adjusting and readjusting herself, then Wil would have thought Katie wanted her to give her some room. But Wil also knew that if she moved away, Katie would complain, hook a leg over hers, and pretend to pout that they weren't going to cuddle.

Wil enjoyed this about Katie. She liked people who were a bit of a show. She liked physical contact of all different kinds, obviously.

So she knew perfectly well that the hand that was currently on her knee, drawing an idle pattern, wasn't meant to make the skin on her chest hot. Even though it did.

"So you *do* want to watch it with me," she said, mostly curious what kind of reaction it would elicit from Katie.

Katie let out a laugh that sounded fully and utterly like a woman's laugh that Wil didn't know yet. When she turned her head to Wil, there was hectic color on her cheeks. "I don't want to, no. Then you'll know much too much. Except there is the part of me that wants you to know everything no matter what happens. I'd say that I can't decide what to do, but I would be lying. Should I pretend I'm watching it like I do at home?"

"How do you watch it at home?"

"Oh, don't ask me that." Katie put the whole side of her body against Wil's, and Wil had to tell herself to relax, to stay cool. Like a fan hoping not to be like all the other fans.

"I did ask," she said. "It happened. Can't take it back."

"Wow. All right. If you're going to be that way, then I will tell you it depends. I'm only allowed to watch your movies one time. I try to pick the right time. Sometimes I watch at breakfast, especially Saturdays, but only if I have something good to eat, which is usually a burrito, and time to myself, and I can really savor it."

"Do you eat the burrito or watch the video first?"

"First the burrito, then the video."

"Other times?"

"Other times, I wait until it's dark out and I'm in bed." Katie put a bit of a rough edge to her voice when she said this and then laughed another one of her grown-up laughs.

"I can't with you," Wil said. "Is this how people are in Los Angeles, just casually devastating each other with sex conversation all the time? Because I have to tell you, here in Green Bay, everything has rolled along as you must remember it. A lot of repression and occasional meaningful glances."

"But who is in the video with you today?" Katie was grinning. It was a version of her smile Wil had only seen in person, never on a screen—big and a little lopsided, sinking a deep dimple into one cheek. "They are from Green Bay, I assume, this person who you propositioned to kiss you. On camera. For an audience of millions." Katie tapped the screen of Wil's phone. "How many videos do you have now, Wil? Are there a hundred yet? Did you find a hundred repressed Green Bay people to exhibitionist-kiss you?"

Wil closed her eyes. There weren't *quite* a hundred videos on there, because there had been more than a few times Wil had let a particularly viral video roll for a couple of weeks, but knowing there were so many and that Katie had watched them alone in her room—just one time each, because that was all she allowed herself—made Wil's phone feel like a bomb in her hand.

Katie pressed her face into Wil's shoulder again. "To answer your question, which I will since you are *blushing*, it is not Los Angeles. It's me. I just like you. Play it now, before I self-immolate."

Wil pushed play. Cleared her throat. "She's my hairdresser."

"That's going to make things interesting next time you go in for a trim."

The screen went from black to full color. *Wil + Mandi* appeared in the caption box, auto-read by the TikTok bot. She and Mandi sat opposite each other on the stools Wil kept on hand because some people felt uncomfortable about standing or couldn't stand.

"Mandi is incredibly hot," Katie said.

On the phone screen, Mandi smiled at Wil. She had a huge smile, teeth that had never been messed with by an orthodontist, which was Wil's favorite thing to look at about Mandi, although Mandi offered a lot to look at. Hydrant-red and pink hair in soft waves to her waist, teased up on top into a half beehive. Winged eyeliner. Tattoos bright against the pale canvas of her skin, all across her generous chest, up her neck, covering her bare shoulders and arms.

Pretty eyes. Wil hadn't noticed until she leaned close and put her hand at Mandi's waist, the smell of her perfume everywhere, as sweet and pink as her hair. She wore black leggings, like Katie, but she filled them out differently, her body lush and big and such an inviting combination of hard and soft, her calves rounded, her belly rounded in a different way, her breasts, her waist, the strong arms she cut hair with, the flare of her hips.

That was what Wil had been thinking about when she caught Mandi's face in her hand and put her mouth on her. Her body, and the way she smelled, and her glossy lipstick.

Katie sucked in a breath.

Wil let her arm come down around Katie before she'd even thought about it, holding her against her side. When they were girls they would often hold hands, put their arms around each other, give each other piggyback rides across the street while cars honked at them for being obnoxious. But she almost regretted the familiar impulse once her hand curled around Katie's shoulder.

Eighteen-year-old Wil must have been much cooler than the Wil she was now.

The kiss was interesting, but not in a way Wil would've been able to talk about, something about how she could feel Mandi's nervousness and her bravado fighting, how she knew Mandi had never kissed a woman before, how she tasted like the gum she'd been chewing when she came through the door.

It was the kind of kiss that made Wil want to take some time. Sit her down for a meal or watch a movie next to her, stroke her thigh or put her hand there and see if it led to more or didn't. But one minute was the constraint.

One minute meant Wil didn't always find out everything she wanted to know.

She found out that Mandi liked her long hair touched, fingers on her neck but not her face, that she didn't want Wil's hands on her body, that she liked Wil's tongue in her mouth and wanted Wil to run the show. And that Mandi was relieved when it was over, not because she hadn't liked it, more because she didn't know what that meant, which made her nervous in a way that became palpable to Wil.

Wil knew things about people in every part of her life that she never would've known if she hadn't kissed them.

After the screen went dark, Wil eased her arm from around Katie, realizing that she'd been holding her pretty tight. "Did you like that?"

Katie turned to Wil, flushed with color up the sides of her nose and blooming between her pretty eyebrows. She breathed in, and she must have been holding her breath, because when she took that breath, the hollow at the base of throat collapsed.

She brought a hand to the side of Wil's face. Wil told herself the cool hand against her hot skin was just more of Katie, *not* the consummation of all of those times Wil had let Katie make her up—soft brushes packed with eyeshadow swirling on her skin, soft puffs of Katie's breath as she blew away excess powder.

Confused longing and mascara.

"I liked that," Katie said, pulling her hand away. "Did you?"

"Which part?" Wil's voice had broken and husked out so completely, it embarrassed her. It sounded like the voice she used after a screaming orgasm.

Katie pushed herself away from Wil enough to tuck a knee underneath her, which brought her up closer, and her huge blue eyes were looking right inside Wil. Seeing everything. "Which part?" Katie whispered. "Wil Greene. Which *part*." She shook her head. "No, I don't think so. Don't deflect. Tell me what it *felt* like to kiss Mandi." Katie put both her hands to the sides of her own face, then slid them back to gather her hair at her nape.

Wil reached over and turned the heater completely off, even though it wasn't why they were both burning up.

Probably.

She cleared her throat and closed her eyes. Her voice came out in a rush. "It felt like she wanted me to be in charge, and like she wanted me but was surprised she did. Or confused that she did."

"God," Katie breathed. "Did anything else happen?"

"After the kiss?"

Katie nodded. In this moment, she didn't resemble the serene, polished, charming Katie Price who'd been on that stage in Chicago, her necklaces softly clacking. Even in her leggings at the Christmas party, with no makeup, she'd maintained some of that polish.

It was a performance. Katie performed herself, performed her celebrity, for the people around her. But *this* Katie, Wil suspected, was only hers.

What a gratifying thought.

"She asked me for one more kiss before she left."

"Did you?"

"Yes." Wil had asked Mandi to initiate it, though. Wil had leaned against the cased opening in the living room low enough that she was nose to nose with Mandi, and they'd looked at each other for a long time before Mandi gave in. That kiss had felt like Mandi was . . . feeling herself. Letting the kiss find something for her. A lot of tongue. They both made a noise at the same time before it eased up and Mandi left.

"What was it like?" Katie pressed her finger into the top of

Wil's thigh, hard. She knew that spot was tender and that Wil
didn't like it. Pressing her finger there was how Katie used to boss-
torture Wil into confessing things.

It hit a little different now.

"It was more," Wil said.

"Does that happen a lot?" Katie was whispering, and the windows were fogging now that the heat was off, so the Bronco really
did feel like a confessional.

"A lot more than I thought it would, but I wouldn't say a lot."

"Did you like watching it with me?" Katie raised both her eyebrows and pulled her legs into a crossed position. Her posture, her
voice, seemed to defuse the tension, and it was a relief.

Wil, despite Katie teasing her about it, needed to *think*.

Katie laughed. "Tell me later. I will tell *you* that I realized I
had been imagining you watching me, or at least imagining that
you knew, *somehow,* I was watching these videos, the whole time."

Wil could've told her that she had been wondering if Katie had
noticed her videos for the last year, but she didn't, because she was
only just now realizing this was true. "I think I would've noticed
if Katie Price had left a heart on one of my kissing videos."

Wil was glad for the cold air that was seeping in through the
deteriorating seals of the Bronco's doors. It reminded Wil it was
December. Katie was here for Christmas, and then she'd go back
to LA. This felt good, and could encourage them to keep in better
touch, but Wil couldn't let herself get confused.

"I didn't use my Katie Price account. I have a secret handle.
Can you guess it?" Katie bit her thumb and smiled around it. The
vulnerable gesture made Wil understand that what she meant
wasn't so much that she hoped Wil had identified her from among
all the comments on her videos as that she hoped Wil could still
see her. The person she'd been when they knew each other. The
person she still was.

It made Wil's skin go tight everywhere on her body, her inner thighs aching all the way up. She thought about opening a window to get more cold air. "Give me a hint."

"I took the handle from a social media name generator. One of the random letters and numbers ones."

It should have been impossible for Wil to guess. There were thousands of accounts like that. Burner accounts. Ad accounts. Spam accounts. Bot accounts.

But Wil knew it.

She'd seen it, a string of six letters and numbers that always liked the videos, always. Sometimes the account left a one-word comment like *forearms*. Or *clutch*. A few times it left an emoji, like the fire emoji or, once, the drops of water emoji.

"Htx345." Wil watched Katie's face the same way she did when she was getting ready to kiss someone.

Katie's mouth came open just a little. Wil could see her tongue behind her teeth. "Yes." Katie shivered and then laughed, but she was breathing hard. So was Wil.

Katie eased back, unfolding her legs and scooting onto her side of the bench seat. But it didn't feel like she was pulling away. Wil thought that maybe Katie was giving herself the same reminder Wil had. The one about Christmas, and LA, and reunions.

"I brought red Twizzlers and pretzels," Wil said.

"Do you know how satisfying it is that you can barely handle me?"

Wil laughed, reaching down to grab the tote where she had put Katie's requested supplies. "Is it?"

"Of course it is. You're Wil-You-or-Won't-You Wil, no last name, wildly popular on TikTok, but also, *also,* you're Wilifred Greene, hottest girl at East High School. Valedictorian of our class. Softball player, fucking *cheerleader* after you quit softball. Student council. Orchestra. You"—Katie put her finger on Wil's

nose—"dated the quarterback, Wil. That is a real YA novel situation you got yourself into there, and the rest of us noticed. We had
thoughts."

"Here." Wil handed Katie the package of Twizzlers. "You're saying these things to me, but also, you have an Oscar. Golden Globes.
Emmys. SAGs. The Grammy from when you played the Appala-
chian blues singer. Oh! And the Tony! My mom went with Diana
to New York to see you on Broadway and had to take two days off
work after. You did that to *Beanie Greene*. A photographer followed
you to the Maldives and took a drone picture of you on a yacht sun-
bathing topless with your cat Trois curled around your head."

"How good was that picture?" Katie asked, separating Twizzler strands and wrapping them around her finger.

"I mean, it was so fucking good, I and the rest of America
deep-dive Google-searched for the highest-res image possible.
That is my point. Somehow, you ended up owning the paparazzi so
hard by looking that good, and also that you're . . ." Wil searched
for the right word, but she couldn't find it, and when she met Katie's eyes, she wasn't sure what to make of what she saw there.

It wasn't pride in being flawless, perfect, accomplished Katie
Price. It was something a lot closer to the way Katie had looked
the day Wil picked her up off the side of the road with red-rimmed
eyes and tangled hair, and they'd sat in the parking lot of the high
school for the first time because Katie didn't want to go home yet,
the wind gusting against the Bronco.

Do you ever feel like you're not real? Katie had asked.

Wil knew exactly what she meant.

Now, Katie was watching Wil the same way she used to watch
and rewatch her Criterion Collection movies in Craig and Diana's
den—as though there were things she wanted to know, and the
only way to figure them out was to keep her attention completely
and utterly on the screen. "Give me your phone," she said.

Wil handed it over. Katie tapped for a few minutes and handed it back.

"What did you do?"

"I logged into my Dropbox so I could grab the hi-res file of the picture and save it to your camera roll."

Wil blew out a breath. "We have really got ourselves into a thing here."

"You're not worried, are you?" Katie pressed her phone to her chest and smiled a new smile at Wil that made her forget this was an extremely temporary diversion made of nostalgia and two confident women trying to out-flirt each other.

"Yes, I am incredibly worried, actually. But I have no defenses against"—Wil put her hand over the phone in the middle of Katie's chest—"you. Wait. Don't lean into me. Jesus." Wil laughed, gently pushing Katie back into her own space.

"Good. I'm glad you don't. Are we going to go drive past Mr. Cook's place or what?"

"I brought us here so we could make a plan. That's how we do this. We sit in the parking lot, we make a plan, we eat junk food. We usually didn't get any further than the plan part."

"We never really did, did we?" Katie put the Twizzlers down and opened the bag of pretzels. "We were terrible stalkers. Or detectives. But now there is a bet. Or at least, there are stakes, and we no longer have a curfew. So what's the plan?"

"I don't know where he lives," Wil admitted. "Like I said, the directory doesn't have anything to run with. He didn't pop up with an address on a quick Google search. We could internet stalk him, but that didn't seem correct."

Katie ate a handful of pretzels one by one, licking the salt off them before she crunched them, which she had also done in high school, but it hadn't murdered Wil's impulse control like it was doing now. If she didn't stop, Wil was going to take off all of her clothes and just exist in the deep end.

"Oh! I know what we can do!" Katie said.

"What is it? Please stop fellating those pretzels."

Katie grinned and licked another one, very slow. "Hmm. What about those things on the internet that save the things on the internet after someone has taken them off? A fan did that to find my deleted LiveJournal from when I was fourteen, which meant I had to talk about my *Grey's Anatomy* fanfic to reporters at Cannes."

"Like a cache? A Wayback Machine?"

Katie shrugged and crunched her denuded pretzel stick. "I'm not internety."

"I'll see what I can do. When is this happening? Once I get the address?" Wil took some pretzels.

"When do you get off work?"

"Tomorrow? Four."

"Pick me up after you're done at work. I want to see what you wear to work and what you're like right after. But I need to focus tomorrow, so don't text me or call. If I think you might text, I'll be wondering if you're going to when I'm supposed to be writing."

"As it happens, I don't even have your number. Seeing as we have not spoken to each other in thirteen years."

"Right. Give me your phone."

Wil handed her phone over again, and Katie programmed herself into Wil's contacts.

Just like that.

Which told Wil it was never that Katie didn't want Wil to have her number. It was that *Diana* feared Katie didn't, or thought it might not be a good idea, or simply had never thought to give Wil access to the daughter she watched over and worried about.

"Fair warning, I used the yacht picture to come up if I contact you," Katie said. "So don't call or text me tomorrow, but I like that you do have my number, and then I can think about how much you're holding yourself back and if you will manage to. Like if you might just lose it and send me a nude."

Wil did not imagine herself sending Katie Price a nude—or rather she tried not to, but did a little bit, and had to squeeze her legs together. "Katie. I'm starting to think you're teasing me."

"I am not. At all." She touched her temple. "I'm just looping and looping and looping up here, all day long. Guess who I like to loop on lately?"

Wil breathed in, slowly. Breathed out. "Okay. What are you writing?"

"I'm trying to adapt a novel. A screenplay."

Then Wil saw something on Katie's face that she was able to identify, the same thing she'd seen a hint of earlier.

Katie felt uncertain.

Uncertain people, frightened people, walked into Wil's house twice a week. Wil had learned a lot about how to connect with, validate, and work through those kinds of ordinary human feelings. "Tell me about that."

"I'm struggling," Katie said. "I've never been like you. School was hard for me. I had to put all of my psychic energy into flattering and impressing Mr. Cook to get the grade I needed to keep my admission to Winston-Salem, and then I didn't go. It's a lot to try to stay positive about doing something I've never done before that no one even wants me to do, especially when it's not going well. And it's not going well. Which is why me and my babies are spending a month in Wisconsin."

Wil took a Twizzler out of the bag and peeled a strip off it. "I have so many thoughts on that, I don't know where to start."

"I mean, dig in. I already feel like a rabbit about to bolt, so this is probably a useful conversation for me to have."

"First off, '*flattering* Mr. Cook'? Do you think that? Because I have to tell you, nobody thought that."

Katie pushed off her Uggs, pulled her bare feet onto the bench seat, and wrapped her arms around her knees. "I spent that whole semester acting like he was the best teacher ever, when literally no one had *ever* liked him. I don't even think anyone had ever *learned* anything from him."

"Sure," Wil said. She thought about that class from Katie's perspective, which she hadn't before. How much Katie engaged with Mr. Cook. Asked questions. Made him feel like he was the caliber of teacher he had never bothered to be. "It wasn't fair. Now that I think about it, it was worse than not fair, like, aren't teachers supposed to be observed sometimes or something? To make sure their talents aren't coming from the efforts of one of their students? But more important, you were *acting*. We were all so fucking entertained by you. I've actually talked to other people from our class about this over a beer, how you razzle-dazzled Mr. Cook into not being a dick for the entire semester. There is lasting gratitude. Jen Diver, for one, who got her IEP accommodations so she could take her tests and quizzes in the library and didn't collapse into a puddle of sensory overwhelm."

"*He* didn't know I was acting." Katie said this in a voice Wil didn't recognize, as though she were speaking for someone else.

Or repeating what someone else had told her.

That gave Wil something to think about. She turned and wrapped her hand around Katie's bare foot. She could feel Katie's pulse throbbing under the soft skin of her instep.

Katie was looking out the windshield at the school building, and Wil looked, too, remembering.

She had put Mr. Cook in the category of a bad teacher, a bully, but she hadn't really interrogated his behavior from her perspective as an adult. Male teachers had so much power. It had been a dicey move for Katie to take up the work of appeasing this grown man who should have known better, who should never have put a student in the position of bolstering him in order to maintain his emotional regulation and ego.

An icy, prickly shiver ran down Wil's spine. Because, of course, just a few months after she left the high school building behind, Katie had met Ben Adelsward.

"I'm sorry we didn't understand," Wil said. "I'm sorry we sat in that class as the beneficiaries of something that should not have been happening." Wil stroked Katie's foot.

Katie tucked her foot more firmly into Wil's hand, an old gesture that meant *massage my foot, you tease,* and shook her head. "It's all why I had the fantasy about getting to the bottom of his secret affair with you. So I could tell both of those women about him. I wanted them to know what a gross insect he is."

"We don't have to bring all that stuff into our getting back in touch now, you know." *Ben,* she meant. But couldn't quite bring herself to say. "I don't need an excuse to want to talk to you." Wil pressed her thumb into the arch of Katie's foot. There was a blustery red mark right under the pinky toe that made Wil think about all the gravity-and physics-defying shoes Katie wore.

Because she was a world-famous actress.

Right.

Katie looked out the window again. Her eyes were too bright in the dim cab of the Bronco, her hand full of pretzels that she'd forgotten to eat. She drew in a shaky breath and exhaled slowly until her shoulders sank down to their usual position. "I want to talk to you about it. I don't think I can right now, but yes. Sometime. What I *can* say is that it got hard for me, after Mr. Cook, and after Ben, to tell the difference between imagining and pretending and acting and—and deception, I guess. Tricking people. Being someone who can do a trick to get what she wants. Not even an especially good trick, just a trick that I was born being able to do, like being double jointed."

Wil stopped herself from blurting out meaningless reassurances. She was holding onto Katie's ankle now, and Katie's ankle felt the same as it always had against the palm of her hand. It was so utterly clear to Wil that this was Katie. The Katie she'd known.

Which meant she'd *never not been.*

Which meant it was *Wil's* Katie who'd gone through all that. It was *Wil's* Katie who'd been drawn into a relationship with a much older, much more powerful man, who had probably treated her terribly, and who had never stopped using the media to harass her. It was *Wil's* Katie who was still going through the kind of thing Wil had seen for herself in Chicago when the press showed their fangs.

Katie had apologized for losing touch, for not being there when Wil's dad died, but Wil hadn't expected Katie to come to the funeral because she'd no longer thought of Katie as anything but a wonderful memory. Someone she sometimes felt angry she didn't know anymore, or wasn't allowed to know.

Do you ever feel like you're not real?

One of Katie's biggest fears. And Wil—along with the rest of the world—had done that to Katie Price. Done it and done it.

"I'm sorry," she started. "I'm sorry I didn't stay in touch and wasn't available to you, if you had wanted me to be, when you were going through something hard. I wasn't a good friend, and all the feelings I had about being mad that I somehow wasn't supposed to talk to you anymore were actually me feeling guilty and regretful and not getting it. I'm so, so sorry. You deserved better from me."

Katie sucked in a breath, and Wil felt her body get very still. Then Katie met Wil's gaze, tears streaming down her face. "Oh, fuck, Wil Greene! I didn't even know I needed to hear that!"

Wil brushed away a tear alongside her nose. "Then I'm extra glad I said it." Wil thought of something else she wanted to say.

"You know that everything about you is real, right? You're fucking smart, you're a genius, actually. You have something, but it's not a trick, and you weren't born with everything you know how to do. Remember, I watched you learn it."

"Say more about that." Katie pushed her foot into Wil's hand, and Wil squeezed it.

"You worked so hard. You were always working. Remember when Beanie and me and Diana drove down to see you play Alice in Milwaukee?"

Katie shook her head and wiped away a last tear.

"Of course not, why wouldn't you? But I do. That was junior year, and I didn't want to go. I'd never minded seeing your stuff, but this was children's theater, and I thought that meant it would be three hours of checking my watch, wishing I was in the backseat of the quarterback's car investigating the contours of my sexuality, because who cares? *Alice in Wonderland* is a kids' story. But I guess there was a way I could love a kids' story. You made me love it. It was all Beanie and I could talk about on the drive back, wondering how you'd done it, how you pulled it off, and mostly what we talked about was how hard you'd always worked."

Katie nodded. "All right. Yes. That's all true, I mean, logically, I know this, and in fact I have a lot of, frankly, arrogance around the work I bring to the table. It's rough, though, when I can't get my screenplay I'm supposed to be writing to do what it's supposed to." Her hands flew up then, floated around in the air in a gesture that shouldn't have meant anything but somehow expressed the three-dimensionality and texture of how the world felt in her imagination. "I *get* the story, I know these characters as well as I know my family. And then I try to make it be on paper, in scenes, with action and dialogue that is right for these people to tell this story, and then I can't. I can't."

She held out her hand for a Twizzler. Wil gave her one. She ate it, looking somewhere into the space between them that was deep inside her head.

"Sometimes I end up petting cats all day," Katie said. "I count that as a good day."

"What kinds of things have you written? Other than your *Grey's* fanfic." Wil was interested in this. She was always interested in problems that she found easy to solve.

"Not a ton," Katie said with a shrug. "Mostly things for school, and my mom had to check everything. If it was worth a lot of points, I took it to one of my college student tutors."

"Do you have a disability?"

"No, I don't think so. My parents got me tested a couple times because I was an early reader and early talker, but school didn't work. I can memorize full scripts like it's nothing. I can focus. I love reading. I have no problem understanding complex contracts. I can learn things I have to do, like how to operate cameras and digital products. I like editing. But I struggle to make what I see and feel, even if it's simple, be writing that communicates what I see and feel to other people."

"See? That's such a very beautiful way to put that, and one hundred percent accurate in every way."

"It is?"

Wil slid forward. "Yes. It means that your only problem is the building blocks—mechanics, process, synthesis—and identifying the right way for you to approach them. This is something you can learn. If you want, I can teach you."

"Yes. I want you to. You know how to write?"

"I don't write creatively, but I'm a good writer. All that pre-law, remember? And three years at the academic center as a writing peer figuring out firsthand that there are a lot of people with a lot to say who just never got the basics from anyone. Ideas into words. I can do that."

"Tomorrow. You'll help me?"

"Sure." Wil wanted to help Katie. She wanted to keep seeing her. She wanted, if she was being honest with herself, to push this temporary connection further than was probably smart or self-preserving, and she wanted to do it in a way that meant it wasn't only Katie who got vulnerable.

Back then, it wasn't just Wil swooping in to rescue Katie and drive her around in the Bronco or introduce her to new friends. Katie had been Wil's friend, too. She'd been the only friend Wil could talk to about the future, because Katie knew that every dream Wil had, every goal she made, came with an asterisk. She'd known Wil was terrified of losing her dad, and Katie *knew* Wil's dad, so she could talk about it without getting weird or running away.

It made Katie probably the only candidate to try where Beanie had failed.

"I will help you if you make me do one thing on my 'Just Fucking Do It Already' list," Wil said. "Which, I admit, isn't fair. As Beanie has already pointed out, making someone else make you do something so you can blame them if you don't do it is classic asshattery. But when it comes to this list, I am already an asshat."

"Wait, this is a real thing that exists? You made this list?" Katie stretched out her toes when Wil pressed her thumbs into the middle space beneath the ball of each foot.

"It is. Beanie helped me. She's recently started to get after me about my languishing."

Katie reached down for another Twizzler. She winked at Wil. "Text it to me when you get home."

"I'll text it to you now. I don't want to get in trouble for texting after I drop you off. It's already tomorrow." She was in so much trouble already. She could almost feel her brain cheerfully compartmentalizing all of her new Katie Price feelings into tidy boxes she wouldn't let herself ever open again after Katie left in a month.

But that was what she'd done last time.

Katie looked at her phone when it buzzed with Wil's list, went quiet, reading, and then looked up at Wil with a smile. "Oh, we're going to have so much fun."

For a little while, Wil thought. She had no doubt they would. They always had.

Chapter Six

Katie was looking at an upside-down Phil while Sue pushed the *All. Done. Mama.* buttons over and over again.

"I am trying to get my yoga on, my babies. Sue, cool it. Phil, move." Katie held the pose, breathing in through her nose. The hem of her T-shirt started slipping out from where she'd shoved it into the waistband of her underwear.

"And . . . scene." Katie slowly curled out of the full inversion onto her feet, just as she flashed her cats, and put her hands in the air as if she had stuck a landing. "Now I can have coffee. And phone. And a half a foot of Mom's coffee cake."

Katie was feeling herself this morning. She'd only slept five hours, which was not great, but the reason she'd slept five hours was the best, best reason, and she woke up excited to tackle this Green Bay Thursday like it was her actual job.

It *was* her job. One of the perks to being Katie Price was that when she wasn't in front of a camera, being Katie was her job. She was done with squandering this enormous privilege on self-doubt and frustrated backspacing. Wil Greene had never stopped being the smartest person Katie had ever met, and if Wil said that it would be no problem for Katie to write this script, then it was no problem.

But first, before breakfast, she did her Katie Yoga, which was yoga, but only the poses she liked, performed in her underpants. Her feet were really fucking cold now because her parents turned down the sixty-two-degree thermostat to fifty-two at night as though they were personally responsible for defeating climate change, but the rest of Katie's body felt amazing. Because, *because*, beyond her new confidence that she would write this script, and it would be as good as she wanted and needed it to be, there was also the fact that at some point between when Wil dropped her back off at the slider doors to her suite and when Trois jumped on her face at six in the morning, Katie had figured out she'd been in love with Wil Greene when she was eighteen.

It made her feel so good to know that. It meant that Ben was *not* her first love and hadn't been her only love.

Katie had sat straight up in bed when she'd figured this out, turning on the bedside lamp so that she could be sure she wasn't dreaming. She'd taken a long drink of water and interrogated herself thoroughly.

It was true. She'd loved Wil. She hadn't known.

Also, she had figured it out at what was an inconvenient moment, because now, now, *now*, Katie was attracted to Wil. She *wanted* Wil. She wanted to kiss her, she wanted to touch her all over, she wanted her own body to be touched by Wil all over, she wanted to figure out what she liked and didn't like and really, really, really liked *with* Wil. And it was not a good idea to layer what she had realized about her girlhood self over a very grown-up emotion, which was horniness. That was how people got hurt.

That was how she could get hurt.

Still, Katie could not help but be fascinated by her own

attraction. She had never felt this way about anyone real. She'd felt this way about characters. She'd felt this way while she was playing a character, but it wasn't the same, it turned out. Desire was much more insistent than Katie had thought. It did too good a job of making her feel invincible. It had a lot of very palpable suggestions that weren't interested in reason.

But, all by herself, in this moment, with sweet coffee cake in her mouth, Katie didn't have to make a plan. She wasn't going to fuck anything up or say the wrong thing or be impulsive. She could just want Wil. Privately. Very much. With a lot of very good mental images.

Though, even logistics-wise, she was thirty-one years old, and thirty-one-year-old rich, professional, desirable women were permitted to meet their desires with a partner. It couldn't be that hard. No one knew she was here yet except April and Madelynn. Possibly someone at the party would leak, although they had been asked not to. Her parents had been very clear, and the guests were people she and her parents had vetted, and there was a reason she'd joined the party completely as her most private self, reminding everyone that she deserved a private self. She deserved to be able to be Craig and Diana's daughter, home for the holidays.

Given all of that, Katie guessed, if she indulged her pessimism, she had about four days before she started seeing paparazzi, as much as she wanted to believe she had a luxurious month. She *might* have had a month, but then she'd asked her mom to have that party. She wouldn't have asked, except that she'd seen Wil in the audience in Chicago. If she were just anyone, she could've asked someone on her team to get her Wil's number. But if she did that, it would have definitely leaked. Maybe not right away, but at some point, probably at a moment when it would make a very not-cute anecdote.

Diana would have given her Wil's number, but there would have been questions, or, minimally, concern. No, thank you.

But! A lot could happen in four days. All those kissing videos told Katie that a lot could happen in one minute. Wil knew all about it. Wil had almost made Katie come in the truck when she'd pressed her fingers into her upper arm at the same time Mandi's tongue finally, finally touched Wil's in that video.

Katie was walking back into her suite after using her multi-head shower when her phone chimed with a text, and her heart stuttered.

Because Katie didn't text much. Only Katie's parents and a few friends had her direct number.

She went through her mental list of who *did* have her real number at the moment. Her team, but they knew not to text. Her friends, but most of them were on California time, and busy anyway with holiday travel of their own.

That left Wil. Who didn't even know that Katie didn't text, because Katie hadn't told her.

So Wil had broken the rules *already* and texted her. It made Katie's entire pelvis literally go hot inside of her body.

She tiptoed over to the coffee table where her phone was lying screen-up. When she saw the text still illuminating the lock screen, she had a brief flash of her hand curled around her purple flip phone, shoved under her pillow, just in case Wil texted her sometime in the night or Katie wanted to text her.

Why the fuck *hadn't* they always had each other's numbers?

But then Katie remembered when she and her mom were staying in the hotel that Katie had fled to from Ben's, after she left in the middle of the night with nothing. The first day, Diana had gone out for a few hours to get Katie some things she'd need, and she'd come back with a brand-new phone that had a brand-new number. Her mom had sat at a desk in the suite and programmed her own number and Katie's dad's number into that phone, and then she'd told Katie that it was going to be important that she be really, really careful who she gave her new number to.

That expensive, shiny phone, feather-light with only two people who could reach her, had given Katie such a sense of safety and freedom after years of Ben knowing where she was and what she was doing at every moment, making her FaceTime him with the background captured in the camera so he knew she wasn't lying, getting calls in her car if the phone tracking didn't line up exactly to where he thought she was supposed to be, and being certain that no matter what she was doing, whatever he wanted would be more important.

The phone her mom gave her had been a magic phone.

Katie forced herself to delay gratification. She ran into the bedroom to get dressed. She put on jeans, a very big flannel, and snow boots. Taking her time, she put product in her hair and braided it into two very tight tiny braids.

None of this was how she dressed in Los Angeles or how she was ever photographed. When she went out in Green Bay, she would put on a hat and a big coat her mom had bought her at Kohl's. She didn't wear her signature winged liner and pink lippie in Green Bay. Or jewelry. She moved her body differently.

Katie could act so that people thought she was shorter, her body shape different. Familiar, but not famous, even when they looked right at her.

It was necessary, but also, a little bit, it was hard.

If she had gone to Winston-Salem, if she'd done all of those student films and crashed Chicago Groundlings auditions, taken road trips for pilot season in LA, started a YouTube channel of acting reels and impressions, Katie might still be an emerging actor, or she might be well-known and famous but in a way that was utterly embraced by her hometown because they had watched her knuckle through Hollywood. Or maybe she would have discovered how much she loved directing sooner, and she would have been, right now, on the cusp of running a show or getting a dream project greenlit.

When she left for Chicago, Katie hadn't known exactly what she wanted, only that she wanted to make stories for audiences. She was eighteen. How could she have known more than that?

But Ben had *decided* to introduce Katie to the world.

He'd set the terms, he'd taught her how to "deal" with the media, he'd taught the media how to look at and think about and talk about her. It meant that Katie hadn't had a chance to make any decisions for herself about what she wanted until after she broke up with Ben, and by then, there were patterns established that she didn't know how to change.

It was one reason why, when she talked to someone like Busy Phillips, Katie preferred to talk about her cats.

No matter how long this trip home was, it was supposed to be about admitting that she was ready for more. Katie had thought *more* meant professionally.

Maybe more was more.

Once she'd finished getting dressed, she sat on the sofa, her babies arranging themselves around her, and picked up the phone, smiling.

I'm not supposed to text you

But I had an idea for you to try today, with writing, and keep things very low-pressure

So forgive me

If you're interested, lmk

Katie smiled.

Yes, she texted back.

She held the phone in her cupped hands like it was a baby bird, waiting. Then the three dots swooped up.

> I want you to pick something on TV to watch. Something short. Then tell me what happened, first by writing it down, then by using this

There was a link.

> Then tell me which summary you like better
> Wld you feel comfortable sending them both to me when you're done?

Yes, Katie replied. She added a heart, then tapped the link. It was to an app, which she downloaded. The app was simple. She pushed the green button and talked, then the red button when she was done. The app transcribed what she said into a document that she could zwoop to Dropbox.

An assignment! Katie loved assignments and constraints of all kinds. She wondered if Wil had guessed this or if she was just very lucky.

She scrambled to the basket where her mom kept the remotes and found the one for the flat-screen, navigated to Netflix, and scrolled around until she found an episode of *Kipo and the Age of Wonderbeasts*.

Katie let herself be completely absorbed in the story and animation, petting her lapful of cats, and then when it was over, she considered if she wanted to write or talk first. She decided to write and extricated herself from the cat pile, apologizing profusely, to get her laptop from the teeny breakfast bar. Having opened a new document, she did her best to explain everything that had happened. Then she opened the app, talked about the episode, and uploaded the much longer transcription document that the app made.

She sent both to Wil before she sat back down on the sofa. She chewed her thumb, waiting.

> Tell me which summary you like better

Oh! Right! Katie was embarrassed she'd forgotten. She went back to the breakfast bar and pulled up both documents.

She reread them both and then realized she was scrunching up her entire face.

> Can't

> Okay. Give me three words about each one

Wil was the best teacher she'd ever had.

> Dry, short, boring

> Feelings, tmi, long

> Good!

Katie squeaked. Yay!

> Do you want a script assignment?

Katie thought about it and realized that she did want a script assignment. She wanted *Wil's* script assignment.

> Yes xoxoxoxoxoxoxoxoxoxo

> Use the app and describe what you want in your
> movie. We'll look at that doc later. Then open the
> long Kipo doc and set a timer for 30 min and take
> out things and correct things until you like it even a
> little or the time runs out. Then nothing else today

K, Katie wrote, with another heart.

She scrolled up in their chat thread to the list Wil had sent her last night and opened it.

After reading through it twice, slowly, she went upstairs and asked her mom for Beanie's number. She promised she would use the landline. Back downstairs, she called Beanie with a few questions about what Katie had decided would be Wil's first mission from the list.

Because that was what Wil had asked Katie to do. She wanted Katie to *make* her do things from her list. Katie didn't entirely understand yet why Wil needed to work through her stuck place in this manner, but she had no objection to meeting anyone where they were at.

Excited again, she texted Wil.

> FaceTime me

> Give me a minute

> K

Katie paced around with the phone until it started ringing.

"Wil!" Katie gasped.

"Katie." Wil smiled. She was wearing what looked like a white button-down under a very plain light-blue sweater with a V-neck. Imagining Wil wearing work slacks with that sweater-shirt combo made Katie horny, which had to be proof she wasn't fooling herself about this inconvenient but privately delicious attraction to Wil.

"So I have an assignment for you," Katie said.

Wil wrinkled her adorable nose. "Okay."

"You have to take a late lunch today and do the Kettle's thing."

"Katie." Wil sighed.

"You *have to,* have to. Because I called your mom."

"You talked to Beanie? Oh my God." She looked away from the phone, then back at Katie. "I can't do the Kettle's thing today. They wouldn't even be expecting me."

"But they are! Beanie's telling her friend."

"Oh." Wil said this with a hint of frustration. "That is . . ." She looked at the ceiling.

"Do it," Katie said. "Would it help if I flashed you right now? As encouragement?" Katie heard a mental tape rewinding in her head, her Reasonable Katie brain horrified, and her neck went hot.

"I'm at work." But Wil was grinning. She already looked 40 percent less irritated, and also like she completely knew Katie was joking.

Which made Katie want to not have been joking.

"Your being at work is what makes it hot." Katie unbuttoned one button of her flannel, watching Wil. Even if she was toeing the line of this teasing exchange, she was an actress, so her body was, in part, an instrument. She hadn't expected anything would happen to *her,* doing a quick flash to make Wil laugh or maybe blush, but now that her flannel was unfastened and her breasts were naked just under it, Katie felt heat race up from her belly button to her throat, and she almost couldn't breathe. "But I'll only do this if you'd enthusiastically *like* for me to flash you over FaceTime on a Thursday morning."

"Katie," Wil said, softly. "You don't have to." Wil's smile was *lovely*.

"Now I really want to, for real." Katie was shaking. She hadn't ever done this before. She'd managed to dig her heels in when Ben requested she do things like this, suspicious of what he'd do with any images, and toward the end he'd taken pictures of her that he shouldn't have without asking, making her glad she'd never *given* him anything like that.

Trusting someone, wanting to, made her skin so hot.

All reactions that belonged to her.

She slid the flannel off her shoulder and felt the cold air of the basement on her bare skin. "Would you like me to?"

"Katie," Wil whispered, then looked at the ceiling. "Yes."

Katie slid one side of the shirt back, just enough, shuddering when the placket grazed her nipple, then pulled it back into place. "I'll see you later. Go to Kettle's. It's been a long time since I went. Maybe they have something edible there now."

"They don't." Wil smiled. Her cheeks were bright red.

Because of Katie.

Because they had both just admitted something to each other.

She really, really hoped she had a month.

Katie disconnected and collapsed on the love seat. She closed her eyes and felt Trois jump onto her stomach, three hard feet pressing in. She petted her cat and thought about herself as though she were a character, the morning she'd had, the day spread out in front of her.

It wasn't, maybe, the kind of story she could tell Madelynn or April. But Katie liked this story for herself.

She spent the rest of the morning pleasantly doing her homework, talking to her phone about the screenplay, editing her *Kipo* document with the timer going, eating delicious chicken enchiladas that her mom had made while thinking about whether Wil had gone to Kettle's, imagining Wil pushing through the door into that coffee shop, imagining her not doing it, sitting in her parked Bronco at the curb, pulling out of the spot and driving through for fast-food lunch somewhere alone, annoyed with herself or with Katie.

There were things she liked about all of what she imagined, but she hoped Wil had gone inside.

"Katie, honey, can I ask you something?" Diana Price scooped another enchilada onto Katie's plate and leaned on the big honey granite countertop, her matching bob swinging forward.

Katie liked looking at her mom, both because she loved her and because she was looking at herself, older, and she had a lot to look forward to. "You may."

"What are you doing with Wil Greene?"

"Ha! That is such a loaded question." Katie spent a moment cutting her enchilada into perfect bite-size pieces and dolloping crema on each one. "Counterquestion. What are you doing with my team?"

Diana raised her perfectly shaped eyebrows.

"Don't"—Katie pointed her fork at her mother—"give me that look of innocence. It is effective, but it is false. Cookies for April? Seroogy's chocolates for Madelynn? I'm guessing there were little notes as well. Veiled, Midwestern-style threats to keep your daughter safe, but in perfect handwriting on holly-and-candles paper."

"I went with wreaths this year." Diana's mouth tightened very slightly. "And I know all of those people and care about them. It's Christmas."

Katie nodded. Nodded some more. "April and Madelynn are worth all of the care. *Family* is a strong word, but it's one you and Dad taught me the value of, and it's one of the things I feel with those two women."

Diana was silent for a long moment. She folded her hands on the table, her face set in the neutral expression she used to keep Katie from reading her mind. "So you're saying yes on cookies and candy, but I should put a lid on the imperious expectations of duty."

"If you would. As far as Wil goes, if we were in a scene together and you asked me, 'What are you doing with Wil Greene?' the audience would lean forward in their seats with absolutely *no idea* where this scene was going next. Will they fight? Will they confess things and cry? Will the mother tell the daughter to stay away from the dangerous internet-famous high school friend, or will she be glad the sheltered starlet has someone to talk to?" She smiled at her mother.

Diana poked her. "You are being very extra right now."

She was. Katie could hear it in her voice—a little bit too much pressure, a feeling like she was reading lines too fast. She knew she shouldn't be irritated with her mother. It was just that she'd wanted to hang onto the good feeling from seeing Wil on FaceTime a little longer. "I know."

"I like Wil very much. I love her. I've known her for her whole life." Diana's tone was apologetic. They didn't fight, or at least they hadn't, not for a long time.

Katie had needed her mother too much to fight with her.

"Yes. I know you do. I also know that there's a *but*. As in, *but* I am only home for a short time, and I am a celebrity, and Wil is not a celebrity *but* has become internet famous in a way that could have consequences for my public image. And also I could hurt her. Or she could hurt me. That's enough things to be worried about that I should, minimally, *think* about what I'm doing with Wil Greene."

Diana had gone still. "It sounds like I'm not a very kind voice in your head."

Katie's gaze dropped to the countertop. She could hear her mom's hurt, and she didn't want to see it. "You're the voice of survival in my head."

"Katie—"

"It's okay." Katie nodded at her plate. "It's okay. I'm not upset. But I mean that. You were the only person I could call. I was sitting in that hotel room with nothing after leaving Ben, and I knew how to survive. I could survive if I called you."

Diana blinked rapidly and looked away, shaking her head back and forth. "You have so much." Diana's voice was soft. "What else do you want?"

Katie made herself listen to that roughness in her mother's voice and feel her heart pounding for a long moment.

Her mom meant, *How else are you going to be hurt?*

Katie didn't know how to find the right words, the right feelings, to express the way she was already hurting. She didn't know how to explain to Diana Price that despite having survived, despite years of therapy, despite all of the awards and accolades she'd earned and having *so much, so much,* she was not okay, because she needed more. Wanted more.

Katie Price was not supposed to want more.

"Did you know that I *liked* Wil my senior year?" she asked, turning this conversation her mom had started about Wil into something with lower stakes.

"Wil? Did I know?" Diana laughed. "Beanie and I suspected. Before Wil, you didn't date anyone or even go to a dance, even with a friend. You were so hardworking and dedicated, I don't think I thought much about that until maybe around your junior year. I had been a bit of a late bloomer also. But your senior year, yes. I could tell that there was something different between you two."

"I was in love with her."

Her mom gave her a look that Katie couldn't interpret. "Did you know that at the time?"

"Nope." To chase away the discomfort, Katie stabbed two bites of enchilada to make a perfect enchilada and crema sandwich. "I didn't. I just wanted to spend all of my time with her."

"Did you figure this out because of how you're feeling about her now?"

It was the worry, Katie realized, that created a small flare of irritation every time her mom talked about anyone new in her life. "Not exactly. I was mostly so happy to understand that Ben wasn't my first love."

Her mom blinked, hard. Then she turned away, reaching up to swipe her face with her hands, and got out of her chair to begin unloading the dishwasher. It was Midwest for, *That is as much as I can talk about this right now.*

Katie smoothed her hand over the frustration in her throat. She wasn't even sure where she was going with this conversation except that she didn't want to feel like her life was a twenty-four-hour vigil against crisis.

She looked out the arched window opposite the kitchen. The house sat on a broad expanse of lawn with a beautiful wrought-iron fence around the property. Her parents hadn't wanted to move. They'd already had their forever home, the cozy two-story stucco they'd bought when Katie was a baby, but Katie's celebrity had made it unsafe for them to live so close to their neighbors, and now they had this beautiful fortress with an unlisted address and a state-of-the-art security system.

She wanted to be proud that she'd been able to earn this beautiful house, the green lawn and the patch of woods in the back that her dad liked to walk around in, but it was hard for Katie to think about the house without thinking about it as something her fame had done to her parents.

It was hard not to think about Ben as something she'd done to her parents.

"I know Beanie so well," Diana said apologetically. "I can't pretend not to know that Beanie's been worried about Wil. She was so close to her dad. Did you know she put off getting the genetic testing to find out if she has Huntington's until this year?"

Katie shook her head, her heart turning to ice so fast, she had to push against her chest to ease how sharp it was. "Does she?"

"No." Diana's eyes filled with fresh tears. "But it was fifty-fifty if she would turn out to have it. You know that Beanie and Jasper didn't know Jasper had it when Beanie got pregnant with Wil?"

Katie nodded. "I think so."

"Jasper's mother had him young, and she still wasn't showing symptoms when Jasper and Beanie were married. Her symptoms came on late and took her down pretty quickly. They didn't have the genetic test for Huntington's yet, so it was a big surprise. If Beanie and Jasper had known, they wouldn't have had Wil. But they did have Wil, and then the testing became available, but Wil didn't *want* to know. She really, really didn't. I think she felt that it honored her dad somehow. Or she was very scared. I can't pretend to understand what a decision like that means to a person. Beanie had to beg her, finally."

Katie wrapped her arms around herself. She thought of Wil's list, and of Beanie helping with it. Of Wil staying here, not moving on. Not going to one of the best law schools in the country.

Wil wasn't stuck. She literally hadn't known if she had real choices to make.

Huntington's was 100 percent fatal and completely, completely awful. Symptoms usually showed up in people's late twenties or early thirties, and then they had ten years left, fifteen at the outside. Katie had done a few campaigns, lending her face and her celebrity presence to fund-raising efforts that Beanie told Diana could make a difference.

But Wil hadn't been tested until recently. Sometime around when she started her stranger-kissing TikTok.

All of which meant that right now was maybe the very first time Wil *could* make choices, or that she felt like she could.

Katie's life, how she had to live, took away a lot of choices.

Diana broke the silence. "I was just thinking that Beanie and I are really good moms," she said. "I have been telling myself to trust, because both you and Wil are lovely people, and the kind of people who will make good decisions. One of the things that always feels the best to hear as a mom, and that moms hear the least, is just, 'You're a good mom.' A long time ago, I figured out that I needed to remember to tell myself that. It's a powerful thing to hear. It's a powerful thing to say. Especially when you have a child who is interesting, exceptional. Like both you and Wil are. When you're a mom who has kids like you and Wil, there's a way that you never feel like you're doing the right thing. But Beanie is such a good mother. And so am I."

Katie rubbed her hands over her knees, then admitted the thing she'd been trying to avoid thinking, even to herself. "I don't know if what I want is good for Wil right now."

Her mom closed the dishwasher and looked at her with kindness in her eyes.

Katie was glad she'd see Wil soon. She needed to, and that was an old feeling she understood. She knew that as soon as she saw Wil, she'd be a little less afraid.

For a little while, maybe it could just be Katie and Wil.

Chapter Seven

Wil walked into Kettle's, wrinkling her nose at the hit of Lysol and coffee that permeated the used bookstore–slash–coffee shop, the mainstay of an awkward neighborhood between downtown and an industrial drag.

Kettle's had carved out a clientele in Green Bay as the default meeting place of the sixty-and-over set, as well as professionals who didn't want to run into anyone they knew, deal with ambient noise, or face a lot of choices about what to eat or drink.

There weren't any customers in the front area, and the ageless brown-haired barista who had worked at Kettle's since Wil used to walk here from East High after school when Beanie couldn't pick her up until five was sitting on a stool behind the counter reading what looked like the Bible, though Wil very sincerely hoped not.

As soon as Wil made it to the counter, she spied the reason she'd come—a couple of tables pushed together with four local attorneys gathered around, their heads bent, talking seriously to each other.

"What can I get you?" the barista asked, putting down her book.

"A coffee with room and . . . the chocolate chip cookies?" The one bright spot at Kettle's was their shrink-wrapped packages of three greasy chocolate chip cookies for a dollar. Most of the time, the cookies turned out to be hard, just tolerable when dipped in coffee, but every once in a while they were soft and falling apart with melted butter and completely worth it.

"Sure," the barista said. "I'll bring it right out."

She would not. No matter what you ordered at Kettle's, you would wait for it.

Wil took a deep breath and turned toward the table in the back.

Beanie was a paralegal, quietly but deeply integrated in the Green Bay legal world. In fact, if Wil's mother had any kind of secret power, it was that a raft of lawyers in the greater Northeast Wisconsin area would die for Beanie Greene, which meant that she could actually get away with capital crimes, corporate sabotage, or ecoterrorism if the mood struck her.

For years, Beanie had done paralegal work for Mike Jerry, the kingpin of legal empires and politics in Green Bay. A small, quiet, elderly white man, Mike was an emeritus partner in the firm he'd founded, housed right next to the courthouse, in probably the late 1800s.

Mike Jerry ruled over a secret cabal of other legal scions in Green Bay, and together, at a back table at Kettle's, they directed the fortunes of every J.D. within a hundred miles.

Careers were ended and made at these tables, according to Beanie.

Wil's mother had been trying to get her to talk to this group for at least a couple of years, convinced that if she did, she might identify a direction for her own career. Get unstuck.

Though being stuck wasn't exactly why Wil hadn't gone to Michigan Law. Beanie knew that, but "stuck" was what Wil and Beanie called the lifestyle consequences of Wil's guilt-shot mortal terror, which had only just begun to ease up and give her some room to breathe.

"Hey," she said. "I'm Wilifred Greene."

Mike Jerry looked up. He gave her a very small smile. His blue eyes were bright and a little terrifying. "I haven't seen you since you started at Michigan," he said. "Sit down. Let me introduce you."

Wil settled into the chair beside Mike. She already knew two of the other people at the table by reputation. One was Mary Lyddle, whose German and Belgian forebears had been lawyers in Green Bay since the first white men arrived and pretended not to understand that all the land belonged to the highly competent First Nations people who had literally guided them to the bay by canoe. Maybe in response to this craven colonization, Mary was notorious for upending Green Bay power legacies whose exclusionary practices held so many in the community back. Wil knew that Jasper had liked Mary very much.

The other was Cord Schiff, a Black man in his fifties who regularly offered criminal law perspectives on left-leaning national news networks.

"And this is Sam Rafferty," Mike said. "He went to East like you, but he's been practicing in Chicago until a few years ago."

Sam was a white guy who looked about forty, but in the way that a fully adult, grown, seriously fucking hot guy looked forty, with the eye crinkles and dark hair shot through with only the tiniest bit of silver at his temples.

Wil wondered if he would be interested in kissing her.

Coming up with two new people to kiss every week created a certain amount of pressure that had taught Wil not to look too hard at these impulses. She just arrowed herself straight at them and let the chips fall. But in this context, with the lawyers, she might need to exercise some discretion.

Sam solved this problem for her. "My girlfriend is obsessed with your TikTok channel." He had a little color in his cheeks. "I benefit from her obsession, so it's really nice to meet you. Don't let me forget to get your autograph before you go."

"You'd both be welcome to *be* on my channel." Wil raised one eyebrow.

Sam laughed. "Hold up. Can you say that again, but I'll record you this time? It would be entirely for points with Robin. I can't be on your channel, I have a minor child. Plus, if these three get their way, I'm headed for the bench. I have to keep myself squeaky clean."

"Aren't you suggesting, then, that my project will create problems for me, should I decide to pursue a career in the law?" Wil made it clear with her tone that she didn't take her own question seriously.

Mary laughed. "Honestly, I think it's adorable that Sam, a rich white man, thinks that kissing an attractive woman on the internet would in any way damage his electability in Wisconsin. Not to mention that his girlfriend is Robin Dahl, who's probably one of the sharpest political minds the Midwest, and especially Wisconsin, is going to see in this generation. If Robin wanted to kiss you, or Sam did, Robin could spin it into a win. Sam's just scared." Mary gave Sam a cutting look.

"I am. All true. Hiding behind my privilege."

"As usual," said Cord. He extended his hand for Wil to shake. "It's good to meet you. I've known your mother for years. Knew your dad, too, and liked him a lot. When he switched to consulting after he had to resign, he helped me out with preparing the VGL Corps fraud case on behalf of the county. My condolences to you and Beanie."

"Thanks. He liked you, too," Wil said. "When you first started doing TV commentary, he'd have me watch it with him. He told me I'd be good at that. I think he liked the idea of me someday verbally eviscerating the bad guys on network television."

There must have been something in the way she said it that betrayed Wil's doubts about that vision of her future, because Cord leaned back and put an ankle on his knee and started looking at Wil in a way that she was sure he had perfected in order to keep people from knowing what he was thinking. "What do *you* like the idea of?"

This meeting had gotten deep much faster than Wil had imagined it would.

Even at eighteen, nineteen, twenty years old, she'd been perfectly aware that she was trying to be the best pre-law student the University of Michigan had ever seen mostly so that her dad—of course her dad, who else but her dad?—would know that she was absolutely going to thrive after he was gone.

When he thought of her, she'd wanted him to feel nothing but pride. Not worry about what might happen to her. Not regret that he wouldn't be around.

Wil had been determined that Jasper Greene know she was going to become what she'd told him she would be, which was essentially what *he* would have been if he'd never gotten sick. She would be Jasper Greene on a bigger stage than Green Bay, the kind of stage that was presidentially appointed and involved Beanie Greene wearing vintage Bob Mackie and Wil going to parties with senators' kids.

One of the first things Wil had been forced to grapple with after she got her genetic testing results, once the euphoria wore off, after she'd taken ibuprofen for the headache she'd gotten from crying, was the realization that now she could get back to going after her dream.

Except that she absolutely didn't want to.

She'd been right to avoid this meeting. She should stand up and walk right back out of Kettle's. She would, if it weren't for the fact that she had never been able to resist the challenge of being put on the spot by smart people asking probing questions.

In this way, at least, she was exactly like her father.

"Maybe I don't have precisely the same idea my dad did," she said.

Cord nodded. "Good." He didn't offer up anything else, not even a clear facial expression.

Okay, then. She was clearly here to prove her mettle to these oldsters. Wil rummaged around in her brain to see if she could pull out exactly what her mettle looked like. Or sounded like.

Mike Jerry cleared his throat. "What we have here, everyone," he said, "is a graduate of Michigan, summa cum laude in pre-law, one of the point-zero-one percent of undergraduates who had an article published in their law journal, who was admitted to Michigan Law, Stanford Law, and a large smattering of ranked-eleven-through-twenty schools, and is working as an insurance adjuster and entertainer."

"Wow," Wil said. "Jump right in, Mike."

"So goes Beanie, so goes my nation." Mike tipped his tea mug at Wil.

"Did you defer?" Sam asked.

"Sure. Eight years ago. Deferred again seven years ago. I think I still have some first-look consideration?"

Sam leaned back in his chair. He was not assessing her as an *entertainer* now. There was some brain there behind the hotness, and it was pointed at her. "Can I ask you a personal question?"

"I don't have the mutation." This wasn't information Wil would normally volunteer, but kissing so many people had made her more attuned to people's faces and the shifts in their expressions, and she could see that Sam Rafferty had big enough feelings about this question that she wanted to spare him having to ask it.

Although maybe that wasn't so much Wil's being hyperattuned to this guy's emotional landscape as it was her own reluctance to let anyone feel anything about the question of whether or not she had Huntington's.

When Wil was eighteen—the age it was recommended she get tested—her dad didn't have a lot of time left, and she couldn't imagine getting tested while Jasper Greene was dying. Having to tell him that what was killing him would kill her, too, eventually? No.

After he was gone, she still couldn't face those feelings. Even thinking about the person at the hospital or lab or office who'd have to call her up on the phone to give her the test result, she couldn't face *their* feelings.

Until Beanie pointed out to her, at Christmastime last year, that Wil was literally never going to be able to face the feelings. Beanie lost it a little, crying, and reminded Wil that after losing her husband and best friend, she would *fucking like to prepare herself.*

Then Wil stopped thinking about lab workers and started thinking about her mom. She scheduled her test for January.

She still didn't know what to make of the fact that the results surprised her.

Or of the fact that her mother's request had made Wil realize that Beanie was *her* best friend. Sticking around Green Bay so many years had meant that she'd spent a lot of time with her mom that they might not have otherwise had together. They'd done the hard things, like sorting through Jasper's possessions and clearing out his office. They'd invented their own traditions and rituals, like going to the Harry Houdini exhibit in Appleton every year and watching all of Katie's awards shows together.

She'd gotten to know Beanie as an adult, and what she'd realized was that she had a mind a lot more like her mom's than she'd ever understood. Where her dad took in the world in the broad, systemic strokes of a warrior, her mom was always looking closely at the minutiae for a way to solve a problem that everyone else had overlooked. It was why she was every attorney in Green Bay's secret weapon. She could find a single leaf on a tree that explained the whole fucking forest.

So could Wil. She just didn't know how to turn that into a future that felt like the right fit for her—and she also didn't know what any of that had to do with the fact that she'd spent the past year absorbed with her project of kissing strangers on the internet.

Although she was starting to have a few ideas about that.

"Do you like being an insurance adjuster?" Sam asked.

"I actually love it."

"Then tell me what you love about being an insurance adjuster."

Wil noticed herself sitting up straighter in response to these rapid-fire questions. She was definitely *liking* this. "I listen, document, solve complex problems simply, usually with money, and talk to different people every day, most of them interesting for some new way they're weird."

Sam grinned. "That's what I loved about criminal corporate law."

"You were a black elevator lawyer?"

That made him laugh.

"I don't get it," Mary said.

"You know," Wil said, turning to Mary, "how the evil, su-pervillain, super-rich types always have a Gotham-esque urban skyscraper lair with a private black elevator that probably also descends to hell?"

"Is that a thing?" Mary looked around the table.

"Our elevator was the blackest," Sam said. "I should say 'is,' because I'm still a partner. I have defended some truly despicable but extremely interesting people. People whose decision-making, looked at head-on, is astonishing in the magnitude and breadth of its badness."

"Sam was telling us last week that he doesn't believe there's any such thing as bad people," Mary told Wil. "Just people who make bad decisions."

"Everyone deserves a defense," Mike Jerry said mildly.

"It's not just that," Sam said. "We know that somebody like you, Mike, or Cord here is going to bring absolutely everything you've got to the challenge of representing the case of someone who's been harmed. That's as it should be. But there's got to be expertise on the other side, too, making sure that whoever did the harming has been identified correctly and that the consequences are proportional. There's got to be someone like me who's the last stop as far as making a corporate defendant *believe* and fully comprehend their accountability, and, as Wil said, fix it with money, which is always going to hurt them more than their conscience will ever sting. I defend in order to redistribute."

"But," Wil said. "*But,* you haven't talked to Fox Valley car wreck people. Fox Valley car wreck people have made some life choices, Sam. You can't even begin to understand how dark the human soul can really be."

He laughed again. Wil liked his easy laugh. It was a shame this man and his girlfriend didn't want to kiss her. "What are you doing now that you're in Green Bay?" she asked him.

"Probate."

"So you can definitely sleep at night now. Probably sleep during the day, too."

Sam laughed again. "Please come to dinner sometime. You would make Robin so happy." He crossed his legs. "I've gathered, pretty easily, that you already know that law is for you." Now his voice was serious again.

Wil let the seriousness of it sink in, and the way all three of these people were looking at her, which was with a lot of intelligent intensity. It was much more comfortable than she would have thought. She couldn't feel anywhere inside her body if she wanted to go to law school, but she could feel that she liked being at this table with these four smart people looking at her.

That kind of thing—not just knowing what felt good but knowing why, and being able to start wondering what it might mean—had been easier and easier since Wil started her kissing project.

Katie appeared in Wil's mind's eye then. Her big eyes, her perfect eyebrows ever so slightly raised as she shrugged that flannel shirt off her shoulder.

Wil had been able to see, on the bright screen of her phone, how fast Katie was breathing.

Katie made that seem so attractive. Doing something different. Being afraid.

"It's December," Sam said. "Application season. All four of us have contacts and expertise that could help you figure out how to get yourself into school this coming fall. If that's what you want to do."

"Wow," Wil said. "I expected so much more beating around the bush from a bunch of lawyers."

Sam crossed his arms. "Do you want it?"

"How long—" Wil's throat had a dry catch in it. "How long do I have to think about it?"

Sam looked at the other people at the table.

"It's the holidays," Mary said. "Maybe a couple weeks for someplace like Yale. They decide early. Michigan's got a bigger window, so you have a bit longer there."

Cord nodded. "The California schools are the ones I know the most about. Pepperdine, Loyola, UCLA. They'll take applications into February, but they stop looking at them about a week into January."

Mike shrugged and looked at Wil. "Two weeks. Give me a call. We know what you need to know to make this happen, and we can introduce you to anyone else you're going to have to figure out how to impress."

"I know Donna at Yale," Mary said. "We went to school together."

"I've got people at all those California schools. It's how I got introduced to all the TV folks," Cord said. "And Sam, don't you have a friend at Harvard?"

Sam smiled. "William English," he affirmed. "There was someone close to him who was in the category of *very* bad decisionmaker, and William was grateful for my assistance in directing him toward redemption."

"Pretty razor-thin deadline," Wil said. Her leg muscles were shaking, even as she tried to joke.

"Sure," Sam said. "Welcome aboard."

"Good on Beanie for figuring out how to get you here," Cord said. "I like a toothy mother."

"She is the toothiest," Wil agreed.

But she wondered what would happen to the conversation at the table if she told them the person who'd made her come today was Katie Price. Or what Katie had done over FaceTime to offer Wil an *incentive*.

The barista interrupted with what Wil assumed was going to be her coffee but was actually a warmed-up cinnamon roll for Mike, and the conversation slid away from her future to Mike's sweet tooth and Sam's nephew, who Wil gathered was some kind of debate powerhouse whose rapid-fire wins had turned all of the attorneys at the table into high school debate nerds.

By the time Wil's coffee and cookies showed up, Mary had already left, and Sam kept checking his watch. "I need to run to the high school." He dug around in his wallet until he found a business card and handed it to Wil. "It was great to meet you. That's my cell number on the back. If you do want dinner and to meet Robin, give me a call or text anytime. I promise not to make it weird."

"I'm fine with weird," Wil said. "I'm actually really good at weird."

He laughed and talked to Mike and Cord for a minute, and then they were all standing up to go, so Wil asked for a paper cup to put her coffee in. It was almost three. She texted Katie.

> Just done at Kettle's, too late to get anything done if I go back to work

> Okay if I come over?

The three dots popped up, then were replaced with Katie's response.

> Yes! but to pick me up bc i'm restless

> need chocolate covered almonds and want to go to costco

> i have a whole system wont be recognized

> youve got it omw

Wil slid her phone into her pocket and pointed the Bronco toward the Prices' neighborhood.

She sipped her coffee and thought about how it could get addictive, driving to pick up Katie. Wil liked how it layered over the way it used to be with how it was now, the high-end neighborhood and the long driveway and Katie coming out of the house in a huge, puffy winter coat, boots, and a dark wig.

Wil leaned over and pulled the handle and shoved the door open for Katie to climb in. Her entire body was singing, just because Katie was getting into her truck.

"Wil!" Katie hopped on the bench. Immediately, she slipped out of the coat and wrestled it into the wheel well. "Why are coats? I try, but I can't. Why?"

Wil put the Bronco into gear. "Probably because it's thirty degrees?"

"Not enough degrees, but I feel like there should be a solution. Like an implant that creates a microclimate around my body. Wait! Stop the Bronco."

Wil put the truck in park at the end of the Prices' drive. "I'm stopped. Do you need me to go back?"

"No. I need us to touch." Katie smiled, but it wasn't her flirting or enjoying the moment, or even relishing a little drama. "*Need* was the wrong word. May we? Or we can pretend I didn't make you stop the truck and ask for a pet like a cat at three a.m."

"How?"

Katie had the same flannel shirt on that she'd been wearing on FaceTime, which made it difficult for Wil to think about anything except what had happened on FaceTime, and how the flannel had slid over Katie's bare shoulder, revealing her collarbone, then a glimpse of bare skin and Katie's unadorned body that had made Wil feel like she couldn't catch her breath.

Katie's wig, under a plain stocking cap, was a very convincing brown bob. She'd done something with her makeup Wil had never seen in any picture of her that made her age undefinable. The coat, close up, had been around the block, and the boots had dried salt soaked into the bond between the sole and the quilted purple nylon. Unless you were studying her *and* were some kind of a superfan, you'd think Katie was a young Green Bay mom, or—at the most glamorous—a stay-at-home spouse.

"Let me back up," Katie said. "A hug. May I have a hug? Maybe a little over-the-clothes?" She scooched closer.

Wil laughed. "A hug would be really nice, thank you."

Katie opened her arms, and Wil reached for her. Katie wrapped her arms around Wil's shoulders but snaked a hand up through the back of her hair, giving Wil pleasant shivers.

Wil hugged Katie tight, spreading her hands over her back so she could feel how her ribs connected to her backbone, feel her breathing.

"People should hug more," Wil said. "This is so good."

"Right?"

Wil inhaled against Katie's neck, pressing her nose into warm skin, smelling whatever Katie's soap and shampoo were perfumed with. When Katie wiggled closer, Wil let her arms band around her so she could feel Katie pressed against her everywhere.

All of the stress melted out of Wil's body. The only muscles engaged were the ones she needed to keep holding Katie, which meant her brain shifted all of its awareness to skin, and warmth, and Katie's cheek against her ear, and how Wil's lips were resting, now, against the spot where Katie's neck curved into her shoulder.

"God," Wil said against Katie's neck. "That feels . . ."

Katie scratched with all of her nails, lightly, from the back of Wil's scalp down her neck. "You like it?"

"The things my body is feeling right now don't belong in the 'like' file." Wil couldn't help it, she kissed, just a little, Katie's neck. Talking against it with her mouth was practically kissing anyway.

Katie's hands stilled in Wil's hair. "Do that again, but ten percent dirtier."

Wil's heart stilled. She hadn't really, exactly, meant to make a move. Part of the pleasure of the hug was sense memory. They had hugged all the time back then. This hug had swept away the last cobwebs obscuring their old intimacy.

But Wil made her brain stop thinking about it so she could get away with kissing Katie's neck, just in case Katie was thinking too much, also. Only the *tiniest* bit of her tongue.

Katie moaned, actually moaned like they were in bed together already, but then eased back, running her hands over Wil's arms as she did. They were still only a few inches apart.

Wil loved this part of kissing people, how she could look at them close in, look at how kissing changed their face. Katie's mouth was soft and relaxed. Her eyes looked different, not so alert, just calm and present. It made Wil unexpectedly tender.

But they weren't kissing.

Katie's face shifted again. She smiled, her eyebrows raised. "Whatcha doing?"

Wil breathed in and breathed out a laugh. "It's just that it comes to me so naturally at this point. You're there, three inches away. I'm here, extremely on board and dedicated. I can tell that you wanted to, which tells me we've been driving in that direction."

"Kissing, you mean." Katie looked highly amused. "Tell me something."

"Sure." Wil was not sure.

"When did we start driving toward this particular moment, Wilifred? Give me the rough date."

"Well." Wil eased the rest of the way apart from Katie, checked her parking brake, and leaned back in her seat. "Not when we talked about it at the party. That's implied. If we had to make a bet to ensure you *wouldn't* come on my TikTok and kiss me, it's fair to say we'd both entertained thoughts."

Katie smiled. "So many thoughts."

Wil grinned and then couldn't hold Katie's gaze, which was too much with her smile and the heat racing up Wil's neck as memories fitted themselves into place, one after another, to make a picture she'd never really let herself see before. "There's one moment I can remember." She managed to keep her voice teasing, but she was sure the color in her face gave her away.

"Tell me, and I'll stop you if I remember it, too."

"We took that super long walk toward Luxemburg because you wanted to try out your new digital camcorder."

Katie laughed. "Stop."

"If I stop, who's going to finish the story?"

"Hmm. I'm not sure, because I have this feeling neither one of us has told this story, maybe even to ourselves."

"Of course not. You were my good friend Katie Price who I had never remembered not knowing, including the time you barfed Kool-Aid onto your birthday cake in kindergarten."

"So keep going." Katie circled her index fingers around each other and grinned.

"Fuck. Okay. So we're walking to Luxemburg along that skinny county road next to the barbed-wire fences that keep the cows in—you filmed a lot of cows, I seem to remember—and I had just gotten Beanie to capitulate on buying me a Roxy puffy vest, which I insisted on wearing with a shirt instead of a coat, so I was freezing."

Katie had leaned back against her passenger door and was smiling at the ceiling of the truck. "I still have that footage. It isn't terrible."

"You noticed one of those railroad bridges with trusses underneath, a little one, over a frozen creek."

"I did."

"You wanted to head toward it, but I didn't want to because we'd have to cut through one of the cow pastures with all the frozen mud and tall grass. Plus, I hate frozen bodies of water. They're creepy, and I have intrusive thoughts about falling through the ice and getting sucked away from the hole by a current."

"God." Katie looked at her. "You didn't tell me that."

"I couldn't. It was only a bitty creek, and I was wearing a cropped puffy vest from the mall with a long-sleeved T-shirt in twenty-degree weather. Obviously I care most about being cool."

"But you did walk with me through the pasture to the creek."

"I did."

"And when I wanted to climb up on that cement culvert and onto the trusses, you followed me."

"Cool people aren't afraid to die, Katie."

"So there we were, sitting side by side under the railroad bridge on a wooden truss, and we could hear the water under the ice. I have footage of that, too, figuring out the zoom."

Wil imagined Katie at home in Los Angeles, playing the old video. It made her feel a pang, nostalgia or loss. They'd missed out on knowing each other for such a long time. "After I stopped being privately freaked, I realized I wasn't cold anymore. I remember it was really pretty. And I was a little bit in awe, in that jealous way that's easy to be when you're a teenager, that you had seen how beautiful it was going to be from all the way across the pasture on the road."

"Is that why you moved my hair out of my face?" Katie had turned toward her. "Because you were jealous of me?"

Here was where it got tricky for Wil, this memory. The moments right after it, she'd quickly covered up with jokes and self-denial because she wasn't . . . *enough* to let happen what had almost happened, or to let it mean what it would have meant. It was as if Wil's instant, total, white-hot flash of self-denial had packed up this memory in layers of paper and sealed the box shut. That meant that opening it, looking at it right now, she had to feel all the feelings she hadn't let herself surrender to then.

"I moved your hair out of your face because I wanted to see your face." Wil had to stop and clear her throat. "And because I wanted you to look at me."

"I did look at you," Katie whispered.

"You did. I think I knew how close together we'd be, sitting on that truss, if you looked at me. It didn't seem like we were *anywhere*, you know? We were somewhere neither one of us had ever been. It was so pretty and cold, it was like nothing was real, and so something I didn't realize I had wanted to do was suddenly taking the chance."

"And that something was . . . ?"

"Kissing you."

Wil kept trying to find the moment, but even now, she mostly remembered when she'd realized her hand was over one of Katie's knees, and that she could feel Katie's breath against her mouth. She had laughed and clumsily dropped her body onto the culvert, turning her ankle but ignoring it, making a joke about movie magic.

The real moment—the moment they had leaned into each other, knowing they were going to kiss, the inevitability of that happening—Wil had lost.

"I had already had my first kiss." Katie sounded farther away than usual. "In a production of *Brigadoon*. I didn't like the actor who I had to kiss. I'd been in shows with him before, and I knew they would cast him and I would have to kiss him. But he was the only person I'd kissed. I remember thinking if you kissed me, I would have wanted you to." She smiled. "That's how convoluted it was in my head. Like, it would be okay for you to kiss me, the thing I really wanted to happen, because I had already, technically, been kissed by someone I found abhorrent." Katie laughed. "I never want to be eighteen again."

"So what happened just now?" Wil asked.

"A much better almost-kiss, I would say." Katie nodded. "You didn't hurl yourself away from me, for example."

"I'm suddenly wondering if I started my TikTok to redeem myself."

"If that was your mission, then consider it accomplished." Katie settled herself back into her own seat again and cracked the window to keep the glass from fogging, which made Wil curious about how much of this was getting picked up by Craig's security cameras and how long they could talk at the end of the drive with the taillights pointed toward the house before Diana walked down with an excuse to get the mail in order to see what they were doing.

"Did you know that a perfect way to make an audience understand desire is to have one of the characters kiss the other's neck?" Katie asked. "A kiss on someone's neck tells the audience that the character wants, *needs,* the other character in a way that can't be satisfied except with intimacy. With sex. It's often more powerful to witness than even a very explicit kiss."

"I am, as of right now, convinced." Wil smiled. "Are you ready to do this mission?"

"Yes."

Wil got them onto the road. "Tell me more about what you were saying about getting the audience to understand desire. I feel like there was something technical there."

Katie readjusted her hat and wig after their hug. "I took a workshop from this amazing acting teacher that was about intimate scenes. Screen and stage kisses and sex."

"They have workshops for that?"

"They have workshops for everything. What I'm talking about are intimacy workshops. Blocking intimate scenes, establishing boundaries, understanding the work of convincing an audience of intimacy. Our teacher's big point was that who we were being intimate with, as actors, was not the other actor in the scene, it was the audience. Every decision we made was about how we made the *audience* feel, because it's the audience who needs to be convinced. It's the audience who all of the feelings are *for*. And that's the same thing you're doing." Katie turned to look at Wil, her eyes big, smiling. "You're kissing all these different people," she said, "but the audience is there for you. They want to see *you* kiss a new person every time. They experience the kiss by witnessing how you react to it."

"But I'm not thinking about the audience."

Was that true, though? Didn't Wil think of the audience when she and the person she was going to kiss positioned the camera? Wasn't the audience a script that was running in the background the whole time, an awareness in Wil's body of how everything that happened between her and this person would look, how it would make people feel?

It wasn't as though she'd ever considered keeping the kissing videos private. The idea had always been, from the minute Wil decided to accept her housemate's comment as a dare, to film and edit and share them. Show them to people. Talk about them and listen to other people talking about them.

The point had been to find things out. At first, about herself, because of the housemate's suggestion that Wil was too casual with relationships and too shallow with her feelings. But it wasn't long before Wil was finding out a lot of interesting things about people that made her realize how much of herself she had locked away as soon as her dad had his diagnosis. Wil couldn't fail to see her feelings when she was working so hard to make someone else comfortable, to try to help them get something they needed out of an experience.

The more people she'd kissed, the more she'd shared of herself. For an audience of millions of people. Wil had made her feelings as big as she could, maybe so she could finally understand them. So she would be able to really see them.

"No. I'm wrong," Wil said. "You're right." Without the last year of kissing, she wouldn't have had access to what she'd felt today with that table of lawyers.

Or to what she felt for Katie.

She hadn't let herself think deeply, carefully, about her feelings for Katie until today. Until the last long minutes at the end of Craig and Diana's driveway. And if what Wil had felt in high school wasn't the same thing she was feeling lately about Katie, it was definitely connected over all these years—their lives rushing past that moment in time, waiting for them to return to it.

It made Wil want to change something, one thing that would let her figure out more about what she wanted and how it might connect up the different parts of her life. Because Wil did understand that all the parts of her life *were* connected, and that she was what connected them.

She wanted the part of her that couldn't stop thinking about Katie—Katie's body, Katie's smile, Katie's mind and how it worked—to talk to the part that was kissing people for TikTok and the part that had just talked to scary-powerful Green Bay attorneys at Kettle's because Katie Price asked her to.

"Katie."

"Yes."

Wil glanced over. Katie was looking right at her. "Will you film my kiss on Saturday?"

At the next stoplight, Katie leaned over and kissed Wil's neck.

Chapter Eight

Katie looked at Wil behind the wheel of the Bronco and ate another chocolate-covered almond from the giant plastic container they had purchased at Costco.

Wil was quiet. Even while they had giggled their way through Costco, she kept retreating to her thoughts. Now they were sitting in the parking lot. No plan yet. No conversation happening.

Katie liked it, actually. Not very many people she regularly spent time with were thoughtful. Intelligent, definitely. Gifted, yes. But her work attracted the kind of people who processed their feelings outside of their minds and their bodies, which included Katie.

She loved how it felt to be near Wil when she was obviously working on something. Her awareness of Katie would surface with her attention for just a few moments because she'd registered something funny Katie had said, or because Katie had deliberately bid for Wil's attention, and then Wil would slide back into herself, her energy curling around some piece of brain grit she was obviously trying to make smooth.

Katie ate a few more almonds, a little bit drunk with anticipation, maybe, waiting for the next time she would get to be Wil's object of contemplation.

"Sorry," Wil suddenly said, her fingers finally curling around a handful of Chicago-style popcorn and pulling it from the bag. "I wandered off there."

"Tell me about your meeting. Don't leave anything out. Especially your feelings."

Wil laughed. "See, if you hadn't said that, I would've told you about the meeting as briefly as possible. Or I would've told you about the secret power dynamics, which were pretty fucking intense, actually. But you want to know *especially* about my feelings, which is the version of my meeting I'm least likely to tell anyone about, ever."

Katie pushed her hands beneath her own thighs. Wil hadn't worn work slacks with her blue sweater. She'd worn dark jeans, the heavy denim tight over her long legs. Katie was dead of Wil's jeans. "Obviously, this is why I asked."

"Obviously." Wil ate some popcorn. "I'm pretty sure the reason I haven't gone to law school is because I knew I'd end up making decisions that felt disloyal to my dad. I could already feel that whatever was going to happen next in my life, it wouldn't be what I'd told him it would. I knew my dreams were going to change, but he's not here anymore to tell me what he thinks of my new dreams. He's not here to say it's okay to be the kind of lawyer I want to be, not the kind of lawyer he would've wanted me to be. So I stayed put."

Wil spoke slowly, taking long breaks to stare out the window, making Katie want nothing more than to gather her up in her arms and pet her hair and the sides of her neck. She told Katie this devastating thing the way she'd always told Katie things when she'd thought about them as much as she needed to, tumbling them over and around inside her head until her thoughts were polished and smooth, perfectly synthesized, and true.

"Tell me more about that," Katie said.

And Wil did. She talked for a long time about the years she'd spent in Green Bay with Beanie, about burying Jasper Greene and learning how to live without him, and about being a daughter and a friend to her mother through the worst of their grief.

What Katie understood when Wil was done was that the stakes of their bet were higher than Katie had thought, because Wil needed, badly, a push. Not into being fully an adult—Wil was already gloriously adult—but a push that would catapult Wil into stomping around in motorcycle boots and doing a montage of hot lawyer things in the Gotham City of her dreams while judges and other lawyers didn't know if they wanted to fuck her or *be* her.

Also, Katie had to very firmly cover the little light that came on in her heart as Wil listed the names of the schools she'd discussed with the power lawyers, as three of them were in Los Angeles.

"I can see why you avoided that meeting," she said. "I think if I knew there were four strangers at Kettle's who could easily assist me in attaining my heart's secret desire, I'd avoid the fuck out of them, too."

"Yeeeeah." Wil exhaled. "A time-out, if you would."

"Poor baby." Katie leaned over and quick-kissed Wil's cheek. Like a friend. Like they had when they were girls. The kiss landed between Katie's legs in a way that surprised her. "We can discuss the investigation."

Wil crinkled her nose in such a familiar way, it made Katie's heart ache. "I'm not sure we have an investigation. I did manage to dig up an address from a cached PTO newsletter from 2013."

"So let's do a drive-by and then work on my script. My mom is making cabbage rolls for dinner."

Wil started the truck, laughing. "I know. Beanie asked me to bring two home for her with mashed potatoes."

"Our mothers know everything. My mom asked me what we were doing today."

Wil stopped at a light. "Did you have to divulge the details of our investigation?"

"She meant 'what are we *doing*?'"

"Ohhh." Wil thumbed the gearshift. Katie was pretty sure Wil was blushing. *Katie* was blushing, too.

"Beanie hasn't asked you?"

"Beanie's been telling me to 'stop by and visit' since the party. But not asking anything."

"At least Beanie trusts me," Katie said, mostly to see Wil's reaction.

She watched Wil process, the streetlights confirming a blush actually bleeding into her lip line, making Wil's lush mouth look very seriously and painfully delicious. "What did you tell your mom?"

"I told her a lot of things. She reminded me that my life is complicated for other people, and she told me Beanie's been worried about you for years. That's Diana making sure I don't impulsively fling myself at your hotness and then Justin Bieber you for the paparazzi with your dingle dongle out for the long lens to capture for the press."

"Whha-at?" Wil downshifted but slipped the gear a little.

Katie laughed. "That's unfair. It was a serious conversation. It made me afraid, actually, because my life isn't easy. Not for me, not if someone else was in it who didn't have to be. I've come of age in front of the world, which is horrible. I genuinely worry if my brain has developed properly."

Wil looked at her, eyebrows raised. "Your brain is solid, Katie. You don't have anything to worry about there."

"Sure, okay, but she talked about what you've been through lately, and she told on you about your testing." Katie held her breath, not sure if she should have said that, except that she felt like Wil had given her an opening when she told her about what her dad had wanted for her and why it meant Wil hadn't moved on.

Mostly, the more time she spent with Wil, which was barely any so far, the more she mourned all the time in the last thirteen years they *hadn't* spent together. It was a little scary, since their tacit agreement seemed to be to spend as much time together as was possible while Katie was here, and Katie wasn't sure how many more feelings she could feel about Wil without exploding.

Or how she was going to go back to LA without her heart in a very pulpy and raw condition.

"Right," Wil said. Katie watched her swallow.

She waited, but Wil didn't say anything more. It made her heart squeeze to think about Wil being worried for so many years, and that made her reckless enough to say, "Also, I told her that when I was eighteen, that spring, I was in love with you."

Wil did slip the gear then, in the middle of a roundabout, and tried to restart the Bronco's engine, which was running, so the truck stalled. "Fuck." Wil frantically waggled the gearshift and turned the key. "Fuck, fuck."

The truck started. Wil put it into gear as a sedan blew around them with a loud blast of its horn. But just when Katie expected Wil to pull the Bronco back into the flow of traffic—just when her heart was racing and she felt breathless and full of regret for surprising Wil with such an ill-timed confession—Wil's shoulders dropped, and she blew out a breath and looked over at Katie.

Just looked at her with her serious blue eyes, all her scary intelligence and intensity, for one long, suspended beat. *"Fuck,"* she whispered.

"I'm sorry," Katie said. "I shouldn't have." She wasn't sure what she meant that she shouldn't have done. If she meant she shouldn't have said it, or if she meant that she shouldn't have loved Wil.

Although she didn't regret either.

"Don't be sorry," Wil said. "I'm pretty sure I was in love with you, too."

Katie clasped her wrist, twisting her fingers around it like the bracelet Wil had sent her.

The loss of that bracelet was still the easiest thing for Katie to feel angry with Ben about. Her rage when she thought of him taking it—hiding it or throwing it away because he knew it was important to her—was utter.

Katie had loved that fucking bracelet.

She had *loved*.

She wished it had been easier—it had even been possible—to understand her own feelings when she was eighteen years old.

She wished she'd known that it *mattered* how safe she felt sitting in Wil's bed, her feet on Wil's lap, laughing and talking for hours. That it *mattered* how her stomach tightened and she got grayed out when Ben kept her late at summer stock for extra coaching, when he stood too close behind her and whispered in her ear and she couldn't see him, could only feel his muscled forearm banded around her stomach, holding her motionless, and his voice telling her what she was bad at, what she didn't understand, what she still needed to learn and he would teach her.

"I didn't mean to never see you again." Katie was a little surprised to hear the strength of her feelings making her voice tremble. "I've never avoided you. I know my mom has been protective. I think—No, I know, for sure, that I put my feelings for you away somewhere that I didn't have to think about missing you. There wasn't any way, when I first was in California, with Ben, to make space for anything that had been important to me before."

The roundabout had emptied of traffic. The road they were on wasn't a busy one. Wil got the truck moving again. She took a deep breath. "When I turned eighteen, I felt like the life I had been living had run out. That's the age you get tested. Before, I didn't have to worry about it. But also, when I had that birthday in April, *you* were there. I was hanging out with you. We were spending all of our free time together, and so it felt like I was getting this extra time. I still had my dad."

"You waited more than ten years after that." Katie didn't worry about how this would sound, she just let herself say it. She felt as though she were sitting on that trestle under the bridge with Wil. They used to be able to talk about anything, everything, without worrying how it would sound. Katie couldn't worry about this conversation. It had been waiting so long for them to finally be ready to have it.

Wil signaled and turned left into a neighborhood that Katie hadn't been to before. She drove a few blocks, quiet, and pulled over at the curb.

"My dad got me to Michigan," Wil said. "Pure ambition and how badly I wanted to make him proud got me graduated, even after he died. Also." Wil cleared her throat, hard. It made tears fill Katie's eyes. "I felt like I was in this race to get as much done as I could before I started having symptoms. The minute I rested, the summer after graduation, it was like I ran out of something."

"Wil," Katie said softly. "Of course you did. You know that, right? That you had to rest?"

Wil looked over at Katie, the rims of her eyes red. "Maybe not?"

Now Katie cleared her throat to keep it from closing up. "Our mothers were correct to worry about us both so much," Katie said. "Possibly, they still are correct."

Wil gave a tight nod, looking at Katie. "Thanks."

Katie knew what her gratitude was for. It was for saying the thing. It was for how easy this reunion was, and how hard. It was for the Katie and Wil thirteen years ago and their confused, perfect, vulnerable hearts.

Wil smiled and pointed through the windshield at a house ahead on the right. "That's where he lives. Or where he lived a decade ago. He might have moved."

"No one ever moves in this town if they can possibly help it. What if you sold your house and the horrible *Bears* fans that bought it turned around and sold it a year later for twenty percent more after tearing down the Packers green-and-gold wishing well that your dad made for the front yard? Could you stand to let a Bears fan steal your investment after you were the one who updated the furnace and paid for that new roof?" Katie sat up and leaned forward. "Turn off your lights. There's a car coming."

Wil barked out a surprised laugh, but she cut the ignition and lights. "It's pulling into the drive," Wil whispered.

"Oh my God."

They watched the silver sedan slowly turn into the drive, where it idled. Both the passenger's and driver's-side doors opened.

"Holy fuck, Katie. That's Brunette."

"It is! Wow. She is holding right up. Look at her ass!"

"*Shh!*"

They watched as Mr. Cook and Brunette met at the trunk. They leaned toward each other. A light in the front yard cast a shadow over the couple where they stood, and Katie couldn't tell if they were kissing or talking close to each other's heads.

"Are they?" Wil asked.

Katie scooted closer to Wil, reaching over to grip Wil's thigh. "I can't fucking see, but do you do whatever they're doing with a friend? Or a colleague?"

"Your hand is on my thigh, Katie."

Katie looked at her. "Do you want me to tell you how many carnal fantasies I've had about you, Wilifred Greene? Because I will do that. I'll do that right now. There were at least six just today. We are struggling, right now, with 'friends.'"

Wil put her hand over Katie's on her thigh, rubbing over Katie's wrist with her thumb. "Do you want me to tell you mine?"

Katie gasped, *want* sluicing over her body in a terrible, hot wave. "Yes. No."

"Look," Wil said, pointing out the window.

Mr. Cook and Brunette came apart, but they were holding hands, and then Brunette got into the driver's seat and started pulling out while Mr. Cook jogged to the front door of the house.

"What just happened?" Katie asked. "What? I don't get it."

"Come on, get out of the truck."

Katie opened her door, still disoriented by her feelings and her sudden horniness, and slid-slash-fell out of the truck onto a neighbor's lawn.

"Are you okay?" Wil shout-whispered, coming around and holding out her hand.

"*Yes.* Shit."

Wil pulled her over to the sidewalk. "We're on a walk. Ladies on a walk." She hadn't let go of Katie's hand.

"You should get out your phone and look at it, and I'll talk to you about something boring. Not sex things."

Wil squeezed her hand and gave her a look that made Katie want to stop walking and press her thighs together, but then she got out her phone.

They approached Mr. Cook's house in the dark, crunching over remnants of half-frozen snow, pretending to be on a walk, Katie talking about if she thought Trois's eye drops were working for a mysterious eye goop issue. As they passed Mr. Cook's house, Katie saw that the front curtains were still partially open. There was a Christmas tree lit up in the corner and a flat-screen tuned to the news on a wall above a fireplace.

A blond woman was sitting on the sofa.

"Katie!" Wil hissed.

"I *know*! I see her."

Mr. Cook walked into the room with a plate, sat down next to the woman, and *put his arm around her.*

Wil let out a small scream and started running, pulling Katie with her. They ran all the way back to the truck and got inside of it, slamming the doors and starting it up, peeling out of the neighborhood.

They got to the stop sign at the end of the street and started laughing.

"What does it meeeaaan?!" Katie finally managed to say. "Wil!"

"I don't know! That we are fully grown women without sense or boundaries?"

"I don't owe Mr. Cook sense or boundaries." Katie felt a spark of rage. "All we've confirmed is that he's managed to hold on to two fucking women for thirteen fucking years!"

"Two that we *know* of."

"Oh my God." Katie made her eyes huge and plastered both hands over her mouth. "This is too much sudden reality in the Mr. Cook department."

"You know why?" Wil asked. "Because tonight is the most actual investigating we've ever done."

"I'm proud of us," Katie said. "Look at our growth!"

They laughed on and off all the way back to Katie's and around the driveway to her suite. It was still at least an hour until dinner would be ready, so there was time for Wil to help with her script. But walking with her to the door into the suite, Katie was hit with the same desperate want she'd felt when Wil touched her hand, when she'd looked at her, and she couldn't pretend it wasn't happening. She didn't want to.

This, right here, wasn't something that Katie had ever gotten. Not the way she wanted it. This swooping, impulsive, buzzing, terrifying, hot bolt of want, of *now,* of *this one*—the sense she'd do anything to satisfy it without inhibition, without thinking, without caring about even the most dire consequences.

She had never felt so absolutely present in her entire life.

"Wil," Katie said, opening the suite's door and pulling her inside.

Wil moved in front of her once Katie had closed the door on the dim suite. Katie glanced at her babies to try to dilute the feeling with a semblance of domestic habit. Trois was grooming Phil's head, and Sue was probably on Katie's bed, sleeping hard. This time of evening was in the middle of her big sleep.

She didn't care, she didn't care, she didn't care.

God. She leaned toward Wil, who smelled like something familiar and good. What was it? *Oh.* ChapStick. Regular ChapStick. Pale pink in a black-and-white tube.

Then Katie thought about kissing it off, rough.

Wil touched her arm. She was studying Katie, and she looked as though she knew Katie was thinking about kissing her, which made sense, because Wil had a lot of experience with knowing when people wanted to kiss her. She was a high-level expert in kissing.

Knowing this made Katie unbearably, unsurvivably, recklessly hornier.

"Tell me," Wil said.

Katie closed her eyes and took a deep breath. "I want you. Understatement." She opened her eyes.

Wil looked all around her face. "Me, too. Not me, you."

Katie let herself put her fingertips on Wil's mouth. The blood bounded in her wrists. "Unfortunately, we have no confirmation on our bet, even after confusing every doorbell camera on Mr. Cook's street. So I cannot kiss you. It isn't permitted."

"That's not the only reason why." Wil reached up and gently dragged Katie's fingers from her mouth.

Why was that so hot? Jesus.

"Because you only do that on Wednesdays and Saturdays." Katie tried to get this to sound flippant, but her inability to kiss Wil was making her want to smash something, and her voice betrayed her frustration.

Wil shook her head. "No. I would kiss anyone I wanted to on any day."

"Oh. That's really good to hear, Wil."

Wil's brows pushed together just a little in the tiniest frown. "But if I ever kissed someone I *wanted*, who wasn't for the channel, who I was kissing entirely for myself, I would never kiss anyone for the channel again. It would mean I was done with that. It would *mean* more than a conversation with a few million people about kissing and intimacy and vulnerability. I told you. About my pair bonding. That's a true thing." Wil's voice was low, and Katie could almost taste her, their faces were so close.

"I can't be on your channel. I can't mess up your life that way."

Or mine. Katie thought of Honor Howell. The Honor Howell who'd wondered aloud if Katie was truly interested in more than the spotlight would not be convinced otherwise by Katie kissing Wil for an audience of millions.

"Yeah," Wil said. "I figured that out. But I don't think you would come on my channel even if it wouldn't cause a circus."

Katie shook her head. "If I kiss you." She couldn't help it. She hooked her hand in Wil's belt. There wasn't a way to tug her closer, but she didn't want her to get away, either. "It would be for the same reason you kissed me."

"Which is?" Wil said this to the side of Katie's mouth, and Katie knew exactly, *exactly* why in scripts, in these moments, one of the lovers would growl. She could feel that growl right at the base of her throat, where her clitoris had tossed it angrily.

"I think we could only kiss each other for the reasons we would've kissed each other under the bridge."

"What if we had? What if we'd kissed?" Wil's voice was low and sexy. Katie felt a tug by her hip and realized Wil had a handful of her flannel. The parts of her body that held her in a standing position threatened to buckle, while other parts that were usually soft came to instant, throbbing attention.

"I wouldn't have stopped," Katie said, without thinking at all. She kept not thinking. "Ever. I'd still be kissing you. Right now, we'd be in some three-bedroom in Ann Arbor, making out in front of the TV after you'd come home from the firm downtown and I had wrapped up rehearsal at a painfully cool local theater."

"Katie." Wil's tone held the teeniest, tiniest bit of warning.

Because what Katie had let herself say was an acknowledgment of how much bigger this was than either of them had a handle on, and of how much, exactly, they both had to lose.

Even in her feverish, blurting imagination, Katie hadn't been able to imagine a world where she and Wil were together and both of them had what they'd wanted. Instead, she'd imagined a world in which she *wasn't Katie Price*. She was a small-time actress in local theater. Wil was someone who'd stayed in Ann Arbor, Michigan, and become an Ann Arbor lawyer, which was a dream of Wil's life without texture or ambition or even creativity.

And still, Katie didn't want to let go of this fantasy, because she *could* imagine the part where they were together at the end of the day. The part where they came home to each other. The part where every day was the biggest day she could imagine for herself *as* herself, as Katie Price, and still, still, still, the best part of her day was Wil Greene.

She just couldn't imagine being allowed to have it. Her life didn't belong to her enough for that to be possible. She had to be safe, she had to be correct, she had to be trustworthy, and even if there were a way for her to be all of those things and still have Wil, being part of Katie Price's life would mean Wil never got to have her own.

"Okay. But," she said.

"But."

"There are so many, many things that aren't kissing."

Because Katie could be *this,* with Wil, now.

She could have what they'd had tonight, just for as long as it lasted until their time ran out. They could have this together, this out-of-time, home-for-the-holidays moment, because the universe owed it to both of them. It would be impossible, ever, to regret it. Katie had never wanted anything this much.

"Come here." Wil led her to the love seat, where she pulled her down to sit. "I'm having a hard time standing up at the level of turned on I am at the moment."

Katie watched Wil shrug out of her coat and put it on the ground. She looked overwarm, flushed, and blonder in her pale blue sweater. The jeans were offending Katie, they were so hot.

Katie took off her coat and then her hat and wig, running her hands through her hair, closing her eyes at how much better it felt.

Wil studied her. "What do you want?"

"I want whatever is the same mood as our whole day so far." Katie thought about it, her body buzzing. "Easy, with both of us doing some first *part* of something. Sexy, but with a little immaturity thrown in. Also, I haven't had a partner, even a casual one, for a very long time, so I like the idea of . . . steps." Katie didn't recognize her voice, and she was someone who had used a lot of different voices over the years.

Wil shifted to lean against the back of the sofa. "Do you ever look at or read erotic stuff?"

"Yes." Wil's question *raced* through her body. "A lot. Not so much look, but read."

"Me, too. Not so much look, but read. You know what one of my favorite kind of stories is?"

"Tell me right now." Katie got closer. Even moving her legs made her have to close her eyes involuntarily at the tension between them.

"Like, there are all different ways to tell the story, but say there's these roommates."

"Yes." She wanted to laugh. *Yes* was what actors were trained to say in improv classes, always *yes,* and this was the best improv scene Katie had ever been part of. *Yes* to talking about erotic stories with Wil. *Yes* to Wil's denim-clad thighs and hot pink white-blond gorgeousness next to Katie on the couch.

Wil laughed. "And they start talking about masturbation. Usually like, *Oh, I never do that.* And *What? You don't? I do it all the time, why not?*"

"The show-me-how stories." Katie laughed. "They are solid gold."

"Yes, and the other part of that kind of story I like is the *Doesn't it feel better when we do it together? Why is that? I have no idea.*"

Katie was extremely turned on. It was terrible. She couldn't stop smiling. "I have an amazing idea."

"I bet." Wil smiled, too. That beautiful mouth. Those blue eyes. Katie felt so lucky.

"How do you do it?" Katie thought this was the best question she had ever asked anyone, ever. Mainly because she was asking Wil.

"I'm extremely old-school," Wil said. "Middle two fingers, indirect pressure, two and a half minutes."

Jesus.

"Unfasten your pants and get those fingers down there."

"Come closer."

Katie got close, leaning against the back of the love seat, inches from Wil.

Wil dropped lower against the soft sofa back, lifted up her sweater, and unbuckled her wide leather belt, making Katie clench everywhere inside of her body. She unbuttoned her jeans, which had a button fly, until Katie could see her barely rounded, pale belly and the very edge of a pair of black panties. Wil slid her fingers underneath the waistband of them. A noise caught in her throat, and her eyes closed.

"Fuck, Wil." Katie watched the small movements, how Wil's knee came up, her hips jerked.

Wil opened her eyes to look at Katie. Her eyes were so soft. "How do you?"

Katie rose up, turned her body, and straddled Wil's thigh, bracing her forearms on either side of Wil's head on the back of the sofa. Wil's free hand came around Katie's back and up her shirt. It was so good to be this close to her. Absurd not to kiss her fat bottom lip with its crease, not to touch her tongue to the depression above her mouth, but Katie loved the constraint. It meant they had to work around it. It meant they had to think, get interesting, get vulnerable, which was something actors liked to talk about and Katie prided herself on knowing how to do, even though it was obvious now that she'd never been vulnerable quite like this before.

She'd never felt so determined and so uncertain. Not imagining what it might feel like to do this, not trying to put herself in the role of someone who felt this way, but *actually* her, settling herself down over Wil Greene's thigh with her hands shaking, caught between desperate desire and reckless laughter.

She let herself push hard against Wil's thigh, one explicit movement, looking into her eyes. "Like that."

Wil sucked in a breath. "I love that." She slid her hand up Katie's back and pressed, so Katie relaxed and put her head against Wil's shoulder, looking at Wil's hand in her jeans, working.

At first, it was so slow and so quiet. Katie felt herself almost floating, tethered by Wil's arm around her and her hot thigh, the *audacity* of bringing herself off like this where Wil could see, in this way she'd done forever, but never for or with anyone else.

It was that precise, peculiar strangeness, though, that suddenly tightened everything, made her rub against Wil harder, and was making her wet. Wil's wrist and forearm, working herself, the noises she was making and how she was moving her body were the next thing that made it all bigger, hotter, overwhelming, close.

"Oh my God, Katie," Wil panted. "Fuck me, just like that."

That worked, too. It really, really worked for Katie. "Wil." She had to close her eyes because she was winding up to that place, much more intense than she'd ever felt. She grabbed the hem of her shirt and pulled it to her collarbones, and Wil's hand moved restlessly over her exposed skin.

Almost there, she put her hand on Wil's where it was under her panties, and Wil made a noise, and her other leg moved up, her foot on the sofa, lifting up her hips, she was coming. That's what did it for Katie. She fell apart, moving hard, Wil's arm under her ass feeling her move. She came, panting against Wil's shoulder.

Both of their bodies relaxed at once, melting into each other. Wil adjusted to hold her fully on her lap. Katie licked Wil's neck softly, kissed it, and Wil shuddered.

"God," Katie said. "Oh my God."

"Was that good for you?" Wil was looking so carefully at Katie with her serious blue eyes, it made Katie's heart hitch. "You're good?"

Physically, she felt amazing, her body humming all over, her heart beating fast. Happy. Easy. It had been so easy to do this thing that she'd wanted, and for Wil to guess how to do it in a way that matched what Katie had told her she wanted it to feel like, and that was perfect.

It was so perfect that Katie knew it was going to take her a while to sort out how it made her *feel*. There was some anger that it had never happened before, that she'd never had this with another person when it was obviously the easiest, best, most fun thing.

"I have so many thoughts," Katie said, barely to Wil. Mostly to herself. "Also, feelings. Yes. Yes, that was good for me."

She should have had it.

She should have known it was something she could have.

The only question now was how long she *could* have this.

Have Wil.

Chapter Nine

Wil curled up in the leather and oak rocker that still smelled a little like her dad's cologne.

Beanie was across from her on the leather sofa, a Tiffany lamp making her white and gold messy bun look a bit magic, digging into a plate of cabbage rolls and mashed potatoes.

"I wish you could've come to dinner," Wil said. "It was nice."

Beanie smiled. "Me, too. Danielle got herself into a fucking mess."

Wil's mom had worked until after ten, helping a firm and its lead on a class-action suit pull together all of its discovery for a deposition the next morning. She'd been called in the early morning as a stringer after the firm's own three paralegals had been found to have botched the preparation. "I hope your bill leaves them gasping for air."

Beanie pointed her fork at Wil. "I put my invoice on the conference table before I left and told them when they opened it, their eyebrows were going to catch on fire."

"Nice."

"You"—Beanie smiled—"went to Mike's club meeting at Kettle's."

"Is there anything I can do in this town that you don't know about?" Wil crossed her arms over her middle. She *hoped* Beanie didn't really know everything, couldn't see everything, but it was very possible she could. Wil attempted to muffle the evening with Katie in the back of her mind in case Beanie could roust out what she and Katie had gotten themselves into.

"Fuck, no. As soon as I realized I couldn't mother you in the ordinary way, I resorted to espionage and bribes." Beanie reached over to pick up her glass of white wine. "You might as well tell me what happened. I'll get it all out of Mike eventually."

"For starters, you should know that while I did ask the hot lawyer to kiss me on TikTok, he turned me down."

"That's because your request probably scared the shit out of Sam Rafferty. He's such a nerd, actually, as hot as he is. I love his girlfriend, Robin. You know she's a teacher at East High?"

"Really?" Wil narrowed her eyes. She might have a reason to use Sam's number for something other than kissing after all. Now that she and Katie's investigation finally had some legs under it.

Wil told Beanie what had happened at the meeting. It was easier than she'd expected, since she'd already talked to Katie. She even included some of her feelings about what had happened, again, because Katie had invited her to articulate them.

Wil had never thought of herself as someone who avoided her feelings, but Katie's relationship to feelings was different. Even in high school, Katie was someone who experienced the world with her feelings all out in front of her. Her years away honing her craft in Los Angeles had only made her more this way.

It was part of what had made it hard for Wil to watch Katie hold herself so firmly in check on the stage in Chicago when the press started asking questions about Ben.

There was a directness and enthusiasm to the way Katie asked for what she wanted that got inside Wil in a way she had never experienced with anyone. It was almost scary the way Katie made Wil's feelings so much bigger, made Wil's body so needy and demanding. Even now, if she closed her eyes, she'd be able to feel the ache in her hands from wanting to grab Katie, the hot place on her thigh where Katie had pressed against her, the rasp in her throat from the way she'd had to breathe to hear every single sound Katie made when she came.

Katie's feelings got in the way of her writing, to some degree, but she'd done good work today with Wil's assignments. Incredibly well, actually. Katie could write. She had vision. She'd won an Emmy for her directing, and what she'd said onstage in Chicago made it clear that this work was a serious passion.

So where was the insecurity coming from? Why wasn't she creaking under the weight of offers and opportunities?

Wil knew what had been holding *her* back, but she wasn't sure about what was holding back Katie. It was a problem that interested her. It was even more interesting that Katie hadn't told Wil herself.

Wil wasn't sure how to make herself safe enough to be a confidante, a genuine friend, for someone like Katie. But she wanted to.

Beanie listened, eating, drinking her wine. When Wil was done, Beanie put the plate on the coffee table between them and gave Wil a long, considering look.

"Oh, no," Wil said.

"You must know that you were going to come right up against this, baby girl."

"I did not know. I work hard on *not* knowing things."

Beanie sighed. "Honest to God, you are like Jasper Greene 2.0."

"But I look exactly like you."

"You look like me, but your insides are all Jasper. It's infuriating for me, I don't mind telling you." This bit from her mom about Wil being identical to Jasper was an old one, wrapped up in both of their missing the bigger-than-life man. Beanie delivered it in her teasing voice, which was a voice she used when she was only 50 percent teasing. The other 50 percent was the dangerous part.

Sometimes, it was grief. Tonight, clearly, it was frustration. Wil had given her mother a lot of reasons to be frustrated with her.

She hoped Beanie and Diana weren't talking *too* much about what Wil and Katie had been up to.

"You'd think it would be comforting." Wil smiled.

"I would never say that my marriage to your father was comforting. Exciting, interesting, fun, loving, hot—"

"Nope," Wil interrupted.

"You can make out with strangers on the internet, but I can't tell you I had a satisfying marriage with your dad?"

"You cannot."

Beanie laughed. "The point, obviously, is that you were born to be a lawyer, and this destiny doesn't seem to care if you're ready for it or not. It's gotten bored with your—I will give you this, incredibly creative and elaborate—avoidance tactics and is now actively hunting you down."

"You're a mother. You could be more fluffy and tender and nurturing about this."

Beanie threw her hands up in the air. "Wilifred! Oh my God! What the fuck do you call the last eight years? I have done so much fluffy, nurturing tenderness! I follow your weird makeout account, and twice a week I *don't* look at it while I put a heart on it! I buy you boring work sweaters! I am done. I have stood by long enough. Too long. If it takes running into Katie Price again to get you to go to that meeting, then I am Team Katie."

"Wait, was this your plan?" Wil asked. "Did you take me to that talk in Chicago so I would get back in touch with Katie and be inspired?"

"Wow. No. I am not orchestrating your life at that level, I'm just doing regular yelling at you."

"Good."

"But," Beanie said, "if I *were* orchestrating your life—"

"I liked it when you said you weren't. I was planning on a topic change." Wil said this in the deadpan tone she used when she wanted her mother to know she wasn't ready to have a difficult conversation, and especially to let her know she wasn't ready to talk about her dad.

But it sounded wrong to Wil, and she wondered if maybe she *was* ready to talk about her dad with her mother. Didn't she owe Beanie that conversation? Wasn't it years overdue? Wasn't it about time that Wil found a way to offer her mom more of herself than just the results of a long-delayed genetic test?

Beanie rolled her eyes, because she couldn't read Wil's mind or hear her thoughts. "If I were, I'd have a lot of questions, also, about Katie."

It felt like the rocker was sinking into the floor. Wil gripped the armrests tight. "What kind of questions?"

"Do you want me to ask them? Because I will. I will ask them and ask them."

Wil had not seen this Beanie in a while. It suddenly occurred to her that her mother *had* been very fluffy and nurturing for a very long time, probably at least in part because of the resources she'd had to use to be such an amazing caregiver for Wil's dad at the end, and then to weather the worst part of her grief.

Wil knew that the last couple of years had been better for her mom. She'd felt it. She'd seen it in Beanie's face—an ease in the way she joked—and, right around the same time, Wil had been having coffee with one of her buddies at work who told her that she'd heard that it took roughly five years after a loss before most people started to feel like they could survive a new normal.

So this was Beanie in her full powers. This was the Beanie who'd told Wil to stop whining about calculus and to try things and, when Wil made fun of a cheerleader, had ordered her to try out for cheerleading. This Beanie had directed a pain-in-the-ass, bossy, loudmouthed kid who got suspended from preschool into a valedictorian with a full ride to Michigan.

Wil felt a little caught out.

But not as caught out as she might have felt a week ago. Which meant Beanie was right about Wil talking to Katie and to the lawyers and, as Katie had said, maybe about everything.

"You have been talking to Diana," Wil tried, as a side door into whatever this conversation was going to be.

"Diana Price has been my best friend for my entire life. I would die for that woman. I would bury a body for that woman myself and use the trunk of my car to transport it. We've gotten each other through some things you can't imagine, but you'll understand someday. Of course we talk. We talk every day. And we definitely talk about our daughters." Beanie crossed her arms. "And what they're up to."

Oops. Wil made herself hold steady. The rocking chair wasn't sinking. She didn't have to get away. She relaxed her grip on the chair's arms. "Okay. Go ahead and ask me about it."

"I will. First question, what happened between you and Katie in high school?"

Beanie Greene was worse than a lawyer, because she was the person who kept lawyers from making fools of themselves. Having a mom who was a paralegal meant that Wil could never get away with anything.

"Technically, nothing."

"That 'technically' is doing a lot of work there."

Beanie's raised eyebrows made Wil want to rub her chest with the flat of her hand and reconsider a lot of the decisions she'd made since she polished off the last of Diana's delicious rolls at the holiday party. Katie's recap of talking to Diana had given Wil a preview of this conversation, but it hadn't prepared her to feel this shaky. This vulnerable.

But that just meant Wil had decided it was okay to be vulnerable with Katie Price and no one else. Not even her mother, who was her best friend.

She suddenly felt over it. Over protecting herself, or her dad's memory, or her life, from risk and the truth.

"I'm sorry," she started. "I'm not apologizing for being flip, I never will. I'm apologizing for not being honest, which I usually think I'm pretty good at." Wil took a deep breath. "Nothing did happen between Katie and me in high school, at least nothing romantic. Nothing physical. But I do think that I loved her. Both of us had been around each other our whole lives, obviously, but I think . . . I think we needed such incredibly different things to grow up, we didn't really notice each other. Does that make sense?"

Beanie nodded. Wil had to look away from her, because her intensity was too much.

"But something clicked at the very tail end of high school, which apparently everyone in fucking Green Bay noticed. The only thing *we* noticed was that we wanted to spend all of our time together." Wil felt her heart release like a wet knot from rope, and then, with that truth confessed to Beanie, feelings she hadn't known she was holding were released, too.

"You didn't know?" Beanie's eyebrows had drawn together, betraying her surprise.

She'd known. She'd known all this time, and Wil hadn't, and they'd never talked about it.

Wil shook her head. "Only in retrospect, and only really when

Katie told me that, in retrospect, she realized *she* had been in love with *me*."

Beanie looked toward the lamp, and Wil caught her wiping a tear off her face.

"Mom. What is it?"

Beanie half-laughed. "It's just that I love you both so much, and it's not simple. So I hate it."

"I didn't say anything about how we feel now."

But hadn't she?

She and Beanie were too much alike, really. Beanie noticed everything and filed things away, thought about them, fit them together, and kept them neatly organized in her head until she finally had a chance to deploy them, sometimes years later. Wil hadn't ever really wanted to know what her mom *knew* about her. But she did now. What if letting the world really see her showed Wil what she needed to know to live her life? She wasn't going to like everything the world thought about her, obviously, but was that what she had been scared of and avoiding all this time? What the world thought? What her dad *would have* thought?

What did Wil think? About her own life? About what she wanted?

Beanie looked at her with her serious eyebrows. "It says a lot about how you feel now if you've both shared how you felt then, and you're sneaking off together in the Bronco like you're eighteen instead of thirty, and Katie's calling me to ask about Mike's attorneys' meeting. I'm not trying to tell you how you feel."

"I know you're not. But you're right. It's not simple."

"If it were simple, how *do* you feel? About Katie?"

It wasn't a fair question. It had only been two days.

But she'd been around long enough to understand that "fair" wasn't a very useful gauge. She'd kissed enough strangers to have learned that some things *were* simple. And Wil was figuring out that sometimes, it *wasn't* that she didn't know something about herself, or that she wasn't sure what she wanted. It was that she wasn't ready to act on that knowledge.

Wil was terribly, painfully attracted to Katie. She loved to look at her. She loved her expressive face and her funny enthusiasm and how surprising she could be. She loved how she was with her cats, how much she thought about them and their cat preferences and habits. She loved the way Katie challenged her and met her right where she was at and made room for Wil to think.

None of that was going to change. All of that was just a baseline, as far as how Wil felt about Katie Price.

"I could fall in love with her."

That was true. Wil knew as soon as she said it.

She *was* falling in love with her, probably, even if it shouldn't be possible. But she wasn't going to say this yet. And she knew the biggest thing holding her back was her fear that Katie didn't, or couldn't ever, feel the same way.

"Wil." Beanie smiled. "Oh, honey."

"Not simple," Wil said. "At all. In any way."

"No," her mom agreed. "As much as Diana has shared with me over the years, talked things through with me, I still find it difficult to imagine Katie's life. Even when she's here, the security on Diana's house, how they have to manage people, and phone calls, and being out in the public? How they've been betrayed by friends and family members, all the private financial settlements to get some family members to go away quietly?"

"Yeah." Wil had to resist a sudden urge to get up from the rocking chair and leave. It was late. She'd had a big week, and the prospect of hashing her way through everything Beanie had just said was too daunting.

"And it seems like no matter how careful they are," Beanie

went on, "the media finds her here and breaks apart the one retreat from it all that Katie has left. Our Katie has navigated and negotiated and sacrificed things that are beyond our ken."

Wil took a deep breath, accepting Beanie's kind dose of reality. "I hear you."

"Look at me, though."

Wil looked up at Beanie, her throat tight. "Yeah?"

"Your path hasn't been simple, either. Don't count yourself out. Don't do that. Don't do this thing where you defeat fear by circumventing it with a reasonable alternative. This is it." Beanie opened her arms wide, indicating the room and the whole world around them. "This is life," she said. "It's all we've got. My Jasper, your dad, he got fifty-two fucking years, Wil. That's all. And he didn't dick around with any of those years, and I loved that so much about him, and you *are* him, inside. You have him in there. He would hate it, *hate* it, if fear about what he went through was some root cause of your not living this life. And honey, my love, you have such a chance."

Wil made herself breathe. It was all she could do, just breathe as her mother choked on a sob, because she hadn't known that Beanie was going to say any of that or that it would land in Wil's body with such a surge of cracked-open, raw grief.

"You got the news he wanted and couldn't have," Beanie said forcefully. "Please don't waste it. Please. Be a lawyer. Be Katie's. Be something you really, really are, but don't be afraid you'll lose it all if you try. You'll at least have had it, even if it was only for a little while."

Wil got up to curl next to her mom on the sofa, and Beanie put her arms around her. "Okay?" Beanie asked. "Okay?"

But she didn't expect Wil to answer. Not yet.

They both knew this conversation was only the first one they'd needed to have, and that there would be more to say. They had more to share with each other. More grief. More gifts.

Beanie had been so patient.

"I love you," Wil said, her voice unsteady but clear.

"I love you, too, Freddie girl."

After hugging her mom for longer than she had in a long time, Wil drove home feeling completely scraped out. She couldn't tell if it was good or bad or if it didn't matter. Just as understanding her love for Katie had come entirely in retrospect, now knowledge of her complacency was barreling down on her, too.

It was as if, when her dad died, or even before that—probably before that, when Wil understood this monster lurking in her family—she'd taken herself to a safe house and left herself there, then carried on day by day *without* herself so that the monster could never find her.

It hadn't worked, though.

Goddamn it.

Wil wasn't in the safe house anymore. Wherever she was, it was better. It wasn't safe, but there was so much more room.

So she was welcoming the scraped-out feeling for now. It made space inside of herself to breathe and, when she got home, to curl around Almond Butter's fat, purring body and actually sleep, which she needed, too.

It was ten days until Christmas, after all, and Wil loved Christmas.

Chapter Ten

Returning to her suite from a disguised coffee run in her dad's Toyota Highlander, Katie was looking through the slider at the floor to make sure her babies wouldn't dash out.

That was why she didn't see her agent chatting cozily with her mother on the tiny sofa until after she opened the door.

"Katie!" April had on her *we'll fight later* face, along with an off-the-shoulder tangerine cashmere sweater and tall leather boots.

"Look who's here!" Diana stood, beaming, her hands around a teal Fiestaware coffee mug because yes, yes, she had made coffee, *in Katie's suite*, and yes, yes, there was a plate of cream cheese Danish on the low table in front of Diana and April. In fact, there was holiday music playing on the sound system, and Katie's babies were scattered about in contented poses because Diana had probably let herself in with a bag of Temptations, their favorite junk food.

Katie smiled without teeth. "Surprise," she said, sitting down in a glider across from them and not very tidily concealing her irritation. "I must have missed a call?"

"Mm." April sipped her coffee. She looked tired. To be in Green Bay by this time of day, she must have gone to the airport early and spent the whole day en route. April hated flying. "This is delicious, Diana."

"I smell Highlander Grogg," Katie said. "Diana Price, did you have advance notice of this visit?"

Her mother kept the Highlander Grogg coffee in what she called the "back pantry" and only pulled it out, ground it, and brewed it for very special guests. It was not something she would do if April had suddenly showed up on her doorstep unannounced.

"April called me from the airport." Diana's eyes dared Katie to be even more impolite than she had been already, thereby corrupting Diana's good-mother image. "You had made it very clear at breakfast that I wasn't to disturb you for any reason because you were writing this morning. So I didn't. When she arrived, you were out." She raised her eyebrows. *I am unimpeachable,* her serene blue eyes told Katie.

"You came a long way for cream cheese Danish," Katie said to April.

"In fact, yes." Katie's agent gathered her mass of curly hair into her hands, twisted it, and wrapped an elastic around it. "Flew first class, also. They're really, really good."

Diana gave April a big smile. "You're so sweet. Thank you. And it's always so good to see you and have a chance to talk. I know you two must have important business to discuss, so I'll see myself out. Just holler if you need anything."

April stood, opening her arms, and Katie watched as the two hugged like sisters separated at birth. Then her mom gave her a little wave and left the suite.

She looked over toward the kitchenette, where her laptop was glowing gently on the countertop, open to the scene she'd been in the middle of when she got to a tricky bit that she couldn't figure out the words to express. Katie had given herself permission to run out for coffee in the hope that driving would help her brain untwist itself.

It almost hadn't worked, but then as she turned into the driveway she'd seen the entire scene in her mind's eye—every line of dialogue perfect—and all she wanted to do was write it down before it got away and hopefully get through the rest of the scene before dinner-time so she could eat the stuffed shells her mother was making—which, it now occurred to Katie, she was making *for April*—and then call Wil.

What she didn't want was this. With April.

Whatever *this* might be.

"Your pages have been breathtaking," April said. "I'm refreshing the Dropbox link every half hour, hoping you've updated."

"That is a very good place to start," Katie said. "I'm hoping you will finish by telling me they were so good you had to tell me in person, and that's why you're here, and then you will leave me alone to make more of those pages, since I am officially *incommunicado*"—Katie made sure to pronounce every syllable of the word—"and on retreat. As discussed. And planned for."

April put her coffee mug down and crossed her legs. Katie had never seen the boots she was wearing before. They looked as though they'd been handcrafted by an angel in the kind of work-shop that could only be located in—

Shit.

"You were in Mexico!" Katie said. "Those boots are from Léon, aren't they?"

"I could've bought these boots anytime. I go to Mexico not infrequently. Three clients have homes there." April was dimpling.

"But you didn't." Katie heard the suspicion in her voice and didn't like it. She'd always been able to trust April. She'd trusted April from their very first meeting when Katie was hurting so much, having panic attacks, barely able to sleep. She didn't want to have any reason, ever, not to trust April.

"I didn't. I took the meeting."

Goddamn it. "With Marisol Gonzales."

April smiled, and Katie knew that smile was about how well the meeting had gone. April had departed from Léon to Green Bay, Wisconsin, excited to share something wonderful with Katie, and very likely there was an explanation for why April hadn't talked to her first.

Katie wished these mental reassurances were doing more to blunt the sharp edges of her panic, but she hated, hated, *hated* when people on her team went off-book. They'd had a plan. Marisol was part of the plan, but the Marisol part of the plan was *not yet.*

"I know Honor spooked you," April said. "But don't forget that the possibility of our snagging Marisol is part of why you attracted Honor's interest in the first place."

Katie narrowed her eyes like she knew what she was going to say, and it was very cutting and business-time, but this was a ruse. She'd walked up to the sliding door with characters' words in her head and then witnessed the car crash of her Los Angeles life rear-ending her Green Bay life, which was happening *a lot* lately, and now her brain was stuffed with an image of April in a handmade tile–decorated sunken living room, talking to Marisol Gonzales without her.

Katie was hurt. She was trying to stem that hurt, and trying to find a position for her body that didn't remind her that she was hurt. She sat up, opened her chest, and dropped her shoulders.

Then she had to wipe away tears.

They were not business-time tears.

"Honey," April said. "I'm sorry. Marisol reached out again, and I figured out, first, that I didn't want to ask you to give me your blessing to meet with her, and second, that I really wanted to meet with her, and third, that we needed to talk. Probably it would've been nice if that all happened in a different order, but it didn't." April leaned forward so Katie would make eye contact with her.

"I thought for a long time on my flight from Léon about why I *didn't* want your blessing, and I think it's because I feel like we haven't made the move from an agent-client relationship to an equal partner relationship. I have to feel like I can make decisions when they present themselves. I have as much invested in our success as you do."

Katie closed her eyes and took a moment to breathe. When she felt settled, she opened her eyes to find April waiting, just like she always had, without judgment, without rushing her.

They were friends. That was why Katie felt scared and hurt and angry. She wasn't afraid that April would betray her or make a bad decision. Katie was afraid that April didn't get how easy it would be for *Katie* to make one wrong move and lose everything for both of them. And then she'd lose April's friendship.

She'd lose April as part of her family.

Katie got up and put a Danish on a plate and carried it back to the sofa. She set it down on the coffee table. "Okay." She nodded at April. "First things first. Tell me why you were afraid to talk to me."

April nodded back. "Thank you. Well, I want to start as we mean to go on, and that means we take calls and meetings with people like Marisol Gonzales, because we are not making something that makes someone like Marisol Gonzales *wait*. Right? We're making something that flings open every gate and door as wide as possible for Marisol Gonzales. We're making something that Marisol Gonzales wants as much as we want her. If we are waiting to satisfy what Honor Howell wants, we will wait forever, because Honor is the money, and money is conservative, and what you and I both know is that no one is going to give money to two women who aren't C-suite for our *ideas*. They're going to give us money because we're already so good, they would look ludicrously irrelevant if they didn't."

Katie had to concentrate to keep her throat from constricting around a weepy hiccup she was *not* going to let out. "That's quite a speech."

"I practiced it on the plane."

"On your way to Léon or on the way here?"

"The one I practiced on the way to Léon was a lot more apologetic and groveling. But the meeting was fire, so I came up with that one on the way here." April patted her knee, and Sue leapt up beside her, making biscuits until she was comfortable along April's thigh. It was something Katie had seen happen so many times in her own home that having April here in Diana and Craig's basement suite started to feel inevitable.

"Who knows you're here?"

"Only Madelynn. Not even an assistant. The nice thing about my work is that even though I'm a stacked six-foot-tall ginger, no one notices me when I'm with the caliber of clients I represent. That means this meeting didn't happen until we both say it did."

Katie bit her tongue to keep from saying that she wished this meeting weren't happening, because Green Bay was supposed to be a step *before*. It was supposed to be the step where she wrote the screenplay so they could say they had exercised the option on a wildly bestselling book. *Then* they committed Marisol. Through both those steps, Katie continued to maintain her status as both the highest-paid Oscar-winning actress in Hollywood and a serious director. *Then* Honor.

The *before* step was the only step that had any space in it for Katie to be Katie. Maybe for the last time.

"Tell me what she said."

April leaned forward. "She told me, stone-cold sober and multiple times, that she wouldn't make this movie without us. She is, right now, being courted by four studios—she showed me the written offers—but she wants us."

"People in Hollywood tell you they can't do it without you all the time. I'm not sure they ever mean it."

But even as Katie said it, she could feel that what April told her was true.

All the steps were happening at once.

She pressed her palms to her thighs.

"While I was here, Madelynn wanted us to call," April said. "I wasn't sure when to get that in."

"Does she have a speech prepared, too?"

April winced. "Not exactly. I mean, I don't know, actually. But for sure she has an *agenda*."

Katie glanced again at the countertop where her laptop was sitting. She'd had her own agenda for this part of the day. She'd liked her agenda. Screenwriting and Wil sounded a lot better to Katie than getting into two uncomfortable conversations in a row with her team.

But also, April was right. This was what Katie wanted. It was just that she'd hoped to keep her LA life out of Green Bay a little bit longer.

Maybe they were still far enough apart.

She made a gesture, and April magically produced an iPad. Then they were sitting on the sofa side by side, looking at Madelynn in an ugly Christmas sweater and wearing an elaborate headset. In the background, there were two other people pacing around with their own ugly sweaters and headsets. One of them looked like he was yelling at the newel post of the elaborate wrought-iron staircase in a beautiful Spanish Colonial home.

"Ignore them," Madelynn said, gesturing behind her. "My dad and brother. It doesn't matter. Katie."

"Madelynn."

"Chicago," Madelynn said.

"Is windy."

"There is, in fact, a *lot* of wind being generated from Chicago. One of those nasty ones that knock over the garbage cans. I think they call it a Ben'easter."

Katie dove toward the coffee table for her Danish and put a big bite in her mouth.

"It's getting worse," Madelynn said flatly. "Ben won't shut up. This is how he's decided to spend the holidays, it seems. As you know, it would be my great delight to take care of this for you. I don't even need you for that. Let me see." Madelynn held up a piece of paper and slid her Christmas tree–adorned glasses down her nose to read. "'He's a dick.' I am happy to run with that. Short, to the point. Exactly, exactly correct. Do I have your okay?"

Katie stuffed what was left of her Danish into her mouth.

Madelynn sighed. "You know who called me this morning?"

"You get a lot of calls," Katie said around her mouthful of Danish.

Madelynn pointed at her through the screen. "I do get a lot of calls. But and however, I do *not* get a lot of calls from Markham Lockwood, president and chief creative officer at New Line Cinema." Madelynn smiled.

April squeaked and clapped her hands.

"What?" Katie looked at April. "What's happening?"

"Power," April said. "Markham would be the one waiting to hear back on the offer New Line made to Marisol."

Madelynn nodded. "And Markham, being exactly what we'd like to see less of in this town, listens to people like Ben."

"Who won't stop talking about what we're doing." April put her arm around Katie.

Finally, Katie understood. "Markham has decided we're serious," she said. "He figured out that our production studio is happening, and Marisol's on board. And if Markham has decided we're serious, it means *everyone* has decided we're serious." Her shoulders got tight.

"Exactly!" Madelynn said. "I hate Ben, but even publicity from a buttwart has a silver lining. His running at the mouth herded you two into a great position."

"Or a terrible one," Katie said, "especially for Marisol. Because if Markham thinks she's turning down New Line and the other studios follow suit, all she *has* is us. And we don't have Honor yet, or a greenlight on this adaptation, so if we don't get them, all she has is *nothing*."

Madelynn snorted and waved her hand like she was shooing away a fly. "Working with nothing is what this town was built on." She smiled. "I think this is the very first time you've provided me with a juicy, flavorful, good-news-bad-news, high-risk publicity situation." Madelynn sighed. "I really like it."

Katie's laptop's screen had gone dark, and it was dark outside, but she could still see sunlight painted on the floor behind Madelynn. It was sunny in California.

In Los Angeles, there would be meetings double-booked over at least two weeks as soon as Katie returned. Directors. Brands. Madelynn's team. Studio sit-downs. Strategy sessions for the PR tour for her next feature release. Designer consults on wardrobe for the upcoming awards season. Her accounting team and wealth manager. Her PA and her PA's assistant.

Katie reached for the dialogue for her scene that she'd figured out on her coffee run—the scene she'd been ready to put down as soon as she came into the room—but she'd lost it. She couldn't remember anymore what it was that she'd wanted to write.

What she wanted to say.

"So we're good," April said. Katie could feel the excited energy coming off her body and brain.

"I can't promise that," Madelynn replied. "For example, Marisol called me an hour ago looking for a guarantee that Katie was not involved, in any way, with Ben Adelsward, and Honor called ten minutes after that, asked after all the news with my family, and then asked me if Markham Lockwood had called me and why."

"Oh my God," Katie said. "What did you tell her? Both of them?"

"I focused on flattering them outrageously."

Katie looked at the ceiling.

Back in LA, she would have to fight for six hours a night to sleep, weighing what appearances she could turn down without taking a hit to the visibility that kept everyone paid, and disappoint people in order to spend time with other people who she actually liked.

People like these two women.

Her heart supplied another name and then, right after, banged against her sternum painfully.

Because that was impossible. Where would Wil live in the middle of Katie's life? How would she go to law school? How would she do all the things that came with law school, the clerkships and internships and social hours and writing? How would she be taken seriously on a campus when there were paparazzi waiting by a coffee cart to take her picture after a long night of studying so the internet could speculate on whether she and Katie were having relationship problems?

Why would she want that, any of it?

And it wasn't how *she* wanted Wil. Which was something like that house in Ann Arbor, that other life, the one that hadn't happened. Except how could she have that and *also* make Marisol's movie and *also* see Wil take on the halls of justice in just the way she was meant to?

It was impossible.

"Katie." April reached over to take Katie's hand.

Madelynn's frown made Katie's heart sink. "It's not going to stop," she said simply. "I can deny and privately reassure until I'm blue in the face, but at the end of the day, no one is going to be able to take you seriously as a creator if Ben Adelsward is behind you claiming to pull your strings. And don't look at me like that, because I know as well as you do that he *doesn't* pull your strings, but Katie, I'm sorry, *it does not matter*. It doesn't matter what's real in Hollywood. It only matters what *looks* real. If it looks like Ben's running your show, if it *looks* like he has the power to make or break your projects, then he does. What people need to see is your power. Marisol's not going to want to sign on with a man she can't control, who you *won't* control, who has the ability to destroy her film. It's a deal-breaker, and not just for Marisol."

There it was.

Katie was a puppet. Ben had found her and made her his puppet, and his control over the early part of her career meant that even though she'd left him, even though she'd worked hard and earned her reputation, even though she'd been good, better, the best, and never allowed even a hint of a scandal to touch her name, it only mattered that she had once been a puppet, and she still *looked* like one.

That was Hollywood.

Maybe she could make it different, one day, for other Katies.

She wouldn't let herself so much as glance at her laptop. She'd had a handful of days making something she knew was good, that made her feel like herself. Made her feel powerful. That was all she would have, because how Katie *felt* didn't make a Hollywood-changing deal.

How she *felt* didn't make a life.

"There's another way," Madelynn said. "And I have never, ever said what I am about to say to any client, but I'm going to say it to you, because I love you. What you have to do is *trust me*."

Katie nodded. She wasn't really listening anymore. She was thinking a little wildly that she'd told more than one person the reason Madelynn was her last publicist was because Madelynn always did what Katie told her to do. She focused on Katie's projects, not on Katie's feelings.

Trust me.

I love you.

Madelynn was asking Katie for a different kind of relationship. That meant Madelynn was telling Katie *she* wanted to be a part of making something other than money and reputation and awards. Something that was a tiny, tiny bit of the Katie Price who ran a cool local theater company and met friends for coffee and held their babies.

"This is not a today project," April said. "You are on retreat. It's not even Christmas yet. The three of us haven't done the thing where we courier over expensive gifts to each other's assistants with glittery cards as big as magazines."

Madelynn laughed. "You know what?"

"What?" Katie sniffed.

"I didn't do that this year. I hope you didn't want a vicuña yarn sweater or a handmade acrostic ring with reclaimed rose-cut gems, because I was feeling . . . well. I was *feeling*, and I got you both gift baskets filled with shit for your cats. That I picked out. Pet stores smell horrible. Like meaty hay. No one told me."

April barked out a laugh. "You hate my cats!"

"But you love your cats, and I love you, so return whatever you bought me from Gucci and get me something sentimental, bitches."

To Katie's surprise, the rest of their conversation was good. Having April in her suite and Madelynn on FaceTime, talking and laughing about Christmas, gave her access to a different way of thinking about her Green Bay life and her Los Angeles life smashing together.

Because LA was home, too. Madelynn and April were home.

That's what Katie was thinking about in the quiet suite after April explained that she couldn't stay for Diana's dinner because she had to make a flight to Chicago that would get her back to Los Angeles overnight.

Then, when Katie didn't want to be alone petting cats anymore, she made her way to the main part of the house to find her mom and make amends for her rudeness, and she heard Diana talking to someone.

To Wil.

Wil was sitting at the breakfast bar in a white button-down shirt and dark sweater vest, destroyed jeans, hair damp from melted snow, but what Katie noticed more than those details, which her whole entire self was greedy for, was that Wil *wasn't* curling her hands around a cup of coffee, though Katie could smell it in the air. She *didn't* have a plate of Danish or Christmas cookies or a slice of the banana bread Diana had made that morning.

Normally, even if Wil had demurred when asked if she wanted coffee or a treat, Diana would've put those things out just in case. When Diana didn't, it was because she wanted that person to leave.

"Katie!" Diana's smile barely touched her face. "I was just telling Wil you had important company, and she was letting me know that she could catch up with you tomorrow."

Wil, to her credit, didn't hit Diana with an incredulous "pardon me" for handling her grown-woman self in such an obvious manner. She only turned in Katie's direction on the stool and directed a *real* smile at her that cut a few taut strings in Katie's neck and made her feel like she could, in fact, handle this situation however she wanted to with Wil's blessing.

Wil was asking absolutely nothing from her. It was one of the best feelings Katie had ever had.

"April left," Katie said. "Wil, I'd love it if you wouldn't mind waiting for me for a few minutes in my suite, and I'll be right down."

Diana grasped her own forearm, closing her body language from her waist in a ladylike, classically Diana way. This same physical movement was one of the tells Katie used with Madelynn's people to get a reporter or fan to move along. "I think Wil said she had a lot to do?" Diana said. "Your law school applications?" She looked at Wil, smiling, and now, to Diana's credit, it was a warm smile, which reminded Katie that Diana *did* love Wil, and so Katie would not have to initiate a nuclear sequence in the next ten minutes.

"I'm happy to wait for you, Katie, so I can say hello and good-bye before I head home. Thanks for keeping me company, Diana." Wil slid off the stool and somehow managed to evaporate into the stairwell with equal amounts of politeness and coolness.

At the last minute, right before she turned the corner to the stairs, she winked at Katie. Which was fortifying.

Once she was gone, Katie noticed the silence first, and then how cold it was in the kitchen. The space around her and her mother felt vast and frozen over. It made Katie so angry—this cold house with its long driveway and its beautiful view, like some kind of grotesque stand-in for the home she used to share with her mom and dad, the childhood she'd lost access to, and the ways that her celebrity was getting in the way of her actual *life*.

Katie crossed to sit down on the stool Wil had just vacated. She looked over to the living room, where, against the wall, not at all coordinating with a tasteful array of leather and ivory boucle and light wood furniture, was the curved-back mallard-printed sofa from her childhood home.

She reminded herself that things were not all fucked here. She could be angry. She could talk. She could be sad. This was her *mom*.

"I think what you and April are doing is very exciting," Diana said. Her voice was soft. She didn't want to fight, either.

Then Katie had to deal with a series of unwanted hot tears.

Her mother stepped closer and put her hand flat in the middle of Katie's back. "Sweetheart, you can try whatever you want to try. That's what I mean." She rubbed over Katie's shoulder blades. "You're at such a good part of your life for trying things, because if it doesn't work out, you have years and years of solid work on your brand and building your reputation to fall back on."

Katie knew what her mom meant. She knew where it came from, even, because Katie spoke Midwesterner.

What Diana meant was that Katie had privilege and money and fame, and so nothing she wanted to do could be truly considered a risk.

Because, after all, she could live the rest of her life as Katie Price, with Katie Price's money, even if she never did anything. She was, in the consummate Midwestern sense, safe.

That was true. It was. But it was only true if it was *also* true that the only things Katie needed to be safe—to be okay—were money and fame.

If she hadn't had that hot obsession with making stories from the first moment a librarian read *Madeline* aloud during a story hour using different voices and real French.

If she hadn't broken her feet in pointe shoes and not told anyone so she could perform in the recital.

If that part of her hadn't looked longingly at the cameras and tools and lights and sets for years and spent frustrating hours with directing mentors who weren't certain why she wanted to know this stuff when she easily had everything she could possibly want.

She could fall back on Katie Price. But Katie Price had never been exactly what she wanted. Not all of what she wanted. *Katie Price* wasn't actually a real person—not to the world, not even to the people she loved.

And it wasn't Diana who had to understand this.

It was *her*.

Her mother was still rubbing her back. Soothing her. "I know it's wrong of me to want to . . . manage things between you and Wil. But the thing is, Katie, I'm not sure you've thought about how much capacity *Wil* has for managing what could happen if the world finds out the two of you are involved with each other."

"Oh." Apparently there were still only a limited number of things that Katie could try.

She shrugged off her mom's back rub and her dangerous and scary remark implying that even knowing Katie, even caring about her, might ruin Wil's life.

"Katie."

"What."

"We're fighting," Diana said gently, "in that way that we fight where I don't really know what's going on."

"If you say so." Katie sighed with obvious irritation. "For the record, I am appalled you didn't give Wil anything to eat or drink."

Diana had the grace to wince. "Well!"

"Very good talk." Katie stood up. "I will look forward to the next one, where we both blubber all the way through the truth of what we were actually fighting about this time."

"I love you," Diana said.

"Don't come downstairs," Katie told her.

She left without looking to see how that landed with her mom. She didn't want to know. She didn't want the hangover from April and Madelynn's talk, she didn't want any of Diana's words and looks and moves, and she didn't want to have to go back to writing her script again in this new world where her retreat was less and less like a retreat and more like a reckoning.

She didn't want to explain to Wil about security and how they pretended like it didn't cause major logistical issues every time Katie only wanted to go to a bookstore or pick out a baby gift herself or fucking *drive*.

She didn't want Wil—in her scalding jeans with torn-off back pockets—to ever, ever have to run, hunched over, to an open car door, with her hand up to block the camera flashes.

She wanted Wil to stomp, to stride, to wink, to dominate.

She wanted to let herself fall for Wil and let Wil fall for her like the only consequences were what they would've been the first time, if Katie hadn't had to leave for Chicago, if Wil hadn't been on her way to Michigan, if Jasper Greene hadn't been dying, if Katie had never met Ben Adelsward.

When she opened the door to her suite, Wil was standing beside the cat buttons with a purring Trois under one arm, Phil weaving back and forth between her ankles, while Sue insistently poked the treat button and then waited for Wil to feed her one of the Temptations from the bag Diana had left behind.

"Hi," Katie said, her heart huge and frantic and worried and half-gone.

Wil turned around. "Kim Kardashian."

"Is a complicated woman."

Wil smiled a tight smile and set Trois down on the floor. She shook a small handful of treats out of the bag and set a few down in front of each cat, then stepped away to signal that the activity had come to an end. "Kim Kardashian is obsessed with getting people's sentences commuted. She's done a lot of political work, and then she decides she'll be more effective with a law degree, so she got a four-year apprenticeship in California with the exact right people to help her get that done and took the bar until she passed it, like failure wasn't an option."

"Yes." Katie had the impression she'd left Wil alone too long. "Kim is a very driven person."

"What do I even want to do?" Wil asked.

Yes. She had left Wil alone too long.

"That is an overwhelming question to ask yourself." Katie walked over and picked up Wil's hand, pulling her to the sofa. She knew it was dangerous to sit on this sofa with Wil, but she was so beyond caring now that she was in the same room with her, holding her hand. She welcomed Wil's careless solipsism. "When you start to look at it that way."

"I always had in the back of my mind, I guess, that if I did this again, I would go to Michigan. Then that cabal of lawyers at Kettle's are telling me that I could go to Harvard or Yale or UCLA or Northwestern or Loyola or Pepperdine, and all of those places are very different, with different opportunities for mentorship and career paths and where I'd live, and I have no idea how to even begin to make a decision."

Katie moved her body closer to Wil's until she could smell snow and mint and the Wil smell of her neck, which had never changed.

"Katie Kat."

Katie straddled her. Wil's hands found her hips. Katie put her nose against Wil's nose. "You haven't called me that yet." It was her name from the bracelet Wil had made her, the name that only Wil had ever called her. Katie hadn't known she'd been waiting for Wil to say it until it landed and lodged against her ribs, making her chest so tight.

"This is really good." Wil squeezed Katie's hips. "It's much easier not to be frustrated about the future when I can feel how hot your thighs are."

Katie smiled down at her. "Here is the question. Do you want to be a lawyer?"

"Yes. I thought so. Especially after Beanie recently got some hooks in that made things more clear. But then I got caught up with thinking how happy I am being an insurance adjuster. It's not that it's hard to imagine myself being happy doing something else. I guess I want to know that I'll be *happier* because I'm doing something that's exactly right for me, and that's where I get stuck."

Katie smiled and kissed Wil's pale blond eyebrows and the line that sank between them when she was distressed. "All of what you just told me is so much better than you even think it is."

"Why is that?" Wil shifted beneath her, putting more of their bodies in close contact and sending up a pulsing ache between Katie's legs.

Katie wanted to lick her. "Because, Wil, you're already happy. You're good at being happy. That means that a lot of different kinds of life will make you happy."

"More." Wil leaned forward, and her hands on Katie's hips slid up to her waist, and Wil's hot, beautiful mouth was on Katie's neck.

More. God. Katie closed her eyes against the shivery, hot, glorious sensation.

"Do you think you could be happy working as an attorney?"

"Yes."

"All of these schools, at the end, do you get to be a lawyer?"

"Yes." Wil's voice was getting a little bit lower every time she answered one of Katie's questions, making the heavy pulse between Katie's legs pound a little bit harder.

"They teach you all the kinds of law you need to know, not just one special kind you pick out right this minute because you figure out *exactly* what makes you happy?"

"Yes." Wil sounded distracted now. Katie had slowly moved her hands to the sides of Wil's breasts, soft under the wool of her vest, and Katie watched how her touch made the hollow in Wil's throat sink and felt her hands tighten on Katie's hips.

Yes.

"So if you make the stakes of this decision as big as they go, then what happens is you leave Green Bay to go to a school that teaches you how to be a lawyer, and you learn about different kinds of law while experiencing what it's like to live in a new location and meet new people . . ."

Katie stopped because Wil had picked up Katie's hands to move them over her breasts. Katie rubbed her thumbs over Wil's nipple and Wil let out a gasp, which led to Katie licking behind Wil's ear. Katie broke out in shivers all over. It took her a moment to remember what she'd even been saying.

". . . and then you either pick what kind of lawyer you want to be and you are a happy lawyer, or you decide it's not for you and return to Green Bay, where you cheerfully resume your career as an insurance adjuster, having had an exciting adventure."

She sounded breathless. Wil was making her breathless. She wanted to kiss her. Katie sank her hands into Wil's hair and put her mouth next to Wil's. Felt her breath on her own lips.

Katie licked her lips.

Wil moaned.

God. God.

She forced herself to stay with their conversation. It was important, and she wasn't allowed to kiss Wil because she knew, too, that Wil would be the only person she would ever want to kiss, and, worse, if Wil kissed her back it would be to tell Katie the same thing, and this, right here, wasn't there yet, and wouldn't be there ever. *This* was a manifestation of yearning they hadn't been able to name years ago. It was honoring that yearning. It was an obliteration of the reality of April on her way to the airport and Madelynn delightedly spinning bad news and Diana upstairs trying to decide whether to bake or run the vacuum because of where Katie had left things with her. It was what Katie wanted, only what she wanted, nothing she didn't want.

She could have this. She *could*.

But she could not kiss Wil Greene.

"You're in a win-win situation," she said breathlessly. "There are no wrong decisions."

But there were for Katie. So many wrong decisions, everywhere she turned.

"That seems too simple." Wil was flushed, her blue eyes liquid, the patch of freckles under one eye darker than it usually looked.

"Because maybe the very biggest decisions usually are," Katie whispered.

Then she pulled off Wil's vest, because she'd reassured Wil with something she didn't believe in for herself.

Only for Wil.

The buttons on Wil's white button-down weren't buttoned under the vest. They'd slipped from the placket, and Katie could see Wil's sheer pale nude bra and bright pink blotches painted over her skin.

"Katie," Wil breathed.

She leaned down and kissed Wil's throat, her neck, her collarbones, every kiss lasting longer, getting closer to Wil's mouth by traveling up her jaw, over her cheekbones. Wil's hands had moved to thread through Katie's hair and thumb over the sides of her neck, a precursor that meant Katie could feel the ache of what Wil's mouth on hers would be like. She wanted it. She wanted it utterly. She wanted to kiss Wil and for Wil to kiss her and for it to mean everything that it would mean, and for that to be exactly, exactly what made both of them happy, always.

It was this thought that made Katie press her lips against Wil's forehead, her thumb already on Wil's lower lip, so that she would stop.

Because *she* was not in a win-win situation. There were wrong decisions in front of Katie. Her life, her celebrity, meant that it was possible at every moment, every day, to make the wrong decision and hurt someone.

Katie eased back. "I'm getting a box of tools FedEx'd to me tomorrow to film your kiss." She said it to remind Wil, to remind herself, that Wil still kissed other people. "It's going to be a step up from your usual production values, so you should prepare yourself."

Wil shook her head as Katie eased herself off her lap, then followed Katie with her body until Wil's face was in her hair and her arm around her, making Katie melt and despair. "I didn't prepare for you," Wil said, her voice still low, unguarded enough that Katie knew she was confused, at least a little hurt, but here. Right here.

Katie huffed out a laugh and squeezed her eyes shut.

You couldn't have prepared for me, Katie thought. *You can't.*

But her heart still insisted it was simple.

Chapter Eleven

Wil stood up from the creaky leather chair in Sam's office, unable to sit there for one more second waiting for Sam and Cord to finish reading her law school file.

Cord laughed. He leaned forward to put his copy of the file down on Sam's desk. "You want to know what we think of these application materials."

"Yes." Wil had moved around to the back of the chair so she had something to hold on to. "Please."

Cord crossed his ankle over his knee and settled back with a particularly loud creak. "I think if I'd had your chances when I graduated from Carnegie Mellon with a transcript you had to squint at to see the potential, I would've been ordering rounds for my friends. But you look like most people do when they're coming to deal with a dead relative's probate."

Wil squeezed the chair again so she wouldn't sigh or roll her eyes. Or run away. It was difficult to subject herself to this kind of scrutiny. It had been extremely difficult to call Sam and Cord to ask for this meeting—to take up their time on a Saturday, to accept the help they'd generously offered.

But she was trying to find her way out of the tangle she'd gotten herself into, and she understood that she was going to need other people's assistance to beat a path through the overgrown mess of it.

She made herself say the thing that was bothering her the most. "I've talked to four people from as many law schools in three different states in the last twenty-four hours." Wil's chest was tight. "It turns out that *all* of them knew my dad, even though he'd spent all but three years of his career here in Green Bay, Wisconsin." Wil picked up her folder from the corner of Sam's desk and tucked it into her bag beside her laptop. "It's a lot."

"Sure." Cord nodded. "But you're not on this earth to replace your dad one-to-one."

Now it was Wil's turn to nod as though she knew this.

She did know. Knowing it wasn't the same thing as feeling it, it turned out.

"What's interesting," Cord went on, "is you and Jasper have both told me the same thing. You said it in this draft of an application essay—that people will always ask for less for themselves than what they'll ask for on behalf of someone else. That it's easier to fight someone else's fight, and it feels *good* to fight a good fight. That the law solves problems other institutions can't, so you better get there first with a worthwhile problem before someone uses it to do harm."

Wil blinked. She hadn't understood herself to be saying any of that, but on the other hand, it sounded correct. It was why she'd once spent a long weekend poring over the TikTok terms of service—because she wanted to be in a position of knowing what she had and what she could ask for.

"Your paper," Sam broke in. "The one you wrote as an undergraduate and was *published* in Michigan's law journal? I've never seen better thinking about NDAs, and I'm a corporate law partner." He smiled. "I've bookmarked it."

Wil cleared her throat. "My dad wasn't sure about that paper. He never said so. He didn't say anything but how proud he was, but I could tell. But it's strange for me to look at it now, to look at all of this"—Wil indicated the folder Sam was holding—"and think about how much I put aside. I feel almost ashamed. Like I'm not up to the person I was then."

"But you liked talking to everyone, I've gathered. Delilah at Pepperdine called me to tell me how much she enjoyed talking to *you*." Cord's phone buzzed where he'd set it on Sam's desk, and Wil watched him pick it up, glance at the notification, and set it back down.

Because he didn't want to interrupt their meeting. He felt that their meeting was important enough not to be interrupted.

This was a very intelligent person, here, making time to talk to her. And he was correct. Wil had enjoyed talking to Delilah at Pepperdine very much. "For real, I didn't come for a pep talk, but yes. Okay. There is clarification." Wil schooled her movements while putting on her jacket and slinging her bag over her shoulder, even though she felt shaky.

She hadn't told them that two of the people she'd talked to also knew who *Wil* was. For her paper and for her TikTok project. They'd been equally delighted about both, which was surprising. Their delight brought into focus what Wil had been thinking about lately—how she would like to use the gifts her parents gave her alongside the ones she had been developing herself, even sometimes without realizing it, for years.

Tackling this project was making her feel more whole, more integrated. It made her feel more like she'd always been heading for something, not running away, not ducking an invisible monster—and that *was* surprising.

The ambition was surprising.

The future was surprising, all by itself. Even after Wil had learned she had one, in the basic sense that her heart would keep beating, her breath would sustain her, she hadn't considered yet what it looked like, could feel like, could contain. Or that she, in any way, was its designer.

Last night, Katie had said her screenplay was going well. She'd told Wil that she'd recently had a private showing of a special exhibit in the Los Angeles Public Library of Carrie Fisher's papers. Katie had spent her entire time looking at how Fisher had doctored and revised scripts. Important, famous scripts. She'd said that learning from Wil how it was that she could write, what she could get on the page, how vision and editing worked together, was the first time she'd understood that she could be capable of something at the standard of Carrie Fisher.

That was what Wil had done for Katie.

But Katie had done something a lot like that for Wil, too.

Later, after Wil had finished talking with Cord and Sam, she climbed into the Bronco and started it up. She stared at the small mountain of snow that the plow had made at the edge of the parking lot outside Sam's office, smelling Katie's perfume in the cab of the truck, or maybe what she used on her hair, something ambery and faint that made sense for Katie and the way her hair shifted color from gold to soft browns. She thought of what it felt like when Katie's attention was on her, the dip above her upper lip and her arched eyebrows arrowing right into every word she said.

Thoughts like these introduced problems.

As she was pulling into own driveway, she got a text from Katie to pull up more because Katie was right behind her. Katie touched her dad's Highlander's bumper to Wil's Bronco and dropped out of the SUV with a big FedEx box, wearing another wig, the big coat, and a slouchy beanie hat.

"Hello!" Katie smiled. "I am extremely early for your TikTok shoot."

Wil took a deep breath of the cold air. The TikTok shoot. Right. "You are! But you're a professional."

"Yes. And I wanted time with you in your house. I'm starting to be very much over my suite. The whole time I've been here, they've had it at icy-cold conservation temperatures. Or maybe menopause temperatures, I'm not sure. Then, today, somebody really cranked it up. But their Nest thingy or their Alexa thingy, whatever they have, refuses to recognize my impression of either Diana or Craig, both of which are *excellent,* and I can't find the manual thermostat. I'm sweating through my coat as we stand here in twenty-degree weather."

"Do you want an ice cream sandwich?" For whatever reason, Katie's nervous ramble regulated Wil's heartbeat.

"Yes."

Wil toed off her boots off and shrugged off her jacket to hang up on the coat tree beside the door while Katie watched her somberly.

"I really, really, really want to erase this day and pull you into your bedroom and not come out until Christmas morning," Katie said. "But I understand that isn't the thing to do here. *Can* we go in your bedroom, though?"

Wil felt everything low in her pelvis swoop and thud. "Should we eat the ice cream first?"

"No, we should eat the ice cream in bed." Katie took her big coat off, then slid her wig and beanie off together to hang both next to Wil's coat. Her hair was in double French braids, a style Wil hadn't seen since they were in high school, and she wore a huge black sweatshirt with a bit of cat hair clinging to its front. She'd put on baggy jeans. She shouldn't be so beautiful, but she was. She was.

Katie followed Wil into the kitchen, looking around while Wil tried not to be self-conscious. The house she rented was very ordinary for Green Bay: a big Victorian four-bedroom with squeaky wood floors that needed refinishing, a collage of windows that mostly worked, and lots and lots of woodwork. None of the furniture matched, all the art was from different eras of housemates, and when it rained, it smelled like the incense a housemate from five years ago had liked to burn.

Wil tried to remember that she found her house comfortable, even cozy, but it was hard not to be self-conscious with Katie looking at where she lived and possibly comparing it to her unimaginable home in Hollywood. While Wil pulled the paper-wrapped ice cream bars out of the freezer, she made herself think instead about why Katie wanted to go to her bedroom.

And why Wil wanted Katie in her bedroom.

They made their way up the stairs, Katie already unwrapping her sandwich. As she led Katie into the bedroom, Wil mentally thanked Beanie Greene for imprinting her with tidiness. Almond Butter rose up from her nap at the end of the bed and arched into a perfect stretch to meow at Wil.

"Almond Butter!" Katie put her hand out, and Almond Butter very obligingly rubbed her head against it, meowing again before flopping to her side and demanding a full pet. "Oh my God, you perfect baby." Wil watched as Katie put her ice cream sandwich down on the bedspread to scritch through Almond Butter's fur with her full attention. "She still makes air biscuits when you scratch her armpits! She did that when she was a bitty baby widdle kitten!" Katie leaned over and kissed Almond Butter's forehead. "You are an elder cat now. You must know so many cat mysteries."

Almond Butter looked at Wil over Katie's shoulder with a vaguely accusatory expression, as if realizing Wil could have been showering her with this kind of attention all along. Even though Almond Butter slept curled around Wil's head when she wasn't napping in her heated cat bed or perched on top of one of the three cat trees in Wil's room, contemplating the view out the windows or the oil painting of herself that hung over Wil's desk.

Katie climbed onto Wil's bed, her ice cream back in hand, to lean against Wil's pink cabbage-rose-print pillows. She patted the spot next to her.

Wil peeled off the sweater she'd put on to meet with the lawyers and crawled into her bed with Katie.

"Scout's honor, I won't take advantage of you," Katie said as Wil lay next to her on her side. Wil wasn't sure how to feel. Even though she hadn't forgotten that Katie was coming over to film the kiss today, she hadn't exactly been thinking about it, either. She'd been preoccupied with law schools, her dad, the future. This plan she'd made with Katie just a few days ago had snuck up on her.

Katie reached over and trailed her finger on Wil's bare waist where her shirt had ridden up. "The problem is, I wasn't a Girl Scout."

Wil laughed and leaned up on her headboard to unwrap her sandwich. "I think I can take care of myself." She deliberately licked her sandwich provocatively. "Also, I won my Girl Scouting Gold Award, so. *You're* safe."

Katie snorted, then adjusted her position and put her feet in Wil's lap, the same way she always had when they were in high school.

"Okay. I'm ready," she said.

"For?"

"To tell you about Ben." Katie finished the last bite of her sandwich. Wil could tell she was trying to keep things light, her calves pressing against Katie's thighs, but her eyes were sad.

"You don't have to."

Katie looked down and laughed, but it sounded more like a big sigh. "I do, because . . ." Katie didn't look up. "Because I don't want it to be thirteen years again. I don't seem to know anything right now, but I know that. I know I want you to know me. Like we knew each other."

"I'd like that." Wil swallowed over a lump in her throat.

Somehow, the way Katie had said *I want you to know me,* the translation wasn't, *From now on, I want you to know me.*

It sounded a lot more like, *For right now.*

Wil wasn't sure what part of her heart had gotten ahead of the basic facts of Katie's visit and Katie's life, but it was a very *big* part of her heart.

"I've never talked about him anywhere," Katie said. "I've told my mom a few things, but I know she wouldn't have shared." She looked at Wil with her eyebrows drawn together. "What do you know?"

Wil thought about that for a moment. "The official story, I guess. That he discovered you at summer stock when you were eighteen years old and he was thirty, *but* you were wise beyond your years and so wildly talented you would be wasted in North Carolina, and so he had no choice but to whisk you away to Hollywood."

"What did you hear from Beanie or my mom?"

"About the breakup? Only that you were having a very hard time. Beanie told me not to believe anything I saw or I read, but she also didn't provide any alternate explanation. I did ask her if I could go out and see you or call you or write or something. I was in college. I wanted to. I'd missed you, and knowing you were hurting was awful. But Diana told me it wasn't a good idea. Through Beanie."

"God, really?" Katie looked away and squeezed her eyes shut. "I would have loved so much to see you. I probably would have climbed into your lap and cried all over you and not even been able to tell you what happened, but it would have been so good to just *have* you."

Wil put her hand on Katie's foot, finding a rapid pulse. "I'm sorry, then. I'm so sorry." She didn't let herself get distracted by the small flare of frustration that Diana had prevented her from comforting Katie. It was a long time ago, and everyone had been doing their best.

After what Wil had seen in Chicago, she got why Diana protected Katie so fiercely.

"It's so much the most ridiculous, worst pile of crap and doom." Katie sighed. "What did you gather from what you read and saw all this time? Go ahead. Say the whole thing."

"Well, when you made it to Hollywood, he got you your first movie, which you were nominated for an Oscar for, and he introduced you to everyone important because he's one of the most important men in Hollywood, and he fell in love with you and was your first everything. He gave you your career. He gave you love as the other half of one of the most glamorous couples in the world."

Katie wrinkled her nose. "Go on. You can say the rest of it."

"And then you became wildly ambitious, jealous of his costars, immature, and you left him. You haven't been able to have a normal relationship since." Wil said this in a rush, her nose burning because it felt like a betrayal.

But of course Katie smiled.

"You're right," she said. "That is the official story. Ben's story. It's a love story." She met Wil's eyes. "*My* story is an abuse story."

Wil squeezed Katie's foot, keeping steady pressure so Katie would know that Wil wasn't afraid to hear this. She wasn't afraid to know.

She'd suspected, of course. More than suspected. But to hear Katie say it rearranged so many things inside of Wil at the same time, it felt like her heart would have to learn how to beat again.

Wil leaned up and reached for Katie, who came to lie beside her. "You don't have to talk about it," she said. "I would never make that a condition of anything. Of friendship. Of anything."

They were side by side, facing each other, inches apart. So

many times, they'd lain like this as girls, talking to each other. Telling each other everything.

"I know," Katie said. "But I'm going to. Tell me first, though, what your number-one question is. That will help me start, because I don't like this. I like being in your bed, and how your pillow smells like you, and how much light is in this room, and the way Almond Butter is snoring like she needs an oil change. But this is a story I hate."

When Wil thought about the trauma that had happened to Katie, there was one mystery that made it easy to know what to ask. "Why is a forty-year-old man still making statements about a relationship he had with a kid ten years later?"

Katie huffed. "Everything is always about Ben. He is the protagonist. And the antagonist. I didn't say anything, and he told our story over and over again, until there wasn't any room left for anything but the story he'd made."

"When did you know he was like that?"

Katie looked at the ceiling, thinking. "He was filming *Creatures* out in the desert about a year after we were together, and he came home the day his costar . . ."

"Alec Wilde." Wil supplied the famous actor's name without thinking. What had happened on that set was still brought up in almost every Wilde interview.

"Yes. That day. The day Wilde insisted on doing the car chase stunt himself, with Lila Watson in the front seat with him, and killed her."

"God." It was one thing to read about something like that happening to people you couldn't imagine. It was another thing entirely to hear it from someone who carried some of its aftermath. "Awful. That's all I got. So awful. Did you . . . ?"

"I didn't know Lila. I hadn't even met her. And Ben wasn't on set yet when that happened, he was on his way. But he was so excited to tell me." Katie rose to one elbow, putting herself closer to Wil. "His phone was blowing up. He was reading me every message, putting every call on speaker, and he couldn't stop telling everyone, telling me, that he 'should've been there.' I realized he didn't mean he should've been there to save anyone, but because he wanted to be part of it."

"Wow. *God.*"

"Yeah. He didn't care that Lila had died. I could hardly think of anything but how tragic it was, how completely awful for her to lose her life on set, doing a stunt, but Ben would change the subject if I tried to talk about it. He didn't even care that Alec's life was probably ruined, and Ben had been friends with Alec since they both came to town when they were seventeen. Ben would've taken any role in it. Alec's, Lila's, the director's. He just *wanted it.* He hated that he wasn't there. And then I realized he was telling the media, letting it leak, that he *was* there. That meant it was impossible to get at what the fuck happened, this terrible thing that every studio is supposed to protect you against and tell you could never happen."

"I remember how confusing the stories were."

"Yeah, because he was making things really fucking confusing, spinning this awful thing that happened to Lila into a way to elevate his own position. He eventually had to stop lying about it after law enforcement and lawyers wanted to talk to him. Even though so much had already happened between us, that was the first time I was scared. That was when I knew I was involved in something I had no control over."

Wil closed her eyes against imagining that feeling. The sick terror of realizing who one was sleeping with. Living with. "Katie."

She leaned against Wil's shoulder, and Almond Butter picked her way up through their legs until she found a place half on Katie's chest and half on Wil's shoulder to loaf herself. "Thank you, Almond Butter." Katie stroked her hand over Almond Butter's fur for a few long moments. When she spoke again, her voice was low and soft. "The two years that came after that were, for me, so hard. So, so hard. But not hard in a way that was *unique* to me. I've learned that what he did to me was very, very ordinary. Because abusers all do the same things."

She looked up at Wil as if for confirmation, so Wil nodded. She didn't know from personal experience, but she'd talked to, lived with, and known a lot of people.

"Abusers tell you stories about your friends and your family that make them sound like they don't have your best interests in mind," Katie said. "Then they call you stupid for calling those friends and family, and they make you doubt yourself, doubt your people, until you don't call anymore. They all have so many endless, important, sensitive needs and opinions that it's just so much easier to make sure everything is done or said or anticipated for *them*. Because you just don't care *as much*."

Wil put her hand on Katie's shoulder. It was hard to know this. Hard to think of Katie Price telling herself that her own opinions, her own wants and needs, were less important than Ben's.

"They all apologize and are so tender after you mess up and react or do something like you used to, before him." Katie said this in a bittersweet way that made Wil's heart hurt. "They all kiss you and keep their arm around you in public, every minute, so you won't talk to anyone or make them look bad. And they all tell anyone who will listen, when you're getting kissed in a gown he told your stylist to dress you in, everything that's wrong with you. Like it's a joke."

Katie's eyes were shining. Wil squeezed her shoulder.

"And they all forget you're real," Katie said in a whisper. "But you are. You're real. You're *real,* and they forget that right up until they can't reach you except through your new agent, and all they have left is the media's attention." Her voice had more power now. She gave Wil a small smile that made Wil miss the chip in her front tooth. Made Wil wish she'd been able to keep this from ever happening.

"It's how ordinary it all is," Katie said, "that helps me keep him as small as I can in my head. So I can be as big as I will let myself be."

Wil slid one trembling hand to Katie's neck and met her eyes. "You have never, not once in your whole entire life, been *ordinary*. Or small. And I hate that this small and ordinary man tried to make you both, like he ever, ever could." Wil felt her jaw lock tight, as though it would keep back the flash of rage Katie didn't need.

"Wil, you look like you're ready to . . ."

"I'm just fucking *saying*." Wil relented to her impulse, and Almond Butter jumped off both of them in alarm. "Let him try to fucking say anything to me. I would like that. That would be so good. I am ready."

Katie laughed. "Oh, you would lawyer him so good."

"I would Midwestern shun him so fucking good, is what I would do." Wil sat up. She was too angry to be prone.

"Yikes. Cold."

"He doesn't even fucking *know* how cold it can get. Where is he from? Jersey or some shit?"

"Pennsylvania. Harrisburg."

"Exactly. Exactly. He never had to come home in the middle of the night with beer breath with Beanie Greene as his mother to have her turn on the living room lamp where she was lurking in the dark and have her say his whole Christian name, not loud, but *softly. Kindly.* He doesn't know the *terror*."

"Never leave me," Katie said, laughing, but then as soon as she said it, right against Wil's neck where she had fallen over laughing, the words hit Wil's skin and traveled over her whole body in a wave. Katie must have felt the strength of Wil's reaction, because she stopped laughing, but she didn't move her face from Wil's neck or ease her body away.

"Katie." It was the only word Wil could manage to say.

"I fought with my mom," Katie whispered. "My agent flew in and surprised me, and I had to talk to her and my publicist without any warning, and my mom didn't offer you anything to eat or drink."

"I noticed that. It wasn't a *full* Midwestern shun, though." Wil was trying to keep it light with a joke, but she didn't feel light.

"Because the thing is, Wil." Katie had a grip on Wil's sleeve, and she tightened it, then let go and smoothed down Wil's bare arm. "I can't. We can't."

"Yeah?" Wil tried to find some fucking purchase. God.

"Everything I do is connected to everything else. And there is no way for us to have this"—she smoothed her hand from Wil's shoulder to her wrist, then touched her fingers to Wil's—"that doesn't also involve the whole entire world."

Katie's life with Ben was why they hadn't talked to each other in thirteen years. That wasn't what Katie had wanted. Or Wil. It was something that had happened to them.

What Wil had been avoiding thinking about—not now, not during this perfect, stolen handful of days and weeks when everything was so good—was if it was too late.

For them.

Both times.

Katie took a deep breath, and then the doorbell rang.

Wil tried to remember what it sounded like when Katie said *Never leave me,* but it had already slipped away from her. "That's Noel. Do you still want to film?"

"Yeah." Katie smiled at Wil, her full Katie Price smile that Wil had seen hundreds of times in magazines and ads and movies and on the internet. "Don't answer the door until I get my wig."

She scrambled over the bed, just like she had years ago, so many times when she realized how late it had gotten. Except instead of running home, she was putting on a disguise so no one would know who she was.

Wil reassured herself that no matter what, she would *always* know.

And maybe that would ache more than it ever had before, but that was okay.

It would be worth it.

Chapter Twelve

Katie felt like every visceral part of her body, her blood and bones and organs, were light and fizzy at the same time. She had retrieved her wig and hat from the coat tree. The wig today was lank, shoulder-length hair that had a very grown-out-looking pink and fading dye job.

"Ready?" Wil was at the door.

"Yes."

She had traded an appearance in a small cameo role with an emerging independent director in exchange for Chichima's agreeing to teach her techniques for filming with an iPhone. Katie hadn't had plans for what she wanted to do with these skills other than the joy of learning and knowing something about them, but now she was grateful.

In the part of the living room where Wil had her photography backdrop, Katie set up a tripod with a miniature camera track that could move her phone steadily in four directions with a little joystick. She snapped on a magnetic wide-angle lens and checked the shot.

She did these things methodically, one after the next, the same way her mother sprayed and wiped down the kitchen countertops after she had a bicker-fight with Craig, because Katie's head was stuck on the conversation upstairs.

It had always been easier for Katie to know how she felt than to put her feelings into words. Her feelings weren't words. Her feelings right now were a whirl of relief mixed up with old shame, the hard pinch of grief beneath her ribs, and a crack through the middle of everything with light pouring through.

The light was Katie's understanding that when she'd told Wil about Ben, what she *didn't* feel was anything like worry that she might be telling it wrong, making Wil uncomfortable, or spinning the story in a way that wouldn't play for the press. It wasn't like talking to Madelynn or April, it wasn't like trying—haltingly—to open up to Diana.

It was just Wil, listening.

It was just Katie and Wil, like it had always been Katie and Wil.

Rosy pillows. Someone who listened to her and heard nothing but what she said. Someone to come home to at the end of a long day who would only, always, be for her. Whose someone Katie could be.

When she left for Chicago, all those years ago, she'd thought there would be more time. She would leave Green Bay, and Wil would leave, too, but they would both come home again. They'd see each other. They'd have more chances.

It hadn't worked out that way.

It wasn't going to work out now. Because Katie wanted Wil to have everything. She wanted that in a very simple and easy-to-feel way.

Everything for Wil.

She positioned her two lights and a portable boom, and then she was ready, standing with her hands open, her posture loose, when Noel came in with Wil.

Wil had told her she met Noel in the fall when she went to a home on the west side of town to take pictures of the homeowner's car, which had been struck by the homeowner's own garage door when she was backing out and accidentally activated the door remote in her purse. Noel was there cleaning the gutters. He'd climbed down from his ladder and stood in the driveway, his hands in his back pockets, listening to the entire exchange, then followed Wil down the driveway to the street, where she'd parked her car, and given her his card.

In case you ever need your gutters cleaned, he'd said.

So of course Wil had asked him, *Would you like to kiss me?*

He looked like every youngish Wisconsin white dude who had ever come to Katie's mother's house to do work on it, which was to say that he was medium height, with medium brown hair, blue eyes, and a snub nose that put him firmly in the *cute* rather than the *hot* category.

Although there was something hot about his directness. Noel was a dude without layers. He shook Katie's hand, barely looking at her because he was busy peering around the living room and asking Wil questions about whether the house was a rental, did she know how old it was, what kind of shape was the roof in, and did the basement ever get water in it.

Wil had told her she hadn't heard from Noel until recently, when he called and said he'd still like to do her "show." His latest ex-girlfriend had told him that he was terrible at kissing, and he wondered if she had a point. He'd confessed to Wil that he thought this would be a good way to find out, like when you take your car to the dealer to run computer diagnostics.

"Noel?" Katie changed her voice to a higher register, letting her vowels flatten into a Great Lakes accent. "Would it be okay if I went ahead and started filming?"

"No, yeah, sure," Noel said. "Go ahead."

While Katie set up the equipment, Wil and Noel had been talking in the entryway, and Wil had gone through a lot of information related to consent. Katie and Wil had debated last night whether Noel should know that Katie Price was filming him. Even though they didn't plan to release Katie's name or whisper a word of her association with the video, they'd decided to let Noel know that the person filming them was someone who, if her name got out, his video would be viral, probably forever.

Possibly, Noel would have guessed who Katie was. But possibly not. Katie had overheard Noel telling Wil that if the video became famous, it was for sure the only chance in his life for such a thing to happen, and maybe it would help the Packers.

Katie was grateful for Noel's disingenuous, pure Green Bay heart. It meant she had the opportunity to film the video, which was something she could do just for Wil. A sixty-second love letter that had all of her best in it. The thank-you she'd never sent for her bracelet.

Katie pulled the stool she'd taken from Wil's kitchen in front of the iPhone, watching the screen.

"So?" Wil smiled at Noel. When she'd taken off her sweater in her bedroom upstairs, Katie had nearly died, because Wil was wearing a white T-shirt, a little loose except across her breasts, where you could see her black bra right through it. The way her hair was cut meant that it was always halfway between messy and curly, and it did things to Katie's insides the same way Wil's heavy denim jeans did. "Sitting? Standing?"

"Let's sit," Noel said. "I'm a bit shaky." He laughed.

"Sure." Wil sat down on the stool she had in front of the backdrop, and Noel took the other.

Katie moved her phone with her joystick to capture how Noel perched on the edge of the stool, one foot fully on the ground, the other up on a rung with his knee bouncing. She zoomed in just a little on how he was rubbing his thumbnail with the tip of his index finger.

But his eyes were on Wil's face. She hadn't looked away from him and hadn't joined his laughter at himself. Katie let the camera see how Wil's gaze and her energy were calming Noel down, second by second. It made Katie's breath hitch.

Before, she'd only ever seen this part in an edited fifteen-second clip. Here, now, the preamble to the kiss spooled out at its own pace, the pace that worked for Noel and Wil, the pace Noel needed to get easier inside his body, for his foot to drop down to meet the ground and his weight to shift forward as he started to think about what he wanted to do instead of how he was afraid he might fuck it up.

That was when Wil slid to the front of her stool, letting her legs interlace with Noel's. Their knees touched. She smiled at him. He smiled back, laughing again, but not so much at himself this time, and he put his hand on Wil's knee. "Okay," he said. "Okay."

Wil put her hand around the cap of his shoulder, bringing her face closer, giving him permission to initiate the kiss, and Katie started to zoom in again slowly at the moment she felt him decide.

She took in a slow, deep breath, watching the screen as Noel's mouth met Wil's gently, softly, and he drew back a little and then came in again, his hand flat against her collarbone as though he needed to feel what might happen next, whether she was moving toward him or away from him, whether he wanted to grip her shoulder or ease his hand down to her waist.

Katie let the camera be her eyes. She kept her gaze on the phone. This didn't scare her. She wasn't afraid to look. She trusted what she felt about Wil, and she trusted Wil, and most of all she trusted what was in the room right now, which was a lot of expansive, beautiful generosity from Wil making room for this almost-stranger to try something that scared him so he could have something he wanted.

Katie trusted. Because Katie was in love with Wil.

She knew that now, watching her kiss this man so selflessly.

Wil put her hand on his face, angled her mouth, and the kiss deepened. Katie pointed the camera where she'd always wanted to look, watching the tension melt out of Wil's face, but not until the camera had already seen Noel's shoulders come away from his ears, his hands ease, his eyes crinkle with a smile that ended the kiss.

Wil had done that.

"You're a good kisser, Noel," Wil said, pulling back.

You're a good mom. That was what Diana had told Katie she'd needed to hear, that she'd learned how to tell herself because it wasn't something the world told her often enough. *You're a good mom. You're a good kisser. You're a good person.*

Katie watched the gratitude fill Noel right to the top. Katie reached up and wiped away the tears that were falling down her cheeks.

Wil Greene was such a gift to the world.

Katie was sorry that she would never get her chance to kiss her.

"Ah, thanks, then," Noel said. He stuck out his hand, and Wil shook it, laughing.

He squinted over to where Katie was, behind the tripod. "Thanks."

"Yeah! Of course," Katie said. She touched the floor switch that turned off the lights, then the boom, and hit the big red stop button on her phone.

"Let us walk you out." Wil touched Noel's elbow. "Do you have any questions about posting the video?"

"Nope, you explained that pretty well and for pretty long, too. I got the form in my email."

"Once you send it back, I'll post, then."

"All right." He smiled. Katie noticed that he looked a bit taller and more at ease. Wil walked next to him, Katie behind them, and as Wil opened the door, a swirl of cold wind wrapped around all three of them on Wil's stoop.

"Katie!" a man shouted. "Look over here!"

She didn't think. Her head moved automatically, pointing her face down and away from the voice. "Hey, Noel, could you come back inside with us for a minute?" Her tone was calm but very firm.

"Sure, sorry." He turned around with Wil, confused but compliant, and Wil shut the door against the knot of men on the sidewalk in front of the house.

One week since Katie landed at the Green Bay airport. Three days since the party at her parents' house. That was how long Katie had thought she might have, because that was as long as she'd ever managed to keep her presence a secret anywhere in the world.

She could never really come home. She'd known that, but Katie had never been more sorry to be right.

She'd never felt more keenly the size and shape of the gap between the life she had and the life she wanted.

It took an hour before her parents made it to Wil's house. While Katie waited, she arranged a rental for Noel and explained he'd have to come pick up his car in a few days when things calmed down.

Her dad borrowed Noel's keys and pulled Noel's car into Wil's garage.

Noel called his brother to pick him up from the back alley behind the house and take him to the rental agency.

Katie's dad drove his car back home. Diana waited for Katie.

By the time they were ready to go, Katie knew, one or more of the men outside would have run Noel's plate and figured out his name, probably his phone number, certainly his social media.

It was what they did. It was how this worked.

Before she stepped through the door to leave, Katie put her hand on the back of Wil's neck, her forehead against Wil's. "I'll let you know when I know, okay?"

Wil smelled like mint. Her skin was warm, so warm that Katie wanted to lean into it.

She closed her eyes as she felt Wil's breath on her mouth, then opened them, even though she was too close to see Wil's face. It was close enough. Close enough for Katie to feel what it would be like to have this.

To have Wil.

"I'm sorry," Wil said.

Everyone always apologized to Katie, as though somehow it wasn't Katie who had done this.

"I had the best morning ever," she told Wil. "We will figure this out, and I will see you soon, because you are the very best one."

Wil laughed, but Katie meant it.

The best.

The one.

Chapter Thirteen

The Nissan electric SUV whirring down I-41 was hushed, quiet. Nothing like the Bronco, with its oversprung bench seat and rough engine. The reliquary of her family's unspoken feelings.

But Wil didn't have even a small yearning for the Bronco, not when this shiny black SUV was gloriously anonymous, pointed toward Katie's house, and she had, for the first time in a long time, a *plan*.

Wil had a plan. She had a goal, a set of steps lining themselves up in her mind and in her chest that she hadn't even realized had been lining themselves up for a long time, as silent as the electric motor of this car, but also, delightfully, as efficient and detail-oriented as Wil had always been. They were easy to follow.

The first step, *Katie*.

Wil hadn't talked to Katie. She was trying to trust that Katie had meant it when she told Wil she'd see her soon. She knew that Katie was still in town. She knew Diana would feel too guilty *not* to give Katie Wil's new number, but maybe not *so* guilty that she would give it to Katie right away.

Wil had been forced to change her number within a few hours of the paparazzi showing up at her house. She was getting so many

calls from the media that at one point, her phone had buzzed itself
off the table.

She'd also had to decamp to her mom's house after hiding
the Bronco next to Noel's car, then talk a cheerful Noel through
changing his number after he DM'd to ask "how in the Good Pete
he could keep these folks from bothering him and everyone else."

It turned out that Noel was not only a good kisser, but also
a great person to be involved in this sort of situation. He didn't
say whether he'd known it was Katie Price behind the camera
the whole time, but Wil thought he must have figured it out. He
hadn't seemed surprised by the revelation. He hadn't commented
on it at all, in fact, except to express a lot of shock that "Hollywood" wouldn't let someone have Christmas with their family,
"for Christ's sake."

Then he'd reminded Wil she could call him for gutter cleaning
anytime.

Noel told Wil that someone in "Katie Price's office" had con-
tacted him to arrange for a "branding package" for his gutter
cleaning and landscape services so that what had happened might
help his business and not hurt it. He didn't think it was necessary,
since he was more a word-of-mouth guy, but it couldn't hurt.

Wil had smiled and teared up because Katie's Christmas was
getting actively stomped, but she had still taken the time to bolster
Noel's business prospects. Because Katie.

Wil had held off on posting Noel's video. Even though she
had Noel's blessing to put it up on her channel, she wanted Katie's.

She wanted *Katie*.

But Wil could appreciate that Katie had a series of fires to put
out. Wil was a problem solver. She understood that problems required time. Patience. Creativity, even.

Wil exited the interstate and made one familiar turn after another until she got to a turn she'd never had to make before. Beanie

had told her about it. She found her way to the chain-link gate at the very back of Craig and Diana's place, which blocked an access road barely visible due to a line of white cedars.

There weren't any other cars or photographers. They would be in the front if they were here. Unless there were drones, they wouldn't know Wil had come to this road.

She hopped out, her boots sinking in the wet snow, and yanked open the gate. Her heart was beating so fast that she made herself take a few slow, deep breaths of cold air before she got back in the driver's seat and found the switch to turn off the lights.

Wil rolled slowly through the gate. Stopped. Hopped out and closed it.

Then she drove toward the back of the Prices' garage, grateful for the quiet electric motor and for all of the good lighting on the Prices' property.

Grateful, too, for their security cameras, because as soon as she parked and got out of her car, there was Katie, tromping over the snow beside the path to the garage, laughing.

"You should have heard my mom's voice when she called down to me to say you were here." Katie's breath swirled in big white puffs in the cold air. "'Katelyn, you have a visitor.'" Katie did a *remarkable* impression of an annoyed Diana Price. "Tell me this is your new car."

"It's my new car." Wil felt better. She was shocked at how much better she felt, just seeing Katie in her falling-off, cat-hair-decorated black T-shirt and leggings. Her glorious movie-star smile. Her freshly washed hair, which had dried without being styled, and which looked so much like her hair in high school, it made Wil's heart pinch. "What are you doing?"

"Packing." Katie smiled again, but it wasn't as bright. "A little bit. Mostly, talking on the phone. Talking on FaceTime. Texting. I think I got a telegraph." She dropped her voice into an imitation of an old-fashioned newsreel announcer. "'Katie! Stop. This is an emergency! Stop. Tell the world exactly how you're feeling. Stop. Maybe a nude? Stop.'"

The *"Wil" Katie Price Finally Get Kissed?* clickbait had started rolling before Wil was even alone in her house, dark in the middle of the day with all the blinds shut. The pictures weren't anything more than a series of shots of Wil and Noel side by side, talking to each other, and Katie a bit behind them, in the wig, looking down. It was easy to recognize Katie in the pictures. Frozen in a photo, Katie's profile, the shape of her chin, and her mouth were all there. The ways she changed how she moved, her accent, her expressions and gestures, washed away.

The story was mostly supplied by imaginative supposition about Katie's association with Wil-You-Or-Won't-You, back-story copy about her career highlights, and fresh quotes from Ben Adelsward.

"I'm so sorry," Wil said.

"That's my line, silly." Katie waved Wil to follow her to the sliders that led to her suite. "Welcome to the Katie Price Show. This time with unwilling special guest stars." Katie slid open the glass doors. "Madelynn, my publicist, told me you're not returning her calls."

"I'm not returning anyone's calls." Wil shucked off her coat and toed off her boots, looking around at Katie's half-packed luggage and noticing that her heart had sped up again. The cats were in a cuddle pile on one end of the sofa, obviously trying to ignore what was going on. Wil could sympathize. "I changed my number."

"You should talk to Madelynn, though. She could help." Katie sat on the floor, then leaned back against the sofa. "She's good at making things go away. I suggested some thin but adorable copy about visiting my old friend from high school who, of course, because we were friends, is extremely cool, and yes, you got me, she has '*the* TikTok'"—Katie made air quotes—"and her gutter guy had stopped by with an estimate." Katie wrinkled her nose. "Harder to make plausible or adorable. Although Noel would receive more bookings than any gutter guy in the entire Fox Valley if we ran with it."

Wil sat on the floor across from Katie, shoving one of the suitcases aside to make room. "That's an interesting angle. Also a lie."

Close up, Wil could see the strain at the corners of Katie's eyes. There was a red place on her lower lip where she'd obviously been worrying it.

Katie didn't look like she had a plan. She looked like she was trying to make the best of a situation that had spiraled out of her control.

Wil put her hand on Katie's knee. "Hey."

"Yep." Katie rolled her eyes. "I'm sorry I haven't called you. I'm sorry about all of this. I'm just . . ." She dropped her head so that her hair fell forward, a curtain that hid her face. "I'm having a hard time."

"Tell me about that."

Katie shook her head. "I usually do a better job. I should have prepared you. I should've told you what would happen."

"You did. You said my life would be divided into everything before I kissed you on TikTok and everything that happened after." Wil made the same gesture Katie had made at her mother's holiday party, one side of her life to her left, the other side to her right.

"That was flirting. It wasn't honestly warning you what this would be like. I didn't"—she swallowed, her voice thick—"I didn't think hard enough about what this would be like."

Wil pushed her hand through her hair. "Neither one of us could've known what this would be like."

They didn't mean dodging the media.

Katie sighed. "I'm sorry."

Wil felt the solidity of the sofa behind her back, the tightness in her shoulders. She didn't want an apology. Katie's apology meant something had gone wrong that Wil couldn't fix. It meant they'd come to the end of the road.

Wil wasn't interested in endings. For the first time in years, she wanted to think about what came next. She wanted to know where she was headed instead of where she'd been. "You keep saying that, but I'm not clear on what you're sorry for, Katie Kat. What is it that you think you've done wrong?"

Katie didn't answer the question, but that was okay. Wil was pretty sure she already knew the answer. She'd had time, last night, to really think about the conversation they'd had in her bed yesterday.

Ben Adelsward was quoted in every single story about Wil and Katie being photographed together. He'd been the primary focus of the stories about Katie's appearance in Chicago—at least at first, maybe until Katie's publicist found a way to spin them away from him.

Late last night, sitting at her desk with Almond Butter in her heated bed beside Wil's laptop, Wil had done a deep dive into Katie's press from the last few years, reading and taking notes and thinking until she finally felt the pieces of what she'd observed and what Katie had told her—their conversations, their past together—begin to click together.

Katie in high school. That day she'd picked her up in the Bronco. Maneuvering Mr. Cook to save the class. What Katie had told Wil about Ben.

Katie walking onto the soundstage in Chicago under the bright lights, the catwalks, with her styled hair and beautiful jewelry, heels and signature pink lips. Confident and untouchable.

Honor Howell.

The rumors about Katie's production company.

Diana. How much Diana loved her daughter, and how fiercely she protected Katie's privacy.

"You have to be perfect, don't you?" Wil asked.

Katie looked away again.

It was cold in her suite. The silence felt cold, too. Heavy. Finally, Katie picked at the knee of her leggings. "I can remember this one night, a few months after I was in my house," she said. "My mom had gone back home. I was alone. It was the first time I'd been alone when I saw a headline. Ben had told the press a secret, what I'd thought of as a secret between us. It was so ugly. The media had gotten really ugly about me. It made me feel like I didn't exist. I wasn't a person. I was twenty-two, and I couldn't understand how it was that I'd been such a singular, brilliant genius when I was eighteen, nineteen, with Ben, but now everyone hated me. I remember thinking I wished—really, really wished—that I could go home. But I couldn't."

Katie's breath hitched, and Wil thought of the hospital bed in the living room of the house she'd grown up in. The hospice people had cleared everything out so quickly, but there had been a span of time—it could have been ten minutes or an hour—when Wil sat in the living room with that bed. The sheets stripped. Empty.

"I know what that feels like," she finally said.

Katie picked up Wil's hand and gripped it hard in hers. "For women, there are only two kinds of movie stars, did you know that?" Finally, she looked up. Her eyes were bright in a way that made Wil feel better. There was so much determined *Katie* in her face.

"What are the two kinds?" Wil asked.

"Tragic and iconic."

"You decided to be iconic." Wil reached out to push Katie's

hair behind her ear, but Katie captured her hand and laid it against the hot skin of her cheek. Her jaw flexed beneath Wil's palm.

"I decided to be beyond any type or category." Katie reached for her hair and pulled it over her shoulder. Like always.

"So that's all." Wil smiled.

Katie shrugged, but then she smiled, too. It wasn't a brittle smile. Wil was glad to see it. "To answer your question, I'm sorry I did this to you." Katie made one of her gestures where just her hand somehow conjured up the paparazzi, buying a Nissan, falling most of the way off the edge into love.

"But." Wil stretched out her legs and leaned back. "It wasn't you. It was me."

Katie raised her eyebrows. "Okay." She made another gesture that said *I don't believe you, but tell me this story.*

Wil was ready to do that. It was part of her plan. "You've heard of ChapStick?"

Katie laughed. "I almost remember it. These days I only anoint my lips with the oil from rare alpine vegetation, of course."

"Obviously. Remember Lynn, on my channel?"

"Yes! Wavy blue hair, tall, looks obscene in a tank top. Grabbed the back of your neck in a way that caught my thighs on fire."

Wil sat up a little taller, pleased with this additional confirmation of Katie's attention—pleased in a way that made her throat and cheeks warm. "I didn't really pay attention, but right before I kissed her, I put on ChapStick. Most of the time I don't even know I'm doing it. And I'm a slapdash video editor."

"For the record, I always notice when you put on ChapStick."

Katie smiled at her in a way that was very unfair and disruptive to Wil keeping track of this story, and Wil laughed. "Don't distract me. The point is that *ChapStick* noticed when I did it in that video, right before I kissed Lynn. And someone in the marketing or social media department at ChapStick had positive thoughts, and these positive thoughts led to my getting a DM inviting me to 'explore opportunities with the brand.'"

"Ah," Katie said. "Once, I accidentally started a three-year fad when I was photographed coming out of the gym with my barrettes clipped to my shirt collar where I'd put them when I changed and forgot to put them back in my hair."

"That was you?" Wil smiled, remembering the inexplicable barrettes-clipped-to-collar fad.

Katie laughed. "Continue."

"Right. So it's a convoluted story, involving some interesting phone calls with ChapStick's parent company, but I'll leave that for another day. Right now, I'm telling you about it because what it triggered me to do wasn't to explore a career as a spokesmodel, but to take a deep dive and make a lot of spreadsheets about influencer contracts, terms of service, and creator content rights."

"Obviously. Because you're Wil Greene." Katie put her elbow on her knee and tipped her head into her hand, and Wil thought, in a sudden flash, that she could look at Katie looking at her like that for the rest of her life.

It made her heart go still and warm, slowing the whole world down for just a moment. A pay-attention moment.

Wil laughed, but she let the shift happen between them. She told herself it was okay. She had a plan now.

She had risked and lost enough to bear how she was starting to feel about Katie Price.

"My point is, if you're leaving, I want to go with you to Los Angeles."

Katie unfurled herself and sat up straight. Shook her head. "Wait. Yes. No. What?"

Wil stood up. Katie did, too. "I didn't think I was going to say that, exactly. Yet. I jumped ahead."

"But you said it was your point!"

"My point was more supposed to be that I'm not stuck. I was wrong about that. When you got here, I'd already started getting unstuck. First, it was just solving people's problems in a simple way as an insurance adjuster. Then I was doing my TikTok, and that sent me into my obsession with fair terms for creators, and that led me to the list that Beanie and I made so I would get unstuck, which meant I went with her to Chicago to see you. Remember, one of the things on the list was 'spend time outside Green Bay.' And then because I'd done *that*, when the reporter asked you about Ben, I was thinking about everything *you* wanted and how the whole world was conspiring to keep you from getting it, and how *I* didn't have that excuse. Not really."

Wil stopped and made herself look at the drop-ceiling panels with their perforated dots. The words were coming out sure and fast, and it felt good to finally be able to say something that felt so completely, utterly obvious and true.

"I tried to keep myself out of the whole world after I lost my dad so I would never lose anything ever again—or that's what one of my therapists said, talking about why I was in Green Bay. But it wasn't exactly right, because I *did* start that TikTok. Over and over again, I kissed people *one time* and let them go. I let myself feel everything I could possibly feel about them, and about myself, and about everything they needed and wanted, and then I let them go. Over and over. The thing is? I never got to do that with my dad, Katie."

Katie put her hands on her heart, one on top of the other, and Wil noticed how fast she was breathing. How intently she listened.

"I never got to go to Michigan Law," Wil said. "I didn't have a chance to get halfway into some important appellate court clerkship and realize it was my dad's dream, not my own, and then talk to him over Thanksgiving about it on the front porch swing with a blanket over us and have him hug me and tell me it was okay to have my own dream. I missed out on that, that whole part of my life. I had to figure out a different way to have it. Does that make sense?"

Katie nodded. Wil could feel her pulse in the palms of her hands. Her heart pounding.

"And you missed out, too!" Wil said this with a quaver in her voice. "Not with my dad, but how you were supposed to get your start. All this perfection you can't let go of because it's kept you safe? It's *good* that you were safe. I'm so thankful for the decisions you and Diana made to keep you safe, but there's always been something you wanted, Katie, and it wasn't safety. *Always.* So my point is, I knew you. I've *always* known you. And I let you go too soon. We already did that once. Right now, it's too soon again. If you go back to LA right now and this ends, it will be too soon for whatever this is that's *not* just a bet, or kissing on TikTok, or flirting with feeling all those might-have-been feelings, but what and who we are now."

Katie made a noise in her throat, somewhere between a sob and a laugh, smiling at Wil.

"And maybe we'll say good-bye to each other anyway." These words came out of Wil more slowly, with more solemnity. "Maybe we'll let go of all of this anyway. Maybe there will be a whole bunch of news stories about how we broke up and someone takes a picture of me crying at a cafe and it's circulated around the world. But even if that happens, you didn't *do* anything to me. I was the catalyst. *Me.* All you did was remind me how big I am, and now I want to remind you how big *you* are. Just you. The original you, the real you. Because if you have to be beyond reproach for the rest of your life, it's going to kill you, Katie Price, and it's just as unsafe as Ben."

Katie had both of her hands against her cheeks, her blue eyes wide. "Wil."

"Unless you don't want me to." Wil's voice was hoarse. "By the way, I didn't plan that speech."

"I haven't heard you make a speech like that since you got vale-dictorian, when you directly imaginary-addressed Supreme Court Chief Justice John Roberts and told him that he was the worst coward who had been walking a tightrope over the true heart of America his entire career."

Wil grinned. "That one got away from me, too. You know it has twenty thousand views on YouTube? I like to think that he's seen it."

Then Wil could breathe again. So she did that for a minute while they looked at each other, and the words Wil had just said settled down between them as one more thing that had happened, dividing the past from the present.

Then and now. Before and after. That kind of division didn't actually make any kind of sense of how Wil felt about Katie Price.

It was like Wil had told her. She'd always known Katie.

Always.

The cats began to meander closer in the silence. Trois rubbed against Wil's leg, and Wil kneeled down to pet the top of her head.

"Where's the video?" Katie whispered. Then she cleared her throat. "Did you get the edited file I sent you?"

"I did. I wasn't sure if it was still a good idea to post it. I didn't want to step on the toes of whatever you and your people decide the message should be. So far, what the media's decided to think about you and Noel being at my house is kind of intense, you know?"

"That's because of Ben."

In one viral video from an entertainment site, Ben had been getting out of his car, walking up to some coffee stand. He said he knew that Katie was "obsessed" with Wil-You-or-Won't-You. The implication was that Katie had sought out Wil's account in her hometown to prove she was still desirable and relevant—to push up her star, break up the cat lady stories, contribute to her enigma.

Ben had made that angle sound desperate.

His statement made it difficult for Wil to be sure Katie wanted the video posted. She wanted to know what Katie *wanted*. It didn't matter if the video went up or never did, as long as Katie was calling the shots.

"Did Noel say it was okay?" Katie picked Sue up off the floor, where she had been shamelessly stretching out her entire body against Katie's leg. She kissed Sue on the top of her head. "I had such a good talk with him. I really like him. I don't want him hurt."

"Noel signed a release form just a little bit ago that took into account everything new. He told me if you wanted to post it, then you should post it." Wil gave Trois one last scratch and stood.

"Right now, either we're in a throuple with Noel, I'm imminently going to be posted kissing you on TikTok in a desperate bid for publicity, or you took on the challenge of going where no one has gone since Ben because of your obvious erotic powers."

"That last one, I thought, was pretty good." Wil couldn't stop trying to lighten the mood, even as her heart had been racing since she'd come through the door.

Katie rolled her eyes, smiling. She set Sue down on the floor. When she straightened, she stood opposite Wil, close. She put her hands on her hips and looked at Wil with all the power of an A-list celebrity tossing out directives to her team. "I want you to know that I'm making this decision for myself. Because, first, the video is good, and if I don't release it, no one will ever see it. I can admit my ego is invested. And second, it's true."

Katie bit that bright red worried spot on her lip.

"It's *true*," she said a second time. "I filmed your kiss with Noel. So if you put out the video with my name attached, it isn't a *story*. It's just what happened. I don't know what happens after we do that, and I haven't even talked about this with my people, but I didn't talk to them about filming a Wil-You-or-Won't-You video, and I should've. Not because of me. Because of you. Because you made something incredible and huge and emotional and sexy and real, and I wanted to and loved being a part of it, and I should've told my team about the *opportunity* I had to do it. So now, I am going to tell the world how lucky I was to get to capture those sixty seconds. In the caption, credit me as the director and cinematographer."

When Katie pulled her hair over her shoulder again, Wil saw that she was flushed along her collarbone. Wil remembered what it was like to have that skin against her mouth. What it was like to feel Katie hot against her thigh.

"Do you want me to tag you?" Even to herself, she sounded far away.

"Tag the fuck out of it." Katie stepped closer, until their noses were inches apart. Too close for the closeness to be for any other reason than the impulse to slide their hands into each other's hair and bite whatever part of them presented itself first to the other.

"I do have a question, though." Wil's voice was a faint rasp.

"What is your question?" Katie whispered this to the corner of Wil's mouth, her eyes closed.

Wil did not have a question. She didn't have a single thought in her head, but she needed to do something to defuse the tension and keep herself from kissing Katie, or Katie from kissing her. Wil had enough experience with kissing to know how close it was to happening. In fact, she'd been in this place with Katie many times more than she would have ever thought, so she was particularly experienced in what it was like to *almost* kiss Katie.

Wil's desire to kiss Katie Price was becoming an all-consuming problem. Kissing Noel had been an exercise in figuring out how to be present enough to kiss Noel when mostly what Wil wanted to do was kiss Katie.

She would post the TikTok, but Wil didn't have anyone lined up for Wednesday. She didn't have anyone lined up, ever, at all.

It was time for the next thing. She hoped Katie would be a part of it, but if she wasn't, Wil was starting to believe she could do the next thing no matter what.

But they definitely weren't supposed to be kissing. Kissing was part of Wil's plan, but they hadn't gotten to that part yet.

Okay. There was the question. "What do you think is our next move with the mystery of Mr. Cook?"

Katie blinked. "I think we're operating with too many unspoken constraints." She sounded like she had that first day at Diana's party, when she was trying to out-flirt Wil. "I love constraints, don't get me wrong, but limiting ourselves to detection that can be accomplished in the Bronco means our progress is slow. Do you have any ideas?"

"We could ask someone who might know the score." Wil said this to Katie's lower lip. Her mouth was slightly open. It was killing Wil.

"Like who?"

"I mean, we've never talked to anyone about this, so, anyone? Like, literally any adult in our circle of acquaintance, for a starting place? But I have someone in mind."

"Hmm. Is that cheating?"

"The better question is if it's cheating to use a bet to give ourselves what we want if we could give each other what we want without it."

Katie leaned her head back and laughed at the ceiling. "You mean that we want to kiss each other. And our bet has been smashed apart by circumstance, reality, and the fact that it was a thinly veiled excuse to see each other as many times as we wanted to while I was here."

"Yes."

"Our real problem, then," Katie said, "is everything that our mothers are worried about." Her teeth dragged over that spot on her lip again. Worry. Worry, worry.

Watching Katie worry released Wil the rest of the way from the kissing spell she'd nearly fallen into, because Katie's worry meant there was something going on there that she didn't *fully* understand and that wasn't part of her plan.

Wil had been slightly behind Katie and Noel when they stepped out onto the porch and the photographer called Katie's name. It had meant that when Katie turned around—her face shielded from the flashing lights and the sudden tumult on Wil's normally peaceful street—Wil had seen, clearly, Katie's unschooled expression.

Devastated. That was how Katie had looked. Utterly devastated.

And even though she'd pasted a new expression on immediately, tossing a practiced smile at Wil, keeping her tone breezy as she walked Noel through an explanation of who she was and what he was witnessing, something about her had changed.

Or maybe what Wil was seeing was how Katie always was. How she had to be when she wasn't *Wil's* Katie.

"If our real problem is our mothers," Wil said, "then it will only freak them out a very unsurprising amount more when we tell them I'm going with you to Los Angeles."

"That's really what you want?" Katie's perfect eyebrows drew together.

"I wouldn't have—"

Katie put her hand over Wil's mouth. "I just realized I don't care as much as I should if you're sure. Because yes, God. Please come with me. Post the video, and we can hole up in my house together and hide from the aftermath."

"Um."

"You have to understand, right now, *out there* is trained on Green Bay, waiting for more. More of me. That's why I was packing. I was planning to ask April to get me out of here without tipping anyone off. If you come with me, it gives us more time. For . . . this. Without . . . all that."

Tension had made its way into Katie's expressive face and dulled it. Her flush had gone hectic.

"College visit," Wil said, trying for humor, trying not to feel like she'd invited herself somewhere she wasn't really welcome. "Isn't that why high school friends fly out to stay in guest rooms on the other side of the country?"

Katie put her hand around the back of Wil's neck, her thumb under her ear, and pulled their foreheads together. Wil felt Katie's breath against her face as a heartbeat between her legs. "This is the worst idea ever, and we are going to get into trouble."

"We never had the chance before," Wil said. "It's about time."

Chapter Fourteen

"Fuck," April said. "This is good." She pulled off her heart-shaped glasses and looked up at her webcam.

"Yeah?" Katie asked. "I wrote and edited all day today. This is it. The first draft. The one I thought I needed at least a month to write, but apparently getting this done only required fifteen to twenty thousand calories of my mother's food, a come-to-Jesus talk from my agent, the realization I've been suffering under thirteen years of longing, a Category Five media storm, and a very Intro to Composition writing lesson that I could've gotten from any tutor anytime in the last eight years."

Conscious of how fast she was talking, Katie made herself take a breath. "But now you have to tell me if it works," she said. "I think it does, but I might have lost perspective. Mainly for all of the same reasons I was able to write it in the first place."

"I'd give this script to you to read, is what I'm saying." April smiled. "Even if there wasn't a lot of money."

Katie closed her eyes. That was good to hear. She trusted April's judgment more than her own wobbly instincts as a writer of screenplays. "I'm so glad. I know it will need revision, but it does feel like I'm really doing it."

"You're really doing it. Green Bay is good for you, TMZ's crash of your idyll *very* much excluded." April put her glasses back on and picked up the script, which Katie realized she'd not simply printed out but actually had bound. It was covered in green ink where April had taken notes. That, more than April telling her it was good, made goose bumps sluice from Katie's scalp to the tops of her legs with joy and pride and interest in making something, her *own* something, and seeing it come together.

It meant even more to see that marked-up script in April's hands, hear the sound of her turning the crisp pages, and listen to April's sharp and incisive notes, because literally everyone around her was having such a hard time ever since Wil's TikTok had posted and set the entertainment news on fire.

Katie hadn't done any of the things she normally would have done. She hadn't circled her wagons, met with her team, or prepared a statement that contained the exact right amount of detachment. She'd been writing. She was letting these chips fall.

But all day, her mom kept bringing her snacks, checking if the basement suite was a comfortable temperature, and pointedly not asking the questions that were filling her eyes with so much worry.

Madelynn had reached out to Katie again, full of rage and ready to lay in wait behind Ben's favorite specialty cigarette shop in Brentwood so she could tear his throat out with her bare hands to present to the Academy.

April put the script down. "What I think is that you give this one more pass, and then we show it to the people who were interested when we bought the option."

"Honor, you mean." Katie's belly went tight with thoughts she hadn't let herself have for the last twenty-four hours since Wil posted their kissing video. Thoughts about how she had strayed wildly from the original plan she'd made with Madelynn, the one that led to the *Hollywood Reporter* profile of Katie in a director's chair and a luscious, dream-making investment from Honor Howell. Thoughts about Honor saying, *I wonder how ready you are for work out of the spotlight*. Madelynn had warned her. Honor wanted evidence that Katie wasn't actually *seeking* these stories about Ben. She needed to know that Katie was more interested in work than in fame. What Katie had done—what she'd had no choice but to do—might have made it so that it didn't matter, as far as Honor Howell was concerned, whether April thought the screenplay was good.

April stretched her arms over her head. The sleeves of her oversized cardigan sweater dropped past her elbows, and gold bangles glistened on both of her wrists. "A script with this much of a vision adapted from a book no one could stop talking about is one of those unicorn first projects for a new production company," she said. "With the right cast, it could mean major profit, distribution, and awards buzz. Especially since your vision for this is cheap—and for that I thank you—so it gives us room to spend money on talent. I'd love to show this to Alison so she can start thinking about casting. She's a vault as far as leaks. She won't even tell you if you have spinach on your teeth."

Katie pressed her hand against her belly. Alison Cornelius was one of the biggest casting directors in Hollywood. Katie had taken more than one very important call from her. April was already talking about spending money. Location. Meetings.

Katie told herself that even if their studio didn't get funded, *she'd* fund this movie herself. She could convince April to let her. She didn't think about how she'd fund Marisol's picture. She couldn't let herself imagine how she might have let Marisol down, and how Marisol would be reminded of it every time she looked at the news. The internet. Social media.

"When will you be here?" April leaned back in her chair. "I'm assuming you're not taking the rest of your month, given the maelstrom. Are you staying for Christmas, at least? Tell me it's not so bad you can't do that."

April must have seen something in her face. The *something* that meant there were photographers camped at the end of her parents' drive, and the police had made the call to say there wasn't much more they could do, sorry, and her dad was checking and rechecking the security system and doing a lot of mumbling under his breath.

It wasn't the same something in her mom's eyes. *That* something was about the TikTok video. It was about how Katie hadn't talked to her mom about it first, or at all, and Katie never failed to tell her mother about decisions she was making, where she was traveling, or who she was meeting with.

That something was about Wil. Who had used the back gate to come and see Katie without calling first. Who had moved, for Diana, from the category of "safe person" to a different category Katie didn't entirely understand from her mother's perspective.

"Wil—" She stopped. She hadn't even exactly, totally, completely confirmed Wil was coming with her to LA. Her soul had said yes, and someplace that was between her throat and heart had said yes, and her eighteen-year-old self had done many, many dances in the middle of the room and in the shower and for the cats, excited as she could possibly be, but it still wasn't something that felt possible.

April leaned forward and grinned. "Can we talk about Wil?"

"I don't think so," Katie whispered.

"Okay. Fair, although I'm putting a giant pin in that. A pin you can see from space. But can we talk about Wil-You-or-Won't-You's post yesterday?"

Katie looked at the small spot on her screen where the bound script of her drafted screenplay sat on April's desk. That, she'd been ready to talk about. But ever since she'd told Wil to post the kissing video—since Katie had let the answer to Wil's question emerge from the ache beneath her rib cage without allowing herself to think about the consequences—she hadn't said a word about the video. Not to anyone.

Talking to her closest friend about it would make it real in a way Katie wasn't sure she was ready to face. "I assume you've talked that to death, to death, to death with Madelynn," she said.

"No." April narrowed her eyes. "I don't mean the press stuff or what Ben said. I'm talking about the post. Your filming Wil and Noel. The actual video."

Katie patted her lap so a cat would get into it. Sue came over and sat near her leg. "I haven't watched it since I edited it."

But Katie was listening.

"I'm not sure I've seen such a powerful sixty seconds of film in a long time, and it was technically perfect." April leaned forward and looked like she was jiggling her mouse. Then she looked at a spot on her screen and broke into a wide smile. "Honestly, I still haven't stopped getting chills. It's beautiful. *Beautiful*. Like a painting that makes you stop in the museum and feel like crying. Which has happened to me maybe one time, ever. I have no fucking idea how you got that kind of light inside a house."

Katie rubbed her chest with her palm.

"Also, it was all you. It wasn't a guest director spot on an established show with its own vision. This was yours. It had the tiniest, tiniest hint of a *signature*." April looked away from the video she obviously had playing so she could smile at Katie.

"It was just one minute." Katie could barely hear herself speaking, her voice was so quiet.

Wil had been just as complimentary. She'd told Katie she'd watched the final file over and over again, fascinated with what Katie had captured, and with the light. With Noel's smile. With how it made her feel. Katie had listened to her search for metaphors and then instead simply tell Katie it seemed like something that was from *her*.

You got into the video what Noel's smile felt like. How did you do that?

"I'll give you a moment to process my love of the video." April held up the script. "Give this another pass. I'll send the scan of my notes. There's work to do in the middle third, but you'll like it. You always like getting notes, maybe a little too much, so be forewarned that if you fuss over my notes too long, I'm going to put an endpoint on your process."

"Duly noted." Katie blew out a breath, relieved. She'd been both excited and worried about this conversation, but it had gone well. While she didn't feel like she was completely keeping up with all the changes in her life, she was at least staying present and trying to let things happen the way they wanted to happen.

She felt good.

Right up until April sat back in her chair and crossed her arms. "Okay. You've had your moment."

"Not nearly enough of a moment."

April grinned like this meeting was fun. "First, strategic planning. Remember when we talked about the Kennenbear joint and the Gloria Latener script, and we were looking at where and when you might want to fit Gloria's movie into your schedule?"

"It was only a few days ago, so yes."

"That's over." April made an explosion gesture with her hands. "No chance. Not happening."

"Why? Did Gloria call you? What did she say?" Katie's mind was racing. She'd always had an excellent relationship with Gloria Latener. She hadn't even considered what the fuss over the TikTok might be doing to her chances for roles. *Good God.*

"No, nothing like that. It's *this*." April gestured back and forth between them. "It's your video. That was such a move! Your name

on that video is giving you the kind of self-generated viral moment we hadn't even dreamed of. Madelynn's over the moon. That
kind of video means you can position yourself as a director beyond
the reach of the studio rivalries. You have your *own* audience now,
and they're hungry for more. It's this screenplay"—April picked
it up and shook it at the camera before dropping it back on her
desk—"and the fact that I'm more than confident it's going to bring
us everything we wanted and more. It's Marisol calling me twice
since the last time I saw you, both times to ask if I could give her
more clarity on the Ben Adelsward situation because she's dying to
make this movie, has been dying to make this movie for years, her
community needs this movie, Hollywood's hairy white ass needs
this movie, and now that she's finally figured out *how* she wants to
make it, she's angry every minute she has to sit at home waiting to
get started. Katie."

She couldn't catch her breath.

"This is happening," April said. "Right now. I can spare you
until Christmas, but then you need to get yourself back to LA to
help me deal with exactly *how much* this is happening. Like, we
need an office. We have to hire staff. Put the lawyers to work on
their reams and reams of paperwork. It's everything we wanted,
delivered with a bow on it and in a way that means we don't have
to beg the studios for favors or get in line or try to remember to be
nice girls. We can do what we want, we can make room for other
good people to do what they want, and we can be part of changing
how this business works."

"Oh." Katie was having a tough time staying present. This was
much more reality than she'd bargained on. "Listen—"

"No." April put her hands to her face. "I know I made it
sound like we were going to be able to take it slower than that,
telling you Alison's a vault, whatever, whatever, but *no*. You're a
director of your generation alongside the new world of directors

of our generation. That's the story now. Remember how Marisol got started, projecting her short film about labor practices on the Mexico City exchange building? There was an actual riot. You made a video of two people kissing that explains exactly why we kiss people, and you put it on a platform that people use for everything from coordinating aid to a war-torn area to how to apply bronzer. *Katie Price* did that, one of the most recognizable people in the world, who everyone wants to know more about, but nobody knows you because you've kept your story to yourself. So I won't let you decide whether or when you're going to be ready to do something when, Katie, *you have already done it. It's here.* There isn't a way to go slow or stay quiet about who you are anymore. You're out there. Everybody wants more of you."

Katie didn't realize one of her hands was pressed against her throat until she swallowed.

"Look," April said. "I'm a very powerful person. I shouldn't be. I don't look like what anyone wants a powerful person to look like in this town. I don't act like what you're told in agenting school makes a powerful person in this town."

Katie cleared her throat. "Agenting school?"

"It's underground. There are ogres." April smiled. "My point is that I am the same redheaded fat girl who binged romance novels and adored her best friend and her cats and whose bat mitzvah theme was 'The Gilded Age' without irony and included posters about notable inventions during the era."

It surprised Katie the way her bark of laughter made her eyes burn with tears.

"Sure," April said. "I'm powerful because I literally *never* walked off my own path. The one without irony and with sugar and romance and cats and nerdery. I let it get bigger and bigger, what was already inside of me, until I became the powerful boss bitch you see in front of you today. And I only deal with the people who respect me, and so it follows that the general opinion is that 'everyone' respects me. This means my life is pretty good, Katie. I don't have to spend time leaning against doors keeping people out. I can just be me, to my highest degree, and I keep my door open, and the people who need me and who I need tend to walk through it."

"You are trying to teach me a lesson," Katie guessed.

"I am trying to tell you that I have enjoyed watching you every single time you went on Busy's show to talk about your cats, because that was the path you had to walk on. But you're on a new path now. It's a scary path, I'll bet, but it's the right one. I need you to keep walking that path."

"I think I'm going to bring Wil with me to Los Angeles." Katie heard herself say the words with no plan or intention to say them. April gasped.

"In a few months," April said. "A year."

"No. When I see you next. Wil will be there. Probably."

April's head started to shake back and forth.

"You *just* said a lot of stuff about walking my own path!" Katie had only meant to mildly call out April's denial, but then she realized April's denial made her angry. "Unless, *unless* you want people like Ben, et al, to stop pushing me around because *you* want to be the one to push me around, all for yourself, and are afraid I'm going to ruin my career a second time by making a debut on the coattails of someone I'm fucking."

"Are you—"

"That's none of your business! But I want Wil to come to LA with me if she wants to." That was easy to say. So easy to say. "And Madelynn says I have to trust her, trust both of you, and I'm working on that, but it also means you have to trust *me,* not only because we're friends and we love each other"—Katie took a breath and checked April's expression quickly, because she'd never said anything like that to April before, but it was okay, April was nodding—"but also because if no one trusts me to *be* anything more than the Katie Price you've known since Ben, I'm not going to make it. I will diminish and go into the east."

It would kill her. That was what Wil had said.

It would kill her not to figure out how to be herself.

"I don't—" April started, then shook her head as if to dislodge a wrong idea. "I thought I was riding the rocket of your video as a viral declaration of your creative intentions. I didn't think—I'm sorry, but I didn't think it was a declaration of your relationship with Wil. Listen, forgive me, but that is a dilution of what this could be. Not just for you." April closed her eyes. "But for me."

Katie rubbed her palms down her thighs and gripped both of her knees, hard.

She was so angry. Instantly, completely enraged by April's comment.

A dilution.

She made herself take a deep breath. Katie understood that April had been focused on the video as an expression of abstract artistry. She understood, too, that expressions of abstract artistry which made people feel things were a *commodity* in Hollywood. April was her business partner, not just her friend, and so of course, of *course* she'd watched that video and seen dollar signs.

And Katie had told her nothing, next to nothing, about Wil. Why would April know her feelings? How could April guess at what was in her heart? Katie herself was still figuring it out!

"I don't even know where it's going with Wil." Katie shook her head. "I do know. But I don't know if I can have it, even if I want it more than anything. And, look, this is scary! I'm just *here*, writing this script and falling in love—"

April gasped again.

Katie held up her hand. "No. Not right now. Maybe falling in love again, or maybe I never stopped, I don't *know*. My point is, if you can go all over Los Angeles and find out if this production company is happening and if people with money are going to take me seriously as a director, then I can go all over Green Bay, Wisconsin, in my high school best friend's Bronco and imagine us in an alternate life, with four cats, making out on a sofa with mallards on it."

"*What?!*"

"It doesn't matter." Katie took a deep breath and closed her eyes. "Listen, I get how you want to use this video. To be honest, I can be grateful that it's a Hail Mary against the likelihood that I've tanked more traditional sources of funding."

"Katie." April sighed.

"No. Hold on. Do it. Let that video take on the cachet of something intentional. Let it be a way to capture the attention of America and convince them I have something new to offer. And I'll—" Katie pushed away an angry tear. "I'll keep it quiet with Wil. So the video means just that, and it's not some . . . *diluted* thing that the Nun of Hollywood did with her new girlfriend as a lark."

Phil hopped down from where he had been napping with Trois in the cat bed and sauntered over to Katie. He had always been sensitive to her feelings. He jumped into her lap. Sue had decided to lie by Katie's thigh.

"I'm sorry. Katie, look, I'm sorry."

"It *wasn't,* you know. A lark. Or some impulsive thing I did that happened to get out." Katie could feel the heat rising into her cheeks from her neck. "The first person I was ever in love with was Wil. She never made me do anything, I just wanted to be with her all the time. I wanted to ride around in her Bronco and listen to everything she had to say about everything."

April leaned forward with her head on her hand. "If you could bottle Wil Greene's presence, it would be a weapon of mass destruction."

"Yes, but you haven't met her in person. Wait until you meet her in person. I don't know what kind of truly enormous tolerance I had built up in high school, but it was gone when I ran into her at my mom's holiday party, and I was confessing to her about how I masturbate within fifteen minutes." Katie took a deep breath, trying to locate herself in the wild drift of her feelings. "Wil asked me to, but *I* want to take her to Los Angeles. Without knowing what's going to happen between us. Just to see if I might, maybe, have enough to offer her."

April's eyes were red and wet. Katie had never seen her cry before. "Once you decide what day you're coming back, tell me, and I'll set up the trip for you. I'll try to give the two of you privacy."

"But not to *hide* Wil." Katie let her agent hear the warning in her voice. She would not be pushed around when it came to this. Wil was too important.

"Not to hide Wil, but *for* Wil. For this chance for you, too." April held both her hands up in a gesture of apology.

Katie was suddenly exhausted. "I love you," she decided to say. Smiling, April swiped at her tears. "You'll have to show me pictures from your bat mitzvah sometime."

They laughed, and after talking about nothing in particular for a few minutes more, she and April said their good-byes and disconnected.

Katie's gaze wandered to the tree that her mother had set up in the basement suite this morning. It had pink lights all over it. Her heart pinched.

She couldn't stay for Christmas. It was too good of a chance to escape. The media would expect her to remain here. Would expect Wil to stay.

Katie closed her eyes and thought of her. Wil.

Hottest girl in school, valedictorian, cheerleader, softball player, orchestra, and, for a little while, Katie's best friend.

And the first person who'd been able to command her attention long enough for Katie to fall in love with her.

She picked up her phone. She started to text Wil, but then, out of curiosity, she went to TikTok first. Her heart was racing. She didn't log in to the Katie Price account—it would have so many notifications, it might not even load. She logged into her lurker account instead, her hands shaking.

Of course she'd filmed the kiss, edited it, watched it dozens of times. But it wasn't hers anymore. It was the world's. And that part, Katie hadn't seen yet.

A lot of Wil's videos went viral. Unsurprisingly, the Noel kiss had gone, well, mega-viral.

But there was lots of conversation, too. Lots of people stitching to it and making their own things, playing it in the background with commentary. Giving Noel some very excellent props, but also, *also,* really seeing Wil and what she was doing.

Everyone who watched Katie's film understood, in many cases for the first time, that Wil was perceptive, commanding, generous, and saw people.

And maybe, well, *absolutely,* there were a lot of people talking about Katie's technique. Adding to the video. Creating whole mini-movies and stories where what she and Wil had made was the beginning, or middle, or end of a whole other piece, story, or film.

She put the phone down and laughed. *God.*

Then she texted Wil.

Wil came over the same way she had the last time, through the secret back gate, still undiscovered by the media.

"Do you remember," Wil asked, stomping her feet, "our last sleepover?" She shrugged off her leather jacket and unwrapped her scarf. Her cheeks were nearly red with cold. "Before you left for Chicago?"

She wore a soft flannel shirt with illegally tight jeans, and her hair spiked and waved around her ears and neck. Katie watched her run her fingers through it, the unbuttoned cuffs of her shirt flipped back, highlighting her new manicure. Her nails had been painted black, with pastel geometric patterns. Something about how she was moving, how the Christmas lights from the pink tree caught her jawline, the tight jeans, superimposed this Wil with *then* Wil, and for a speechless moment Katie was overwhelmed with what felt like a thousand feelings—all of them tender and hot and excited and familiar and new and *welcome.*

"Yeah," she finally said. "We told our moms we were going to pick up a pizza and got distracted. Didn't have our phones. Came back three hours later after laughing so hard the whole time my scalp hurt, then got yelled at while we ate cold pizza."

Wil grinned. "No. Not that one."

Katie tried to push away all of her Wil feelings so she could focus, but it was impossible when Wil was standing right in front of her with so much cleavage giving that flannel a life it had never dreamed of when it was sitting on the shelves at L.L.Bean. "Um?"

"The sleepover we *called* the last sleepover."

"Oh!" Katie looked at Wil. "*Oh.*"

"Yeah. *Oh.*"

"The tent. After we swam in Lake Michigan."

Wil laughed and stepped closer. "What were we up to?"

"I mean," Katie said. "Nothing *happened.*"

"That is not how several recurring dreams over the last thirteen years remembers it."

"*Technically.*"

"Technically, it was two friends sharing a tent and s'mores," Wil said, stepping even closer, and *God,* she was extra-super *Wil* tonight, and Katie could not take it. "But I am really starting to understand why I started a TikTok where it was a foregone conclusion I would get to kiss the person in front of me."

"And also maybe why that almost-kissing part lasts so long in those videos." Katie cleared her throat. "I forgot about . . ."

"Did you, though?" Wil put her finger on Katie's collarbone.

"I absolutely did not forget," Katie admitted. "However, I did maybe *submerge* the memory a little. So that I could survive, probably."

Wil traced her finger along Katie's collarbone, tracing up her neck when Katie shivered. "I don't have any kisses lined up right now. With anyone who is not you."

Katie studied Wil's face, wanting to memorize the way she looked after she'd said that.

Good. That was how she looked. So good that Katie wanted to keep the movie of it in her head forever.

"I'm happy to hear that." Katie caught Wil's fingertips where they were sifting through the hair behind her ear. "State your business, then."

"You told me you wanted to go for a ride." Wil raised her eyebrows. "I have a lot of buttons undone to signal I can provide a good one."

Katie laughed. "In your new car. The one parked by the garage that looks like the Batmobile."

"Where are we going?" Wil bent over and grabbed her jacket.

Katie waited until Wil was facing her again, then slowly fisted the front of the flannel, pulling Wil to her. "One last time, we're going out investigating Mr. Cook, but really getting distracted. Not by anything in particular, just by being us, together. We're going to do that before I put you on a plane with me to LA, because once we go to LA, the whole world is going to change all over again. I think those two girls in the tent should have one last drive."

Wil kissed Katie's neck. "I like it."

Katie kissed Wil's forehead.

Then they ran out into the snow.

Chapter Fifteen

Cy Newhouse, the unbearably beautiful and extremely famous bisexual place-kicker for the Green Bay Packers, sat across from Wil in one of the leather seats of the private plane he shared with several other Packers players, including just-as-beautiful, just-as-famous former Packers quarterback Joe Starr and his increasingly famous girlfriend, Angela Goossens. Who were also on the plane with Katie. And Wil.

Surreal.

Cy Newhouse and Joe Starr and Angela Goossens were not flying to LA. They'd just come out to see Katie while the crew got the plane ready, to "visit," Katie had told Wil, as though she were describing Diana dropping by Beanie's house with a plate of casserole for ten minutes of conversation, barely worth mentioning.

That was what Katie was doing now, visiting with Joe and Angela in a separate bank of seats. Catching up with her friends.

Wil had never been on a private plane before. She had also never met one of the Packers, unless you counted standing in line behind a recently drafted running back at the Chipotle near the stadium, which she did not. She had certainly not anticipated meeting Cy Newhouse, ever. Or Joe Starr. Her father's favorite player.

Wil's father's favorite player had told her to call him Joel. That was his real name. Wil had known that already, because it was something the color commentators liked to mention during the games, and therefore something her dad also liked to mention.

Her dad would have been so interested to hear everything about what was happening to Wil right now.

"I had my agent call you!" Cy leaned forward and put one finger on Wil's knee. He smelled amazing. His eyes were just as blue as they looked in photos, and his dimples were a crime. Why did a six-foot-tall man with gorgeous brown skin and blue eyes and broad shoulders need dimples? What for? Killing her with? "How did that not work?" he asked.

Wil had no idea. She'd like to think she'd answer any kind of call from anyone representing one of the most photographed sports heroes in the world if it meant she'd get to kiss said sports hero, who looked like he knew how to excavate several layers of eroticism out of a sixty-second kiss.

"I get a lot of people contacting me about the channel," she said. "I can only think that I didn't believe it was real. There are a lot of prank calls from inside Green Bay."

"Sure." Cy nodded. "You have to protect yourself. What you're doing is powerful, and that means assholes are going to notice." He put his hands on his cheeks. "But Wil Greene. *Wil Greene.* I've been wanting you to kiss me for almost nine months. And now you're in my plane, but you're with Katie. My life isn't going my way."

Wil could feel her heart beat in her throat, and in her palms, a good kind of ache—but that ache wasn't about Cy's direct gaze and what he said he'd wanted from her. It was that he'd said, *You're with Katie.* She wanted to ask him if he'd seen something between her and Katie that had told him, *Wil's with Katie.* Maybe whatever he'd seen, he'd taken a picture of, or could describe to her, so she could keep it no matter what.

No matter what.

"I feel like it can't be true, what you just said," Wil replied. "I'm thinking your life goes your way more or less all the time."

Cy grinned at her. "It's pretty good, but I want to complain about this." Cy turned his attention to Katie, pointing across the plane at her and raising his voice so she'd hear him. "Katie Price! You've known this woman the whole time!"

"Yes and no," Katie said. "It's complicated."

"No," Cy said and laughed. "It's not."

He met Wil's eyes, and Wil did, in fact, at least *feel* what he had seen. Because even though this was Cy Newhouse, and she, along with millions of other people, had been arresting on the vision of his oiled, naked body in athletic shoe ads for many years, what she'd found out in the last half hour was that he was amazing to talk to. Insightful, kind, and funny.

Cy was very good friends with Katie. In fact, he and Katie had already made New Year's plans, as they did every year when Katie was home and the Packers' schedule put Cy in Green Bay.

Wil hadn't known that. But she liked it.

Even more, she liked realizing that she, herself, would love for Cy Newhouse to become a friend.

In the years since she'd moved back to Green Bay, Wil had grown close to Beanie. She had a big network of hometown people from growing up who were glad to see her or meet her for a drink. She'd had housemates—so many housemates—who had been the usual mix of fantastic and cringe, and a lot of them were still people to grab a meal with or catch up with periodically. Doing her job, she often met people she liked, and she had coworkers she was friendly with. But she, Wil Greene, famously social, hadn't even *tried* to make real friends. Deep friends. Ride-or-die friends.

What's more, it hadn't been on her list.

Yet it turned out *Cy* had been wanting to stand across from her in her living room and let her kiss him.

Wil would have absolutely kissed Cy Newhouse. Before.

The entire last thirty-six hours had felt like no time and endless all at once. Then she was in a car with Katie, being driven to a private hangar at the Green Bay airport while finishing a conversation she'd barely started with Beanie over text in which Beanie was trying to be supportive and not worried while Wil was also trying not to freak out because Katie wasn't herself.

Or, at least, she wasn't the Katie who Wil was familiar with. Maybe this Katie was perfectly herself, and Wil hadn't met her yet. Which was fine. Except the tight feeling in her belly didn't think it was fine. It thought Katie not being herself was a reason to be as worried as Beanie that Wil was flying with Katie to Los Angeles because it was the only way to know if . . .

It was the only way to know what they needed to know.

All of that was a lot to keep up with, and they hadn't even closed the plane door yet. But Wil kept checking in with herself, and except for being worried about Katie not being entirely *Katie* enough, Wil kept discovering she was good. Better than good.

She hadn't felt this *interested* in her own life for so long.

Looking into Cy's pretty blue eyes, Wil smiled. Cy had famously told the press he would leave the NFL when he met his true love, which had earned him the nickname "Cynderella."

"I hate to tell you this, but I don't think I'm your Prince Charming," she told him.

"Damn it." Cy studied Wil's face for a moment. "No, yeah, I think you're right." He put his palm over his heart. "Stings, though. I've been nurturing a serious Wil-You-or-Won't-You crush for ages. But fill me in." Cy leaned forward. "You've known each other and not known each other this whole time? Because if I'd had any idea there was someone out there who made Katie let down her guard this much, I would have played matchmaker so hard."

"We've known each other our whole lives. But parallel." Wil gestured a side-by-side trajectory with her hands. "Then, senior year, something happened."

Cy took Wil's hands and smashed them together. "Something like that?"

Wil laughed. "Then, we didn't really see each other or talk for thirteen years, until last week."

Cy leaned back and crossed his ridiculously long legs. "You two must have had a lot to say your senior year." He held up his hand when Wil started to try to fill in more. "You don't have to. This is the kind of thing I *get*. The media likes to play, but I'm serious. When I find my person, then That. Is. What. I'm. For. I don't want anything else taking first place." He aimed his million-dollar smile at Wil. "So what are you doing now that you've found her?"

"I'm making her take me home with her. I've cashed in all of my vacation, sick, and PTO time at work, but I don't think I'm coming back. To my job, I mean. I couldn't tell you, right now, what LA will be for me in any kind of long term."

"You're scattering her defensive line." Cy nodded. "It's not as deep as she thinks it is. But I think you already know that." He put his big hand on Wil's shoulder, squeezed it, and smiled.

Wil smiled back, but her heart had done a flip. He made it sound simple. He made it sound like the story of Katie and Wil was always going to end the same way.

She hoped so.

The flight attendant, an adorable, auburn-haired white person who had introduced themself as "Mace, nonbinary, they-them," emerged from the cockpit, and Cy waved and began sauntering in their direction. Katie and Angela were sitting together, their heads bent toward each other, looking at pictures on Katie's phone while

Katie told Angela something about her California garden and an avocado tree. Wil watched as Joel Starr leaned down to kiss Angela on the temple and said something quiet in her ear.

Wil felt as though she was mostly handling the reality of Cy Newhouse and Angela Goossens on this plane, but she couldn't quite make herself look straight on at Joel-not-Joe Starr. His celebrity, combined with his extraordinary sandy-haired, full-lipped prettiness, like a young Robert Redford, was proving difficult for Wil to accommodate.

It did help that he kept getting out of his seat to kneel on the floor and talk to Katie's cats inside their cat carriers, poking his long fingers through the grates to pet their tiny faces. Joel was famously an animal lover.

When Almond Butter yowled from her carrier, Joel laughed and withdrew his finger. "All right," he said gently. "I was only being friendly."

"That's Almond Butter," Wil made herself tell him. "She's sixteen, and she's never been on a plane. I couldn't decide if I should sedate her? The vet and I decided no, not unless she started to seem distressed. But I'm a little bit freaking out."

"She's a beautiful cat for sixteen. She looks like she has a lot of years in her still."

"I hope so." Wil looked away for a moment. "I'm supposed to be planning for the end of her life, but I get mad when I try to. My dad got her for me. He died when I was in college."

Joel nodded solemnly. "It's very loving to plan for the golden years of our animals. It helps them feel like they still have a role, even if they don't get around the same way or like the same things." He spoke deliberately, with a beautiful honey-laced Southern accent. "I have a donkey who's quite elderly, Marianne, and she used to act as a guard for a group of goats that lived on a farm in Elmhurst. Marianne has arthritis and can't work like that anymore, but with medicine and a very warm stall, she's comfortable, and she's found that she loves treat puzzles. So I devise new puzzles for her every day and make it seem like it's very important for her to solve them. It means we both have something new to do and something new to learn about ourselves." He glanced at Wil a little bit sideways. While he spoke, he'd been looking at Almond Butter.

Because, Wil understood suddenly, *she* made *him* nervous. "That's an incredibly helpful perspective," she said. "I'm going to give that some thought."

"All right. What does she like?" he asked, eyes back on Almond Butter. "Not having her chin scratched."

Wil cleared her throat against how this conversation was making her tearful and tender and overwhelmed with the goodness of life. "If you hold out your finger, she'll rub against it if she's interested in claiming you as her own."

Wil knelt down next to Joel and showed him, and just like that, Joel Starr, *Joe Starr,* was making friends with Almond Butter, making kissing noises at her, telling her she was a good girl, and looking at Wil with delight.

Wil's heart lurched again. Not because Joel was gorgeous, or for how close she was to him, or because she'd looked over and seen Katie and Angela were sharing one chair, their legs hooked over each other, Angela touching Katie's hair, or because Cy was flirting with Mace so hard that Mace had just reached out to touch the placket on Cy's shirt and Wil realized that the two of them had some kind of history that was pleasant for them both.

Her heart was thudding and skipping because she liked how vulnerability had inveigled itself into new parts of her life since she'd connected with Katie.

And because these were Katie's friends. This was Katie's real life, a tiny slice of what Katie's life was like as *Katie Price, Hollywood Triple Threat*. And Wil *liked* it.

The part of her that was Jasper Greene couldn't be more thrilled to meet and talk to these fascinating new people.

The part of her that was Beanie Greene loved the idea of learning the ins and outs of a completely new way of life, synthesizing everything she learned, and filing it away, ready to deploy when the moment was right.

Mostly, though, it was the most *Wil* part of Wil Greene that loved sitting on the carpeted floor of a luxury jet, talking to Joel Starr about her cat. Because she'd gotten herself to here. Her life had. Her experiences. Her kissing project, even, for how it had taught her to meet new people exactly where they were at.

And Katie. Wil wouldn't be here if it weren't for Katie. It was talking to Katie, *being* with Katie, that had given Wil the gift of all this curiosity about her own life.

All of this hope.

"I hate to break up the party," Mace said, guiding Cy's hand from their waist to their hand and squeezing it. "But if you're not flying to LA, you'll have to say good-bye for now." Mace looked at Cy and winked.

By the time the flight took off, it was dark, with only a slash of sunset in the distance that the plane continuously chased. Katie was quiet once her friends left, and a rule-follower on the plane, and so was seat-belted properly into a wide leather chair next to Wil, obviously lost in her thoughts.

Wil kept putting her fingers on the window where that fading strip of pink and orange light wouldn't quite go, their westerly flight literally carrying them into the past. She imagined that if the plane could fly a little faster, and then even faster than that, it could spin the whole world around until she could hug her dad again.

Or take her back to the last night in the tent by the lake before Katie left for summer stock.

Wil had almost kissed her that night. It was the second time she'd almost kissed Katie, the first time she'd known what she was about to do.

They'd had a golden day together. They took a long swim in the lake as the sun began to set, the pinks and oranges of the sunset making Katie's skin glow, the gathering dark making her teeth flash extra white when she smiled wide at one of Wil's jokes.

A stiff breeze had come up off the lake, and they'd thrown their bodies out of the water, squealing with cold, their feet squishing in the sand mixed with fishy-smelling lake mud right at the shore. They'd sprinted to the outdoor rinsing station to blast the lake off their bodies with freezing water, exaggerating all of their reactions until someone at a campsite yelled into the twilight for them to *shut up, already! Jeez!*

Which had made them laugh more.

They made s'mores over a little spirit stove, too tired to try to figure out how to start a fire with the campfire wood bundle they'd bought at a Kwik Trip on the way, and then they'd collapsed into the tent. Wil could still remember the exact color of the air inside the yellow tent, how it mixed with the deep purple sunset and the cheap camp lantern to make their skin glow blue and the shadows go black.

Their swimsuits had dried, and in the cramped quarters of the tent, they didn't bother to really change, just hiked on their sweatpants and T-shirts and dove into their sleeping bags to talk.

Wil could still see Katie's face through the dim light when she'd turned off the lantern, and all she could hear in that sharp, crystalline, time-stopped moment was Katie's breath and the waves hitting the shore.

She'd known she wanted to. All day. And all day, it had seemed like they'd been one single gyre of energy, snapped together by a look or hand-holding or laughter like they couldn't move an inch out of the spin.

Your hair's gotten so long, she'd said, and she touched it, tracing it over Katie's shoulder with her fingertips until Katie shivered.

Goose bumps, Katie had whispered. She didn't have to whisper. The next campsite couldn't hear them have a conversation over the hum of insects and the lake.

Wil didn't know how long it was like that before Katie said it. *You can.*

She didn't know, either, why that broke the spell—Katie's admission she wanted the kiss, too—but Wil had found herself suddenly unzipping her sleeping bag and putting her arms around Katie, not to kiss her, but to lay her head on her shoulder and squeeze her in a hug even while she wanted to, she still wanted to, but not as much as she wanted something with Katie that would never end.

It had ended anyway.

Gazing out the window of the plane taking her with Katie Price to Los Angeles, it seemed to Wil that every single kiss of her life had been measured against that kiss that didn't happen.

She didn't want to wonder anymore how things might have been different. It wasn't an interesting question.

The interesting question was what kind of life she could make with Katie now.

When they landed, a van was waiting for them, and a driver ready to take on cat carriers and luggage. There weren't any photographers. Katie had said her agent, April, had made the arrangements so they could arrive in the city "without any fanfare," which Wil understood to be code for "without showing up on the celebrity gossip websites four minutes later."

The van traveled up into the Hollywood Hills, past landscaping lights and lights on gates marking the turns, until it pulled into a long, narrow, blond brick drive that widened to something that looked more like an exhibit in an Asian garden than a house, all glints of glass and twisting, miniature trees.

Wil had seen pictures of Katie's home, but they were pictures a mother would take. The pool. Pretty flowers in the yard. Stained glass in a door.

This was different. Dark. Shadows. A hint of glass. Very private and strangely still. When they got out of the van, a coyote yipped in the distance, and Almond Butter complained about it loudly.

Katie had been so quiet during the flight and in the van. But she hadn't let go of Wil—her hand, a loop in her jeans, her knee.

"This is where I live," she said. The front door responded to Katie's fingerprint on a complex security pad. She had Sue's carrier in one hand. Wil carried Almond Butter. There was a light on in the entry hall and flowers on a low table by the door. They smelled amazing. Wil could see straight down the hall, through what looked like it must be the kitchen and dining area, through an open door to the glowing turquoise pool.

The contrast to the incredibly nice basement suite Katie's parents had put in at their home in Green Bay couldn't have been more stark.

Who had Katie or April called to turn on the lights, buy the flowers, and leave the door to the pool invitingly open? There were lights floating in the pool, even, and a pitcher of something that still had condensation beading on its cool surface on a table by the pool with glasses at the ready.

Everything was very beautiful—colored glass and art, natural materials in magical layers that made it feel like they had stepped inside a millionaire's treehouse—beautiful in a way Wil had literally never seen or experienced in someone's home.

And this was Katie's home. Katie from East High School.

"Do you like it?" Katie put the carrier down. She pulled out her phone, tapped it, and it did something to the lights. Everything was suddenly bathed in some kind of perfect, warm-colored, after-dark indoor glow that made them both look like they were in a movie.

Wil almost laughed, and then she saw Katie's face.

It was a real question. Katie wasn't sure.

"Katie, it's objectively the most gorgeous house I've ever seen close up and in person." Katie wrinkled her nose. "But maybe it would be easier if you showed me the parts of it that you want me to notice. I heard you tell Angela you have a hundred-year-old avocado tree. Is this house a hundred years old?"

"Almost!" Katie beamed. "It's from the forties, but it had a big expansion in the fifties and got renovated again in the nineties. They built the conservatory around the avocado tree, or at least that's what the real estate agent told me. Let's get the rest of the cats, and I'll show you. I think Almond Butter will like the conservatory. She can pretend she's in the forest."

Then it was better. Katie showed Wil how the security system worked, they brought the cats inside, and Katie had Wil carry Almond Butter into the living room where there was what she called a "neutral area" that she felt would be a good place to make the introduction between all of the cats.

Sue came over and smelled Almond Butter and went to the credenza with her AAC buttons and said, *Home. Mama. Mama. Home. Cat.* Then she pressed another button that made a "Hmmm?" noise, indicating a question.

Sue approached and smelled Almond Butter again, this time with her tail in the air, until Katie told her, "This cat's name is Almond Butter. Would you like me to make a button for her?"

Sue returned to the credenza. *Yes.*

"Okay, my baby. I will get on that tomorrow, and a button for Wil, too." Katie pushed the buttons, *Tomorrow. Yes. Hmm?*

Yes, Sue pressed. She left the room. Trois, in the meantime, had already smelled Almond Butter all over, rubbed her entire side against Almond Butter's body, and run away, rounding the corner at a high rate of speed and disappearing into another part of the house.

Phil was perched in a window that looked out over the thickest part of the garden, taking in the night view.

Wil held out her hand to Almond Butter, who rubbed her face against Wil's fingers. "She seems good," Wil said. "She's met a lot of cats over the years because of my housemates, and she's always the cat who keeps the peace. But she'll need her heated bed wherever I'll be sleeping."

Wil glanced at Katie, her belly deciding at that moment to flip over and then make everything in her body ache.

"Come here," Katie said.

Wil stood, and Katie pulled Wil close. Her cheeks were flushed. There was still a mark on one of them where the seat belt in the van had pressed in when she'd used it like a pillow.

"Hi," Wil whispered. She reached out and put her hand at Katie's waist.

"Hi." Katie took a deep breath. "I have three guest rooms, Wil. All of them are ready, but I think if you took one of them I would"—Katie laughed—"I think I'd just invite myself in, probably half an hour after you went to bed. But I am a grown woman? You can have your own space. If you want."

Wil put her hand against the side of Katie's neck. Under her jaw. She rubbed Katie's jaw with her thumb. Katie closed her eyes, because it wasn't a neutral place to touch someone. It wasn't where your friend would touch you. It wasn't *how* a friend would touch you.

It was a touch that asked permission for something else.

When Katie opened her eyes, she took a quiet breath and laced her legs between Wil's so that she was close enough for Wil to feel her breath against her lips. Wil put her other hand on the other side of Katie's neck, feeling the goose bumps break out under her fingertips.

"I've seen you do this before," Katie said, soft. "On your videos. I've seen you hold someone like this."

Wil smiled. "Usually only if I'm pretty into them."

"I got that impression," Katie said. "Watching the videos. I always wanted to be the one you kissed who you held like this before you did it. Those kisses usually got pretty . . ."

"Interesting?"

"No. I mean, sure. But I was going to say 'hot.' Like, very, extremely, horny hot."

"Can I kiss you, Katie?" Wil moved her hands gently, her fingers to Katie's nape, her thumbs over her earlobes. Because she was done. Done with their bet, which had only been an excuse for them to get close to each other anyway, and done kissing everyone she'd kissed since Katie got famous but not kissing Katie.

"You can," Katie said.

Wil's heart stopped.

Then Katie reached up and grabbed onto Wil's wrists to pull her the last half inch to her mouth, and Wil was kissing Katie, or Katie was kissing Wil, but either way, they both moaned at the same time like they'd been waiting thirteen years and seven days to kiss—which they had, exactly that long, and longer. Katie's mouth was so soft, and they kissed softly, just kisses, just three times, and then Katie was sucking Wil's bottom lip into her mouth and Wil was tasting her, and Katie let go of Wil's wrists so she could slide her hands up under Wil's shirt, making her shiver when Katie dragged her nails up her sides.

It had been so long, so *long* since Wil had kissed someone and it felt like this. Wil had felt tender and turned on and interested and surprised and hot and sexy when she'd kissed people for her channel, but she hadn't felt those things like they were for *her*, like she was taking something for herself, getting herself off and getting touched and letting go all the way, letting herself go and trusting that who she was kissing wanted her to let go and wanted to let go, too.

It was so fucking *hot*.

Wil was touching Katie everywhere now. Everywhere she had always wondered about. Her hips, then over her breasts, which were naked under her loose shirt. Wil was so wet, then wetter when her thumb against Katie's nipple made them both gasp into each other's mouths and made Katie move to Wil's neck, where her kissing slowed down and got very explicit just as she reached up and unhooked Wil's bra.

"God," Wil breathed, and laughed. "I'm actually dying, Katie."

"Not yet." Katie kissed Wil's throat and slid her hands under Wil's loosened bra to touch the sides of her breasts, which made Wil grab at Katie with no specific intent other than to prevent herself from puddling to the floor, broken by unmuted lust. "Don't die yet."

"Okay, but you're going to have to take me to a second location," Wil said. "I can't maintain any posture that's not helping me put all of my concentration on coming for the next two hundred years."

Katie laughed. "It worked! I am a kissing genius. That's good, because I didn't love the plan where I snuck into your bedroom."

But there was something in Katie's expression, something eloquent that made Wil think about the fact that Katie hadn't had partnered intimacy in a very long time, and she was also a very physical, and definitely sexual, person. What they had already done, on the prim HomeGoods love seat in Diana and Craig's basement, was one of the dirtiest things Wil had ever gotten herself into, and they had been fully clothed, and no tongues had been involved.

Wil might not actually *survive* making love with Katie Price.

Katie moved in again, and Wil kissed her. Kissed her more, let Katie crumple the front of Wil's shirt in her hand, which made Wil clench so hard that she almost touched herself, putting pressure where she needed it, but she didn't. She wanted to see what would happen if she waited.

Katie stepped away just a little and took Wil's hand. "Come on."

Wil followed her down the hallway, catching her breath.

Reminding herself of everything she knew about Katie, and had always known, and leaving room for what she didn't.

Chapter Sixteen

When Wil put her hands against Katie's neck, it was the most exciting thing that had ever happened to Katie in her entire life, and Katie's life was a case study in excitement.

She'd watched Wil Greene kiss a lot of people—watched carefully, watched rapturously, watched enviously. The kisses had turned her on or made her laugh or made her cry. She had learned what Wil did to make herself safe, to encourage the other person, to reassure them, and sometimes, every once in a while, to let them know she wanted them.

With her hands gently against the sides of their necks.

Katie didn't know why it *surprised* her so much that Wil wanted her, and wanted her so badly. She was surprised, though. Wil's hands had been shaking a little, but she'd been smiling at Katie with her indecent, terrible, ruthlessly hot mouth, and then surprise whooshed up through Katie's body and she thought, *it's me, it's me, it's me.* That's what she'd tried to give back to Wil in her first kisses—*it's you, it's you, it's you*—until everything started to fray at the edges and a pulse hit her down low so hard, she couldn't breathe.

Until she had one hand driven into Wil's hair and the other

clamped onto the T-shirt at her waist and was pulling her in the direction of her bedroom, Wil's tongue rubbing against hers, both of them making noises that Katie marveled at because these were *their* voices, they sounded like themselves gasping and moaning, but also like an entirely new thing they were making together.

"This is my room." Katie pulled Wil to the bed and sat down on the edge of the mattress, kissing Wil's neck and her jaw before leaning over to find the switch for the lights beneath the floating shelves that gave the room a romantic glow.

In the light, she looked at Wil. Her kisses had swollen Wil's lip line into a gloriously pink mess without definition, and her hands had destroyed Wil's hair like they'd been to bed already.

God. How long had she wanted to see what she could do to Wil Greene? To have the attention of Wil's brain and her body and her racing heart?

How long could she have this? She'd already let it go once, before it had even started.

"There aren't any windows." Wil was looking around, her eyes flicking from the textured cream duvet to the array of shelves around the bed to the open doorway, but she had kept the same grip on Katie's hip that she'd managed as they'd gotten to the bed, and her voice was husky and impatient.

"They're up there."

Katie pointed until Wil's gaze found the ring of clerestory windows and the skylights set into the ceiling. "For privacy?"

Katie nodded and leaned close to Wil. It was so quiet in the house. In Green Bay, there had always been the Bronco's engine or the sounds of her parents' footsteps and activities above them. Here, she had Wil to herself, which had always been what she wanted. "And because sometimes I have to sleep at odd hours. There are motorized blackout blinds that can turn the room into a cave, and, like, this white noise machine so I can make it sound like I've been tossed up on a beach in the blackness, which is kind of amazing or extremely annoying, depending on my mood."

Katie wasn't tracking her own words. Wil's eyes on her face had gone dark blue and hot. The pulse between Katie's legs got so insistent, she was pretty sure she was seconds away from her clothes rending themselves from her body and fluttering to the floor, charred at the edges.

Wil's indulgent smile told Katie she had not failed to notice how fast Katie was talking or how many words she was making about nothing. "What's your mood right now?"

Wil sounded so calm. That was how she got, Katie knew, when things were overwhelming. She was going to be an alarming attorney.

"I feel . . . excited?" She showed Wil her trembling hands and laughed. "Maybe a little nervous? I haven't . . ." Katie looked away for a moment, trying to think how to capture the feeling in words.

It wasn't about how long it had been since she'd had sex. She'd already had sex with Wil in a way that very much counted to her, and hugging Wil in the Bronco counted, and watching the kissing video with her, and watching Wil's videos on her own while she was thinking about Wil.

Katie knew her own body and what she liked. Her life had not lacked sensual pleasure or intimacy with other people, even if she hadn't been sexually intimate with anyone but Wil since Ben. She wasn't afraid of Wil's experiences or hung up on worrying she lacked them.

It wasn't about Wil's gender or sexuality, either, some perceived difference between man-sex and woman-sex that didn't feel remotely real or important to Katie inside her body.

"It's the knowing," she said, squeezing Wil's hands. "Sometimes I get like this in my trailer on set when I'm about to do a scene and I *know* what it's going to ask of me and what it's going to give me. I know I'm ready for it, because I can feel that inside my body, and I'm intensely looking forward to it. But I'm also afraid. Because I know it's going to roll through me and use me and knock me over like a wave. And because, maybe, I know that's what I'm for. It's why I'm here. Why I'm alive."

She looked at Wil's blond eyelashes and her pale hair swooping down over her forehead, almost covering one of her blue eyes. Her mouth was so serious. Wil's serious listening face. Then she smiled, and it made Katie want to laugh because she knew this smile, too.

This was how Wil smiled when she was pleased with whatever had just been dealt to her.

"Oh, no," Katie said. "I mean, I think I just made it sound like it's my life's purpose to have sex with you." A snort-laugh escaped her, and she covered her mouth with the back of her hand. "Which sort of feels true at this moment, but is probably not the coolest thing I've ever said."

Wil laughed, too, but then she slid her hands up Katie's thighs with enough firm pressure and intent that Katie's eyelids began to feel heavy. "Can you do something for me?"

"Probably, yes, I will do whatever you ask me to do."

As soon as she said it, Katie knew it was true, and it was something she could hang on to.

She didn't know what would happen next. There were a lot of things, a *lot,* that she hadn't been able to keep herself from worrying about, including her mother's reaction to the news that Katie had decided to miss Christmas and take Wil home to Los Angeles with her, which was not the reaction Katie had been hoping for, and the way April's face had looked when Katie told her about Wil, and everything, really, about the future.

But she would probably do whatever Wil asked her to. Katie knew that.

She knew what it meant.

"Can you keep talking to me?" Wil asked. "Tell me what you like. Tell me what you want. I don't want to lose track of you."

"I'm good at talking." Katie put her shaky hands on Wil's shoulders. "I want you to take off your shirt."

Katie had been thinking of Wil in her bed in Wisconsin, the pink and red flowery sheets that she wouldn't have guessed Wil would have, the color matching her cheeks. Lying down in Wil's bed to tell her about Ben and eat ice cream sandwiches, with Wil's T-shirt riding up and her full breasts spilling from that black bra underneath, Katie had discovered another patch of freckles, secret freckles between her breasts, and she'd looped and looped on kissing them and on touching Wil's nipples, imagining them almost as pale as her skin.

Katie had liked everything about how soft Wil looked, seeing her hidden body at the same time as her beautiful, familiar face, and how . . . It was more a feeling. Almost an aggressive one, but velvety and big inside of her. Katie was so comfortable with bodies, with nudity, with thinking about how everyone around her was using their body and using her own body as a way to tell stories, that the clumsy and obsessive lust she felt about Wil and about her body was completely delicious and the right amount of scary.

Wil took off her shirt, this one a long-sleeved T-shirt with raw hems where a collar and cuffs should be. Tight and black. As she pulled it off, the warm, dark vanilla, powdery Wil smell of her body, the wintergreen of her breathing out, her bra still unhooked and loose at her sides, the way her belly curved down toward her belt—Katie caught herself trying to record and memorize all of it, as though this were a video she would only let herself watch once.

"It's off." Wil smiled. She shrugged forward and out of the bra. It was black, too. There was a flush spreading over Wil's chest. Katie reached up and traced it, feeling the heat of Wil's body against her palms, and Wil closed her eyes. "What else?"

"I don't want this to only happen once," Katie said. "What if we don't get to do everything I want to do? That's too much pressure. I can't take it." Whatever was making her spine white-hot and everything ache deliciously was ferocious inside of her.

"Katie Kat," Wil said. "Even if we don't do anything but this right now, we'll get to whatever we want to do." She unbuckled her sturdy belt, and the thick leather running through the brass buckle was Katie's new favorite sound.

"It's just that your body is like . . . you know Bay Beach?"

Wil laughed, her zipper down. Katie noted with interest that the edge of the elastic of her panties was also black. The low light caught a shadow from her belly button to that elastic that Katie wanted her mouth on. "Yes. I know Bay Beach."

Bay Beach was an amusement park on the shore of Lake Michigan that was owned and operated by the City of Green Bay. Most of the rides cost one or two twenty-five-cent tickets, and there was a big Ferris wheel and an old-fashioned wooden roller coaster whose claim to fame was that it had been Elvis Presley's favorite.

Katie had a lot of feelings about Bay Beach.

"Remember the very first time you went on your own, and your parents got you an extremely fat amount of tickets and told you to have at it—" Katie swallowed as Wil leaned over, her breasts pressed against her thighs, her face still looking up at Katie while she pulled off her short boots and then her socks.

Wil's toenails matched her manicure. It was devastating.

"I remember." Wil didn't take her eyes from Katie's while she shimmied out of those extremely tight jeans. So *much* happened to Wil's body when she shimmied.

Katie laughed, mostly at herself, as Wil slid close to Katie in only those extremely tiny black panties. "So many tickets that you kept folding and refolding them to figure out how they felt the best between your fingers and in your pocket, and your parents were just going to sit on a bench and have coffee, and it felt so bad and incredible and dangerous and filthy and . . ."

Wil laughed against Katie's neck. "Filthy, huh?'"

"Filthy," Katie repeated. "Completely. There were too many choices, all of them could be yours, you would never run out of tickets, you were tall enough for every ride."

"Okay." Wil's thighs were a roller coaster, a Viking ship swing, a gravity spinner, dusted everywhere with pale blond hair. "Filthy Bay Beach."

"That's what this is, right here. I have so many tickets to spend on your incredibly filthy amusement-park body, I might lose it."

Wil put her hands on Katie's shoulders and pushed her down, then crawled over top of her and backed her up the mattress while Katie wiggled and squealed. "I'm going to undress you."

"Yes. Do that. Take a lot of time over it. Or don't. I can't decide. There are just two pieces of clothing. It makes me wish I'd invested in some kind of high-necked, multilayered Victorian costume." Katie was certain she'd never been this wet in her entire life. She had never been this turned on, of that she was sure. She'd only had a very theoretical idea of what turned on even was until this moment.

"Ready?" Wil kissed Katie's neck with a very satisfying amount of tongue.

"I am the perfect amount of ready and not ready." Katie said this with more confidence than she'd had before. She *did* know her own body, her own heart. She *did* have a lot of experience with letting herself feel, letting emotion and sensation overtake her.

Then she took a look at what happened to Wil's body on her hands and knees, and her hips lifted up, practically involuntarily, because she was one giant, throbbing ache from the tops of her knees to deep inside, where she felt luxuriously slippery and hot. She pulled off her own T-shirt.

"God," Wil said, and got closer, holding herself up on her forearms, pressing their breasts together, which made both of them
make a good noise. "I'm just going to kiss you for a minute."

"Two minutes," Katie said.

Wil laughed, and then she was kissing Katie, her weight pressing down, and Katie soaked in Wil's taste and her heat and her
mouth, letting her hands roam over Wil's silky back, the shapes
of her shoulders, Katie's knee coming up so she could rock against
Wil's hard thigh over and over again.

Katie fisted her hands in Wil's hair, breathing hard, her clit
starting to pinch and start up the climbing, climbing sensations.
"Hold up."

"Yes." Wil was panting, too.

"I inadvertently got close."

"Was it inadvertent?" Wil asked. "Because I feel like I was
helping make something happen."

"You were." Katie palmed one of Wil's breasts. "Oh, fuck.
That just made it worse. Don't move."

"Don't move what?" Wil kissed her forehead. "Can we get
your pants off?"

"Yes." Katie maneuvered herself to the top of the bed so she
had a pillow behind her head and skimmed off her leggings, then
immediately had to press her thighs together tight because she
couldn't stand the look on Wil's face. It was too promising for her
almost-come to handle. "Your panties, too."

Wil reached down and pushed them off. "Can I touch you?"
She put her hand on Katie's thigh.

"Yes." Katie moved onto her side, looking at Wil all over. Her
blond hardly darkened, not between her legs, not over her shins,
not under her arms. It made Katie want to slide all over this fucking golden bear she'd managed to get into bed with her.

"What are you thinking?" Wil said this while stroking the

back of her hand over Katie's belly, her hip bones, her voice betraying amusement so that Katie knew she'd been caught up in her thoughts in a way that was obvious to Wil.

Katie told her.

Wil laughed. "Oh my God, Katie."

"Well. I mean, I'm lasered. I have been for years because it's just easier with the costumes and stylists. And so then I get thoughts like that, and I don't even know. I'm a babe in the woods, Wil. I am a raw sex nerve that you have made with your body. Show me mercy."

Wil did not. She moved closer and put her hand between Katie's legs, her fingers very explicit, suddenly, and terrible in their knowledge. Katie had to hang onto the duvet and bite her lip for dear life, and she made a noise anyway that made Wil laugh, so Katie had no choice but to grab her by the back of her neck and get serious about kissing her for long minutes while she pressed against Wil's fingers and died.

"Do that forever," she said. "Do that until I come, I don't even care anymore." They were both on their sides. She lifted her knee to give Wil better access, and Wil hooked Katie's leg over her hip, moving close enough to press against Katie everywhere.

"Is that what you want?"

"It's one of the things I want." Wil slid her fingers between Katie's legs, skating over every sensitive place, finding a rhythm. Katie lowered her head and licked Wil's pebbled nipple. "But I want *you* to come, too, so you're going to have to figure out the mechanics on that." She stroked between Wil's legs experimentally, breaking out in goose bumps when she found her wet.

Wil reached down, cruelly taking her fingers away from Katie, and slid her hand over where Katie was touching Wil. "Put these two together, and press . . . there. God, *God,* exactly like that, and then when I'm close, go inside me if you want. You can't do it too hard." Wil's voice was somewhere between a whisper and gravel, distracted.

Katie groaned. That was too good, hearing Wil suffering as much as she was, feeling her at the same time, and Wil's hand returned to Katie, touching her confidently, soft, but in a way that made everything buck and clench, but then Wil came back with only the heel of her hand against her, and it was exactly right.

"Fuck against me like that," Wil whispered, kissing her. "Do you like anything inside when you get close?"

"I am close. I have been close since the dawn of time." Katie was already moving against Wil's hand. "Also, yes. Sometimes. Now is sometimes. But then kiss me. Kiss me and kiss me."

Wil did, and Katie felt her entire center meld into Wil, just the way she liked it when she was connecting with someone but in a way it had never, ever been when she'd done this. She let her fingers follow Wil's hips and gasps, and she got herself kissed, so kissed, while Wil pressed with her hand and slid so cleverly inside of her with fingers.

It didn't take long. It took forever. Katie had no idea, but if it stopped, she was going to be angry, or so happy, who knew?

She hadn't known before. She was so glad to know, finally, about *this*.

Then Wil bit her bottom lip, and everything got hot under Katie's fingers. She slid down, inside, and *oh*. She'd had no idea how much she was going to like that, love that, being inside Wil, feeling her get tighter and tighter, and then Wil was inside her, and Katie pressed her thighs together to keep her there.

It felt like she came for a long time. She knew she was saying Wil's name. At least once, her whole name, including middle, but there was nothing to do because the sound of Wil coming against her neck, on her hand, while Wil's fingers were inside her, was the best thing Katie had ever heard.

The best thing she'd ever felt.

Wil was the best thing.

"Katie," Wil breathed. "Are you . . ."

"We live here now," Katie panted. She put her hands on Wil's waist and dug her fingers in so Wil would know she was serious. "In this bed. Everyone will have to adjust their own insurance, do their own lawyering, and hire someone else for their *Sarah, Plain and Tall* remake set in 1980s Brooklyn." Katie pushed the damp hair away from Wil's neck and kissed her.

Kissing her. So easy.

"I really liked that one," Wil whispered. "I cried for hours."

"Everyone does." Katie didn't know if she was sleepy or spinning or if this was just what it felt like when you wrenched open your heart. "That story is a nuclear explosion of longing and miserable love." She kissed Wil's neck again.

"Katie." Wil pulled back and looked at her, her face a little bit serious.

"Yeah." Katie cleared her throat against some feelings that were there—not exactly, *exactly* a nuclear explosion of longing and miserable love, but something she was afraid could end up in that neighborhood.

She didn't want to be afraid. This was Wil. It would be okay. It would. Because it *was* Wil, and when she was with Wil, she was Katelyn Rose Price. She was Katie Kat. They had both decided on this together—for Wil to be here, dipping her beautiful manicured toes into Katie's life, so that Wil could learn what it was like, and so that Katie could . . . could find out. Could know.

But she already knew.

"I have to settle Almond Butter in and sleep," Wil said. "I'll stay here with you. But in the morning, can we talk more about me here? In Los Angeles? I'm glad to be with you. Don't look like that.

I've been meaning to talk to you all day about how you're doing and what you've been thinking about. But . . ."

"I know." Katie slowly rolled over and looked at the ceiling's raw wood beams, the dark glass. She watched Wil lean over the edge of the bed and realized she was reaching for her shirt.

"No. Don't. Hold on." Katie got up, the room too cool against her skin and too bereft of Wil, and pressed the panel in the wall that opened her closet door. She turned the lights on in the dressing room to grab a robe for Wil and her favorite jersey nightshirt for herself. "For you."

Wil belted the robe on and held her arms out. "Come here."

Katie took the hug. "Can I just say a little bit? So I don't freak out?"

"Yes. Follow me around while I deal with Almond Butter."

Katie did. She followed Wil to the living room and watched her squat down beside her beautiful geriatric cat and scratch her neck. She thought about Wil on the plane. She'd been cautious at first, but then she'd relaxed and laughed and talked with Cy.

Katie thought of how Wil had looked sitting next to Joel by the cat carriers, listening to Joel say more words in a row than Katie had ever managed to pry out of the man, even though she'd met him several times because he was Cy's best friend.

She thought about Wil in her robe, Wil in her house, Wil in her bed, and it felt so completely, perfectly *possible* that Katie didn't know what to say, after all.

It was hard to know what was right for yourself. She'd gone to hundreds of therapy sessions to learn how to figure that out—how to identify her feelings and know what to do to help herself feel them and make choices.

But Katie had never learned how to know what was right for someone else.

Their luggage was in the entryway where the person who drove the van had unloaded and left it. Wil found the big duffel bag where she'd packed everything for Almond Butter. She located Almond Butter's cat bed and heat pad and food dish and a bag of special cat food.

It would be Christmas in three days. Katie had spent Christmas a lot of different places, a lot of different ways. She'd thought she would be spending it in Wisconsin this year, so she hadn't asked for her decorations to be brought out of storage.

"Have you ever spent Christmas away from home?" she asked.

Wil turned to look at her. "No. But I've spent Christmases feeling like my home was away from me."

Katie swallowed over a sudden burn of tears.

She should've been there. Where had she been that first Christmas Wil and Beanie spent without Jasper? On set? Overwarm, her feet rubbed raw from her heels at an industry party that was super important to be seen at because of her next project? Hosting a charity event? She would've been twenty-two. Four years into her career, a year since she'd left Ben. It would have been her first Christmas since she'd arrived here that she'd spent *without* Ben.

She remembered. She'd fought with her mom at Thanksgiving in Green Bay and then flown to Iceland for the location shoot. She'd stayed through Christmas, by herself in a condo with a view of a cliff and the sea, even though she didn't have to. She could've gone home. But she hadn't, because she was mad at her mom, and mad that she didn't know what Christmas meant to her anymore.

If she'd gone to Green Bay, she would've heard how hard a time Wil and Beanie were having, and she would've seen them, even if it was only to be kind. And she would have realized soon enough, probably on the way over to their house, that all she wanted was Wil.

Home. That was what Christmas was supposed to mean.

Wil had been her home, or she'd almost been. They'd almost been that for each other, but they were still children, with only the experiences of children, and no one to tell them what they were about to lose.

Katie stepped close and touched her forehead to Wil's. "The good news is that we can do absolutely anything you want. You want a tree, we can have a tree. You want to drive out to the desert and lay on a blanket under the stars? That is an option. Beach bonfire Christmas. You name it."

Wil smiled. She slid her hand up and pressed it against Katie's sternum. "I like the idea I'll spend Christmas with you." Wil pulled away and kissed Katie on the mouth, just a short kiss. But it was an *I like you* kiss, and maybe that was the best one Katie had gotten so far. "Show me where to plug this in, okay? Your bedroom walls are mysteriously smooth."

Katie led her back to the bedroom and showed her how the outlets were hidden. Wil set up Almond Butter's cat bed and put out a dish with her nighttime snack after checking to be sure Katie's cats wouldn't get into it.

I love you. That was what Katie really wanted to say. *The part of me that loves you has always loved you. I feel like it just keeps getting bigger, and pretty soon it will be all of me, all of me will love you for always, and I want you here with me for the rest of my life.*

Katie couldn't say any of that.

Not when April had all but secreted them to LA, when her mom had texted while they were in the car from the airport that the media still thought Katie was in Green Bay, when Katie knew that April had already spoken with Alison about casting and scheduled three other money meetings.

Katie had lived for so long with the feeling that she had to do one more thing and do it just right, do it to win the next thing, just so that the world would tolerate her fame another year, and then another. It scared her to try to imagine what it would take to spend another run of years like that with someone else. It made her feel like she would be sure to hurt them. Sure to hurt.

That was what her mother had said—lovingly, sadly—when Katie told her she would be taking Wil to Los Angeles for Christmas.

I love you both, and I don't want you to be hurt.

Hurt was everything Katie had worked so hard to never feel again, and definitely not to do to another person.

To Wil, who was—who was *her person.*

"You're sleeping in here with me, then?" Katie tried to make this sound casual, but her talents failed her, and it came out more like, *You are sleeping in here with me or I will throw myself against the guest room door like a cat shut out of the bathroom.*

Wil had stood up from petting her cat and Trois, because Trois had shoved herself into Almond Butter's bed, and now Almond Butter was grooming Trois's head.

"Of course." Wil laughed, which meant Katie had sounded exactly as demanding as she thought she had.

"Good. Okay. Are you hungry?"

Wil laughed. "You saw how much I ate on the plane, right?"

"It was barely anything. I don't want you to be hungry, even a little. I can have anything delivered you want. Korean barbeque? Tacos? Caramel corn?"

"Katie." Wil put her arms around her. "I think you need to get into bed with me."

Katie closed her eyes. "Was I too impulsive, bringing you here? I don't know."

"I invited myself here, if you'll remember." Wil took off her robe and climbed into the bed. It was extremely distracting. Katie hadn't gotten a good enough look at Wil's ass before, and Jesus Christ, it was the ass to end all asses, like an actual peach emoji, including the flushed color. Wil had two big dimples in her lower back where the swell of her backside started up. Katie was mesmerized.

"Are you staring at my butt?" Wil climbed in on Katie's usual side, but that was okay, because maybe Katie's imprint would soak into Wil's body and cast a spell on her.

"How am I supposed to stop myself?" Katie slid into the unfamiliar other side of the bed. "I'm big spoon. You have to let me, because I want to hold all of your deliciousness in my arms, and also when *I* am spooned, I feel like I'm suffocating."

It was the first time Katie had overlapped her experience of being with Ben with being with Wil. It made her stomach drop a little, realizing how much there might be in front of her for her and Wil to navigate, to learn, to work out.

And what if it didn't work out? The lessons she'd learned being with Ben were such hard ones.

But Wil just laughed, a low rumble that sounded to Katie like being liked, and she let Katie wrap herself around her from behind. Wil's skin was warm. Katie put every one of her limbs around her, aroused all over again.

Wil fell asleep first, and as soon as she did, Almond Butter hopped up on the bed and made biscuits on Wil's pillow until she was satisfied, then curled around Wil's head. Trois came up next, and then Phil, confused to find a new person in the bed but happy to make his usual cat circle with Sue at the foot of the bed.

Katie reached for her remote and turned on the white noise machine with the timer. She just wanted an hour of the ocean. She could be a castaway with Wil and their four cats curled up around her. She could pretend they were alone here in the big dark world, with only the basic things to figure out.

She fell asleep wondering if she knew enough to build the life she wanted.

Chapter Seventeen

Wil woke up like she usually did, with Almond Butter snoring in her face, except when she reached up to gently move her away from the top of her head, it wasn't Almond Butter snoring in her face.

It was Katie.

Katie Price, who had ninety-five million followers on Twitter, an Oscar, an armful of Golden Globes, a shelf of Emmys and SAG Awards, and a Tony nomination, slept with her mouth open, sawing logs like she was building a cabin.

Which, Wil remembered, she always had. Why would she have stopped?

Katie's arms and legs were still wrapped around Wil, and Wil wanted nothing more than to kiss her awake and touch her everywhere, taste her everywhere, but even in the dim light from the clerestory it was obvious there were purple smudges under Katie's eyes, and her snores were long and slow.

Katie should sleep more if she could.

And Wil would be happy to be Katie's sleep buddy, except that she was still on Green Bay time, and it was well past the hour she needed to get up and pee.

Wil extricated herself one limb at a time, ultimately swapping her warm pillow for her body in Katie's arms as she scooted away, pausing between each removal so Katie's breathing could slow down into deep sleep again.

Katie's robe was on the nightstand. Wil belted it on. She knew that Katie's room had an en suite through the walk-in closet, but she couldn't figure out how to open the invisible door. She decided to creep down the hall to where she'd passed a powder room the night before.

All four cats thumped off the bed one by one and followed her out of the room. They were waiting outside the bathroom door when Wil finished, looking like a jury box, and then she was their parade leader into the kitchen, where Katie's cats lined up where Wil assumed they must have their breakfast. They looked at Almond Butter with terrible envy, since she was already placidly crunching her special older cat food in the spot Wil had set up last night beside the floor-to-ceiling windows that had a view of the pool.

Sue meowed mournfully, and Phil and Trois followed suit.

"Okay, niblets," Wil whispered. "Give me a minute."

They watched her open and close smooth wood cabinets with a grain that looked expensive and rare until she found one full of different kinds of cat food and treats organized into clever trays and baskets. She couldn't locate cat dishes, but she divided up the breakfasts onto the small plates she did find, trying not to think about how she might have just served the cats breakfast on appetizer plates that cost more, each, than the Le Creuset Dutch oven Wil had splurged on recently, feeling full of herself and grown up.

She opened the refrigerator that showed her what was inside of it on a big digital display, got out a fancy flavored water, and nearly drained it, standing in the kitchen while the cats ate.

Katie.

God. Wil hadn't counted on . . . She didn't know how she ever could have been prepared for that. Kissing Katie. Her body, the way she moved, the way she moaned. Her hands trembling. Her eyes on Wil, staying right on her the way they always did, like there was nothing else to look at in the world.

They'd both been nervous, or, if not nervous, they'd both been completely overspilling with a lot of different kinds of feelings.

Wil hadn't felt that much of any kind of emotion since she lost her dad, and grief was so opaque and obliterating. It had dulled all of her senses and left her with one sharp, keening loss to stare at and stare at until she forgot there was anything else to look at or to feel.

The grief had been so preoccupying and steady, there was a way it stood in for her dad. She'd relied on it to keep her place, to keep her weighted to the earth, even as that was the only thing it did.

But how she'd felt kissing Katie, touching her, making love to her, was overflowing the way something fizzy overflowed. It was champagne. It was effervescent, with lots of transparent colors, with Katie's deep blue eyes and blondy-brown hair and her skin washed over with pale flushes. None of Wil's feelings had stayed put. She'd felt hot and sexy, then tender and shy, and then like she wanted to hold Katie down and suggest dark things they could do together right before they told each other everything in their hearts.

When everything was love.

When everything was what *in love* felt like.

When everything was loving Katie.

Wil loved Katie.

Loving Katie was easy.

It was everything *else* that Wil didn't know how to do yet. Now, all by herself, it was a little intimidating to stand here in Katie's beautiful, almost unreal house. The light wasn't the same light they had in Green Bay in December, and the fact that it was dancing over the water in the pool meant Wil wasn't in the Midwest anymore.

Her fear felt overfull, like a bowl she held in both hands that she had to be careful not to spill. Wil had to keep reminding herself that she'd been afraid before. Last night, falling asleep, she'd told herself that in the past, when she'd done things that scared her, they often ended up being the things that mattered most.

She was glad for the cats. They helped.

She walked across a huge space, the floor a dark, swirly cork that was utterly silent to walk on, to a rough-edged wooden table. There was a laptop at one end, a little arrangement of succulents in a tabletop garden, and a row of *Los Angeles Times* newspapers starting the day Katie left for Wisconsin.

Katie read the paper.

That was funny. Craig, Katie's dad, had a big ritual around the newspaper. He got the Green Bay paper and read the whole thing every morning with his breakfast, and on the weekend he went to the cigar shop and newsstand, Bosse's, to buy a copy of the Sunday edition.

Wil hadn't known that Katie read the paper, but it made sense. She liked her little routines, her breakfast burritos and morning yoga. In high school, she'd carried a case in her backpack that contained her phone, six perfectly sharpened number-two pencils, a black pen, a red pen, a blue pen, and an immaculate pink eraser.

Wil had always liked learning Katie's little routines. She'd bought the Twizzlers and the pretzels, she'd memorized the routes Katie liked to take between classes so she could walk with Katie during passing period, and even in the years she didn't know Katie, she'd seen all of her movies, watched her at the awards shows, and followed her press.

It wasn't going to be difficult for Wil to learn about Katie's life in Hollywood. It was going to be a pleasure.

Then she realized her cheeks were flaming hot, because her brain had fed Katie's cats and seen her newspapers and then wandered off, whistling, as though this was it. Her and Katie.

She took a deep breath. One thing at a time. The newspaper. Then, the three gazillion things before her and happily ever after.

Wil padded to the entryway. In the daylight, it was filled with a rainbow of different colors of light from the stained glass. The entry was a huge wooden door that was hinged to swing from the middle, and Katie had already shown her how to arm and disarm the alarm system, so Wil disarmed it and stepped outside.

It had to be in the high sixties and sunny. She could definitely get into that after thirty Wisconsin winters.

The wide part of the blond brick driveway where the van had parked last night was shaped like a giant kidney bean, surrounded with beautiful landscaping that set off the house like it was jewelry made of glass, wood, and color. She didn't see the paper anywhere on this part of the drive, so she made sure her robe was belted, then padded down the narrow part that came up from the street toward the wrought-iron gate at the bottom. She wasn't worried anyone would see her. The drive was long, and the landscaping, rock walls, and fencing created a secluded space.

The bricks were warm, and there were so many different kinds of flowers and plants to look at that she didn't notice the tight group of men clustered around one of the brick pillars of the gate at the bottom of the drive until it was too late.

"Wil! Wil! Wil Greene! Are you involved with Katie?! Wil! Did you spend the night? Are you—"

The shouts and the sounds from them were awful. They made Wil heat from the bottom up, made her feel completely naked, humiliated, like she had broken something expensive and everyone was looking at her.

She turned around and walked back up the drive, the photographers shouting, and as soon as they were out of sight, she ran to the door, shaking, unable at first to figure out how it opened until she remembered Katie had said that when the front door shut behind you, the alarm rearmed. She went to the display, but it didn't know her. It didn't know her fingerprint.

She could still hear them shouting.

She had to push the option to alert the homeowner. She heard the small electronic tick of cameras from the security system training on her. All she could think of was Katie, warm in her bed, sleeping, oblivious, her arms wrapped around a pillow she thought was Wil, getting some kind of alert and seeing Wil on the cameras in front of her house in nothing but a short robe, in *obviously* nothing but a short robe, panicking and trying to get inside.

Wil felt terrible.

The lock clicked, and Katie pulled the door open. When she'd made it through, Katie opened her arms. "Shh. Shh, it's okay. Good morning, sweet baby."

"I was trying to get you the paper." Wil's throat felt raw.

Katie squeezed Wil. "Oh, never change, you ridiculous Wisconsin dad. Were there a lot of them?"

"So many. Are they there every day?"

"Most days. At least a couple of them." All of the concern in Katie's face was for Wil—or, at least, that was how it seemed. But underneath, there was something Wil didn't like, something that made her think at least a small part of Katie was *acting* right now. "If there were a lot, that must mean either they were covering their bases, given everything going on, or someone tipped them off."

Katie said this more to herself than to Wil.

"How bad is this going to be?" Wil asked. "Am I going to be on the front of grocery store tabloids in this robe?" She glanced down. "Do I look good in this robe?"

"You look good in everything. Look at your tits. They're

outrageous. If I had tits like that, I would never wear clothes at all. I'd just parade about naked all the time. But to answer your first question, I don't know. You *will* be on the internet. Whether or not you make it to print tabloids depends on what is most interesting between now and when they go to print."

Yes. Katie was definitely acting, or at least, smoothing. More than likely, she was doing it *for* Wil, trying to minimize whatever ripples or tidal waves what Wil had just done was going to create for her.

Wil's concern from yesterday rose up from her heart, tightening her throat. She could appreciate that Katie was a kind person. This was a kind decision. A little bit, though, it would've *helped* her to know how Katie really felt.

"Look," Katie said matter-of-factly, "there was always, always, always going to be public interest in you already because of your channel. You already had the prank calls, the disgusting offers. And I directed one of your kisses, so the world knows that we know each other, and if you've seen even a fraction of the chatter about it, you know the speculation is intense. I think your followers have quadrupled."

"I've been kind of distracted, and I didn't really look at anything from my channel after I posted. I think of it as running my TikTok in a very French manner."

Katie looked at her, brows confused. "French?"

"You know. Like I put up the video, and then *Oui—*" Wil mimed taking a drag off a cigarette and flicking it away.

Katie burst into laughter, and then laughed some more, crossing her legs and holding her middle. "Oh my God. Oh my God. Madelynn is going to love you so much."

"Madelynn?"

"My publicist, remember? Also, your publicist. Welcome to Hollywood."

"Oh, shit."

"Mm." Katie pulled Wil down the hall. "First shower, then strategy. I'm assuming you fed the cats."

"I fed the cats. I couldn't find your bathroom in the wall, so I used the hall one. I couldn't figure out the flush."

Katie stopped and wrapped Wil in another hug. "I promise it will get easier. You won't feel like this for long. I'm sorry I didn't show you how to find my bathroom. No one's ever slept in my room before!" She grinned, but Wil could see the strain behind it. "I will be a better hostess today."

Wil stopped. She almost spoke. Then, she shook her head.

She'd started to tell Katie that she didn't want Katie to be a *hostess* of any kind.

But wasn't that what Wil was, a guest?

And as Katie pulled Wil toward the bedroom, where Almond Butter was curled up in her cat bed again and the covers were still rumpled, Wil realized that Katie had stepped so quickly into the role of cheerful minimizer, into gentle reframing, that Wil almost hadn't noticed it wasn't like Katie at all. This was something she'd learned in the years they were apart. The Katie who Wil knew had always *reacted*, run through every scenario twice, exaggerated. She still did that, but only when the stakes were essentially zero.

It meant there were stakes here, and Wil didn't know what all of them were.

She and Katie needed to talk.

Katie pulled her through her massive closet, then into a bathroom that was legitimately bigger than Wil's bedroom. She worked another keypad that turned roughly three thousand showerheads on. They pointed in every direction inside a massive shower covered with tiny, pale holographic tiles. The light from the small windows around the room caught on the tiles and made them look like rainbows. There were shelves set in the shower holding plants, and one with a pristine row of fancy products.

"Wil." Katie put her hands around Wil's face. "Look at me for a second."

Wil did. It *was* a relief. Wil let her eyes wander around every familiar part of Katie's face, let herself remember that she understood this woman, and this woman had lived here for a long time and made this home. Wil knew that whatever Katie hadn't been able to share with her, she *had* shared important things, incredibly special things.

They trusted each other. They always had.

"I'm sorry," Wil said.

Katie shook her head. "If I seem like I don't think it's a big deal, it's only a coping mechanism."

Katie pulled her hair over her shoulder. Something unknotted in Wil's chest. "I'm actually glad to hear you say that."

"Tell me why." Katie stepped closer.

"Because I only want to be protected or handled if I've asked to be, or if I'm told you or someone else are doing so for reasons we've agreed on."

Katie reached out and touched Wil's hand, worrying her bottom lip with her teeth. "*I'm* sorry. I actually have no idea how to . . . smash all of this together." And then she made one of her gestures, and it did, it *did* encompass the whole world they were living in right now.

Wil kissed Katie's forehead.

Katie closed her eyes. "They *are* scary. I think I rushed you through a few steps. Would it be okay with you if we talked to Madelynn? You can constrict the conversation however you want. We can only talk about how you want to handle the publicity with the video I directed. Or open it up to being in California with me. Or—"

"About Ben?" Wil unbelted her robe.

Katie pulled off her nightshirt, shaking her head. "Whatever he says about this, he won't know what he's talking about, and whatever he says doesn't have anything, for sure, to do with us."

Wil wasn't so certain.

Katie pulled her into the shower, and that helped, too. Nothing was too hot or too cold, and being massaged all over and getting clean was a real, solid feeling, and so was Katie as she turned Wil around and washed her hair, scraping her nails over her scalp.

Wil let Katie put some kind of conditioner in, too. She let her rub her with soap and a mitt that felt scratchy in an amazing way. Wil kissed her whenever she could, letting herself have what the kisses gave to her and what it did to her to touch Katie's body, sliding soap over it.

Then they were just kissing, touching, and Wil could focus on Katie, excited in a way that was safe, familiar, and known, loving her. Loving the way Katie's waist curved under her palm, the way she arched her back into Wil's hands, the way she opened her mouth for Wil, twined her arms around Wil's neck, thumbed over Wil's hard nipples, bit her neck, breathed and moaned and said *yes, yes.*

Just when Wil had backed her into the tiled wall, her thigh between Katie's, her hand between her own legs, the water stopped. Wil and Katie's kissing was suddenly loud in the tiled space.

Katie giggled. "My shower's on a timer for water conservation."

"Do you want to get out?" Wil kissed her again.

"I do not want. Keep doing what you were doing."

"What am I doing that you want me to keep doing?"

Katie smiled, but she was breathing hard. "Just—Wil-ing yourself all over my body."

"Do you want to—"

"Yes."

Wil laughed, gripping Katie's waist. "What was I going to say?"

"You were going to ask if I wanted to frottage myself on your thigh while you got yourself off? But also, yes to literally anything else."

"Can I try something?"

Katie nodded.

Wil softly ran her hands down Katie's body, getting on her knees. Something hot and slow and huge pulsed in her as soon as her shins touched the cool tile and she rested her forehead against Katie's belly. Katie put her fingers into Wil's wet hair.

"I've thought about this," Katie said, breathing hard, touching Wil's hair all over. "But I was the one . . ."

"Do you want me to?"

"Yeah, yes."

"Is there anything you like? Or don't?"

"Wil, I don't even know. What you're doing now is working already."

Wil smiled and then tasted her, the scent from her soap and Katie. Wil could tell that Katie felt shy at first, which was different, so Wil went slow, touched herself because she was incredibly turned on, and then Katie reached down and showed Wil something, and together they got it, a little of what this could be like for them, both of them getting there in a rough, fast, stumbling way that made Wil's feelings for Katie big and precious and good.

Katie came with the sole of her foot against the wall, talking nonsense to Wil, and how it sounded pushed Wil the rest of the way over.

The tall ceilings and the silence and the dripping water made everything feel more explicit. Wil just gave herself up to it, happy to have this simple thing, her immoderate lust for Katie, her delight in her body, in her Katieness, in her.

She rested her head against Katie's thigh until Katie tugged at her hair. "Come up here, gorgeous creature. I need a kiss, and then we have to put clothes on or I'll just drag you back into bed for the rest of the day."

"That's a bad idea?" It sounded like the easiest way for Wil to handle the day in front of them, and easy was an appealing endcap to good sex.

"Such a bad idea. We would get weird by two o'clock, probably I'd order a lot of food I didn't want to eat because I'd waited too long, and then I would pick a fight with you and cry. I do so much better as a human if I put clothes on and eat meals."

"That's good to know." Wil stood up and kissed Katie. "You pay attention to your body really well."

"If I don't, I have a hard time with emotional regulation. Can you do something for me?" Katie smiled. Her face was wet, water dripping from her eyelashes to her smile crinkles.

"Yes."

"Can you tell me one thing you'd like to do so that I can make it happen and feel a teeny-tiny little bit like I can offer you something one percent as good as your driving me around in your Bronco? Or buying a car so you can come over to visit me?"

Wil's heart pinched. "Can you find me one of those famous social media influencer nail artists so I can get my nails done LA-style?" she asked. "I've got a fresh mani, but I love those accounts." She touched one finger to Katie's mouth.

Katie squeezed her eyes shut and grinned. "Yes! Yes! That is exactly something I can do! Probably all of the nail artists in town want to do your nails, Wil, you know that, right? To be perfectly honest, you should tell your nail artist to move here and leverage all of those tags you gave her into big business." Katie pulled her out of the shower and then handed her a huge, perfect towel.

"Maybe I will. My nail artist works in the mini-mall by the Burger King, the Starbucks, and the automotive supply complex. She's nineteen years old. She probably would love to do that." Wil thought about D'Vaughn and wondered how big of a thing she could make happen for her.

It was a nice thought to have, a reminder of how much she'd liked meeting Katie's friends on the jet. Cy Newhouse had texted her when they landed and told her to tell him if there was anything she needed, and he'd make it happen.

Wil made herself balance that bright spark of something good against everything she couldn't seem to keep herself from worrying about.

After they dried off, Katie showed Wil where she could put her clothes, and Wil let her help her unpack, because Katie definitely wanted to do that. They looked around the house for a good spot to put Almond Butter's fluffy mat, which was where she liked to take naps in the afternoon, and they decided on a spot in the hall-way near the conservatory that got a lot of late-afternoon sun but wouldn't be too hot.

Then there was breakfast, which Katie took out of the fridge and warmed up in a small countertop oven with another app. They drank fresh-squeezed papaya juice and tall glasses of flavored water with crushed ice and ate delicious rice bowls with tempeh and grilled Asian vegetables outside on Katie's poolside patio near the birdfeeders, where they could watch the birds come and go.

"Do you get used to it?" Wil asked. "Also, if you do get used to it, what's it like to not have it, to be living in a trailer on a set or sleeping in your parents' basement?"

Katie smiled and speared a piece of tempeh with her fork. "I don't know how to answer that. At least not how you mean. Some of this"—she waved her fork around—"is just Los Angeles. If you want a house of a certain size with a certain level of security in Hollywood Hills, you end up with a pool and beautiful landscaping and an indoor avocado tree, all of which are enjoyable to have, but they don't make me feel any different. It's more like how, if you go to Chicago, you eat deep-dish pizza."

Wil shook her head. "It's got to be more than that."

Katie put down her fork. "Yes. You're right," she agreed. "I don't mean to make light of it at all, because another whole part of it is about inequality, injustice, and capitalism, and whiteness. My accountability to that is a big part of how I think about what I want to do, how I want to try to make a difference or, if I can, change things for the better."

"I'd love to hear more about that." Wil watched a bird with teal feathers land on one of Katie's feeders. "Especially about whether you're thinking about breaking the system or making a new one, because, you know, millions of people—not *your* level of millions, but millions—have been paying attention to me for a year, and all I can think about is the system. Who's being exploited and who's doing the exploiting. I asked *one* question about ChapStick, and then I had so many more questions. It made me start thinking that trying to fix everything that's wrong from *within* the same system that made it is the worst kind of whack-a-mole. Not to mention a waste of time."

Katie took a sip from her juice glass, then looked out at the hills past the pool. "April likes to tell me that Hollywood isn't a *good* place to make movies, but unfortunately it's the *best* one. But I don't know, I think a fucking lot more good could be made with a system that didn't hurt people so much. I'd love to be part of a system that knew what was good in the first place, instead of only what's at the top of a killing, supremacist hierarchy." Katie bit the inside of her cheek, and a pink blotch appeared on her throat.

So Wil had understood correctly. Katie *had* gotten to the part of her career in Hollywood where she understood she couldn't fix it from the inside, or at least that trying to do that would be a waste of her time and talent.

Interesting.

Wil was glad to know it.

"The thing is, Katie, for too long, all of this was a thought experiment. But what's obvious to me now is that I want to start something. I don't want to whack-a-mole. I want to use the hammer thingy and let all the moles free."

Katie snort-laughed in surprise, which made Wil laugh. "You're mixing metaphors pretty freely, here. Like, in this story, the moles are exploited creators who you're rescuing?"

"Yes. But I think you must want to start something, too, something bigger than just your script, and you haven't talked to me about it. I'd love to know about that. I want to hear about what part of the making-or-breaking cycle you're in."

"What makes you think I'm *really* making or breaking? Maybe I'm fine with drinking fresh-squeezed juice in my trophy room and running off at the mouth about this town?" But Katie was smiling a very Katie smile.

"I saw your Oscar at your mom's house, first of all. There is no trophy room. There are a lot of well-organized cat treats. But also, you were *glowing* in Chicago, and the only thing that made you dim was that reporter. Ben."

Katie made a weary gesture.

Wil shook her head. "I'm pretty sure there's more going on than Ben. You know," she said carefully, "I've noticed that all you've done since we've reconnected is push me to get what *I* want."

Katie looked over the pool into the house, where Wil could see Trois pressing herself against the window, staring at the bird-feeder. She sighed. "It's what you said before. About perfection.

And it's how I got started here, as Ben's girlfriend." Katie cleared her throat. "But you're right, it's more than that. There's a lot."

"That you're not saying," Wil guessed.

"That I've never done and don't know if I can do." Katie wrapped her arms around her middle. "I haven't figured out how to be a catalyst in my own life. Not without blowing everything up."

Wil put her hands to her face, which was hot. It wasn't the sun or a leftover flare from her excitement from talking about what she'd like to do with her life. It was realizing that everything Katie was afraid of, controlled for, protected herself against, was sitting across from her at this breakfast table.

Which was *Wil*.

Katie was afraid of the kind of life she imagined they could have together, even if she had no idea about the details.

Katie was afraid that what she wanted, what was *good,* would blow everything up.

And it wasn't that Wil didn't understand. She did. She'd protected herself, too, telling herself for eight years that she needed to stick close by her mother, that she was happy with her life as an insurance adjuster. Even the Bronco.

"Come here." It was the only thing Wil could think of to say.

Katie straddled her in the chair, and they put their arms around each other.

Wil hoped all of this *everything,* including all the everything Katie wasn't telling her, could smash together just like her and Katie.

Holding on tight so they didn't have to ever let go.

Chapter Eighteen

Katie knew that Wil's walk outside for the morning paper had precipitated a true crisis when Madelynn walked into Katie's house with what Katie called her "big bag"—a huge leather messenger that contained an oversized laptop, multiple files she didn't want digitized, and phones. Madelynn always had more than one phone.

Katie waved at her. Wil was in a chair in the back where they'd had breakfast, with earbuds in, taking a call about law school with one of the people she'd had a meeting with in Green Bay.

It seemed like a hundred years since Katie had called Beanie and asked her to set up that meeting on Wil's list. As though it had happened in a completely different life. That day with Wil, Katie had only been spending time with an old friend. Testing to see if it still felt the same as it used to. Thinking about paths she hadn't taken.

That wasn't what she and Wil were doing now.

Wil had been on the phone an hour and a half, making Katie a little tiny bit nervous, since this meant they hadn't talked since they talked over breakfast, and that was an intense conversation.

As Wil had correctly intuited, Katie's entire sympathetic nervous system had been hijacked by the run-in with the paparazzi and what it meant.

This beautiful, unfurling, delicate, dangerous thing they were making between them had just become global news at the same moment that April was talking to investors, to Marisol, to *everyone*, in order to convince them Katie would innovate the director's chair and make movies that changed Hollywood and keep it relevant for the next generation.

When she'd let Wil back into the house this morning, Katie's heart had broken to see Wil's panicked face. Ever since, she'd been trying to remember that there was nothing real or true about the idea that her relationship with Wil was scandalous. She'd been *angry* with April for suggesting that Katie's relationship with Wil diminished the power of the video Katie had filmed for Wil's channel.

But Katie was spooked. Worse than spooked. Petrified.

Until she caught a glimpse of Wil pacing along the pool, her earbuds in, her big phone in the back pocket of her jeans, gesturing to the person she was talking to, and she was so beautiful, Katie couldn't even take in a whole breath. Wil had always been beautiful, but Katie had only ever basked in it. She had never felt Wil's beauty could have secrets for her.

Like how her brows furrowed together when she came, lifting up the corners of her eyes and softening her mouth.

Like the way her wrist bent when she was sleeping.

Like how she bit the side of her tongue when Katie let her see how turned on she was.

Even the way her tiny patch of freckles faded in a pale flush when Wil was frustrated with *Katie*.

Which was new.

Like everything, everything else.

"Katie." Madelynn set up her computer on Katie's dining room table. "Nice to see you."

"Is it?" Katie sat down on a chair and crossed her legs, smiling at Madelynn. She had gotten herself in "Katie Price" mode, blowing out her hair, winging her eyeliner, and putting on her brightest pink lip. She'd dressed in tall jeans, tall shoes, and a sweater Harry Styles had sent her when she hearted it on his Instagram. "Because I'm conscious that Christmas is in two days, and perhaps you would rather be with your family than coming to my home to put out the fire I started."

Madelynn looked at Katie over her kelly green John Lennon glasses. "My family are all publicists."

"Right."

Having organized her secret files, Madelynn dug for a pen. "My dad's Linden, Webber, and Soh, and my mom founded Adelaide Communications, naming it after my sister, Addy Soh, who you may have heard of as the communications director for the governor of California. My brother is based in D.C., where he puts out fires for politicians, and my niece is an intern at Beeker International."

"Oh my God." Katie leaned forward. "I *knew* this, but I didn't understand how . . . a *lot* that really is."

"All of us will be working through the holidays. The holidays are traditionally our biggest billing days of the year. People get themselves into some things over the holidays." Madelynn smiled. "My family celebrates Christmas at the end of January. Always pretty quiet then."

"Wil's on the phone. She'll come in soon."

"Good. We can talk about you."

Katie blew out a breath. "I would love to fast-forward to the end of January. I'm really looking forward to finding out how nicely everything will have settled down by then."

Madelynn tapped her lip, considering Katie. "And I would have loved to hear, from you, that you'd known Wilifred Greene since you were children, since you were *infants,* and you attended the same schools, and your mothers are close friends. Best friends, according to my sources. Minimally. I might have spun such an excellent story out of that. *Home for the Holidays* meets *Sweet Home Alabama*. Perhaps then April's scheme to label your short film directing debut as a Banksy-esque art drop might have been embroidered with a little folksy lace."

Katie willed her pulse to slow. If it didn't, she was going to pass out. "Things got away from me. Events took a turn."

"Where we're at now, unfortunately, is in a defensive position. Not my favorite position."

"No," Katie agreed. "You like to play offense." She watched Trois leap down from the living room sofa and run at full speed down the hallway toward the conservatory. Trois and Madelynn did not enjoy each other's vibes. "You have in fact begged me to allow you to play offense, and I have turned you down over and over again, and here we are."

Madelynn's mouth twisted in wry acknowledgment. "Indeed. I expect we'll see press from Ben within the next thirty minutes. The photos of Wil in her robe in your driveway are already making their way around, and because the rumors were primed by your involvement with Wil's channel, this news is like pouring a ladle full of paraffin on a campfire."

Katie glanced through the glass door to the back patio, where Wil had stood up. She was smiling, nodding. Wil's body language said she was wrapping up the call.

"However, Wil's platform is sexy, popular, and that perfect blend of progressive and transgressive. We both know April's in meetings as we speak, and I trust her to keep the focus on the vision despite being forced to jettison our initial strategy of separating the obstacles of your professional future and your love life. Ben Adelsward is going to paint himself in a very unfavorable light within the hour. I would love, really *love*, to have your permission to make it clear to the public, minimally, that we have noticed he's a wankhammer, and our policy from now on will be one of zero tolerance. He is an obstacle that is best obliterated completely and forever."

Wil came through the door to the table and slid into the seat beside Katie, and Katie breathed in sun and vanilla and felt her pulse slow down. "You must be Madelynn." Wil held out her hand. "Wil Greene."

Madelynn gave Wil's hand a brisk shake and introduced herself. "I enjoy your TikTok. My niece sent me the link back in June."

"Oh! Thank you."

"You have four million followers and no publicist. I'm going to act as your publicist now." She reached into her big bag and handed a form to Wil. "Look this over and sign it. Give it to Katie or one of her assistants to get it back to me. I'll bill Katie."

Wil looked from Madelynn to Katie. "Those were all orders," she said mildly.

Madelynn placed her hands on the table and gave Wil a polite smile. "Would you like me to make them questions? I forgot you're from the Midwest."

Grinning back, Wil shook her head. "No, that's okay. I understand I'm out of my depth. I've been working as an insurance adjuster for years. The robe incident was a car crash. You're the expert. I assume you're going to solve my problems with knowledge and money. I'm also going to assume that Katie has read every word of this agreement, since you wouldn't ask me to sign anything she hadn't already signed. Yes?"

Madelynn nodded.

Wil glanced at the form, scanned the table until she saw Madelynn's pen, picked it up, and signed. She slid the form back across to Madelynn. "Save me from myself."

Madelynn smiled. "I'm good at that. I was just sharing with Katie that I'd love to use this opportunity to take a shot at Ben Adelsward."

Wil turned to Katie. "What do you think of that?"

Katie opened her mouth, then closed it again, suddenly adrift in feelings she hadn't planned for.

Her throat tight. *Shame*. Her chest too floaty. *Humiliation*.

Also, her stomach sick with guilt, because she hadn't told Wil anything about what she had planned with April, or anything about the stakes. Sitting at the same table with Madelynn and Wil made it obvious to Katie how many secrets she had been keeping. How many parts of herself she was protecting from Wil.

From *Wil*.

"I don't want anything to be about Ben right this minute," she said. "I need to tell you that there are things I haven't told you about that I don't want you to hear from anyone else but me."

Wil had been sitting with her arms crossed after signing the form, but now she leaned forward and planted her elbows on the table. She looked from Madelynn to Katie. "I've known that," she said, her eyes sad. "I did try to ask."

Katie straightened up so she wouldn't cry. "I have a professional goal I've been working on a long time, that you know parts of, but you don't know all the parts that have been working under the surface."

And then Katie told her. She told her that she had been counting on Honor Howell's money, but that didn't seem likely to come through. The photographs taken outside Wil's house had fanned the flames of the public conversation about Katie's personal life at the exact moment when Katie needed to reassure Honor that she would be a director and filmmaker who centered work above everything else. She explained that April had the idea to use the video Katie had directed to attract alternative, less conservative types of funding—a strategy that would work only as long as the video was disambiguated from Katie's love life, which wasn't supposed to exist.

She told Wil that this was the reason they had been secreted to Los Angeles. The real reason.

And Katie told her that they now had to pivot again, because there were pictures of Wil in nothing but a robe in front of Katie's house when Katie was supposed to be in Green Bay.

But also that Ben was likely to make it almost impossible to pivot, because Ben knew things about Katie and Katie's life, and the story he liked to tell about her was one that highlighted her incompetence, salacious drama, and insecurity.

Once she'd stopped speaking, Katie couldn't tell what Wil was thinking, only that the patch of freckles under her eye had become flushed.

One of Madelynn's phones lit up with a notification. When Madelynn slid it closer to herself, the second phone lit up, too. She swiped and frowned at her screen. "There it is." She put the phone down on the table and pushed it across to the space between Katie and Wil. "If you want to see it. Katie, I know you usually don't, but this might be a special circumstance."

Wil leaned forward to read the screen. "Damn," she said. "That is fucking *cold*." She swiped at the screen a few times. "Although I have to say, even though I hate the clickbait, I'm not mad about the pictures." She swiped again. "I should request a hi-res copy so I properly remember my own hotness."

Wil slid the phone back, pushed her hands into her hair, and sighed.

Madelynn watched Wil, her face perfectly impassive.

Katie didn't know what to do or say. She wanted to sink into the floor. The feeling of having disappointed everyone, *everyone* in her life, and having ruined everything, was so intense that it brought tears to her eyes, and her chest got tight, tighter, until she coughed, her eyes stinging, and realized she'd forgotten to breathe.

Wil turned in her chair, her hand on Katie's arm until Katie had taken a few slow, deep breaths.

The room was completely, totally silent when Wil finally spoke.

"When you went to summer stock," she said, "you were my best friend. More than that. You were *mine*. He took you."

Wil let her hands drop.

What she had said made Katie's heart feel like it would never land another beat again. There was color rising up Wil's neck into her cheeks, painting them scarlet, and Katie wanted them against her own so badly, she ached.

"My name's in his mouth."

Katie closed her eyes. "What did he say?" Her voice sounded small to her own ears.

"Can I ask you something first?" Wil revolved her entire chair toward Katie, so that their knees touched. When they got dressed, Wil had put on a different pair of tight black jeans, but these had holes slashed in them all the way up, revealing a mosaic of edible thigh and a black tank that Katie suspected Wil had spent not a little money on. She looked like something Katie wanted to press between the pages of her diary and keep flipping back to for the rest of her life.

"Okay." Katie took another deep breath.

"Wait. Before I ask you my first question, there's another thing, which is that I have to tell you I do feel sad and angry about what I didn't know. I know I'm not part of your professional life, but I feel like at some point there was an intersection of *us* with your professional life that I missed because I didn't have your help to know we'd gotten there. And that meant I couldn't do everything I might have done to help *you*."

The tears that Katie had been hanging onto started to fall.

"But I think we'll have to get to that when it's just you and me," Wil said quietly.

Katie nodded.

"Okay." Wil rubbed her hands together. She was making the face that Beanie called *thinking face*. "*Second* first of all is Mr. Cook."

Katie gave a faint laugh, surprised by her own shaky amusement. "Oh my God. Our very important investigation."

Madelynn had startled at Katie's laugh and was now poised to take notes. "Who the fuck is Mr. Cook?"

Katie and Wil answered her question at the same time.

"A bigamist."

"An adulterer."

Wil gave Katie an amused look and tapped one fingernail on the table. "Yep. In other words, Mr. Cook is like the most impossibly average white man in America."

"We could literally swap him out for another completely different middle-aged white guy and no one would notice," Katie said. "And for the last thirteen years, he has maintained a relationship with two different, objectively banging women."

"Which should be impossible," Wil said. "Right? Can we agree on that? Impossible. My guess is we would like these two women. They're probably interesting and do amazing things. The ass on that brunette is a poem. I caught myself nodding along to all of Official Wife's Facebook reposts, and some of her self-generated content made me cry. These are objectively powerful women. Tell me, Katie."

"Yeah?" Katie said, leaning forward.

"What has Mr. Cook got that they even need?"

"Nothing."

"Nothing," Wil concurred. "Absolutely nothing. Say it again."

"Nothing. I love that song." Katie couldn't help but notice that some of the dark despair had lifted out of her voice. Wil was purposely cheering her up.

Because Wil was a lovely, generous person who deserved

someone who was just as generous. Someone brave who didn't keep secrets.

"Me, too," Wil said. "My point is that we're interested in Mr. Cook not because we're interested in Mr. Cook. No one cares about him. No one. We care about these women. Our fantasy, when we were kids, was to figure it out and then tell the women. Right? We didn't even care what happened to him as a result of our intrusive meddling. Probably he would disappear, or die. Whatever."

"Any recent meddling?" Madelynn asked. "Do I want to know?"

"Definitely not," Katie said. "We're safe. People only get worked up about *men* who randomly show up on their doorbell cameras after dark. Plus, I wore a wig."

Madelynn's eyes had gone wide, but Wil kept her attention squarely on Katie. "The thing is, Ben Adelsward is essentially just Mr. Cook, scaled up. In Mr. Cook's classroom, you were the most interesting thing. *You.* He used you, in the sense that he accepted your flattery even though he'd done nothing to earn it, in the sense that you made his class work for him, and he got all the credit. Ben used you, too, to scale up. He still is. All Madelynn wants to do is point this out. You don't even have to tell the whole story. It's the chance to say to Ben, and to all the Mr. Cooks out there, 'Oh my God, just fucking find something else to do! Be worthwhile! *Why* are you? You think you're so great, but you keep harassing girls and women so that everyone else thinks you're great, too!'" Wil looked at Madelynn for confirmation.

"That's a version," Madelynn agreed.

Katie barely heard her. She wanted to understand what Wil meant, but the comparison of Ben to Mr. Cook only made her notice that she couldn't think about either of them without feeling failure and loss.

Wil's blue eyes narrowed. She seemed to understand that Katie wasn't with her yet. "So, here's an observation. In high school, you *started* with the goal to distract Mr. Cook from being a bully in class with your overly interested questions and compliments. But it wasn't long before you were making sure everyone in that class had at least one good hour in their day."

Katie frowned. "I don't remember it like that."

"I do. Before that class, no one we went to school with had really known who you were. I had known you since I was born, and *I* didn't really know you. You'd been so preoccupied with acting and singing and dancing. No one has the kind of passion you did in high school, and when kids don't understand something or someone, they avoid it or lash out against it."

Madelynn had stopped taking notes and was listening, not like Katie's publicist, but like a friend. Katie made herself take a deep breath and tell herself that right now, she was safe.

"But there you were in that class," Wil said, "with this objectively bad person at the front of the room who had all the power, and you stepped up to him. You met his power with your power. And what you did was show us that you were this person who wanted to know everyone's story. You wanted to hear what they had to say. You wanted everyone to have an experience. You made it so it wasn't Mr. Cook's class anymore, and that was *important*. That's why people still talk about it. Every class get-together, every reunion you're not at, they come up to me, they sit down, and it turns out they want to talk about Katie Price in Mr. Cook's class. Even before they talk about your career. Because it meant something."

"I don't . . ." Katie's chest felt warm and tight. She reached for words but couldn't find any.

Wil smiled. "So that was my long-winded way of saying that you have to remind everyone, exactly the way *you* would, and not like anyone tells you to, that your own story belongs to *you*."

Then, Wil gave Madelynn a look that meant, *I'm more right about how she should do this than you could ever be.*

Which Katie loved, because Wil was establishing the dominance of her love with one of the most powerful publicists in California, and she made Madelynn smile with approval while she did it.

Katie loved Wil.

Wil had come to California. After all these years. She'd come here. Beanie and Diana and the whole entire world, including Katie, had been uncertain, but Wil had come, and she'd brought Almond Butter with her, even. She'd bedazzled Cy Newhouse and Joel Starr, admired herself in a paparazzi photograph, had a mysterious meeting with law schools, charmed Madelynn, and gotten the truth out of Katie.

God. *God.*

What if Katie let the people who loved her *love* her?

"I need some air." Katie looked at Madelynn, who nodded agreement. Then she reached out her hand to Wil. "Walk with me?"

She was relieved when Wil took her hand.

She took Wil outside, along a brick pathway that wound behind the pool house and terminated at a gate in the wall behind her property.

"There's a trailhead a few yards from here. It's a three-mile loop, but sometimes I just follow it for the first mile, then take a cut through that's a quarter mile. It's steep but very pretty. Is that okay?"

"Sure."

Katie put in the code for the gate. She sent a message to her security and turned on tracking on her phone so her people would know where she was.

She stepped out with Wil under a huge desert willow and crunched through some gravel to the trailhead.

For the first half mile, they just walked. The trail was narrow and steep, sometimes with a few wooden stairs. All the trails near Katie's property had a lot of trees, which she'd learned the names to after a whole life in Wisconsin, where a stand of birch trees was exotic. If she didn't need forgiveness, she would have pointed them out to Wil and showed her all her tiny favorite places along the way.

Katie moved her hair away from her ear and around her shoulder. Then she did it again, moving her hair to the other shoulder. All of her muscles felt a little too big and hot. She was glad for a cool breeze. California was making itself pretty for Wil.

She looked at Wil's curvy, muscular arms in the tank top and her artfully shaggy hair. She'd put something in it this morning in front of the mirror in the bathroom, pulling it and twisting it this way and that, and Katie had nearly tackled her to the floor in a sharp fit of lust and wanting and aggressive possessiveness.

"What did he say?" Katie finally asked. Out here, with the big sky and the trees and Wil's strong body, she felt fully accountable to her own life.

"I was just thinking about that," Wil said. "I haven't been with you, or here, for even, like, a minute, so I can't comment on what Ben said except to say what we already know. But that's because I know the real story. No one else does. Also, I have just learned firsthand that holding on to helpful information in a bid to protect yourself or other people is something you do, and I have to ask, is that *working* for you, Katie?" Wil looked at her. Her eyelashes had gone pink in the golden sun.

Katie didn't gasp, but it felt like all the air in her lungs disappeared from her body. "I thought so," she said. Katie let go of Wil's hand and stopped by a cairn of stones, some of which had been colorfully painted by other hikers. "Until I wanted more."

"You want more, but how are you going to *have* more? Because I'm interviewing with Pepperdine after the New Year, and I have a good feeling about it. I'm empathetic to your predicament, since I did something similar, which was tell myself I was fine with what I had until I really, really wasn't, and then have to change everything all at once instead of in more manageable increments."

"Pepperdine is in Los Angeles," Katie said.

"Yes. It is. But unless you want me, unless you want *us,* want *this,* all of it and its mess—because it is going to be so messy, Katie—and you want it out in front of everyone, without holding back, I'll only be one of your four million neighbors. Who used to know you. Way back then."

No.

For a long moment, her hands balled into fists, Katie could only think of one angry syllable, *no,* just *no,* not again, not ever. No.

She'd already lost Wil once. She'd lost Wil's bracelet. She'd lost her way. She would not be *neighbors* with Wil Greene. She'd burn down the whole world before she allowed that to happen.

But Wil was right. She had to make a choice, and it wasn't about keeping Wil or giving her up, it was about whether Katie would ever, ever decide that she was allowed to have her life.

Now. She was allowed to have it now.

She wasn't here to make room for other people to have the life she'd wanted but failed to earn. She wasn't alive—her heart beating hard in her palms, her mouth full of cotton and her throat so thick, she couldn't swallow over how scared she was—in order to make one safe choice after another until she died. Her life was not an apology. Her heart, her body, were not an apology for what had been *taken* from her.

Wil had asked her if she was making or breaking things.

Yes.

She was making and breaking things. Or at least, in her *heart* she was, but with her life, she hadn't yet.

But she had everything she needed. And so she could.

For the first time, Katie felt it—a delicious kind of anticipation and eagerness and urgency of ideas that made her want to open her laptop and write an *original* screenplay, that made her want to fly to Mexico and have strong coffee with Marisol and talk all night long, that made her want to tell Honor Howell to go fuck herself if she couldn't let go of her money so that Katie could make the greatest movie of all time. So that everyone in her studio could make the greatest movies of all time. So that she could break it all down and make it all back up again.

"Wil," Katie started to say, grabbing her hand tight.

"Wil!"

"Katie!"

Wil looked at her. "That sounded a lot like Beanie."

"And Diana," Katie said. "But I am not done having my moment!"

They turned around and, yes, it was Beanie and Diana, a little pink-faced, wearing ugly Christmas sweaters that were much too hot for midday in Los Angeles.

"We're here for Christmas," Beanie panted. "I flew first class."

"We wouldn't have come after you on your hike, but there are a lot of people in your house, sweetheart," Diana said. "April and Madelynn. And Honor Howell, with her dog. The cats are unhappy."

"The babies," Katie whispered. She turned and put her forehead against Wil's. "I'm making and breaking. We will never be neighbors. More at eleven."

Wil laughed and pulled her down the trail toward their mothers, who were already bustling toward the gate, and when they stepped into the house, yes.

There was April, beaming, sitting with Madelynn on a FaceTime call.

Diana was in the kitchen, pulling a pitcher out of Katie's fridge, directing Beanie to retrieve glasses and a silver serving platter from the cupboard.

Sue sat on top of the credenza with the communication buttons, pressing the same button over and over again. *No. No. No.* Phil and Trois were on the floor in front of the credenza, looking *definitely* freaked, hiding behind Almond Butter, who was nonchalantly grooming a front paw.

And there was Honor, in tapered jeans treated with something silvery so that they shone, paired with a crisp white blouse, tucked in, but open to her belt. She wore her hair in a natural style Katie had never seen before, and when she saw Katie, she stepped toward her and Wil, huge diamond hoops gleaming, and took off her glasses.

"What the fuck is this I hear about you counting me out?" For the first time, Katie noticed the Chihuahua Honor held under one arm. The dog looked just as pissed at Katie as Honor did. "Do you know who I am?"

"Honor Howell," Katie said over the parched lump in her throat. "You're in my house."

"Only way to get your attention, it seems." She gestured over to where April and Madelynn were still on FaceTime, which Katie could now see was connected to Marisol and a slim man in dark glasses whom Katie had met several times. Diego. Marisol's companion. He never spoke, but Marisol never made important decisions without him. "Have you not even rented a space? What is this? You can't run a production studio out of your dining room! You need a receptionist." She pointed a finger at Katie. "A cold one."

"I thought . . ." Why couldn't she complete a sentence? Katie was an actress. She couldn't recall *ever* being at such a loss for words in a professional situation.

"I can guess what you thought." Honor reached her hand toward Wil and smiled warmly. "Honor Howell. It's nice to meet you, Wil Greene."

"I'm honored." Wil said this with a wry, teasing tone that Honor picked up on and *winked* at, and Katie watched Wil shake the hand of one of the most important people in Hollywood like she'd been doing it her whole life, with an easy grin, and one muscled arm running her hand through her hair at the same time.

If Katie hadn't already fucked Wil Greene, she'd do it right now. She'd kick everyone out, Honor included, and do it right here on the dining room floor.

Wil's grace gave Katie her spine back.

"Who told you I was counting you out?" Katie asked. "Because I don't remember calling you."

Honor raised an eyebrow at Katie. "I have a feeling you misapprehended me in Chicago, and I know I have a reputation for pulling my investment when people misbehave. But tell me, Katie Price, how have *you* misbehaved?"

For some reason, the question made Katie think again of the white cardboard Priority Mail package that had come to her in Chicago, the box Wil had sent with her Katie Kat bracelet, and how she'd had to open it in front of the theater nerds who she'd hoped would be her friends but who hated her because she'd captured Ben's attention.

Even though Katie had never been able to control Ben Adelsward.

She hadn't been able to keep him from paying attention to her.

She hadn't been *capable* of telling him no.

She hadn't been in charge of him in any way through the entirety of their relationship, and after she left him, she couldn't stop him from talking about her however he wanted, whenever he wanted, forever.

She hadn't been able to understand, because she was a child—because she was a child, as Wil had pointed out, with passion and ambition—that Ben was wrong. What he did was wrong. What he wanted was wrong. How he treated her was wrong. And because she couldn't understand, she'd done the only thing she could do, the only thing that was in her control.

Katie had made herself responsible for all of it.

She'd never, ever done anything wrong, which she *knew,* but she hadn't let herself live her life like she knew.

She hadn't let herself live. She couldn't, in the shadow of carrying guilt that wasn't hers.

She was done. She was fucking done.

"I am not a dog." Katie glanced nervously at the Chihuahua. "Or a naughty cat. Or a man with too much power and not enough good ideas. I don't misbehave. Everything *I* do is either what I wanted to do, or it's my own mistake. Which you can believe I am learning from. I'm not chasing fame. Everything I said on that stage in Chicago is true—I'm in this for the work. I'm in it to tell stories that need to be told. I'm in it to center and lift up other storytellers so the world can see them. And if it's time for me to speak up and advocate for myself to finally put a dart through Ben Adelsward's ridiculous obsession with me, then that's what I will do. I tell stories, Honor. I can certainly tell my own."

Then Katie looked at Wil, who had leaned against the counter, and who was smiling at her.

Wil didn't look worried, not in the slightest. She looked incredibly, extremely cool.

Because she was Wil Greene, everywhere, forever.

"You'll be all right," Honor said. "I was hoping you'd get to here"—she gestured at Katie, a sweep of her hand seeming to encompass Wil and Diana and Beanie, Madelynn and April, and most of all what Katie had just said about herself and the strong, proud way she'd said it—"because I couldn't genuinely believe that all of the folderol about Ben Adelsward was something you *wanted.* But all I've ever seen you do is dodge it, and I *did* need to see that you're a fighter, Katie. I wish I didn't. There simply isn't a way to make films in Hollywood that lift people up if *you're* not willing to go to the mat. Particularly when your mission is to include artists Hollywood has counted out." She scratched gently behind her Chihuahua's ears. "You and Wil should come to my house and have dinner with Melinda and me before the New Year. We'll tell you both all about the mistakes you can make when you fall in love and have no sense."

Katie smiled, finally, and then realized her mom and Beanie were talking to Dale, her landscaper, in the entryway, and then realized they weren't talking, they were helping him haul in a truly giant Christmas tree.

"Oh my God," Katie said.

Diana looked up, changing her grip and getting needles all over the floor. "Well! You didn't have one. Where are all the presents supposed to go?"

Madelynn got up from the call, waving good-bye to Marisol, and then joined Katie, Honor, and Wil. She held a glass of the herbal tea Diana had no doubt made.

"Listen," she said, and the grin on her face was one that Katie had never seen before. "I have an amazing idea."

Chapter Nineteen

Wil waited in a metal folding chair in a dressing room in a TV studio. She'd been dressed and had her hair and makeup done. She was miked.

Beanie sat next to her, her hands clasped in her lap. Every time Wil met her eyes, she broke out into a huge grin and squealed, "Busy!"

Beanie Greene was a *giant* fan of Busy Phillips and her show. Whose greenroom Wil and Beanie currently occupied.

"You're going to make me more nervous if you keep doing that," Wil said. "You're not a squealer."

Beanie took both of Wil's hands in hers and swung them from side to side. "Don't make this less fun for me. I've never had the opportunity, in my motherhood, to be wildly worried and wildly excited at the same time."

"I did go off to college."

Beanie made a scoffing noise. "You went to Michigan and came home all the time. Your dad knew most of your professors, who treated you like a prodigal son. Your success was overdetermined. *This*"—she whipped her hand around the greenroom, and then opened her arms to indicate the general state of Wil's life— "this, you could really fuck up. You could get your heart broken.

You could *fail*. And that is what I have been waiting for, Wilifred Darcy Greene, for so very long. My work is done."

"Oh my God." Wil glanced in the mirror at the room behind her. It looked like these rooms always looked on TV and in the movies—the long mirror surrounded by lights, a chipped white Formica countertop that had been through some things, a couple of folding chairs, black carpet. There was a flat-screen near the door that showed what was happening on set with a countdown to when they'd come for Wil.

Five minutes.

Katie had been here and was gone already, and so had Madelynn and a lot of studio people. Wil had briefly met Busy Phillips, who was gracious and looked like she did on Instagram, and they'd talked to each other for ten minutes while four different people listened and took notes so they could come up with scripted-not-scripted questions for Busy to ask later.

The hair and makeup and stylist people were familiar with Wil's TikTok and had a clear sense of her personal style. They'd put her in tight black pants that had tucked seams sewn horizontally across the legs from midthigh all the way down below her knees, for an effect somewhere between "military uniform" and "kneepads." Wil wanted to keep them. After the stylist showed her a bunch of different tops, Wil picked out a stretchy pullover made from multiple thin, semi-destroyed overlapping layers of gray and black jersey, with long sleeves that came down over her hands and drew attention to her new manicure.

They'd done her hair like she always did it but made it shinier, a little messier, a little spikier.

She looked like she was playing herself in a postapocalyptic zombie movie in which she had become, over the course of ninety minutes, increasingly jaded and fierce, having killed too many undead to keep count.

Beanie was right. Wil looked like she could fail.

She was into it. Lately, she felt like that version of herself a surprising amount of the time.

"Listen," she said. "Since you're here, I need to do a thing."

Beanie clasped her hands together, her eyes wide. "Is this when you tell me I shouldn't have come without warning or permission? Because obviously I should not have. It was a gross invasion of your adult privacy. But and however, I will say that Diana talked me into it by promising to put us up at the Beverly Hills Hotel, and you know I have always wanted to stay there."

"You have?" Wil narrowed her eyes at her mother.

"I have always since Diana showed me the place online when we were on the plane, yes."

Wil laughed. "No, I'm not going to give you a hard time for *chasing me across the country* due to your maternal misgivings—"

"Really Diana's maternal misgivings," Beanie interrupted. "I'm her ride-or-die, remember? I already told you how I feel about this absolutely wildly impulsive situation, which is positive."

Wil felt her heart skip. "It's not . . . wildly impulsive."

Beanie smiled and kissed her forehead. "I know, Freddie. I do know. If I seem flip, it's only to soothe myself. What I know about you is that you know you. What I know about Katie is that she will learn *whatever* she needs to learn to make a good thing work. What a beautiful place to start."

Wil's eyes had begun to burn. "Listen, I am wearing at least three layers of mascara."

"Noted." Beanie smacked Wil's thigh. "Only squealing now."

Wil took a deep breath. "I just wanted to say that I've been thinking a lot about how much Dad would really, really like this." She gestured at the room. "All of this. I met Joe Starr, for example. I think we're going to be friends. I can't . . . like, *right now,* I can't talk about Dad. But I wanted to tell you that I can. I can talk about Dad. If you want to. Really talk about him."

"*Stop*," Beanie said, and looked away, pressing her fingertips under her eyes. "My God." She looked at Wil. "I wish he could see this. He wouldn't just like it. He would *love* it. He'd love it, Wil."

Now Wil pressed her fingertips under her eyes.

Lucía Gomez, a PA who Wil had met earlier who had a long, high ponytail, perfect deep red acrylics, and an earpiece, came to the door. "They're ready for you." She took in Wil and came to an abrupt halt, frowning. "Shit. Do you need makeup?"

Beanie and Wil laughed, and Wil sniffed and stood up, shaking her head.

Wil followed Lucía's swinging ponytail upstairs. There was a mark she was supposed to stand on. There were other marks taped to the floor to show where she had to walk, where she would pause for Busy to get up and hug her, and where she should stand for a minute for the first back-and-forth exchange of greetings and a joke before she sat down.

She'd been here all day. She hadn't been alone with Katie for longer than a minute since they were interrupted yesterday on their hike. There had been at least half a dozen people moving in and out of Katie's house at all times—Katie's personal staff, April's agency staff, Madelynn's agency staff, folks Honor sent over—and conversations Wil could only halfway follow about messaging, contracts, and unions, although she kept up the best she could, fascinated to have this glimpse of Katie Price's life in high gear.

Finally, Wil had wandered off to sleep in one of Katie's guest rooms when it became clear sometime north of 2 a.m. that Madelynn and April wouldn't be leaving, and Katie didn't intend to go to bed.

Tomorrow was Christmas. Wil couldn't imagine who watched late-night TV on Christmas Eve, but Madelynn said it had been one of the highest-rated nights the last two years on Busy's show, and the point wasn't the viewers anyway. It was getting Wil's story out there so that people could read the highlights and watch clips from the interview on the new phones and tablets and laptops they got for Christmas.

The biggest hurdle, according to Madelynn, was the sit-down between Katie and Busy that Wil hadn't been a part of, where Katie tried to make Busy understand what was at stake and asked Busy if she truly wanted to put her own capital into those stakes. Katie had chosen Busy over everyone else because she believed she would get it, even if she couldn't do it.

But Busy *had* wanted to do it, and Wil hoped that gave Katie some confidence in owning a big part of her own life.

She toed the mark on the floor. They'd let her wear her own motorcycle boots, although someone had whisked them away to be oiled and conditioned and shined up. The lights were hot. There was a studio band backing an extremely young singer-songwriter who'd already performed her single and was now covering Mariah Carey's "All I Want for Christmas Is You" with a lot of style.

Wil really hoped this wasn't a mistake.

But as soon as she had the thought, she realized she would be okay even if it was.

It was a funny thing. She'd spent so many years nerving herself up to make any decision at all—big ones, small ones—but now that she had, she wasn't worried about what would happen next.

She was just so glad she'd gotten herself here.

The song finished. The audience applauded, and then Busy was saying her name, talking about her and her TikTok channel, and Lucía gave Wil a little shoulder push. Wil followed the tape path onto the stage, smiling at Busy, careful not to look at the floor, careful not to trip, careful to keep her hips loose and look casual and keep it cool.

Busy opened her arms. Wil hugged her. She smelled amazing. Wil hoped that when she inevitably sweated through this shirt, it wouldn't show.

Clapping and smiling, Busy bounced up and down. She wore an

adorable short-sleeved green dress with a pink belt, and her blond waves were loose around her shoulders. "I'm so excited to meet you!"

"Thank you! I'm excited to be here," Wil said.

"I'm such a big fan! I follow your TikTok. I've watched your kissing movies a million times, like a million, million times. I have sometimes watched them in the bathtub?" She leaned closer to Wil and stage-whispered, "Do you understand what I'm saying? Am I being perfectly clear, Wil?"

"I get you," Wil said with a wink. "You're not the only one doing that, from what I hear."

Busy made her eyes big. "I am not. I did a poll of all of us on the set. Wil, I asked *everybody. Everybody's* doing that."

Wil laughed. She'd already heard this joke, but that didn't keep the flush from crawling up into her cheeks. Her heart was pounding. Busy pushed on her shoulder, a light tap like they'd just shared a funny moment together, and Wil remembered she was supposed to sit down. She flopped onto the blue sofa next to Busy.

Sit up straight. Sit at the edge of the cushion. Face your body forward, but keep your torso angled toward Busy. Keep your chin up. Don't fiddle with your clothes or your hair. Don't interrupt. Wait for the audience's reaction. Smile.

"Okay, so, Wil." Busy gave her a coy look. "You're from Wisconsin."

"I am. Green Bay."

"You're from Green Bay, Wisconsin, and so are most of these people you're kissing, so that's my first question. Where are you finding all these hot people in Green Bay, Wisconsin? Should I be moving there? Should America be paying attention? What's going on with that, Wil? It's almost alarming."

The audience laughed, and Wil held her smile and didn't rub her sweaty palms on the thighs of her designer army uniform kneepad pants. "I wouldn't have thought so when I started my project, but coming up with two people to kiss every week makes you look around at other people in a very different way."

"Yeah, I can feel that." Busy flattened her hands over her chest, her blue notecards with her prompts and questions stuck between her fingers. "Tough job."

"Interesting, too, because it turns out when you're really *looking*, there are a lot of completely, incredibly kissable people where you least expect them. I asked my hairdresser to kiss me. This guy who cleans gutters. I even propositioned a dude at the DMV, although he turned me down."

"He turned you *down*?" Busy made her eyes wide again. "He turned *you* down?"

"He did. Told me he was happily married. I get turned down a lot. But that's important, too, right? Asking the question and being okay with hearing no."

Busy leaned close and grabbed Wil's arm. "I'm just going to say before I lose my nerve that I would not turn you down, Wil Greene."

"Let's put a pin in that," Wil said, because that's what they had planned on her saying when Busy told her she wanted Wil to kiss her.

With Busy so close, though, Wil did take the opportunity to really look at her. Not like a famous person, but to connect with her.

She had really good eyes. There was a lot of *Busy* in her eyes, and a steely kind of centeredness that told Wil the woman sitting beside her was more than on board for the places this conversation would go.

That felt good.

"Okay," Busy said, smiling again. "Because there might actually be someone who hasn't seen what you do—though I'm guessing there are a bunch of people who are on their phones right this minute trying to get a peek—we do have a couple of your videos to share. Wil, can you tell me about this one?"

While soft transition music played, Wil and Busy turned their bodies toward an oversized screen on the set. One of the PAs near the cameras in front of them blinked a small light to cue that the video was starting. The position of the lights meant that Wil couldn't see what was on the screen, but a prompter played the video next to the camera, where she had been told to look.

It was comforting to see Molly on the prompter screen in the familiar video. It grounded Wil in the moment.

"This is Molly," Wil said. "She's a vet tech who specializes in elderly cats, and she does checkups for my Almond Butter, who's sixteen."

A picture of Almond Butter flashed up on a different screen right behind Busy, and the audience gave Almond Butter her due.

"Molly had seen what I was doing with the TikTok, and she'd just gone through a breakup, and she told me she wanted to remember that she knew how to feel something."

"That's kind of amazing," Busy said. This part wasn't scripted. Busy hadn't wanted it to be. She'd wanted her reactions to the video and what Wil said about it to be a surprise to her so that it could elicit genuine emotion. "I love that. I love that this could be that for her, because it can be so hard to identify what you need when you go through something like that. Okay. Let's watch."

There had been an argument about how much of the video would be aired, because a minute was a long clip for live television, but Madelynn had been very firm, and ultimately Busy's team agreed that it would be worthwhile to show the whole thing, in part because of how it began. Which was with Wil and Molly sitting across from each other on stools, and Almond Butter in Molly's arms, and Wil telling her, smiling, *You have to let go of Almond Butter now.*

Molly glanced at Wil from beneath her full eyelashes. She was a tall woman with broad shoulders, brown hair, and brown eyes, one of these Germanic Wisconsin white women who was built to survive the woods and the prairie. She had blunt-cut bangs and

huge eyes and those unfair eyelashes that Wil had thought were
fake, but up close she'd seen that they weren't.

*But she's doing such a good job of protecting me from what I've
gotten myself into,* Molly said.

You don't have to kiss me if you don't want to, Wil told her.
*There's no point at which it's too late to say no. Even with the video
rolling, you can say no. You can always say no.*

She'd waited until Molly met her eyes.

Do you want to say no, Molly?

But by that time, she hadn't meant the question seriously, and
you could hear it in the video and see Molly's gaze lock with Wil's,
and the way her lips parted just a little bit, and she leaned closer
and set Almond Butter gently on the floor. Wil's cat trotted obe-
diently out of the frame.

Then, when Molly sat back up, she grabbed the stool between
her own legs and yanked it closer to Wil's, and put her hands on
Wil's shoulders, smoothing her palms down Wil's arms.

I want you to show me how you do this, Molly said.

Like I'm teaching you? Wil put her finger on Molly's knee.

Molly shook her head. *Like you're—like you're seducing me.*

That was what the rest of the film showed. Wil figuring out
what seduction looked like, felt like, sounded like to Molly. How
she wanted to be touched. How she liked to be kissed. The way
she hummed her approval, her hand at the base of Wil's throat, her
head tipped to the side, her eyes closed, and her knees locked onto
either side of Wil's thigh.

It was a good kiss. It had felt good, but mostly Wil remembered it had made Molly feel good, which was why she'd picked it
for Busy's show.

Wil had also picked it because she remembered that on the
morning when she filmed herself kissing Molly after breakfast,
before she had to go to work, she'd understood for the first time

that something was happening with her project that she hadn't expected, and she liked it.

"Um. So. Wow," Busy said, as music played as an outro when the video faded to black and the audience reacted. "I mean, of course it's sexy, right? But really, I'm thinking that it's powerful. Tell me why you decided to do this project, this channel, this thing."

She and Busy had also talked about this question, and Wil felt like it was incredibly generous of Busy to throw herself under the bus by asking it.

"There isn't a *why*, and there doesn't have to be," Wil said. "I had an idea, and it was obviously a good one, because millions of people have seen these videos. It's powerful because good ideas are powerful, and because I'm real, I'm a real person, doing something vulnerable and real that happened to be a fuc—an effing good idea."

Busy leaned forward and laughed. "Such an effing good idea. And good ideas don't need a why, do they?"

"They don't. No one needs permission for a good idea. Honestly, cis white men have a lot of bad ideas, and they don't ask permission, either. Maybe they should." Wil crossed her legs as the audience hummed with approval and scattered applause.

Busy reached out across the sofa and took Wil's hand. "With that in mind, let's watch the video everyone's talking about."

"The one that Katie Price filmed."

The audience went quiet.

"Yeah. The one I have bookmarked in a special secret folder of bookmarks." Busy said this with a laugh in her voice, like a close friend sharing an inside joke.

The video came up, and even though Molly's video was powerful, was hot, was interesting, was in every way a good idea, it was immediately clear on this big screen and in this context that there were many more layers of talent, vision, and gifts on display in the video Katie had filmed.

It wasn't just that she had the right equipment, whereas Wil just had her phone and a fifteen-dollar phone tripod she'd bought online. It was that you could follow Katie's eye. You could see and appreciate the very heart of Wil's project.

Katie had *asked* the audience to focus, in this video, on what Wil was doing. What Wil was giving Noel. On what Wil wanted the audience to believe about themselves.

In one minute, that was there. Which meant that Katie had, of course, always understood what a minute of film felt like, what it could feel like, and what it could do.

Wil hadn't expected it, but as she watched it from the stage, the hot lights burning into her scalp, she cried.

Busy and Wil looked at each other at the same time after the video ended, now without any outro music in order to focus the audience at home's attention on the reverence in the studio. Busy had tears in her eyes, too.

"That's just so incredibly beautiful, isn't it?" Busy asked. "It's like I'm looking at this incredible thing you're doing, Wil, and at the same time, I'm seeing the birth of one of the most important filmmakers ever. I can't even with it. It's so big, and I'm so honored that you and Katie would come to LA and come to me and share this with everyone."

This was, Wil knew, an important part of the messaging that Katie and Madelynn and April had hashed out—the idea that Wil and Katie had flown to Los Angeles together to share Katie's video with the world in an expansive, generous way. It was a message to counter the competing narrative, forwarded by Ben, that turned Katie's video into a pathetic bid for attention.

"Thank you."

This felt good so far. Wil tried to imagine Katie in the green-room, where she'd said she would be watching with Madelynn. She hoped it was good for her, too.

"There's this other thing that I don't even want to talk about," Busy said.

"Yeah. Why would you? Why would I?" Wil smiled so the audience would know it was okay.

Busy took a deep breath. "Like, there's some bullshit? Out there? Namely from the ex types? About your project, and your coming to California, and of course, Katie Price. Do you want to talk about that?"

Wil did. It was a big part of why she'd agreed to do this, that she would get to talk about Katie from her own perspective. "A lot of it isn't even my story, but I'll tell you what is. I've known Katie since we were babies. Our moms are best friends. They're out there right now."

Wil grinned into the audience. She couldn't see anything but lights and cameras, but she knew Beanie and Diana were there, and the cameras would find them.

"Katie was always around," she continued, "but she and I weren't, like, best friends, because let me tell you, just from my perspective, Katie was working so hard all the time. And it was all her. Katie's mom, I think, would have loved it if Katie did what I did, play some high school sports and be a cheerleader and date and have a lot of fun. But Katie wanted acting and voice and dance lessons. She watched movies—No. She *studied* movies. She messed with cameras. She was always making movies and putting on plays and being in plays. She traveled and did this stuff that to me was unimaginable. So it wasn't until our senior year of high school before she went to Chicago to do summer stock—"

At that, the audience interrupted Wil, not with applause or anything loud, but with a kind of hum that meant they knew what had become the apocryphal story of Katie Price.

Summer stock. Ben Adelsward.

"It wasn't until our senior year that we became friends," Wil continued. "Best friends. We were doing everything together, and in so many ways it was one of the highlights of my life, because I don't know if anyone's noticed, but Katie is incredibly compelling."

The audience laughed.

"Right? And I was compelled. On the surface, it didn't seem like we did a whole lot more than ride around in my Bronco and eat Twizzlers, but we were telling each other stories about ourselves and each other. She was so excited to go to summer stock. To go to this elite acting program in North Carolina. The rest of that story doesn't belong to me, but we reconnected recently, and you know those people you can just pick up with where you left off?"

"Yes," Busy said. "So much of me depends on those people."

Wil squeezed Busy's hand. "Yes. You know, I think. And we've been doing a lot of riding around in that same Bronco and talking about why neither one of us should have to ever answer the question 'why.'"

"Because you're allowed to just have ideas and to do them."

"Yes. And because we both are powerful women with our own stories."

Wil wished she could see her mother in the audience then, just because it felt good to say it. She was a powerful woman with her own story. It was what Beanie had raised her to believe about herself. It was the only thing Diana had ever wanted for Katie.

And here they were.

Then Wil thought of the dozens of people who'd been in and out of Katie's living room and kitchen last night, talking animatedly, waving their arms around, strategizing and arguing with each other as they worked toward this moment that would, they all hoped, make a *change*.

"I'm wondering if I could do something on your show," Wil said. This was a little off-script, and Wil hoped she didn't fuck it up.

What Busy and Wil were supposed to be talking about right

now was what was next for Wil. Everything that had happened so far was what the team had set up to make a favorable foundation for what Katie wanted to say in a statement or other interview. Also, to make something worth talking about to take over the commentary about Ben's statements and Wil's pictures. All of that was Madelynn's idea.

But Katie had shared an idea with Wil that was entirely her own.

"You can do whatever you want on my show," Busy said. "Right?" She asked this of the audience, and they whooped and cheered. "Like"—Busy squeezed Wil's hand—"for real, for real. Whatever you want. It's Christmas."

"I wanted to give someone a kiss. On your show." Wil watched a flush travel up Busy's neck. Wil was thrilled to give Busy's show what were going to be stratospheric ratings, and she was glad Busy was catching on.

The audience lost their minds.

"Like, someone from the audience?" Busy asked.

But she *knew*.

The audience lost their minds some more.

"Like, this would be my last kiss," Wil said. "My retirement kiss, really."

The audience rose to their feet.

"You're killing me, oh my God."

"Merry Christmas, Busy." Wil winked. Then she stood and looked at the wings, and she smiled.

Katie smiled back.

Wil was going to kiss the love of her life on national television, and for whatever reason—or for all the reasons—it felt exactly right.

Chapter Twenty

Katie had made a lot of good entrances. She'd stunt-rolled out of a moving car, she'd dropped through a ceiling, and one time she even did a cartwheel, but she didn't think she'd ever enjoyed an entrance more than this one, walking into Wil's open arms.

"Hi there," Wil said. She wrapped herself around Katie's body.

Katie pushed the tip of her nose into Wil's. She didn't have a microphone, but it didn't matter. This wasn't a speaking role. She took Wil's face in her hands, then smoothed her fingers over Wil's ears and down her neck to wrap her hands around her nape. Wil's hands found Katie's waist and pulled her closer until their legs touched.

The audience had collectively lost their minds.

A little bit, so had Katie. She'd missed this. Missed Wil.

She'd been on so many stages and so many sets, she was used to thinking about a hundred things at once. How she needed to position her body for the cameras. What the director had asked her to convey, what the script said, what her goals were for the piece, what the character needed from her, and of course the other actors—what they needed, how they felt to her, what their faces and bodies projected and how she received them, took their energy, changed it and gave it back.

But never like this. Katie had never done anything like this.

She'd never been in love and watched the woman she loved go on live television and be so sexy and charismatically *commanding*. Katie should have expected it, because she'd seen the videos, a year's worth of kissing videos on Wil's TikTok, but she hadn't, still. She couldn't have imagined Wil would be like *this*. She hadn't known Wil would hold the audience and the host herself in the palm of her hand.

Katie felt Wil's thumbs brush under her eyes, across her cheekbones, which was how she knew she must be crying. She smiled at Wil. "I love you," she said.

It was so easy to say. It was the truest thing, the easiest thing, the most beautiful thing she'd ever had.

She loved Wil Greene. She always would.

"I love you, too, Katie Kat."

Wil didn't say the words aloud. She mouthed them, because she'd been miked, and these words were only for Katie. They landed against her beating heart with a soft thud just at the same moment that Wil kissed her.

Wil's mouth was soft, her fingers tangling into Katie's hair. Katie dropped her hands to rest against Wil's chest where she could feel Wil's heart beating hard beneath her fingers, and she forgot to keep track of anything but how right it felt to kiss Wil, how glad she was that she'd had to wait so long and go through so many things, because it meant she could feel that. The rightness. The goodness of it, of the two of them together. The rush that was always, always the same but just kept getting bigger.

She closed her eyes, and Wil angled her head and kissed her jawline and her neck, and Katie thought of how Wil had looked at the buffet table at the holiday party, walking right up to her, smiling and saying, *Guess what?*

Like time didn't matter. Like the past hadn't happened.

Like nothing mattered but Wil and Katie, forever.

They pulled apart at the same time, the audience roaring, and laughed.

"You are doing Los Angeles so incredibly well," Katie said. "You *are* Los Angeles."

Wil just smiled.

Busy approached them, laughing and crying, and they both turned and gave her a three-way hug. A producer ran onto the stage and miked Katie, and then they all sat on the sofa.

Producers were working the audience to get to a place of calm, and Katie waved at them and held Wil's hand.

She'd told Madelynn the plan a few minutes before she saw that Wil was going to execute it. Madelynn had been delighted. She was completely unconcerned that Wil or Katie would fuck it up. *I've been waiting for this moment ever since I met you. No. I've been waiting for this moment my entire career as a publicist. This is it, Katie. Let them interview you after, and speak from your joy. Speak from your big, expansive heart.* She'd taken Katie's hands in hers. *Show them who you are, Katie Price.*

The truth was, Katie had always known who she was. She would never lose track of who she was ever again. She would live her one wild and precious life, and she would tell her own story, no matter how messy.

"Katie!" Busy squealed. "Katie, Katie, Katie!"

"Busy, Busy, Busy!" Katie bounced and clapped her hands. "I crashed your show!"

"You did!" Busy mock-pouted. "I didn't even know you were coming. I was kept out of the loop."

"But you loved it," Katie said, "so you can't complain."

Busy shook her head. "I'm speechless. It's not my usual condition." She waved her blue index cards in front of her face. "There's nothing on here for this eventuality. Okay. Katie. You are here

with Wil. That was a kiss to end all the kisses. What have you got
to say for yourself, girl?"

Katie looked at Wil, who reached over and took her hand. She
looked back at Busy. "I mean, you've seen her. She's always been
like this." She waved her hand to indicate Wil's entire selfness. "In
high school, everybody was just out of their minds about her. I'm
only human, Busy. I was always at play practice, but when I finally
slowed down a minute and we took a class together, that was it. I
attached myself to her. She couldn't get rid of me if she tried."

Busy leaned forward. "Did anything . . . you know, *happen*?"

"Almost," Katie said, with the perfect amount of coy in her
smile. "But I won't say more, and I'm not sure I would've known
what to do if it had. You remember what it was like back then. We
didn't have Instagram or TikTok to teach us all the important stuff,
we just had MySpace and, like, Tumblr."

"Oh my God, Tumblr," Wil said. "I had a Tumblr."

"You did?!" Katie turned to see Wil blushing. "What was on
your Tumblr?"

"I can't talk about that on national television." Wil Greene had
never looked cooler. She was impenetrably, impossibly cool, confessing the existence of her secret, probably sexy Tumblr on live TV.

Katie would ferret out this Tumblr. She would assign a PA to
the task. But that was for later.

"Wow." She turned to Busy. "See, this is what happens when
you go off-book. You learn things. But my point is, I didn't know
what I was feeling. I didn't understand it, I didn't have a way to
understand it. I only figured out much later that Wil Greene was
the first person I ever loved."

Katie was careful to use the same language Ben had always
used. *I was the first person Katie Price ever loved.*

She made sure that she slowed down when she told the world
her version. Her story. Her truth.

Wil squeezed her knee.

Busy leaned around Katie to make big eyes at Wil. "Do you have anything to add, Ms. Greene?"

Wil laughed. "Yeah. Same."

"And now?" Busy asked.

"*Now,*" Katie said, "we are kissing on your show, and that's all you're getting. The rest I will tell you on my patio with a lemonade, because, if Wil gave me a retirement kiss, this interview retires any national discussion of what is now my very amazing love life."

"But I have questions!" Busy said. "So many questions."

"You can ask two," Katie said, and laughed at her own imperiousness. She'd probably give Busy almost anything she wanted. Busy was genuine and adorable and always had been. There was a reason Katie had come on her show a dozen times.

"I only get two?!"

"Look at your poor producers! We've made everything chaos, and we might go over time, and they probably still have Barbie Dreamhouses and cat trees to put together when they get home tonight!"

Busy and Wil both laughed, along with the audience. Katie loved this. It had been a long time since she'd had this much fun on TV. She'd worn a red dress with a white collar and tall black boots, just in case her plan with Wil worked out. She liked a theme, and Busy did, too. Santa was a solid theme, always. Now she crossed her legs and grinned at Busy, ready for the first question.

"Wil told me the part of the story she said was hers to tell," Busy said. "What about you?"

Katie took a deep breath. She'd known this might be coming. She thought about what she'd prepared to say, what she and Wil had talked about. Scripted. Safe.

But then she remembered that Madelynn had asked her to speak from her big, expansive heart.

Her story belonged to her.

"You know, Busy, it's Christmas," Katie said. "So I'm going to level with you. It's been nine years since I had a relationship with Ben Adelsward or said a single word in public about him, and just this morning, I saw one of those split pictures with my head on one side and his head on the other, and I'm just, like, *really?*" Katie cocked her own head to one side, her expression blending bewilderment with irritation. "We're still doing this? Why are we doing this? Who wants to look at their head next to their ex's head forever?"

The audience had gone completely silent, but they were listening, and their listening felt generous. They were leaning into her anger.

She hadn't really let herself feel it. She'd needed more, something bigger, to contain it.

"Mm-hmm, mm-hmm." Busy spun her finger at Katie. "Tell me more about that."

Katie looked out at the audience. "I feel like you guys get me. I know I'm not the only person who sees these articles and this story just going and going and thinks, *Come on!* You guys have thought about this, right? Why someone may not want to talk about her ex who started 'dating' her"—Katie made air quotes—"when she was eighteen and he was thirty years old? How there are probably some legitimate reasons. Private reasons. Personal reasons. *Real big reasons.* But the most likely explanation probably *isn't* that she's jealous and immature and sabotaging? Because is that any kind of explanation? Ever?"

"If we're talking about immature," Busy said wryly, "I'd point out that his girlfriends aren't getting any older."

The audience bottomed out in applause and hoots and delighted screams.

Katie put her head down, but she smiled. "There can be a way where, if one person is telling a story, it feels true. It feels like the story. But the minute I got behind the camera on Wil's channel, you could see, right? That there was a completely different story that Wil hadn't been telling on her channel. *Hers.* Her story. All it took to see it, and to understand it, was someone else looking at it. *My* story isn't Ben's. It never has been. You know who I'd love to be centered in my story, Busy?"

"Tell me."

"Diana Price. My mom. She's such a good mom! Because she drove me to all those acting lessons and voice lessons and dance lessons. It made her a little nervous. She worried I wouldn't have a real childhood, and she wanted me to have a good life. But she believed in me when she might have kept me safer in Saturday soccer and Girl Scout camp. She sat through my auditions, and held me when I cried when I didn't get the part, and when she probably would have rather I quit than put myself through all that, she told me that it had to be someone. Why not me? *She* was why I came to this town, and I made a movie, and I got nominated for an Oscar when I was nineteen years old. Diana Price. My acceptance speech, in case I won that first Oscar, was all about her. I didn't get to give it, but I just gave part of it now."

Katie looked out to the audience where she knew her mom was sitting. "I love you, Mom!" she called. She could just make out her mother's pale hair and Beanie next to her, waving one arm so that Katie could spot them through the lights. Katie beamed in her mom's direction. "You're a good mom!"

The audience cheered, and Katie smiled, her heart so full. When it quieted down, she said, "So that's part of my story no one has ever heard, and Wil told you the other part." Katie looked at Busy, then out at the audience again. "Put it together." She let her voice get firm, building slowly toward a crescendo so the audience would know to pay attention. "My first love, ever, was Wil Greene. My mom gave me my career. And there are good goddamned reasons why a twenty-one-year-old who moves out of their boyfriend's house in the middle of the night—keep in mind, those are Ben's words, not mine—doesn't say anything about it, and it's not because she's sabotaging or jealous. It's because she's *scared*." Katie looked at Busy. "Right?"

"Right!" Busy nodded. "A hundred percent."

"And I'm not the only one with that story. We all have to remember to look at every part of a story, and if we don't have the ability to because someone is quiet, or focused on something else, or may be hurting, I don't know, maybe we shut our mouths?"

Busy got up from the sofa and pounced on Katie to give her a hug, and Katie hugged her back, laughing.

After the audience finished calming down, Busy sat on the sofa again. "I get another question!"

"Oh, yikes." Katie laughed. "Two feels like so many questions now."

"This is a good one. Tell us what you're doing next! We're dying! And we need to know how your cats are handling these changes in your life. I'm worried about how Phil is coping with your new romance."

Katie clapped her hands. "My babies are good! They have a button for Wil, and Almond Butter has taken her rightful place as their wise and experienced elder."

The audience exploded again, this time with hoots and laughter.

"I feed them breakfast," Wil said. "They've figured out I'm a softer touch than Katie. This morning, Phil looked at Almond Butter eating her special geriatric cat food, and then he looked at Sue—"

"—who is the spokescat," Busy interrupted. "Right?"

Wil leaned back against the sofa cushion, utterly at ease, and draped her arm along the back behind Katie in a way that casually claimed her as Wil's own.

Honestly. Wil Greene was a miracle.

"Right," Wil said. "The next thing I know, Sue goes up on the buttons and says, *Wil. Breakfast. Cats. Want. Yes?* So what am I going to do? That's brilliant, right? That is some genius cat behavior. I had no choice. Everybody got some of Almond Butter's food."

"No one told me," Katie said. "I was otherwise occupied, or I would have intervened. But to answer your question, Busy, what I'm doing next is starting my own production company with my former agent, now founding co-partner, April Feinstein. It's called Talking Cat Pictures—"

Someone in the audience whooped, and Katie waved, laughing.

"—under the Cineline Carnegie Howell parent company. I've written an adaptation of the worldwide bestseller *Obstructed View,* which I'll also direct, and Marisol Gonzales has committed her biopic of the artist Emma Tenayuca with us. And that's just the beginning."

After that, there was a lot of pandemonium, a few more hugs and smiles, and Katie put her finger through Wil's belt loop and dragged her off the stage, mostly for the audience's enjoyment, although Wil's outfit was a *lot,* and Katie couldn't really help herself.

Also, she couldn't help pulling Wil into a corner and kissing her again, just the two of them in a dim, comparatively cool spot, Katie's back against the wall, Wil's hips pressing into hers, her mouth hungry, her hands roaming over Katie's back, her hips, her waist. When Katie pulled away, she was panting, her heart racing, every pulse point hot and aching. "I want to go home," she said.

"Yes. Hard agree."

They had to find Madelynn and April in the greenroom first, because Madelynn had arranged their transportation, and then Madelynn told them to wait a few minutes for their mothers, who were coming to the greenroom to talk to them.

"That was the best Christmas present anyone's ever given me,"

Madelynn told Katie. "I can take down my dartboard now. Nothing will compare to the utter annihilation of that interview."

"It was super fun," Katie said. "Would do again."

"I hope so," Madelynn said. "But go home and rest. Take the holiday for your family, and then let's make some time for all of us before the New Year." She kissed Katie's cheek and shook Wil's hand before one of her phones rang, and she walked away, already talking.

April held her arms out to Katie. "Come here, you incomparable creature." April hugged her once, hard, lifting Katie to her tiptoes. "You just did that. I can hardly believe it. How do you feel? Are you dead? Did it kill you?"

"It didn't!" Katie watched April—her business partner, her *friend*—wind her red curls around themselves into a self-adhering springy bun on the top of her head. "It felt really good."

"Are you scared about what happens next? Because Madelynn's got this, and even if she didn't, I would. Marisol was watching with Diego. She's been texting me. She's happy. Honor's happy. But I want to make sure *you're* happy." She braced Katie by the shoulders, searching her face.

Katie shook her head, smiling, completely at a loss for words. Standing here in the greenroom with Wil by her side, with Madelynn and April, with her mom and Beanie on the way, the biggest thing she felt—the thing she noticed, because it was new, and because it was *everything*—was that she wasn't afraid.

She wasn't afraid.

She couldn't remember when she'd ever, ever felt so safe. Not because nothing bad could happen to her, but because she knew that whatever happened, she would be loved, and she would keep telling her story and living her life until she took her last breath.

"I'm so happy," she told April.

April reached out suddenly and took Katie's face in both of her hands. She looked into Katie's eyes, her own eyes brimming with tears. "Good," she said. "Finally. Katie. This is so good."

Then she stepped back, letting her hands drop. "Have the best Christmas. We'll talk in a few days. I'm lying. Probably tomorrow. Maybe tonight on group chat. Pretend I have boundaries."

Katie laughed.

There was a knock on the greenroom doorframe by a PA, and then Katie was wrapped in her mom's arms, the familiar smell of her Emeraude perfume like an aura of love and safety. "I'm so proud of you," Diana whispered.

Katie leaned back. "Yeah? Because that wasn't—"

Diana shook her head. "I can be a good mom and be wrong, especially about things that scare me when it comes to my kid. I can't wait to see and be a small part of everything that's coming your way, Katelyn. It's not going to be easy, but you know what? I think it's going to be a lot easier and a lot more fun than what you've been doing." Diana looked over at Wil, who was making Beanie laugh. "She won't let anything happen to you." Her mom's mouth got firm. "I can see that now. I like that. I should have seen it sooner. I know Beanie, after all, and she's terrifying."

Katie laughed. "Are you two meeting us at the house?"

Diana smiled in a way that made Katie's cheeks warm. She raised her eyebrows. "Is that what you want, sweetheart? For us moms to come to your house tonight and make tea and start a batch of cinnamon rolls for tomorrow morning, and talk to you two for hours and then sleep in the guest rooms in the same hallway as your bedroom?"

"Hmm," Katie said. "Hmm, hmm, hmm."

Diana laughed. "No. I'm going back to the hotel with Beanie so I can call your father, who's having the utterly silent and contemplative Christmas of his dreams, and is currently participating in an online Sotheby's auction for rare baseball cards. He'll fly here sometime soon. Beanie and I both have midnight massages booked, and Beanie already marked up everything she wants to order from the room service menu like it was a particularly messy brief, so after our five-hundred-dollar breakfast tomorrow, we'll come over for lunch and presents. If that's okay with you."

"Yes," Katie said, and hugged her mom again.

Katie and Wil were led to a back door of the studio to get in their car, but of course there were photographers. Instead of looking down, she looked at Wil, who was looking at her, and they laughed and then tumbled into the car, the shouts of the paparazzi muting as soon as the door closed.

Every stop in traffic felt like it might actually kill her. She could hardly look at Wil, because when she did, Wil was being outrageous, sitting in the leather backseat of the car with her extreme beauty and hotness. She hadn't changed out of her amazing clothes. Her skin glowed. Her tits were a crime. It was horribly rude and upsetting in every single way.

By some mutual recognition of the horny energy between them, as well as the lack of a divider between them and the driver, they were not talking or touching.

After almost a thousand years, they were going around the loop drive to Katie's back gate in order to avoid the cameras at the front. Katie had never been more glad that she had her phone managed, and that Wil had changed her number, so their phones weren't blowing up in their bags.

At least for a while, they could just have each other.

The car stopped. They got out by the back gate and walked through the pool area. Quiet and still.

"Hey, Katie?"

"Yes." She looked at Wil.

"That was really something."

"It was."

"And it's Christmas Eve." Wil's voice was serious, but she sounded happy, as though she couldn't quite believe what they'd managed to pull off for themselves.

Katie couldn't believe it, either.

"It is. Tomorrow is Christmas." Katie pushed the door open and leaned against the jamb. "There's no staff. Just us." Katie grinned. "Until our moms descend on us earlier than they told us they would, and everyone starts calling me for 'just one thing,' even though it's Christmas Day."

"Good." Wil slid her hand over Katie's neck in a slow and illegally erotic way with a smile Katie wasn't quite prepared for, and so she blushed, and instead of executing her devastating plan of stripping by the pool and diving naked into it, surfacing to crook her finger at Wil, she bustled into the house, snort-giggling.

Then Wil was right in front of her, all shadow and silver and glittery in the low light. So Katie said it, thinking about the thousands and thousands of times she would say it in the years ahead of them. "I love you. I never stopped."

Wil smiled. "I love you. In front of a live audience and also right here in your kitchen." She leaned forward, grabbing Katie's dress, and pulled her closer.

This kiss was different.

Wil wanted *her*. That's what this kiss meant. It meant Wil wanted her, and Katie really wanted Wil, and Katie felt like they should get a special present, because they had exploded Christmas into tinsel, into stars, into colored smoke.

She pulled away and looked at Wil from over her shoulder with the look she had imagined she'd give Wil by the pool. Wil followed her to her bedroom.

"Let's take off all our clothes," Katie said. "Then I want to do the thing I've been thinking about."

Wil toed off her boots and started wiggling herself out of pants that if she knew cost $1,500, she would die. No one in Wisconsin owned $1,500 pants. Well, no one but Cy Newhouse.

"What thing?" Wil asked.

Katie shucked off her dress so she could watch Wil look at her. But she had miscalculated, because Wil was wearing the most miniscule thong she had ever seen in her entire life, and she had seen a lot of small underwear.

"Wil." Katie pulled Wil to herself. "What the fuck is that thong?"

"It's my confidence thong." She turned around. The strings were like cobwebs. "Do you like it?"

"Fuck me, Wil."

"Okay." She laughed and pulled her shirt off, and her bra matched. It was black and see-through. Katie wondered what the fuck with this woman.

"No. I want to do my thing." Katie had been experiencing some intense fantasies lately. Something about watching all those videos for a year, thinking about Wil, feeling what happened when she touched Wil, filming Wil with Noel, had made Katie want to imprint herself onto her. She wanted to taste her and bite her and command her and overwhelm her. She wanted to have Wil's complete, utter, compulsory attention, because Wil was so powerful, so interesting, so everything.

It made Katie ache and her heart race every time she thought about it.

"Tell me what you want, Katie Kat."

Gah.

"Get on the bed." Katie meant to make it sound outrageously commanding, but in reality she whispered it. Still, she was glad to see that Wil's breasts went pink. She crawled onto Katie's bed, still in that terrible thong and bra, her hair extra messy from the studio styling. Then she lay back, holding herself up on her elbows.

"I don't know how to do what I want to do," Katie said. "But also, I feel like it can't be that hard."

Wil laughed. "I mean, it has a bad rap for being a high-level-of-difficulty activity, but its complexity is way overstated."

"It turns me on just to think about it." Naked now, on the bed, Katie licked Wil's knee, and Wil closed her eyes.

"That is such a good start, Katie. Go with that. If it helps, it's something I really, really like, and my delight in getting it tends to fill in where the technique could be better. I've never—oh fuck, fuck, fuck."

Katie had experimentally dug her hands into the insides of Wil's thighs to open them up, but then that looked so pretty, she did an experimental bite. Then Wil bucked and swore at her, so this was good.

Katie wasn't nervous anymore.

She curled herself up between Wil's legs and didn't bother to take off the confidence thong. It was tiny, and it was already wet, and it looked amazing. When Katie tasted Wil for the first time and Wil started making noises, moving like she was desperate, the entire world narrowed to one point, and Katie felt so strong and fierce and hot that her entire body unfurled, her hands between her own legs, her mouth on Wil, everything sliding and building and throbbing.

When they were both close, Wil wanted it hard, and that was so good. It was so good. The way it made Katie feel was so good, and so much locked into place about Wil inside Katie's heart. Inside her body.

This woman. For her.

It was such a great story.

The very best one.

Chapter Twenty-one

Wil knew that as soon as they left Sam Rafferty and Robin Dahl's house, Katie would want to discuss Robin.

First of all, Katie had said after the first time they'd had dinner with the couple, *she has Bambi eyes and falling-all-over hair like some kind of pearl dust–painted silent film star crawling out of a bed in lingerie.*

From there, Katie had talked for a long time about Robin's rhinestone-bedazzled shot silk romper that she'd worn with Ziggy knee socks. Katie had said Hollywood would *lick Robin Dahl off a spoon and ask for more.*

Where do you find these people? Katie had wanted to know. *This woman teaches at our old high school! I can barely stand it.* Then Katie had been quiet for a few long moments, the Bronco rumbling, before she started up again. *Also,* also, *she talks fast and sharp, like Katharine Hepburn's long-lost Wisconsin sister. She's luminous!*

Wil would be jealous, except this was how Katie talked about a lot of things these days. She and April were surrounding themselves with incredibly talented people who had richly textured life stories, amazing ideas for projects, and it was clear that Katie was in a near-constant state of inspiration. More and more, she let herself react. She chattered and emoted and waved her hands around, making her incomparable gestures, even when there were stakes. Especially then.

It was so good to see. It was both a return to how Katie had always been and a new thing—an expression of how Katie was leveraging her position in Hollywood. When they were in Los Angeles, there were not a few dinner parties that ran late enough that Wil would have to beg off and find a quiet place to study, listening to the laughter and conversation from the patio, the dining room, or their sunken living room.

It was everything Wil had never let herself want.

Tonight, they were in Green Bay at the beginning of a three-week summer break from Pepperdine before Wil would start an internship at a law firm in Culver City that worked primarily with entertainment clients. Katie didn't actually have any time off at all, but she had habituated to herself to taking "vacation days" to line up with Wil's schedule. She treated Wil's law school breaks as sacred, given how little time Wil would have once she started practicing.

As if this were their long, last, senior year.

Katie had *also* come here with Wil to Green Bay because Robin promised that the next time they came to dinner, she would tell them a story that resolved, once and for all, an old and extremely important mystery.

They were at the coffee-and-dessert part of the evening, which was very chichi Wisconsin. Wil was snuggled next to Katie and listening to her eat the crème brûlée Sam had expertly concocted, making small noises that sounded like she was . . . kissing Katie, so Wil was nice and buzzed on that sound, and excited because Robin was finally getting to the good part.

"I started at East High when you guys would've been . . ."

"Our sophomore year," Wil said.

"Okay, yeah." Robin's hair was tamed tonight in two big buns on either side of her head, and she wore a green velvety top with huge swooping sleeves like moth wings underneath a pair of denim overalls. She sat beside Sam on their black leather sofa, her thigh tight against his. "The class load I had at first was mostly everything the rest of the social sciences instructors didn't want to teach. It was multiple preps, whatever, a nightmare." Robin waved her hands around frantically. "Doesn't matter. That's the kind of thing you're supposed to do when you're twenty-four years old and a woman because no one thinks you're real. The only advantage to that position, of course, is if you're not real, then no one is paying any attention to you, and that means that reconnaissance is an available hobby." She put an imaginary fedora on her head, squishing it down over her big hair with a sly smile that made Katie laugh.

"How could no one notice you?" Katie leaned forward. "I can't look at anything else in this room except you and Wil, and that's only because I'm in love with Wil."

Wil laughed. Katie's flirting made Robin blush, which just made her prettier. "That's a good question," Robin said. "You should ask Sam that question."

Katie swung her gaze to Sam, narrowing her eyes. "What did you do to her?"

"Jesus." Sam choked. "Go easy. You *know* I didn't tell her how I felt about her in high school and then didn't see her for twenty years."

Katie sighed. "And you know I have no argument against that excuse." She reached out her fist to Sam to bump. "Solidarity as ding-dongs."

Sam bumped it and smiled.

"But watch yourself." Katie pointed at Sam and hooked her leg over Wil's. "You're going to have to earn Robin Dahl every day for the rest of your life."

"That is actually my personal philosophy." Sam leaned over and kissed Robin's neck. "Carry on."

"So Andrew Cook was obviously in my department," Robin said. "I knew right away that he was the worst."

"Thank you," Wil said. "And a bully."

"Agreed," Robin said. "He doesn't mess with me anymore, and he's been put on notice more than once, but you'd be surprised how many times a mediocre white man can fail up."

"I wouldn't," Katie said. "I'd be more surprised if he didn't have a bunch of teaching awards and made the top of the pay scale."

"Point and point." Robin smiled. "So it won't surprise you to know that, yes, Andrew Cook managed to get the attention of two women."

Wil shook her head. "Standards can be so low."

"When I started teaching, he was married to Cynthia Cook. She's an executive assistant high up at Georgia-Pacific. At that time, their marriage was very seriously not doing well. Like, fighting over the phone in the breakroom, the principal having to take Andrew aside—that kind of not doing well."

"Cynthia Cook. The blonde?" Katie looked at Wil, her eyebrows raised. Her cheeks were flushed, and Wil put her hand over Katie's knee.

"Official Wife," Wil confirmed. Her heart was beating a little fast.

"That's right. But they had two kids. He actually *complained* about keeping things together for the kids, but I think that's what Cynthia was doing. Her job was very demanding, and she'd worked hard to get into an assistant position to the bigwigs over there. I got the sense she was concerned that if she had to try to co-parent with Andrew, she'd end up having to give up her job because he was so hopelessly incompetent."

"Good lord," Sam said, with genuine annoyance.

Robin hooked her arm through Sam's at the elbow. "So they were limping along, and then Andrew was suddenly happy. I was sus."

"No shit." Wil had to keep herself from leaning her whole body forward in anticipation. Beneath all the levels on which the Mr. Cook mystery had been a pretext for spending time with Katie, it turned out there was a level on which Wil quite desperately wanted to get to the bottom of it. "How did you figure it out?"

"There would be a moment, Wil," Robin said, leaning toward her with incredible magnetism, "that any fucking nitwit could figure it out. Andrew Cook is not wily, let's say. Kindly. But to answer your question, I followed him." She said this with satisfaction, as though any pure-blooded Midwestern high school teacher would have done the same.

"I love you," Katie said, with all sincerity. Wil laughed.

"I love you, too," Robin replied. "So I grabbed all my grading, and I told my husband at the time I'd be late, and I followed Andrew Cook across town and saw him having cozy drinks at one of those fish fry bars with Jess Heidelman."

"Brunette!" Wil said.

"That's right."

"So I'm the winner!" Katie said triumphantly. "It's an affair."

"At first," Robin agreed.

"A-ha!" Wil was laughing, but didn't even care, because Katie's hair smelled like Wil's own shampoo, which Katie had borrowed this morning, and it gave her feelings—rich and big and grateful and horny feelings—that Katie was claimed and cozied into Wil's life in this manner. Last night, she and Katie had hung out with Cy and Joel and Angela at Joel's farmhouse with all of Joel's foster animals. Wil had flirted outrageously with Cy, and Katie had told her later that she had been wrecked with delighted concupiscence the entire night over watching Wil's *moves* and *coolness* from afar.

Wil kissed the top of Katie's head, huffing her shampoo smell.

"So Andrew's happy," Robin said. "His teaching notches up from grossly incompetent to mediocre. His wife is happy, because Andrew isn't talking about divorce anymore and is probably a better dad, because men. And I hope Jess is happy. She's the one who can be most confusing to me, to be honest. But of course it isn't long before Jess and Cynthia figure it out."

"Not wily," Katie said.

"Not at all. My friend Carla was at Festival Foods one Saturday morning—she's a science teacher at East and my best friend—and she ran into Andrew. She was talking to him, as one does, and then Cynthia comes up, so she's talking to both of them. Everything's cool. Then she carries on, is in the frozen section, and she sees Andrew again. Pinching the ass of Jess. She's appalled—and I should say here that Carla has no filter and assigns all consequences to men—so she goes tearing around Festival, looking for Cynthia. Finds her. Tells her that she saw Andrew getting handsy with another woman. Cynthia raises one eyebrow, cool as a fucking beer stein, and says, *I know*."

Wil burst out laughing. "I'm so happy right now. Sam, I need another one of these." Wil held up her empty crème brûlée ramekin. Sam's hobby was baking, and he was magical at it.

Sam got up, collected glasses and plates and Katie's empty lemonade bottle, and disappeared into the kitchen.

Robin's eyes were bright with conspiratorial excitement. "Now, Carla doesn't have a chance to get the whole story, and we're left in the dark for a few *years*, you guys. I did my best. I'm ashamed I couldn't figure out more. All I can say is, if you can't figure something out, assume it's because a woman doesn't want you

to, because men can't hide anything for shit." She pointed one finger at Katie. "Which, speaking of—and I've never mentioned this,
but I can't *not*, because I'm all worked up talking about Cook—I'd
been listening to Ben Adelsward talk about you for years and ap-
plying a very jaded perspective to his bullshit. Like, yes, Ben, keep
telling me about how your eighteen-year-old girlfriend has failed
to appreciate your unique qualities as a life partner. What was that
again about how she left you in the middle of the night? Was she
barefoot also? Did she have to crawl over broken glass, you massive, arrogant prick?"

"Move to Los Angeles," Katie said, laughing. "I can't be without you."

Robin grinned. "So say many. I'm pretty great. My point is just
that I know it wasn't just me who felt that way about Ben. It was
lots of us. *Lots* of us were waiting to hear you confirm what we all
knew, and anybody who wasn't was being deliberately obtuse."

Katie wound a strand of hair around her finger. "Thank you
for saying that."

"Anytime." Robin dusted her hands together. "All right. So it's
also the case that Carla and I were being deliberately obtuse about
Cynthia and Jess. They had to tell me the deal themselves. Then it
was so obvious."

"How did this happen?" Wil's mind was racing with possibili-
ties, and she almost wanted to ask Robin *not* to tell them so she
could think about it until the next time they got together, just to
enjoy the mull. Katie would never go for it, though. "Keep in mind,
at this point, I would believe anything you said for any reason."

"I was at a conference, a teaching conference, in Minneapolis.
The school had gotten some grant and was sending more of us
around for professional development, so it was a pretty big deal.
A hotel room, conference hotel, buffet—it takes so little to keep
teachers happy, honestly. Andrew was at the conference too, and

you could pay extra to bring your spouse. Cynthia was there. And then I ran into Jess at the hotel bar, late." Robin grinned.

"Oh!" Wil shouted, delighted with this plot twist. "Oh! Oh!"

"Yes. But wouldn't you know it? She wasn't meeting Andrew there. She was meeting *Cynthia*. I had parked myself at the end of the bar to monitor the situation behind a pillar, very *Harriet the Spy*, and Cynthia comes up. They hug, then proceed to have a drink, laughing, what have you."

"This really happened to you!" Katie said. "I love that this happened. I'm so overjoyed with this story. Tell us every single detail."

"Obviously, I can't stand it anymore," Robin says. "I walk over and am basically like, 'I'm dying. What's the deal?'"

"That would be the only thing to do." Katie nodded.

Wil closed her eyes so she could savor the scene for a moment—Robin Dahl, in one of her signature outrageous outfits, stepping out from behind whatever hotel bar pillar she'd been hiding herself behind so that she could walk up to two women who were near-strangers and insist they tell her the details of their most private emotional and sexual arrangements.

Also, Katie Price saying, *That would be the only thing to do*, as though Robin's move hadn't been completely shocking.

Wil loved this. She loved Katie. She loved having clever, interesting friends like Robin and Sam, Cy and Joel and Angela, and of course Madelynn and April. Sometimes, when she took a hike in the hills behind Katie's house, she talked out loud to her dad, telling him the most interesting and provocative details of her new life with Katie, the ones that would have made him pontificate or roar with laughter. It just felt right to Wil, now, to make him a part of her happiness.

"At first they were kind of cagey," Robin said. "Understandably. But it's me, so eventually I get them to tell me. Turns out, Cynthia had found out about Jess basically right away. Because men, and because Andrew was so happy. And I mean *happy*. Like, his and Cynthia's marriage and *indoor sports* were better. There were moves happening in their indoor sports that he had not previously attempted or proved himself capable of. That kind of thing."

"Ew." Wil shuddered. "Just, ew."

"Mm-hmm. So she calls Jess, and at first Jess is denying it, but then they start talking. Really talking. They like each other. And Jess tells her that she had a horrible marriage, and a horrible divorce, and she never wants to get married again, but she likes the companionship and sex on her terms, and maybe the both of them can work out an arrangement."

"They are going to fucking time-share Andrew Cook?" Wil's bafflement was utter. "Like, anyone else on earth, fine. But Mr. Cook? What?"

"I can't account for anyone's predilections," Robin said. "Cynthia had almost finished raising two kids, she had the job of her dreams, and she wanted to focus on her own shit without dealing with men or dating. She wanted Andrew Cook to remain her husband so she didn't have to deal with the enormous fucking hassle he would be if he *wasn't* her husband. Jess was done with it all except for this one thing she wanted, but which she didn't want in *her house* permanently, ever, *ever*. What I am saying is, it was all less about Andrew, and maybe not about him at all, and more about these two women finding each other, understanding and *believing* what the other woman wanted, and realizing they had a way to give that thing to the other woman without a lot of cost to themselves. They saw that as an opportunity, and a rare one."

"Oh my God." Wil wiped suddenly at her eyes. "I'm crying."

It wasn't about Mr. Cook.

Of course it wasn't, because it had never been about Mr. Cook. Not for Katie, not for Wil. But also not for Cynthia and Jess, the two women who'd drawn Wil and Katie's attention so long ago.

It was about *them*. Their lives. Their big, important stories and how they wanted to live them.

Katie was sniffling. "Me, too! Crying. God."

"I also cried," Robin confirmed.

"And Andrew?" Wil asked.

"He's never found out. He thinks he's fucking James Bond."

Sam came back into the room with another dessert for Wil and drink refills. "What did I miss?" He sat down beside Robin and squeezed her thigh. "Why are you all looking at me like that? Oh, no."

"It's nothing," Robin told him. "I mean, it's something amazing, but you wouldn't immediately get why it's amazing, you'd ask too many questions, and I don't want to explain it to you." She kissed his temple. "But I will tell you that you look very handsome tonight, if that makes you feel better."

"It makes me feel like a sex toy, but I'm good with it."

They talked for a while longer. Wil took the opportunity to grill Sam about her course selections for her second year at Pepperdine while Katie learned everything she could about Robin Dahl and her life story, probably so she could write someone like Robin into a movie.

Katie's head was full of movies these days.

They stayed late at Sam and Robin's, probably later than they should have, until Robin was yawning and apologizing, and Sam mentioned that she had to be up early to teach in the morning.

Katie and Wil held hands on the way to the Bronco, parked on the street across from the house.

"Drive me around, Wil." Katie skipped ahead, then turned to face Wil and walk backward against the setting sun, so that Wil could see the outline of her body through her short floral dress. Wil had been wiggling into stiff, raw denim jeans that Beanie had bought her and were the exact brand and type Beanie had as a young wife. Wil had always thought those jeans were very cool in old photographs of her mother, how they were broken in by her mom's body. It was a little warm to wear jeans, but she knew Katie liked the way she looked in them, and that was an incentive.

Wil got in, opened the door for Katie, who crawled in, her dress hiking up over her thighs.

"Do you want to park?" Wil asked. Because *yes.*

"I do. Don't you feel like this Bronco hasn't been properly christened? Like, there is all of this intense *energy* inside of it, but the energy is unconsummated. It needs to be consummated so that the Bronco will be comfy on its trailer being carried to our love nest in Los Angeles."

Getting the Bronco out to LA was the last stage of Wil's move. On earlier trips back to Green Bay, they'd packed up Wil's things at her rental house, and Wil had said good-bye to her landlord—an unexpectedly tearful coffee meeting at Kettle's, since Brenda had been accepting Wil's rent checks for eight years, and it turned out they'd grown closer than either Wil *or* Brenda had realized.

"I know a place." Wil pointed the Bronco toward the bay, and they drove past their old high school, past the new mural in the area the city was trying to turn into an arts district, past the neighborhood where Diana and Craig used to live and Beanie still did, and to the new neighborhood where Diana and Craig had their big house. But instead of following the road to Katie's parents' driveway, Wil made a series of turns until she had to put the Bronco into a low gear to navigate driving it over a bumpy field that was well behind the house, though you could still see Diana's kitchen lights were on.

A couple of big construction vehicles were parked near a square hole, not so big, really. Just big enough that with two stories, there could be a bedroom that looked over the patch of forest, and a main room downstairs to put the mallard sofa, a TV, and lots of cat trees.

Green Bay wasn't Jackson Hole or Aspen. It wasn't a ranch outside of Austin. But what it lacked in glamor, it made up for by belonging to them. This was where they'd met and grown up. This was where their families lived. Sometimes they came back and soaked in nostalgia. Other times, like tonight, they made new memories.

Big and messy and glorious memories.

"Oh!" Katie clapped her hands. "Look at what they got done today!" She peered out the windshield. "They moved around more piles of dirt!"

"I'm sure they are very important piles of dirt." Wil couldn't honestly tell if anyone had been here recently. But she was sure Craig had this project well in hand, since it was mostly what he talked about on the family group chat. A lot of long, dry texts about footers and when Brown County would be putting various lines in.

Wil smiled at Katie. "I love you."

"Come here," Katie said.

Wil pulled her legs up on the bench seat and crawled to Katie on her hands and knees, then kissed her neck.

Desire washed over Wil in a warm rush. She let Katie bite her a little, stroke her hands over Wil's shoulders as she settled in next to her, and then Wil did what she'd wanted to do when she was in high school, more than once, even when she couldn't admit it.

Which was kiss Katie Price.

Wil thought the energy in the truck must have been breaking up, because as she kissed Katie and let her feel how much she wanted her—kissed her until they were both finding places to touch each other that they knew the other liked—she felt a little of what she might have felt back then.

If she hadn't let Katie go, not for even a moment.

They fogged the glass. And so, panting, Wil rolled down the

window Katie was leaning against, and the cool air of a June night in Wisconsin came rushing in. The fabric of the bench seat's upholstery was rough on her knees when Wil shimmied out of her jeans, so there was nothing but her underwear and a tissue-thin T-shirt between her and Katie, who had impatiently shucked off her dress several kisses ago. There wasn't so much room, but that felt correct, amplifying the illicit feeling of being out late somewhere they shouldn't be—at least, not doing this, sliding fingers beneath Katie's panties, finding ways to touch each other that made them both rock and gasp, made Wil moan against Katie's neck.

When Wil came, she remembered their last sleepover before she went to Chicago, the night in the tent when Wil had looked at Katie in a new way and whispered her name, their faces close together, and Katie had said *You can* and made Wil's heart pound so hard, she could barely breathe.

She'd been so afraid, but there hadn't been anything to be afraid of.

Only what she wanted. Only this.

It took them a while to come down. The cab started feeling cool, and the noise of insects was loud. Katie had been so still, Wil wondered if she was asleep.

"Katie?"

"Yes?" She turned her head toward Wil and smiled, her hair everywhere and her neck shining with sweat.

"I have something for you. A present."

Katie sat partway up and opened and closed both hands at once. "Give it to me right now."

Laughing, Wil reached down to find her jeans in the dark wheel well and pulled her present out of the back pocket.

She handed it to Katie.

Her bracelet. Her Katie Kat bracelet.

Katie started crying.

Wil kissed her forehead and helped her put it on. "It's not the very same one. I tried to remember what the colors were, and I think I got it? Beanie still had my kit with all my thread, and this was one of the last bracelets I made, and because I was a teenager, the skeins I used were sort of shoved on top of everything else. There's even the same button, because when I bought them, there were two." Wil smiled at her. "Don't cry. Look, it's on."

"I have to cry, because right this moment, I am literally feeling the whole universe button into place," Katie said. She held her wrist to her heart and closed her eyes. "Now we're bracelet married."

"Katie." Wil laughed and kissed her. "If that's true, we're also Bronco married."

"Absolutely we are. I'm not kidding." Katie examined her bracelet again. "I can't even with this, Wil. You are the most romantic person on the fucking earth. When did you even find the time?"

"You've been writing until late, and you have to do it in your study because you use the voice app, so once I got my little kit in the mail from Beanie, that's what I've been doing while I read law. Reading law and knotting embroidery thread and starting over ten thousand times because I've suffered some skill slippage in the past thirteen years." Wil's voice sounded thick with emotion even to her own ears. It was only an embroidery floss bracelet, only a small gift to say she'd been thinking of Katie, but of course it meant something big.

As big as the foundation of the home they were building together.

As big as the whole future.

"Are you ready to head to my parents'? Or to your mom's?" Katie's voice was rough with feeling.

They'd been dividing their time between Katie's suite in her parents' basement and Beanie's spare room. The media had no idea they had *ever* stayed with Beanie, or possibly even imagined that Wil had a mother, so it was an unexpected respite. Wil often wondered if Beanie had done some kind of nationwide string-pulling to make her home invisible to the media. She wouldn't be surprised.

"Your place," Wil said. "Your mom will have chicken and dumpling leftovers in the refrigerator. Consummating the Bronco burned off my pasta and crème brûlée."

"Yes. Let's go there, and that way we don't have to gather up the cats. I think there's still some apple crisp. We can get a giant plate of chicken and dumplings and a bowl of apple crisp and eat all of it naked in bed."

"That's the dream, Katie." Wil put her hands on Katie's face. "I love you."

"It's *my* dream. I have a lot of them, actually. You're in all of them because I love you so much."

Wil kissed Katie, trying to make it as good as she always did, trying to give her everything that she needed and wanted. In this kiss, and later.

And forever.

Acknowledgments

The opportunity to thank others for their part of a wonderful, humbling, hard-won milestone is an overwhelmingly beautiful feeling.

Our children, August and James, are continuously supportive and proud of us. They don't mind that we write at the dining room table and obsess about our book and how stories are made. Instead, they share their fan fiction and fan art with us, and tell us about books we should read after breathlessly telling us the whole plot, and talk about how video game lore works, and litRPG, and introduce us to *Owl House* and the queer narratives and framing of *Undertale*. They contribute, daily, to a creative household that feels good to be a part of, and they help us make a safe space for trying, failing, singing, drawing, writing, taking a step back and listening, and seeing everything as queerly and inclusively as possible. They are good teachers and lovely humans.

Likewise, Barry and Barbara have provided unparalleled support of our journey as authors, reading some of the first books we wrote together, talking about them over dinners, and celebrating wins and booing the setbacks. They listened to what we wanted, a kind of listening that is much too rare, and it had the tremendous impact you can imagine.

Our agents, Pamela Harty and Tara Gelsomino, have tirelessly introduced our work to so many editors with enthusiasm and confidence, and have been equally excited about our cowriting projects as our solo ones, encouraging us to think big and write what we want. They've found us wonderful places and people for our work and answer our many questions nearly instantly with reassurance, experience, and accuracy born of expertise and research.

Susan is both a god-tier aunt to our kids and the dearest of dear friends. She reads everything we write, often more than once, and loves it, brags about us, and generally makes us feel like we may be cool people even when obviously Susan is the cool one. She gives good group chat, which is invaluable, and considers hanging out with us and our kids, eating, having quiet time, and discussing various wellness interventions while eating chips to be an especially good time—which makes her the perfect friend for any writer. We are so lucky she is ours.

This book was really, truly, perfectly *seen* by our editor, Alex Sehulster. Her immediate connection to Wil and Katie's love story in all of its awkward, lush, confused, yearning, funny emotions was a connection that meant she understood how to make this book's heartbeat palpable. Alex is genuinely inspiring, and this story would not be the story it is without her gifts for how to identify what makes a book work and how to make what works sing for a reader. What's more, she's sensitive, intuitive, and has been encouraging and supportive of our ideas. She is a part of efforts to reshape the landscape of publishing to be inclusive, expansive, and celebratory of all kinds of stories and voices, and her efforts shine in every note, email, and conversation. Our gratitude for where she took this book is enormous, and we can't wait to see how much we can accomplish with her vision.

Other authors are such welcome companions on what is often a very strange quest to write and make books. They are the first to validate the choking tears of disappointment and insecurity, your voice, your wins, and your need for rest. We were so moved by Kate Clayborn's and Ashley Herring Blake's early and warm endorsements of this book. Both authors have been our comfort, inspiration, and teachers through their own work, and so their willingness to lend their support was the best, best feeling.

Finally, a book passes through so many hands before it's in a reader's. We have had such warm collaboration from the people at St. Martin's Griffin, whose love for books is evident at every single stage of publication, from manuscript to print and beyond. They are excited to share their authors' books with readers, and they really get that every author's career is unique and without comparison. So much thanks to Cassidy, our behind-the-scenes guide, and to everyone else on the team who has been responsive, kind, and expert.

Our cowriting name, Mae Marvel, is a name that refers to powerful women in our family's tree who made their own way through considerable challenges and trauma while reaching out and loving so many others around them. This author name is a reminder to ourselves to keep working, and to protect and take care of others, make community and connections, include, learn, choose love, put down attitudes and biases that don't serve, and write stories about the very best lives and loves of women and our queer community. This book is inevitably a part of the love we share with each other—a love that has made so much possible, so much easier, and so much more fun with more kissing.

About the Author

Alyssa Lentz-Underwood

Mae Marvel is the alias of cowriters Ruthie Knox and Annie Mare, bestselling authors of more than a dozen acclaimed romance novels between them. Mae lives with two teenagers, two dogs, one cat, four hermit crabs, and a plethora of snails and fish in a witchy century home in Wisconsin whose extravagant perennial garden gives them something to look forward to in the depths of winter. In addition to romance, they also write mystery novels and cannot promise not to branch into new novelistic territories at a moment's notice. They can be found online at maemarvel.com.